BLOOD IN THE VALENCIAN SOIL

Love and hate hidden in the legacy of the Spanish Civil War

CAROLINE ANGUS BAKER

Bella Figura Publishing

Also by Caroline Angus Baker

NIGHT WANTS TO FORGET:
Internal struggles beneath 'La Bella Figura'

Bella Figura Publishing
Auckland, New Zealand

No part of this publication may be reproduced by any means, graphic, electronic, or mechanical, including photocopying, recording, taping or by any information storage retrieval system without the written permission of the author except in the case of brief quotations embodied in critical articles and reviews.

The characters and situations in this book are purely fictional and are not based on any person, living or dead.

carolineangusbaker.com

Copyright © 2012 Caroline Angus Baker

All rights reserved.

ISBN: 978-1475280982
ISBN-13: 147528098X

For my father, Scott

Thanks to you, I know who I am and where I fit in.
Rest in peace, Dad

Then I realised I had been murdered. They looked for me in cafes, cemeteries and churches …. but they did not find me. They never found me? No. They never found me.

~ Federico Garcia Lorca

Cuenca, España ~ marzo de 1939

"Come on, Luna! They will be here by now!"

Luna Beltrán Caño looked away from the window of her bedroom. Her view looked across the gorge towards a monastery, which rose from the fog that sat between the mountains on the chilly spring day. Cuenca was once a medieval fortress precariously built on a hilltop, and now was an isolated little town. Fog shrouded the deep gorge of the Huécar river that surrounded the town. Any evil could lurk down there, the same kind that caused the original inhabitants to wall around the town for protection 1300 years ago.

She picked up her unassuming brown coat from the only chair that adorned the sparse room. She was lucky that she owned something to keep her warm. Luna was a young woman with many luxuries in her life, like her single bed that had two blankets on it this year, and she was even able to wash them semi-regularly. On the wall over a small wooden table where she kept her diary, she had hung a mirror. Her father had bought it for his wife, but now Luna had inherited it. She looked at herself, with her curly black hair in a ponytail. Her cheeks had thinned over the winter; the shortage of food in the town wasn't new. The farm labourers ventured further and further from the safe outskirts of the town into the mountains in search of places to grow crops or herd livestock. Many never returned. Every day there seemed to be fewer men in the town. Families had fled the town for Catalonia or the Basque country in the north, and they were never heard of again. Nowhere was safe during a civil war.

The war had raged for almost three years now, and its intensity continued to grow. Cuenca was flanked by the Republican stronghold of Madrid to the west and the Republican port of Valencia to the east. The Republicano zone continue to lose ground to Franco's rebel fascist troops, or Nacionales as they called themselves, and stories of immense atrocities spread far and wide.

Now the threat of Franco's army crossing the mountains and into Cuenca was about to become a reality. Men ran from the town in pursuit of adventure; to support the Republican fight against Franco and his brutal army, only to become barbarians themselves as their blood spilled into the soil that they fought to rule.

Fighting and instability was all Luna knew. She was 20 years old, and her whole life, her world had been fighting. The war may have just been three years old, but she couldn't remember a time where things were calm. She knew how lucky she was – they lived in town and they owned a home. Many did not. Most had been at the mercy of landowners, nothing more than peasants who worked for the wealthy. People were treated like slaves, traded like cattle, their desperation for work and food exploited. No wonder España's population had divided themselves and decided to rise up to defend themselves. Luna was 12 when revolution came in España, not old enough to understand. She had never been to school, couldn't read and write at that time. She was lucky that her father was educated enough to teach her as she grew older. The Second Republic, founded in 1931 promised an equal society, but that never came. She remembered her anarchist father getting her mother, Isabel, to vote in 1931, when women were first given the chance. Again, no change came, just in-fighting. People were poor, humiliated, unheard. No wonder civil war came in 1936. Franco's rebel army had flooded into Spain from Morocco and the bloodletting had begun. The group, supported by fascists, monarchists and religious conservatives couldn't just take España, because the Republicans were prepared to hold on to their country. Luna's mother had been a Catholic, but her father's new-found hate of the church and State meant that Luna couldn't find solace in her religion anymore. The church was seen as oppressive, as was the army, who hated anyone who had an opinion on anything other than the unity and control of España. The fabric of society had well and truly broken down over the course of her short lifetime. The socialists, anarchists and communists who worked together under the Republican flag had held on to parts of España, with the help of a large group of international volunteers. But now, three years on, España was weary. Her people were weary. The Republican spirit had faded to the oppression of the Franco army.

Luna stepped through the door that separated her own room from the rest of the house, passed through the room that her brother and his wife occupied, and through into the living space. The Beltrán Caño family was one of the blessed families who had managed to avoid starvation throughout this difficult time. The textile business that their father Juan Pablo help run, along with the town's anarchist co-operative, had managed to stay afloat, thanks to the supplies he bought from Barcelona. At least the supplies were still in demand in the region of Castile-La Mancha. Her father was away in Madrid, which left her with just her older brother, Alejandro, and his wife, Sofía.

"Sí, sí, I'm coming!" Luna replied. Her sister-in-law stood at the front door of the house across the small room. Sofía was a nurse, and her uniform was tight now that she was nine months pregnant. "You know Alejandro will come right to the house, don't you?"

"I want to be there when he gets out of the truck," Sofía said impatiently, and watched Luna put on her basic black shoes. The puddles that formed between the cobbles outside were a real pain, because their shoes leaked. Sofía was on her damp feet all day at the hospital and so uncomfortable because of her pregnancy. At least Luna's skirts were not as long as the full-length white ones Sofía had to wear at the hospital. Sofía's dress soaked up the dirty water on the steps that made up the narrow streets between the house and the hospital, which only added to the misery of her life. But none of that mattered; today her husband of only six months was home from Valencia again. As long as Sofía had Alejandro at home in Cuenca, nothing else mattered to her.

Luna checked the fire in the stove, and the two young women stepped out onto the narrow road that was cold and damp in the shade. The women walked up the streets made of countless rows of stone steps. They were all alone on the street, all the other houses around them still shut up tight.

"I'm so glad they're back," Luna said. "I'm not sure how much more of this I can take."

"Because you miss your brother or because you miss Cayetano?" Sofía teased.

"I worry for Alejandro, of course! He's my brother. He engages in these dangerous trips, and the worry keeps me awake at night."

"I know the feeling. With Alejandro back in Cuenca, I will be sure to keep him awake in bed," Sofía giggled.

"But you're pregnant."

"I know that, Luna. How do you think I got into this dilemma with your brother? You're the most innocent 20-year-old girl."

"I know how it works, Sofía. Remember that I have to sleep in the next room. I'm not a little girl."

"Do you need to confess some impure thoughts again?"

Luna threw her a sly look. "I won't share anything with you again. Besides, the day of being able to seek guidance from the church is long gone. Not since the mobs burned the church and killed most of the clergy here. We may be fighting for a liberal society, but yet I don't find anyone fighting for my rights or beliefs."

"And that's why your mind is occupied with dreams of the moment you make your way into Cayetano Ortega's bed?"

"Oh, would you stop! Papá has arranged for me to marry Ignacio in Madrid."

"The man is a bore, Luna. He looks so ill all the time."

"Yes, but if marry him, then Papá's business and Ignacio's family's business can merge and do well together. Times are hard enough. We need to own a business once the war is over, for our own safety and survival."

"They don't need your marriage for that."

"No, but Papá thinks that Ignacio would make a suitable husband. Plus they need someone to carry on the family name."

"So you're willing to pop out babies for the sake of textile businesses? That's cold."

Luna sighed. "I like Ignacio. He is a gentleman. He is sophisticated, friendly, considerate, and wealthy. I could do worse. Much worse."

"You forgot love, Luna. Ignacio is a Falange member. Your father is just getting cosy with the enemy for his safety. He is a pig, you know that, don't you? Juan Pablo is playing with fire."

"I will love Ignacio. But he lives in Madrid, I never get to see him."

"Then why don't you just move to Madrid?"

"And leave you and Alejandro? I wanted to be with Mamá until she died."

"I know," Sofía said and placed her hand on her best friend's shoulder. "I'm not trying to be nasty. I'm not."

"Alejandro told Cayetano unequivocally that he has to stay away from me. Ignacio should be the man for me."

"Alejandro says that because he knows what kind of man Cayetano is."

"Yeah, Ale and Caya are as bad as each other!"

"We all have different expectations in life, Luna. In a few weeks from now, we could all be dead. It's that simple. You saw what happened when the Republicans first claimed Cuenca for themselves..."

"Yes, they dumped priests' bodies in the street while the church burned."

"If I'm going to be raped and murdered when the Franco army sweep through here soon, I want to know that I married the man I loved while I had the chance. Alejandro is not perfect, but he's a hero."

"He drives people from Madrid to Valencia! Hardly a noble task!"

"That's all Cayetano does! The trip from Madrid to Valencia is dangerous, Madrid is surrounded on three sides, and they bombed the roads to Valencia. It's a risk. Cayetano is a drinker, and a womaniser, just like

Alejandro was. They are more noble than any fascist bastardo. But we love who we love."

"Alejandro loves you, Sofía. There is no doubt about that. He is my brother, and I love him. I don't care what he does for money, the same way you don't care. Alejandro and Cayetano be may not be in the Republican army now, but they fought in Madrid, Jarama, Guadalajara, Teruel... they're lucky to still be alive."

"I think Alejandro, Cayetano and Scarlett do a fantastic thing now! The more people they can help out of Madrid and to Valencia, and then off to a safer place, the better. Maybe we should be the ones fleeing to Valencia while we still can."

The pair turned a corner and stepped into the pale spring sunshine. There on the edge of the hillside was the small truck. Alejandro and Cayetano stood next to the open door at the front of the vehicle, and Scarlett sat in the driver's seat. Alejandro glanced over to see his wife and sister coming in his direction. He dropped his cigarette on the path and dashed over to Sofía, and gathered her and their baby into his arms.

Luna stood back with a smile. Alejandro and Sofía were so in love. She could see her brother's face wet with tears as he held his wife. He had been gone three weeks, but the roads from Madrid to Valencia were the next target for the Franco army and the front lines of the war were just miles from Cuenca now. There were soldiers ready to shoot anything that moved in every valley. It would have been the most dangerous trip yet. Alejandro Beltrán Caño knew the obligation he had to his family, but he wanted adventure. Alejandro had wanted to fight the army and the onslaught that they brought to his nation. He wanted to look a Falange member in the eye as he speared the life from him, and had done so many times during the war. The Republicans desperately wanted to save their country. With the aid of his friend, Cayetano Ortega, he had almost built up enough cash to ferry the whole family out of España while the war raged. People in Madrid would pay what little money they had to have their families and their belongings driven from the uncertainty and starvation of Madrid to Valencia in the back of a small truck, so they could set sail for Francia.

"Buenos días, Señorita *Luna*."

Luna turned at the sound of Cayetano's voice. She savoured every word she heard from the man's mouth. His voice was deep, and it sent a sensation through her body that she wasn't sure she could trust. She was reluctant to look him in the eye for fear of what it did to her. "Buenos días, *Cayetano*," she said, and dared to look at the tall man. He held his dirty brown cap in his unwashed fist as he tried to tidy his uncombed curly black hair with his *other hand.* "Welcome home again."

"How have things been here? How are you?"

"I'm fine," *she shrugged.* "Sofía has been unwell."

Cayetano nodded. "I saw your father in Madrid. He is worried for you and Sofía. But he is too busy to come home. We suggested that he stays in Madrid for a little longer."

"Papá is safe? I have been so worried."

"Your father is fine. Alejandro will try to get back to Madrid next week with the truck and visit him. Your Papá will be okay. The Beltrán family will be back together soon."

"Luna," *Scarlett said, her voice stern. Luna looked over at the woman and squinted in the sunlight. She wasn't sure what to make of Scarlett.* "I'm sorry to hear that your mother passed away last month."

"Gracias," *she mumbled in return. Luna found her intimidating. Scarlett Montgomery had been a nurse with the International Brigade based out in Huete. But after the camp had been bombed, she travelled the 60 kilometres to Cuenca to work at the hospital, where Sofía befriended her. Scarlett was from a far off country, Nueva Zelanda, and had sailed to España in the hope of aiding the less fortunate caught up in the war. But now Scarlett had become disillusioned and had left nursing to help her friends Cayetano and Alejandro get people out of the country. Luna had no idea what Scarlett did with her share of the money. Now that her husband, Ulrich, a German soldier with the International Brigade, was dead, who knew what her plans were.*

"Now that Isabel has passed away," *Scarlett continued,* "what are you doing?"

"I help Sofía."

"She needs help, Scarlett," *Cayetano said. He knew that Scarlett didn't like Luna.*

"I'm aware of that," *Scarlett said as she got out of the truck.* "But a woman like Luna could do more to help save her country from invasion than just sit at home." *She folded her arms, which pulled at her oversized dark green shirt. It revealed the curves hidden under the androgynous clothing she wore.*

"Me? How?"

"Women are no longer confined to the kitchen, Luna. Women take up arms to fight alongside their brothers. They run political activism groups and set up charities for orphans. You are a caring person, perhaps with some training you could even be a nurse."

Luna looked Scarlett up and down. Her luscious deep red curls were pulled back from her face into a long ponytail. Her face carried a deadly serious expression. Alejandro had told her that Scarlett had come to España with three fellow countrymen who were eager to fight. They were all killed soon after they left Barcelona, which left Scarlett alone with no language skills. The woman had come a long way in two years, but it was easy to see that her heart had been darkened by the experience.

"Luna will marry Ignacio Reyes Paz, remember?" Cayetano said. "Luna will be going to Madrid with him. To associate herself with the enemy."

"Is that wise?" Scarlett asked.

"I thought that," Alejandro interjected. "Perhaps you would be safer in Valencia. Papá's plan to marry you off as a safeguard for our survival is ridiculous." He gave his sister a massive hug, happy to see her again after his hair-raising expedition.

"I don't know," Luna said once her brother had let her go. "I haven't spoken to Papá or Ignacio..."

"Or you could be more than a wife and fight for the Republican cause," Scarlett interrupted her.

"Leave Luna alone," Sofía said. "She's an innocent."

"I'm not a fool!" Luna bit back. "I know things and have seen things that I should never have had to experience because of this war, just like the rest of you. If there is a way I can help España, I will do it, but I care about the people I love first. Don't berate me for that."

Scarlett rolled her ice-blue eyes, and turned to fetch her bag off the seat of the truck. "I'm going home for a while. Are you coming or not, Cayetano?"

"I'll be right behind you," he replied.

"We might head back to our house for a while," Alejandro said. "You don't need to be at the hospital right away, do you, Sofía?"

"No, I have hours left yet," she said with a cheeky smile.

"I might go for a long walk," Luna said and threw a look at her sister-in-law. "You need some space."

"Cayetano," Alejandro said firmly. Cayetano smiled back at him when Alejandro threw him the 'leave my sister alone' expression.

As Alejandro, Sofía and Scarlett headed back down the hill in the direction of their homes, Luna noticed that Scarlett looked back over her shoulder at Cayetano. Her gaze also looked Luna up and down. She felt relieved when Scarlett disappeared around the corner and out of sight.

"I was wondering," Cayetano said, "do you have an escort for the fiesta next week?"

"No." Luna couldn't help but smile. "Besides, there was talk of it all being cancelled this year. Parties aren't exactly a priority. Last year they tried to hold it and it ended up being a riot. Sixteen people died!"

"Would you care to accompany me if your brother permits it?"

"Will you ask him that?"

Cayetano cringed. Alejandro's words rang in his ears. *Stay away from my sister. She deserves better than some bastard who has nothing to offer her except being a husband who will be dead before the end of the war.* "Perhaps we can meet at the fiesta," he offered. "Alejandro wouldn't object to us dancing. Besides, he is so caught up in Sofia. I have a suit, and I can use the bathhouse before then."

Cayetano at the bathhouse by the river? The poor young girl shivered at the thought. Imagine catching a sight of him while doing the laundry. "I would very much like to dance with you," she stuttered.

Cayetano grinned so much that he started to laugh. "Excellent. I will meet you at Plaza Mayor then."

"But won't you be taking Scarlett?"

"We live together as friends. Her husband only died six months ago. Even if it was appropriate to be romantically involved with her, I wouldn't be interested. Scarlett doesn't care what people think, and I'm not sure if she is even going to the fiesta."

"Scarlett doesn't like me."

"Scarlett doesn't like anyone. She has earned the right to not trust people. The pain she has suffered defies belief."

Luna watched Cayetano put his torn cap back on again. Luna could mend that hole in his cap. A little thread, a little time. "I will let you go and rest, you have had a long trip from Valencia."

Cayetano took her little hand in his, brought it to his lips, and gave her a tender kiss that was full of promise. "Until we meet again, Luna," he said in his deep, sensual voice.

She bid him a polite farewell, and decided to head in the direction of the river for a walk. The nation that Luna lived in burned around her in fear and bloodshed, and the fire in her heart had also been awoken.

Madrid, España ~ agosto de 2009

Mañana, mañana.

Luna groaned as she fought her way through the busy Madrid streets. *Mañana, mañana.* Procrastination at its finest. Bloody Spanish. *Sure, I will put everything off another day,* she had yelled at the woman at the desk of the *Registro Civil*. *Sure, I will come all the way back to Madrid another day, just because you're closing for siesta.* August was unofficial holiday month in Spain, so Luna should have been grateful the place had been open at all. Shit.

The trip to the New Zealand embassy after the trip to the registry office had been painless, but she couldn't get anything she needed from them until she had a copy of her grandfather's birth certificate from the *Registro Civil*. That place was like a zoo for humans. She had sat for hours amongst whining Spaniards, fussy babies and dozens of other irritations, only to be told the woman at the counter couldn't be bothered to help, because she was off to a bullfight that afternoon. Unbelievable. So typically Spanish. Work to live, not live to work.

Luna had walked 16 blocks in the 40-degree heat through the crowds for nothing. Now she had walked another 12 blocks back towards her hotel. Her white blouse and long, deep purple skirt clung to her tiny frame, and the sweat that poured from her made her feel awful. Her long curly black hair was tied up in a high ponytail, but it was stuck to the back of her neck. Even the folder of paperwork she carried was damp. She stopped at the pedestrian crossing and glanced through her black sunglasses at the electronic thermometer sign across the street. The red numbers read 43. It was still getting hotter.

That was August in Madrid for you.

The lights changed, and Luna set off across the street with the other tourists, and the locals who probably weren't going back to work after *siesta*. Luna was on Calle de Alcalá, the main road alongside Las Ventas, Madrid's famous bullring. People jostled and hurried to get into the ring for the fight that was due to start. The air was mixed with cigarette smoke and frustration as people tried to get out of the sun.

Over the sounds of the bustling Madrid streets, Luna heard her phone ring in her bag, and she stopped on the edge of the path, eager to answer it. She had left her twin sons, Giacomo and Enzo, at home in Valencia. It was the first time in their lives - all five years of it – that she had been away from them. Was something wrong? What if something horrible had happened? Her heart pounded in fear any time they were out of her sight. She felt guilty not bringing them along – there was so much to explore in Madrid.

"Darren?" she answered the phone. "Is everything all right?"

"Of course," his warm Australian accent said back to her. "Lulu, you need to stress less."

"Yeah, good luck with that," she muttered as she glanced up at the terracotta coloured bullring across the street. "What's up?"

"I just wanted to check and see how everything is going in Madrid."

"Miserable. The city is full, the people are rude, the embassy couldn't help me, and the *Registro Civil* was a fucking nightmare! The woman in the line ahead of me, she stood for 20 minutes, telling the woman who worked there her whole damn life story, and then it turned out they were cousins anyway, so she already knew the whole thing! What the fuck was the point?"

"So, it's much like the bank here?"

"Like the bank, or the pharmacy, or the phone company, or anywhere. Oh to be Spanish and have a friend who works somewhere that could be useful to you."

Darren chuckled as he listened to her little upset voice. "Calm down, Lulu."

"I don't want to fight the Spanish bureaucratic system!"

"Come on, you love a good fight."

"Not today."

"What did the embassy say?"

Luna started to walk along the path again; head down as she tried to concentrate on the conversation. "They said that if I have proof of my Spanish grandfather, then I am eligible for Spanish citizenship. I should be granted a permit. I haven't gotten into any trouble on my work permit in ten years, I have a job, and have children that were born here. But when they run my name through the court system database, Luna Montgomery flashes up."

"None of that was your fault."

"The embassy guy, he was a New Zealander like me, and he knew who I was. That kiwi woman in Spain who fought the legal system…"

"Don't be ashamed!" Darren replied. "You campaigned for harsher sentences for drunk drivers, that's not a negative thing."

"Yeah, I know…" Luna was tired. The last few years had been difficult in ways she never imagined. "If Fabrizio hadn't been killed…"

"It's okay, Lulu," he tried to reassure her. "Once this is done, everything will be under control, and we can live our lives together."

Luna sighed. Thank God for Darren James. He was the best friend anyone could hope to have. He had moved into her apartment with her and her twins when her husband Fabrizio died in a hit-and-run accident. Since then, he had helped her with the kids and been her support. "What if they don't renew your work permit next year? You will have to go back to Australia."

"No way, I will get my professional cycling contract renewed, and they will let me live here while I train. Don't worry, Luna. I'll never let you down."

"I guess I could get my citizenship and then marry you, so you could stay in Valencia with me," she joked.

"At least let me propose to you!" Darren had imagined it multiple times before, propose while they took the kids to school, or stood and laughed in the kitchen together, or just sat on the balcony of their apartment to watch the world below them. Many times Darren had imagined what it would be like if Luna loved him back, but it always seemed too soon after the death of his colleague and friend, Fabrizio Merlini.

"Well… you never know what could happen… a year from now."

"Indeed not," Darren replied with the sound of satisfaction in his voice. He could wait. "So, is your work in Madrid complete?"

"No! I couldn't get the birth certificate of Cayetano Ortega, this alleged grandfather of mine, so the trip is wasted. I'll need to come all the way back another day."

"That's a pity, but at least you have the rest of the day to enjoy Madrid. How is the hotel?"

"The hotel is excellent. You didn't need to book me into the Ritz. But… I think I might just get the train home. I could be home in five hours."

"No! Lulu, no, you wanted to spend a day in Madrid, so you should do it. And before you say it, don't worry about the kids. They have been fine all day, and they will help me cook dinner, so they say. I have finished all our housework. My godfather role is important to me."

"You're too kind to me. If you and the boys were here I could enjoy it…"

"Pity we don't have our babysitter available, or I could be there with you," Darren said. Stay the night in the hotel, just the two of them… away from the kids… a chance for her to understand how he felt about her. Luna would never agree to that; she worried about the kids too much.

"You're my babysitter," she chuckled. "Okay, I will stay. I think. Maybe."

"Good. Go to the Prado, even though you know every painting in the museum. Wander in the park. Browse the bookstores if they open after *siesta*. Relax. I'll call you later to check on you."

"Okay. I love you, Darren."

"I love you, Lulu." More than you realise.

Luna stuffed her phone into her bag and continued to step between the ambling masses. Luna Montgomery walked with purpose; no matter what the activity. There was no time for a stroll, no time to admire, no time to stop and relax. Shit, it was hot. The last thing she felt like doing was to fight crowds after an already difficult morning. She turned onto a shaded side street, a narrow cobbled lane that was protected from the blaze of the summer sun by the buildings and their leafy balconies. She started down the quiet street, a moment's peace away from the Madrileños and tourists.

Luna didn't feel the man come right up behind her, didn't hear a single sound. He shoved her and she stumbled, but knew what he wanted. It wasn't the first time someone had tried to steal her bag.

She grabbed the leather strap as he yanked it from her. The sudden pull caused her to drop her folder full of paperwork everywhere as she wrestled with him. But when he struck her in the face with a closed fist she had to let go. Luna fell to the ground as the wretched man ran off down the narrow lane.

"*¡Oye!*" A deep and full-bodied voice echoed down the street. Luna looked up to see a tall man dart out from a bar a few doors down from where she sat. The man pushed the bag-snatcher hard against the stone wall across the street and grabbed the bag from him. She watched as the man paused for a moment, undecided about which way to go – chase the man who had made a run for it, or come to her in the other direction.

Luna looked down at the path, and her heart sank. In the fall, her silver watch had come off her wrist and smashed on the smooth cobbles. Everything in her bag didn't mean a fraction to her compared to her watch. Silent tears, the same that accompanied her everywhere, every day, started to fall on her cheeks. She didn't have power or desire to stop them as she picked up her battered watch.

Through the haze of her tears, a hand appeared. Just as her stubborn nature was about to refuse the gesture, she glanced up, and the gentleman knelt down beside her. The olive features of his face accompanied a gentle but genuine smile. His jet-black hair was messed from his impromptu scuffle. A curl had fallen forward, and covered one of his honey brown eyes that gazed at her. "*¿Estás bien?*" he asked in a soft tone.

"I'm all right," Luna replied, her Spanish momentarily forgotten. "*Perdón...*" she apologised.

"I speak English," the man's rich voice replied. "Please don't cry, *preciosa*, I have your bag for you."

Luna almost felt a smile come to the corners of her lips. Just the word precious coming from his mouth made her feel better. She looked at the man who was right in front of her. Luna had blue eyes, but not just any blue eyes. They were a bright ice-blue, and they stopped people whenever they looked at her. With black hair, pale skin and cold blue eyes, her features were striking, and this handsome man had noticed. She took his outstretched hand. It felt like the first time in an age that Luna had accepted any kind of assistance.

"I'm Cayetano." He could feel the dampness of one of her tears between their hands. He glanced down for a moment and saw a wedding ring on her other hand. He let her hand go, and handed her the bag back.

"*Gracias,* Cayetano," she said. "I'm Luna."

"Let me get your papers, Luna," Cayetano replied, and bent over to scoop them up.

"No, please, I can do it," she pleaded, but it was no use. Cayetano had gathered them all together for her.

"Come and sit down with me," he said, and tried to tuck the papers back inside their folder. "My friend has a bar, just here…"

"No, I should keep going…"

"I insist."

Luna looked the man up and down for a moment. He was handsome. He hadn't shaved for a few days, and combined with the shining eyes, the cheeky smile, and concerned tone, he enticed her. No one enticed Luna. She glanced down at her broken watch felt a pang of guilt for even looking at this man. "No, I should go back to my hotel."

"You must come and sit with me. I don't want you to get the impression that Madrileños are unscrupulous people."

"I don't think that, assholes are everywhere."

Cayetano laughed as they reached the wide open doors to the small bar and the cold air-conditioned air that greeted them. "Please, Luna, reward me for my good deed and let me buy you a drink."

"Is that why you did it, for a reward?"

"Not at all," Cayetano replied. He gestured for her to go and sit at the table right at the back of the bar. "The fact that you are very lovely does make the victory far sweeter."

"Cayetano, *que fue impresionante,*" the man behind the bar said.

"No, it's nothing," Cayetano muttered as he glanced over his shoulder back onto the street. Not that fucking impressive, he hadn't caught the guy, which disappointed him. He turned to see his friend open his mouth again, and he shook his head. Shut up.

They sat down opposite each other, and Cayetano watched Luna with her broken watch in her fingers. He frowned; it was a bulky watch for a woman to wear. It looked like an expensive sports watch, and it looked too big for a small wrist like hers. She wore it on her right arm, he could tell from the slight tan line just above her hand. He wore his watch on the right arm, too; an unusual thing, even for a left-handed man like him. "Your watch is broken?"

"Yes," she sighed. "The clasp has been damaged for a while, but I didn't fix it. Now it's ruined."

Cayetano could swear she was about to cry again. She hadn't minded that her bag had been taken, and she didn't seem to mind her paperwork all jumbled and screwed up, but the watch hurt her. "Are you alone in Madrid?"

"Sí."

"Is there someone I can call for you? Perhaps your husband? He would like to know his wife is well after being hit in the face like that."

Luna brought her little hand to her face for a moment and looked up at the concerned man across the table. "This is my husband's watch."

Cayetano nodded. "I'm sure he won't mind."

"I suppose not," she replied, and tucked it into her large handbag that was on the spare chair against the wall. "He died almost three years ago."

"Oh," Cayetano stumbled. "I'm… I'm sorry."

The conversation was stalled by Cayetano's friend behind the bar, who had come and put two small glasses of red wine on their table. "Cayetano," his friend said in a cocky tone, *"ésta es hermosa."* He gestured at Luna.

"She can speak Spanish," Cayetano replied.

"Perdón, Señora," he said and excused himself from the table.

"I'm sorry," Cayetano said to Luna. He leaned forward over the small square table. "Please pay no attention to him."

"There are worse things than someone saying that I'm beautiful," Luna smiled. She picked up her wine and sipped it. She needed it today. "This is his bar?"

"Sí, he is an old friend of my father. My father helped him to decorate it years ago."

Luna looked around, the walls adorned with bullfighting memorabilia, photos, posters, the customary mounted black bull head over the bar. "He's a big fan of *corrida de toros.*"

"He is. So am I. Do you like bullfighting?"

"I have been a few times."

"How well do you know the bullfighters?"

"Not well," she confessed. "I only know Pablo Ortez Cantera, who is famous in Valencia where I live."

"I know him!" Cayetano said. "He's a terrific fighter. I have worked with him a few times."

"Doing what?"

Cayetano frowned for a moment. "I work at the Las Ventas bullring."

"You don't need to work today? Isn't there a giant fight on?"

"My day off. Tomorrow and Sunday are the main fights."

"Do you have to deal with all the tourists?"

"I… I work with the bulls. My father, he breeds bulls for fights."

"I would rather work with bulls than tourists," Luna quipped.

A smile spread over Cayetano's face as he sniggered, and she returned it. "Excuse me, *preciosa,* but wouldn't you be one of those tourists?"

"Me? I am just a *guiri.*"

"A dirty foreigner you are not," Cayetano said. "Where are you from?"

"New Zealand, but I have lived in Valencia for ten years. But I will always be a foreigner. I work as a tour guide, showing mostly Northern Europeans around the Turia park in Valencia by bicycle."

"A bicycle tour guide?" he asked. "Unusual job."

"It's a very, very long story." She twisted the platinum ring on her finger. It felt gratifying to be out for a change.

Cayetano watched her fiddle with her wedding band, and decided not to ask any more. "So why are you in Madrid?"

Luna groaned and placed one hand on her jumbled folder of paperwork. "That is an even longer story. I need to take on the Spanish bureaucratic system."

"I fear you never leave the city."

"I have been at the *Registro Civil* this morning. I thought there was no worse hell than the Valencia office, but Madrid is all new misery and laziness rolled together."

"My sister works at the *Registro Civil.*" He watched Luna's pretty face cringe, and he chuckled. "My sister has also long been known as lazy, so she is perfect there. Did you get what you needed?"

"No, I need a birth certificate, and it seems that the Madrid office doesn't have what I need, which is a big problem." She watched him take a sip of his wine. His dark eyes looked over the rim of the glass at her. His fingers that held the glass looked so scarred, but tanned and strong. She watched him lick his lips to take a single drop of wine from them, and rubbed them together. This scruffy stranger sent a spike of something through her that she hadn't felt in a long time. *It's okay to admire a handsome man, Luna. Don't tell yourself otherwise.*

"Would you like me to walk you back to your hotel?"

"You mean in the interest of my personal safety?"

"I can't save the damsel and then send her on her way, without knowing that she's safe."

"How do I know that you are any good for me?"

"I'm not good, Luna," he said. "People who are good, they are usually that way out of fear of some kind. I have no fear of anything. I have an immense respect for many things, but I don't choose to conform. That way I don't need to be good, and instead can be open to experience life."

"Sounds like a bachelor's excuse to misbehave."

"It could also be that," he nodded with a smile. "What you were supposed to say was that you were astounded by my bravery with the guy who took your bag."

"Oh, I see." It was rather impressive how he had shoved the guy. It was clear that Cayetano was a strong and agile man. It didn't matter that she didn't know him, because she was attracted to someone, for the first time in a long time. "That bastard hit me in the face!"

"Yes, he did," Cayetano replied with a half-smile at her delayed reaction.

"*Gracias.* Did I say that? Thank you for getting my bag back."

"*De nada.* Are you sure you don't need me to walk you back to your hotel?"

"I wasn't going back to the hotel. I was going to go to the Prado."

"It will be busy this time of day. Perhaps you would enjoy a walk in El Retiro with me instead."

"You're persistent," Luna replied, and she watched him shrug. "Okay, a walk in the park."

It was busy in Buen Retiro Park on the August afternoon. Locals looked for shade from the heat, and mingled with sunburned tourists, who wandered around in wonder of the city oasis. Cayetano seemed to want to walk away from the main paths and people, so they walked from one shaded spot to another beneath the lush trees. The cool grass that tickled Luna's feet between her sandal straps was such a contrast to the heat.

"What's in the folder that you hold so tight?" Cayetano asked. "I saw something about the *guerra civil.*"

"I'm interested in the Spanish civil war."

"That can't make you popular."

"Why do you say that?"

Cayetano shrugged. "I was raised to never talk about it. I was born just before Franco's dictatorship ended, and my Papá, he wanted me to never talk about anything Franco related."

"I'm a foreigner, so I don't even get an opinion on politics in Spain."

"You can have an opinion." Cayetano smiled. "Whether anyone listens is another thing. So, what interests you about the war?"

"A mystery."

"Interesting."

"It is. A mystery and a mighty long, sad story. One I had hoped to clear up today at the *Registro Civil.*"

"What do you need? Maybe I could ask my sister to help you."

"I have to come back to Madrid one day and try again," Luna said. "But thank you. I needed my grandfather's birth and death certificates. But he died in the war, and the records are not complete."

Cayetano nodded. She was clearly a foreigner, because she had just spoken of the civil war in public. It was better, and far more polite, not to talk about the war. That was the case in the family he had been brought up in. "You're Spanish?"

"So the rumour says," she half-smiled and looked over at him. His expression was hidden under his sunglasses. "My grandmother was a nurse during the war. She got pregnant to some Spanish guy, and I only have his name and nothing more. My grandmother went home to New Zealand, and my father was born three months later."

"And you want to find out who your grandfather is?"

"I need to prove I have a Spanish grandparent, so I can be granted permanent citizenship in Spain. My work visa is about to expire, so it's time to become permanent here."

"You don't want to go home?" Cayetano asked. They turned on to Paseo de la Argentina, a beautiful tree-lined pedestrian avenue, adorned with white marble statues that glistened the sun in the clear sky over them.

"I have nothing to go home to."

"No family?"

"No." Luna took a deep breath. The pain of that fact followed her around.

"You are the opposite of me," Cayetano replied, and placed his hand over his heart. "I love my family very much, but they are around me all the time."

"A bit smothering, is it?"

"You have no idea."

Luna looked around; it seemed as they walked, everyone took a second glance at them, and it seemed strange. She turned and looked to Cayetano who walked with his head down. "Do you get the impression that we're being watched?"

"Maybe they're thinking, 'why is the beautiful woman hanging around with that *revoltijo?* That will be it."

"You're not a mess." Not at all. He may have been unshaven, with messy hair, but the clothes he wore were an expensive kind of casual. The sunglasses on his face were not a cheap pair.

"We are walking the right way to your hotel, *¿no?*"

"*Sí.* I'm staying on Plaza de la Lealtad, at the Ritz."

"I'm not sure I'm classy enough to walk the lady to the Ritz."

"But you are my *acompañante,* my chaperone, here to keep me safe on the mean streets of Madrid," she joked.

"I couldn't leave a lady on her own. By the way, Madrid is the greatest city in the world."

"After Valencia, yes, it is."

"I'm sorry, but if you believe that, we can't be friends. Valencia greater than Madrid? Never."

"Spain is like sand, it slips through your fingers when you try and hold onto it. It changes in the blink of an eye. While Madrid is busy feeling smug, Valencia could easily be bypassing Madrid as it continuously evolves."

"No chance; never going to happen," Cayetano said as they stopped to cross the street that separated the park from the street to the hotel. They started across the street with the crowds, and were relieved to be back in the shade between the buildings of the narrow street a minute later. The small curved street that the Ritz dominated was quiet. They came to a stop outside the hotel, and Cayetano nodded hello to the doorman who stood very astute in his black suit.

"I shall leave the lady for the rest of her day," Cayetano said formally, and Luna giggled. "But in all seriousness, I hope you're all right, Luna."

"*Gracias,* Cayetano. I will treat myself to a walk through the Prado museum to see my favourite painting, and forget the whole incident."

"Which is your favourite painting?"

" 'The Garden of Earthly Delights' by Hieronymus Bosch."

"Ah, 'El Bosco', I know his work. It's the one full of naked figures to depict sexual freedom? That big triptych, *¿no?*"

"Yes," Luna said with raised eyebrows. She was impressed that he knew that.

"It has the lovers in the glass ball. Pleasure is as fragile as glass, is that the expression?"

"Yes it is."

"Would you like to go out for dinner with me?" Cayetano asked. The words practically fell from his mouth. "The Goya restaurant here in the hotel is excellent."

"The Goya restaurant here is phenomenal. A little too fancy for me."

"Nonsense, I can get us a table, I promise… unless you need an excuse not to have dinner with a humble bull-minder?"

A smile spread over Luna's smile as she sniggered. The humble bull-minder was an intriguing man. A handsome man. *Live a little.* "All right, dinner."

"Good. How about I meet you at midnight? Is that convenient for you? I'll meet you in the lobby, by the staircase."

"That would be good. Are you sure midnight is not too early?"

"Perhaps, but I can try and show up on time. It's a date, as they say." He placed his hand on her arm. "See you soon, *Señora.*"

"*Hasta luego.*" Luna couldn't contain her smile as the doorman opened the glided main entrance to the lavish hotel, and she left her new friend. *Hang on, a date?*

Madrid, España ~ agosto de 2009

Cayetano stood full of impatience in the lobby of the hotel under the soft lights dotted around the room. In one moment, this woman had bewitched him, just there on the path in a daze. He had gone home and tidied himself up, and then he realised that was a mistake. Dressed casual and unkempt made it easy to fit in, and Luna had taken to that look, which surprised him. But now he looked like himself – the 'himself' that everyone knew. Dressed in his finest black suit, with his hair combed back, and his face smooth, he had become recognisable now. He was about to dine in a restaurant that was a place 'to be seen'. Once Luna knew who he was, the whole thing could go rather different to what he hoped for. The unassuming way he had met Luna was a breath of fresh air. She hadn't heard of him, didn't know what he did, she didn't know who his family was. Imagine if his wife knew where he was.

Luna walked into the lobby of the hotel, her purse held tight in her hand. She had spent the rest of the afternoon in the air-conditioned halls of the Prado art gallery in peace. She was never alone, not with two five-year-olds, so this was new for her. She missed her boys and had called them before their bedtime. They were in Darren's safe hands, but after she spoke to each of them, she did wonder why she hadn't just gone back to Valencia on the train. Just because Darren thought she needed a night off – her first in five years – didn't mean it was a bright idea, fancy hotel room or not. She had stood at the mirror in her ornate 100-year-old room, and wondered what the hell she was doing. She hadn't come prepared for a date. In fact, all she had to wear was the outfit she had packed for the following day, a simple ice-blue dress. With luck, it would make the grade for the Goya Restaurant.

She stood on the spot in the lobby, and twirled one of her long black ringlets in her fingers and tried to spot Cayetano. Maybe he had changed his mind. While her mind told her that would be a good thing, it hurt to think she wouldn't see the engaging man again. Her eyes spotted him across the room by the staircase, just like he had said. The man she met on the street was gone. Stood before her was an impeccable gentleman. She watched him take swift steps towards her with a smile on his face. Did this man want dinner with her? He was the man that all women had in mind when they imagined a tall, dark and handsome Latin man who could whisk them away. She had that fantasy a few times herself, as cheesy and predictable as it was.

"*Buenas noches, preciosa,*" he purred.

"Good evening. I almost didn't recognise you."

"In that case, let me re-introduce myself," he said, and put his hand out. "I am Cayetano Morales. I'm pleased to meet you."

It occurred to Luna that she hadn't even got his surname earlier. "Luna Montgomery," she said and shook his hand.

"Shall we, *Señora?*" he said with a tempting smile and offered his arm. She tucked her hand into his elbow, and they set off toward the restaurant. "I hope you don't mind, but I ordered for us already. The degustation menu, so we can try a little of everything."

"Been here before, have you?" she asked as they were greeted by the waiter at the entrance.

"Once, with work colleagues, they brought us for dinner." Slight lie there, it was your wife's Christmas party last year.

"Just for the record, I would have been just as happy going to a little tapas place, to laugh at Spaniards who toss their little napkins on the floor."

"What else are we supposed to do with them?"

"Put them in the bin?"

Cayetano scoffed. "Foreigners, you just don't get it."

They were seated in the corner, the silver of the cutlery and the sparkle of the crystal wine glasses glistened in the dim light of the candlelit tables around the high-ceiling room. Cayetano felt relieved when the cava, a sweet sparkling wine from the Catalonia region, was poured. For the first time in a while, he felt nervous. It had been a while since he had been on a date, and the beautiful creature across the table enchanted him. They sat there through the small courses of their dinner, the meal full of light and relaxed chat about anything that seemed to come up, but Cayetano was so taken with her that he didn't pay too much attention to the polite conversation. Silence would fall over on the chit-chat at times, but he hadn't minded. He was comfortable to sit there with her.

"So how did you become a bicycle tour guide?" he asked as the final course was cleared from the table, which left them with the remainder of the second bottle of cava.

"It was the only job I could get," Luna cringed. "I needed a job, and I like bikes and can speak Spanish and English. Plus I know Valencia well. It's shift work, which is what I need."

Cayetano frowned. She seemed ashamed of what she did for a living. "What did you do before this?"

"I was a road-racing bicycle mechanic on the European pro-racing cycling circuit."

"Wow! That's new to me. How did you get into that?"

Luna shrugged. "I just always like riding bikes. I used to ride with my father when I was a kid. I got a job after school at the bike store close to home, and it was fun. I like working on bikes. Then, when I was 18, the world changed on me."

"What happened?"

"There was a professional cycling event on in Australia, and my father and I decided to fly over and watch. It was the racers from Europe who came to compete. For me, as a kid, it was so exciting, and a chance to see my heroes. When I got there, I happened to meet a guy, Darren. He was my age and had the same job as me."

"Sounds like a romance."

"No, no," she dismissed him. "But Darren had a friend who worked on one of the cycling teams. He managed to get us through to where the riders were and see the bikes that we were in awe of. That is where I met Fabrizio Merlini."

Cayetano sat back in his plush chair for a moment. That name was familiar.

"You have that look," Luna sighed. "The one everyone has. The 'why do I know the name Fabrizio Merlini?' look. What did he do to get his name on the television?"

"He died," Cayetano said as it came to him. Of course, the famous

Italian sportsman killed in Spain. That had been hot news. "A cyclist killed by a drunk driver in Valencia." In the bar earlier - the watch. It was my husband's - he died. He looked up at her, and her sweet, alluring smile had gone, now just a stiff expression. "You were married to Fabrizio Merlini?"

"Yes," she said awkwardly. "A few years after we first met, I managed to get a job on his cycling team, so we got to spend more time together. He was based in Valencia for training so that is why I moved to Spain not long after we got married. When he died I needed to find a new job. I couldn't face going back to work with his team."

"I'm sorry. The guy who killed him went to jail, didn't he?"

"I don't like to talk about that guy, it's…. it's pretty raw for me."

"Yes, I'm sorry…"

"It's okay," Luna replied. Her gentle smile came back. "Perhaps the story of how you work at the bullring is more compelling. What do you do when there are no fights on?"

"Well…" Damn. More lies. "Bulls need to be bred for fights. We also breed horses, but I don't have much to do with that side of the business."

"That is a very unusual job." Luna leaned forward onto the table as she spoke. "How did you get into that?"

"My father gave me the job. Now I just do whatever he tells me."

"It's like a family business?"

"Yes, my father used to do it. But now I am the… bull-minder … of the family."

"Wow. I guess you like animals then."

"No, I don't," he confessed with a smirk, and watched her laugh. He leaned forward onto the table again. He wanted to get closer to her and her perfect smile. There was something about her, something so captivating, and he was attracted to her in an understated but powerful way. But she had just lost her husband, so whatever carnal male thoughts he had been having earlier about the end of a date with the pretty woman were on hold.

"So, have you had any more ideas on how you will solve the mystery of your grandfather?" Cayetano asked. His hand had drifted from the base of his wine glass in the direction of her delicate fingers that rested on the white linen tablecloth.

"No," she replied, and frowned. "I'll come back when they find something on him in their records, but I do wonder if the whole thing is pointless."

"Perhaps you need to marry someone to stay in the country," he teased.

"Yes, well… that has been suggested."

"Have a man all lined up, do you?"

"No," she smiled. "I can get my work permit renewed. But I want to gain my residency here. I want to do this for myself. From what I know, this man, my supposed grandfather, Cayetano Ortega, owes his family something. It seems he wanted nothing to do with my grandmother when she got pregnant."

"How much do you know?"

"Not much. My mother died when I was young, so I was raised by my father. He lost his own mother when he was young, so family was a subject he didn't want to talk about."

"It sounds as if your father had a very painful time."

"He did. He died 10 years ago. My mother had passed away 15 years earlier, and he never got over it. He would talk about her all the time, but I never knew her. He had lost his own mother, and his father was some man named Cayetano from a country he had never seen. We were on our own."

Cayetano gently ran his thumb over the back of her little hand. She again wore her wedding ring. "I'm sorry, Luna. Family is valuable. It must have been so hard, to leave behind his only child."

"I had just got married when he died, and my husband had promised my father he would take excellent care of me. I think that helped."

Cayetano watched Luna take a deep breath. Only the husband hadn't taken care of her. The conversation had become deep again, and it hurt her. There had to be a way to ease it back again. "You're right. This Cayetano does owe his family something. Do you know where he was from?"

"My grandmother, Scarlett, she worked in Cuenca when she got pregnant. My father thought that Cayetano was from somewhere around there."

"Perhaps you need to go to Cuenca," Cayetano suggested. "Have you ever been?"

"No. It's not that far from Valencia, but I've never visited. I came to live in Spain for reasons that had nothing to do with my heritage, so until now I have had no reason to find Cayetano. It seems that information is hard to find. It seems he just vanished into thin air. That is why my grandmother returned to New Zealand at the end of the war. He just abandoned her."

"Are you sure he died? I mean… maybe he just ran off?"

"You mean, am I sure that he wasn't dragged from his bed in the night, murdered and stuffed in a shallow grave?"

"Given the time period, anything could have happened."

"I guess anything is possible. From the way my father spoke, his mother must have told him that his father was dead. I can only trust what she said. Of course, I have no one I can ask these things." She watched as his fingers curved along the back of her hand. When he touched her, it had sent a sharp spike through her senses. Far from home, far from reality, it seemed natural to be out with a man.

Cayetano shrugged. "I have both of my parents. I also have my mother's parents in my life. I'm blessed. Even so, if I asked my grandparents about the war, they would not speak of it. *El pacto del olvido.*"

Luna held her tongue for a moment. The pact of forgetting. Nobody wanted to talk about the civil war, or even of the 35 years that the dictator Francisco Franco held on to Spain after his victory. Franco was a subject that was never discussed. She looked at the man across the table. He was probably about 40, so born in the late sixties, a time where the years of starvation were over in Spain, yet still a time of exceptional difficulty and atrocious crimes were still committed against innocent people. The Spain they sat in today and the Spain that Cayetano would have been born into were very different. Generalissimo Franco had died in 1975, a year before Luna was born. Spaniards born before Franco's death, and those born after had totally different lives and upbringings. It was not something she had ever discussed with a Spaniard. *La Transición,* the transition to democracy had been achieved by smothering the past and Luna knew she was up against decades of fear when looking for her grandfather.

"Enchufe," Cayetano said.

"What about it?" Luna asked. "I'm a foreigner, I have no *enchufe.*" *Enchufe,* knowing a person who knows someone who knows someone who could get you whatever you want. A little nepotism never hurt anyone. Except those who had no *enchufe.*

"But I do. My sister, Sofía, she works at the *Registro Civil.* I'll call her, and see if she can help you. You can't run back and forward between Madrid and Valencia for a piece of paper that may not exist."

Luna glanced down at her hand again. Now, all of his fingers caressed the back of her hand. His large fingers more or less covered her entire hand. She glanced back up at Cayetano; he had leaned right forward over the table as he looked back at her. His honey brown eyes were soft as they gazed back at her, and flecks of green in his eyes sparkled. Luna became aware of how revealing her low cut dress was. She had brought it to keep her cool in the hot weather, but with the fiery eyes of the Spaniard on her, it turned up the heat. "I don't know," she said. "I think Madrid was worth the trip."

"I would like to think so," Cayetano replied. "You never know what you will find in Madrid."

"Maybe something I didn't know to look for."

"Perhaps." His fingers began to trail up her arm, and they delighted every inch of skin they touched. "How was 'The Garden of Earthly Delights' at the Prado? As sexually liberating as you hoped?"

Another playful smile graced her face. "Yes, thank you. I'm a believer in sexual expression."

"Really?" he asked with a raised eyebrow. He hadn't expected that.

"I just think people should be able to express themselves how they like, with whoever they like."

"I think I should have come and looked at these naughty paintings with you, it would have been quite an excursion."

"I'm interested in 18th century Spanish art and 15th and 16th century Italian work. Most of it is religious, or dark."

"The humble bull-minder can't keep up with that."

"Humble isn't a word I would use."

Cayetano couldn't help it. His lips were stuck in a broad smile. They had been most of the night. He wasn't sure what it was, but the foreign girl had him in trance and she didn't seem to realise it. "Maybe I could seduce you into some dessert?" he asked.

"I think you mean convince."

"No, I meant seduce."

"I've never been seduced."

"Never? Do you like to be in charge instead?"

Luna nodded once and watched the grin on his face. It was fun to play with him. He was charming and flirtatious. *What the hell are you doing, Luna?* You don't even know this man. Somehow that didn't matter, he stirred an emotion in her that had been dormant for years, and she didn't even feel guilty about that.

"*Perdón,*" came the voice of their waiter. Cayetano and Luna sat up straight again, surprised at the intrusion. "*¿Necesitas algo?*" he asked politely.

Luna glanced at Cayetano and shook her head. "I don't need anything. I'm done with dinner."

"I know I am," he replied. "*¿Puedo tener la cuenta, por favor?*" he said to the young man.

"No, I will pay," Luna interrupted. "I'm the guest here."

"You will not, a gentleman wouldn't allow that."

"Are you always such a gentleman?"

"*Claro.* Of course. Will you allow me to walk you to your door? After all, you have been attacked once today already."

The bill settled, Cayetano and Luna walked through the silent lobby and took the short elevator ride to her floor. The ride was made in silence, but Luna was well aware of how close to her he stood. His whole body radiated a masculinity she hadn't been able to appreciate in a while. It was a raw attraction, something she didn't realise she was brave enough to indulge in until now.

"This is my room," she said and gestured to the door only a few steps from the elevator. He had held the door for her. Nobody did that anymore.

"I told you that it wasn't safe for you to walk on your own," he joked. "Lucky I was here."

Luna leaned back on the door of her hotel room and held her breath. Cayetano stood right in front of her, one arm against the door, his elbow just above her shoulder and leaned into her. "You didn't have to walk me to my door."

The most lascivious heart-pounding smile poured over Cayetano's face. He ran one finger over her bottom lip, and felt the palpable tremble that ran through her. "Is it true, what you said earlier?" he asked quietly. "That you have never been seduced?"

"It's true. I don't get myself into positions where men think they can seduce me."

"Have you ever wanted to be seduced?"

"Many times," she whispered as Cayetano brought his lips to hers. It was such a soft and gentle kiss, a hesitant moment as their flirtations came together for the first time. He ran an arm around her waist, and she weakened to him, folded into him while he poured his lips over hers. His addictive and captivating taste surged through her as her hands grasped at his shoulders. His tongue parted her lips, and she let herself yield to him. Now was time to think up an excuse to stop being so reckless, but her mind no longer cared. *Damn you, cava.*

"This is the time that I politely say goodnight, isn't it?" he asked, his lips almost touching hers. He didn't want to move from his spot against her.

"I suppose it is. Though I was about to I invite you in… to enjoy the view."

"I'm already enjoying the view," he whispered.

Luna's hand fumbled to get the door open, and the two of them stumbled into the dark room. Having his body against hers sent a deep ache through her, an ache she hadn't felt in a long time, and she realised how desperately she missed it. She didn't even know this man, yet he set her on fire. The last time she had felt like this, she had only been a girl, awakened by the man who would become her husband. Her husband.

"Wait," she stumbled, and pulled her body from his. They were entangled in a frenzied fumble of hands and mouths, and it was too much. When did she become this woman? This weakling who couldn't decide what to do? Luna wasn't soft, she was fiery. For almost three long years she had been a quiet, prim and proper mother of two. For almost three years, her risk-taking nature had been suppressed by pain, and it saw an opportunity to be wild and stupid. So why couldn't she just take it?

Cayetano stood with his fists clenched for a moment and tried to maintain some level of composure. "I'm sorry," he said through a deep breath. "I am. If you want me to leave…"

"I don't know what I want," she replied. She was in danger of being swept away by him, and maybe that was what she wanted. "But I'd like to find out what I want."

Cayetano stepped forward and brought her back into his embrace. He wasn't about to screw up his night of guilty pleasure. This wasn't cheap sex, they had spoken of seduction, and that was what he wanted. It had been so long since Luna had felt a kiss from a man; he knew that. He had to be soft yet strong, gentle and firm, loving and passionate, all at once. He wanted to touch her until she felt dizzy, as if she would to melt into him. He brought her lips to his, a sincere and resounding kiss, and when their lips parted she gasped for air. Kisses and cava, an intoxicating combination. She wanted to be seduced tonight. He held her against him and kissed her again, eager to taste her supple lips that were happy to accept his affection, happy to surrender to what he wanted to give her. She felt vulnerable in his arms, and he didn't dare to push her further than she could handle. Her hands dropped the buttons of his jacket, and Cayetano felt a jab of need shoot through him. She wanted to undress him, and God, he wanted that himself.

Luna felt overpowered by the situation she found herself in, and she didn't care. She was dizzy on the sensations of his warm body against hers. She held her breath when she felt him unzip her dress, and the blue fabric pooled around her feet on the floor. The cold, lonely voices in her head were lost to the heat her body experienced against the bare flesh of another person. She had thought that she would never feel like that again. When you meet the love of your life, you don't move on from that. Luna wasn't the girl she once was, she was now a woman who yearned for the physical power of a man. All of her senses took the man in, one urge at a time. Her eyes drifted from his, down to just below his right shoulder to a huge, violent scar that disfigured his skin. Her hand instinctively went to the wound and followed its lines over his defined chest, further and further down his body. It was a horrific injury once. Luna's hands stopped when they reached the button on his trousers, but she knew the scar went further, and she wanted to see all of him.

Cayetano watched as her ice-blue eyes came back to meet his. The look on her face suggested she had abandoned her guard. "Indulge me," she murmured.

With one quick sweep, he picked her up in his arms and carried her over to the bed. He wanted her, even still half-dressed that was obvious, but there was no rush. There was so much to touch, so much to elicit. He gave her a slow and powerful kiss when she began to undo his trousers. While she seemed ready for the passion he could show her, she was still was stunned as him at the spontaneous emotions that they invoked in each other. He felt her tremble as his hands ran over her skin and curved in between her legs, and she cried out through their hungry kiss. He knew that he should slow down, but the awakening she brought in him must have rushed through her as well, and any rational thought was long gone. Her hands were on his body, curving over him, and the way she touched told him how much she wanted him. She wanted him just as much as he wanted her. She was no shrinking violet.

Cayetano took his time with Luna, despite the mutual craving they felt. She wanted to be indulged, to be seduced, and yet that was what she was doing to him. He was being swept away by the power of a woman he didn't know. She had been blown into his life, and that only served to make it more eruptive. Cayetano had taken many lovers in his time, but none of them had sent such a message of desire through his veins as Luna did. The patient and sensitive nature to their passion defined the night in his mind forever. It was a powerful and satisfying seduction. He was so exultant he would have forgotten his own name if Luna hadn't called it out. The desperate way she struggled to breathe when they moved together made him shiver. The way she dug his fingernails into his skin sent excitement through him. The way she curved her legs around his, and held on to him when they rocked against each other delighted him. Luna wanted the night of guilty pleasure as much as Cayetano did, and it shattered every sense in his body when they worked their way over the edge of satisfaction together.

The whispers of morning light had come in the window when Cayetano woke. It had been a long time since he stayed all night with a woman. Usually he found an excuse and left, but after he had made love to Luna, he simply didn't want to go. He had sat up on one elbow, and listened to her while she spoke to him. His hands continued to trace along the inside of her leg during the light and intimate conversation. He had fallen asleep when the exhaustion of their union had taken its toll. It was not the night for him to be up late – in fact, it was now early morning and his world would be wondering where he was. He jolted awake when his body realised where he was, and in the process, he had woken the sleeping beauty in his arms.

"I'm sorry," he said in her ear. "I have to go, *preciosa.*"

"Oh," Luna said, and sat up, and held the sheet against her chest. "Of course, yes."

"I have to go to work." Cayetano sat up next to her. "I must be running late already. Sorry."

"No, it's fine," she stuttered. "You go."

Cayetano ran his hand against her cheek and cupped her face in his hand. "It isn't because I want to leave, I promise you."

"It's no problem," she smiled. "We don't have to pretend this is any more than it is. You should go and do what to you need to do."

"It's not what I want to do," he whispered, and brought his lips to hers. The second they touched he felt the power of their connection again. The way her kiss seared into him made him ache. He didn't want to go anywhere. His hand drifted away from her face, and took the sheet from her fingers, and let it fall so his hand could touch her body. His fingers grazed past a nipple as his hand clutched at her breast, and he knew he wasn't going anywhere. Before he knew it, they were in the bed again, entangled in each other. He could swear that tears were going to come to his eyes. Inside this hotel room was a stolen season of life. No one would ever know what happened, and he could forever enjoy the astonishing moment of raw passion he felt for this woman. To hell with work. To hell with obligation. Pleasure was as fragile as glass. Like glass, this spell had to be broken, and they both knew it.

4

Valencia, España ~ agosto de 2009

No matter how smooth the train trip from Madrid to Valencia was, Luna thought she would be sick. She sat curled up in her seat with her head against the window. The view out across the plains of Castile-La Mancha, with the fields of sun-scorched earth stretched out before her, but she couldn't even open her eyes. She wanted to bawl, cry out the agony of what she had just done. Her eyes were wet under her huge dark sunglasses, and she didn't dare move a muscle, or the droplets would pour down her face. She could barely move her muscles anyway. Her body ached, awakened when Cayetano had made love to her. She must have held on to him tight with all four limbs, because every time she moved, everything burned in pain. She throbbed from the inside out from what they had done, whether that was from the physical act that they had committed – twice – or from the guilt. She had slept with a man who she didn't know. A few cheeky glances and a few flirty lines and she was on her back. Luna wanted to wake up this morning and feel good about herself. She had overcome a massive hurdle in moving on after the death of her husband, but she had thrown herself away on a mistake. Luna wasn't cut out for this; she wanted to love someone. Sure, when she lay in bed at night she wanted a man there, but a physical partner wasn't enough for her. Since there was no man for her anymore, a sexual substitute didn't suit at all. She felt conflicted in so many ways. Cayetano had asked for her phone number, and she had given it to him, but she didn't expect to hear from him. She wasn't sure she wanted to hear from him, but if she gave out her number it meant that she could fool herself and think that they had just had more than a cheap one-night stand. None of this made any sense. Last night it had seemed like a great idea. To have him close made her feel alive again. She had woken up to another world. A world where she wasn't miserable, and that only brought on more guilt. Her husband was dead. *You shouldn't get over that and be happy.* This man, this Cayetano, was dangerous. He had brought feelings she didn't know she wanted to have bubbling to the surface.

'Have you ever wanted to be seduced?' 'Many times'. Many times? How could you say something that ridiculous? Sure you think it, you don't say it! In one night, Luna had ruined what had been a private adult life. The only man that had ever laid a hand on her was her husband, and now she had let herself be used. God, it had felt good. Caught up in the bed sheets, the way her legs felt weak when he opened them, the throbbing that pounded its way through her veins as he took her. The way his lips bit at hers as his hands ran over her naked body. The way he growled when she had placed her hands inside his firm thighs to touch him. She had done that.

Luna took a deep breath and unlocked the door to her apartment, eager to see her family. What had happened in Madrid could stay there. She needed to go into her apartment and back into her life. The moment she stepped through the door she saw her gorgeous redheaded sons run from the living room into the entrance way with enormous smiles.

"Mummy, you're back!" Enzo squealed, and wrapped his little arms around one leg. Enzo was her soft, gentle one, the sweet soul, a total angel.

"We missed you," Giacomo said. "You're home early. Did you bring us presents?" Giacomo was the boss of the two boys, so he thought. He had begun to develop a personality much like Fabrizio's, which amused his mother.

"I did," she said, and they moved into the living room, where she unzipped her case to pull out the puzzles she had brought them, to more squeals of delight. "Where's Darren?" she asked them. He should have been with the boys.

"He's in the shower," Enzo said, without looking up from where he had sat at the table with his puzzle. "He said he would be quick."

"I will go and see if he's out," she said and ran her hand through

Giacomo's curly red hair. "Can you boys play here for a moment?"

"Yep," they both replied quickly in unison.

Luna headed down the hall, past her office and the children's room, past her own bedroom, and down a second hallway to Darren's room. He had a large bedroom and bathroom in a separate part of the apartment, away from the bustle of children. Luna had given it to him when he moved in, in case he had a girlfriend to bring home and didn't need the interruption of his best friend and her two kids in the way. Darren never had given her any indication that he was seeing anyone. Ever. Not once in the almost three years he had lived there since Fabrizio had died. She knocked on the partially open bedroom door, to no answer. She went into the empty room, but she could hear a noise in the bathroom. She sat down on the end of the bed. Then it hit her - she couldn't tell Darren about last night. Imagine how hurt he would be, that she would do something like that behind his back. *Behind his back? You aren't with Darren, Luna. You should be with him, and you know it. That is why he doesn't bring women home – you are the woman in his life, and you let him think that.* Luna watched Darren come out of the bathroom in just a towel, and his face lit up in a mixture of shock and surprise. "Lulu! What are you doing here?"

"I live here."

"I was going to meet you at the Estació del Nord."

"I got the early train instead. I wanted to come home this morning."

"I was watching the kids, I swear. I was in the shower for only a few minutes. I thought they would be fine," he stuttered.

"Of course they are," she dismissed his worry. "You have done a great job with them. I appreciate it."

"I have something to tell you," he said as he tightened the towel around his waist. "But... it's quite serious. About Giacomo."

"What?" she frowned. "What happened?"

Darren crossed the room and poked his head down the hallway, to make sure the boys weren't in earshot. He turned back to her and ran his hand over his mouth. "This morning, I made them breakfast. When I gave Giacomo his cereal, he just looked up at me and said, 'thank you, Papá'."

"Shit," Luna said slowly. Giacomo and Enzo didn't know their father at all, and never would. Luna and Darren had never given them the impression that Darren was their father.

"I guess the other kids talk that about their fathers at school, you know, talk about their home lives."

"The day had to come where they started asking questions." There he was - Luna's best friend since she was 18. The man was gorgeous, stood there in next to nothing, his toned athlete body still a little damp. Luna knew how he felt about her, but she always felt too guilty to act on it. If she could whore herself out, she could take her relationship with Darren up a gear. Her kids thought he was their father. He had done so much for her. He knew her so well. He was the one she had to be with in a relationship. *You can move on, and the perfect man is right in front of you.*

"I have to confess, I didn't correct him," Darren said, and watched her stand up. "I didn't know what to say, so I just let the moment pass. I... I didn't know how you would react."

"They do what they feel is right," she replied. She took a few steps to stand right in front of him. "You're the male role model in their lives."

"I take it seriously."

"Thank you for giving me a night off."

"You're very welcome. Do you feel better for it?"

"I have had a lot time to think," she replied. "About me, the kids, you... did you miss me?"

"I did. I put the kids to bed last night, and then had no one to curl up with on the couch."

"Would you like to curl up with me now?"

"I think you know what I want." He didn't touch her, in case he frightened her off. He had hoped so many times that she felt the same way he did, but he had never been sure, and couldn't push her. Not after all she had been through with Fabrizio.

This is where you belong, Luna. Forget last night. Do you want a man in your life? Make the logical choice. She reached up and grazed her lips against his, and hoped he would take the lead from her. She kissed him just a little, just to try out the moment that would take them from friends to something considerably more. She felt him respond, and kissed him again, fuller this time, and he took over the power of the moment. He brought his arms around her and pulled her into his embrace and thrust his kiss on her lips, which opened her unguarded mouth with his tongue. For the first time in 15 years, he was able to explore what it would be like to kiss her. Luna ran her hands around his bare body, to knead his flesh with her fingers. It didn't have the excitement she had hoped for, but she could feel that he enjoyed it far more than she did.

"Mummy!" they heard Enzo call down the hallway, and they pulled themselves apart. Darren tightened his towel again just as the boy appeared in the doorway. "Mummy," he said again. "Can we go to see the dolphin show again today?"

"Sure, why not," Luna said.

"Are you going to come, Darren, or do you need to go riding?" the boy asked innocently.

"It's a family day, of course Darren could come, can't you?" Luna asked.

"I don't want to be anywhere else," he replied.

"We should let Darren get dressed," Luna said and ushered the boy from the bedroom. Last night may have been a secret, a stolen season, but it had opened up Luna's world and attitude all of a sudden.

The day had passed like any Saturday in the Montgomery house. Luna and Darren took the kids to the aquarium for a family day out. They had sat either side of the boys at the dolphin show. Darren's arm was stretched out around the boys, and he twirled a lock of Luna's black hair in his fingers while they sat there. She didn't dare move the entire time. Every time she closed her eyes she could see last night, and she was full of guilt.

The boys were tucked up in bed at their usual time, exhausted from a day out in the Valencian heat. Luna cleaned the kitchen as Darren read the twins a book and put them to bed. When Luna had finished in the kitchen, she wandered out into the living room, where Darren sat with his feet up on the couch in front of the television. He glanced up over his shoulder when she came into the room, and gave her a smile without a word. Luna stood for a moment, and wondered what to say. Her spot was right next to him in the evenings. She would sit against him with her head on his shoulder. To start with it had comforted her night after night while she cried after the death of her husband. Then she began to feel better, and now it was… habit? Comfort of another kind? Just 24 hours ago she didn't need to question anything. "Where am I supposed to sit?" she asked him. Darren pulled his feet back, and she sat down next to him. "What are you watching?"

"The news has some story about a bullfight in Madrid. It was a big one. One of the most revered and admired *toreros* in Spain."

"Ooh, sexy matadors."

"Not matadors, they're *toreros*. Remember your Spanish."

"Don't pick on my Spanish! Fine, *toreros*. Either way, you've got to love those tight pants."

"I thought that's what you loved about us cyclists."

"Yeah, I like you boys for that. Yesterday was crazy in Madrid. They enjoy their bullfighting season." Cayetano was probably there at Las Ventas tonight. He had rushed off for work. *Just don't think about him.* "Who is this bullfighter that we are waiting to see?"

"The one and only *'El Valiente'* Beltrán."

"*'El Valiente'* is his nickname?" Luna asked, sceptical at the cheesy title. "I guess we're about to see how brave 'the courageous' one really is when faced with a bull."

"Apparently he is pretty good." Darren glanced back to her, and she looked right at him. "Are you going to tell me what this morning was about?"

"Did you not like it?"

"I think you could feel how much I liked it."

"I don't know what that was about."

Darren reached out and took her hand. "Why don't you come here and try to explain it?" he suggested. She moved over to lie against him as the two of them reclined on the couch. The atmosphere between them had changed. Wasn't that what she wanted when she kissed him? She looked at her hand that sat on his chest. "I'm confused."

"What can I say that might help?"

Luna looked up at him, and he stared straight back. "I know you are in love with me. I know you have been the whole time you have lived here. I know you were even when I was married."

"I will apologise for that, but I won't apologise for loving you now."

"I have thought about moving on after Fabrizio died," she said. "But… it never seemed the right time to do that. The whole thing is still so fresh."

"Only you know what is right for you, Lulu. I'm never going to ask anything of you."

"I'm lonely. I'm lonely in a way that a friend can't help. I want to take my life back. I'm angry about what happened to me. I'm upset Fabrizio is dead. I want to be myself again, not the widow. Not the single mother. Last night, in Madrid, I was myself."

Darren chuckled at the determined yet cute look on her face when she spoke. Luna wasn't a sweet girl. She had a temper. She was strong. She obviously wanted her feisty nature back, just like Darren did. "Maybe it was time I just said what I think every time I look at you."

"What?"

"I love you. Every time I look at you, I know I love you. I want to be with you. I want to be with the boys. I love everything you do, every time we are together, no matter what you're doing. I want you. When I am away for work, I want you to come with me. I am in love with you."

Luna leaned forward and kissed him just once. "I want you to show me where we go from here," she whispered against his lips.

"I don't want to push you."

"I want you to push me."

Darren swamped her lips with his, and brought her body on top of his. He placed one hand on the back of her head and gave her a furious kiss. It was the woman he had yearned for, at last letting him follow his desires. She kissed with all the power he imagined. She was no shrinking violet under his spell, and her strong will was behind every move. He got his hand up under her shirt, but just as his fingertips dipped into her bra cup, the television roared, and it broke the spell.

"Cayetano is down!" the presenter yelled at the top of his lungs. "He's injured, this is incredible!"

"He got gored!" Darren exclaimed. He looked past Luna at the screen. "Typical, all these years of watching fights and now a guy gets gored, and we missed it!"

"His name is Cayetano?"

"Yeah, Cayetano *'El Valiente'* Beltrán Morales."

Luna scrambled from Darren and stared at the screen. Sure enough in the close up shot, there was Cayetano. Her Cayetano. Works at the bullring, he said. Helped with the bulls, he said.

Cayetano was a *torero*, a matador. Not just any bullfighter, but the best. Her eyes could barely keep up with what she saw. The replay was of Cayetano doing the *faena*, the display with his red cape and sword. He was dressed in a red and gold *traje de luces*, his suit of lights. It was so well-fitted to his muscles. That was the man she had been with last night; only now he was a whole new person. His face was stone cold with concentration, his curly hair slicked back. She watched the replay as the bull rammed its horn into his thigh, and blood spilled onto the dusty earth beneath him. She watched as the bull was chased away by the *cuadrilla*, Cayetano's entourage of fighters, but he lay in agony. The medic crew had rushed to his aid. "Oh my God," she muttered.

"He will be all right," Darren said. "It looks as if the bull grazed him. It's not a full goring."

"I cannot believe it!" the Spanish presenter cried, as excited as a starving dog who could see dinner. "Never has Beltrán suffered a loss of concentration like that!"

"He has paid for it!" the other presenter said. They had to yell over the cries in the full arena. "Rumour had it this morning that he was late to his preparations, and was out last night. He could be tired out there in the ring today."

"That is not behaviour typical of Beltrán," the first presenter said. "But if it's true, he has paid dearly."

"How would they know he was out last night? How would anyone find that out?" Luna asked. Oh shit. He had been tired from last night and messed up, and it could have killed him.

"Maybe they guessed," Darren shrugged. "If you watch the replay, he does seem a little slow out there."

In the replay, all Luna had seen was the fire in his eyes, the honey brown filled by the flecks of green, just like she had seen the night before when they had sex. This whole thing no longer seemed like a stolen moment. Now it had a consequence.

"His wife is down at the ringside," the presenter said. "She will be able to see him once they take him from the ring."

"His wife!" Luna cried. "This guy is married?"

"Yeah," Darren said. "To that woman on Tele 5, who fronts that lifestyle programme. María something. María Medina? Why?"

"Nothing," she snapped. "He's a fool. A fuckwit who kills animals for entertainment."

"Are you okay, Lulu?"

Luna turned in her seat and faced Darren. Now the mistake she had made was a thousand times worse. Stupid fucking girl. "I'm not good enough for you," she shot out in an abrupt subject change.

"What?" Darren frowned. "Why would you say that?"

"I'm an idiot. You need a woman who will treat you the way you deserve."

"That sounds like a bullshit way of giving me the brush off."

"It's not. I just… why would you wait for me to make my mind up about us?"

"Because I love you," he shrugged. "It's pretty simple."

Luna glanced back at the television for a moment. She would have felt sorry for Cayetano if he hadn't been married. She turned back to Darren, who sat there full of expectation. To tell him about the night before wouldn't to do any good. She did feel guilty, and she wouldn't feel that way if she didn't have feelings for Darren. "I love you, you know that, right?"

Darren inched across to sit next to her again. "I know, but maybe not the same way that I love you."

"Maybe it's time I stopped feeling guilty. Fabrizio is dead. I'm not sure how much he loved me when we were married."

"He loved you, but not as much as I love you, and he knew it," he whispered, and brought his lips to hers. Darren had been in love with Luna for a long time, and he hadn't imagined what was between them.

From the time they first met as kids until now, there had been something there, but they had missed their chance. Fabrizio had appeared at the wrong time. He was gone now, and neither of them had any reason to hide their feelings. Fifteen years of trust, love, respect, friendship, and now it was meant to be more. They had all the hallmarks of a great relationship, so why couldn't Luna just take the leap?

5

Madrid, España ~ septiembre de 2009

Luna took a deep breath and turned the handle to the office at the Madrid *Registro Civil*. The stark and disorganised government building was awful on its best days, and today, another Friday, it was busy with couples there to get their wedding licences. The last thing Luna needed was to see happy couples with their families, all dressed up for their momentous day. That day wouldn't come for her. She shouldn't have felt mad at others for their fortune in love, but she did.

The noisy building was one thing, but the sight that greeted her on the other side of the door was quite another. The room she had visited two weeks earlier, a windowless beige room with about 30 chairs, was empty. The desk where a single staff member worked was unattended. *Oh, for Christ's sake.* She had fucked up. The door closed itself behind her while she looked at the piece of paper with the date and time written on it.

Viernes de 1 septiembre. 14:30. Nacimientos y muertes de la oficina de matrimonios. No, she was in the right place. Birth, Deaths and Marriages. Last time it had been full, and now it was dead.

"Luna Montgomery?"

Luna looked up to see someone at the desk, an irritated-looking woman in her mid-thirties. She was attractive, but her obvious disdain for having to be at work during *siesta* clouded her pretty face.

"*Sí, soy Luna.*"

"I'm Sofía, I can help you," the woman replied. "Who do you need to find?"

"I need Cayetano Ortega. Born in or around 1914."
"Full name?"
"Not sure."
"No date of birth?"
"No."
"Birthplace?"
"No. Maybe Cuenca?"
"Parents names?"
"I don't know."
"Occupation?"
"I don't know that either."

"*¿Por qué mi hermano quiere que le ayude?*" Sofía muttered. "Wait here, I will go and check the records."

Luna frowned as the blunt woman left the room. Why did her brother want to help? That was a good question. The door behind her banged open, and Luna turned, surprised that Sofía would be that quick. No such luck. There stood Cayetano, the Cayetano she knew anyway, with his left leg bandaged. The man's strong body now relied on crutches. He looked awkward as he got himself through the heavy door, and hobbled over towards her. "Luna, *buenas tardes*. Has Sofía met you here?"

"What are you doing here?"

"*Enchufe*, remember? I asked Sofía to stay and help you. I thought it would help you to find your *abuelo*."

"How is your leg after the accident?"

"You saw?"

"I saw the whole *'El Valiente'* Beltrán fight. How has your wife coped with your injury?"

Cayetano swallowed hard. He hoped to come in here and see Luna again. He didn't have the courage to ring her after lying about who he was. He hoped that if he helped her today it would maybe ease some of that. He wanted to ask her out again. Now it would be ugly. "Can I explain?" he asked.

"No." She raised her hand in his direction. "There's no need."

The door opened again, and Sofía was back. "Cayetano! How did you get up here on your own?"

"I can walk," Cayetano replied in his sister's direction.

"This woman is a friend?" Sofía gestured towards Luna.

"More of a casual acquaintance," Luna said coolly.

"I'm not much help to you, Luna," Sofía said. "There are no records. I suggest you go to *Registro Civil* office in Cuenca for original documents. Anything else I can do?"

"No, thank you so much," Luna said. "Thank you for staying late to help me. I won't bother you anymore."

"Luna," Cayetano said, and reached out for her. She stepped around him, and he was unable to reach her, and stumbled on his crutches. She was gone from the room in a heartbeat.

"What did you say to her?" Sofía asked her brother. "Did you just get me to do a favour for a girl you're interested in?"

"Would it matter if I said yes?"

"Imagine what Mamá and Papá would say - the golden child has betrayed his wedding vows."

"Since when do you ever talk to our parents?"

"I don't want to have that conversation. Do you need a ride home?"

"No." He turned himself on his crutches in the direction of the door. "Thanks, Sofía. I need to go and apologise to Luna."

"So you did say something to her," Sofía commented and opened the door for her brother.

"It's more what I didn't say," he sighed. "I'll call you tomorrow. Maybe you could come to family lunch on Sunday?"

"Would they want their family's disappointment there?"

"You're not, not to me," Cayetano said. "I have to go. *Hasta luego.*"

Luna stood on the narrow cobbled path and pondered her next move. The next train from Atocha station back to Valencia wasn't for another hour. When she had got a call from Sofía's office, she had thought they had something of interest for her. Why couldn't they have just called her? Cayetano also had her number, and he could have used it. But he didn't. He didn't call her. He lied and slept with her behind his wife's back. So why lure her here under the pretense of having some information, when, in fact, Cayetano Ortega may as well not exist?

"¡Luna, *espere!*"

Luna shut her eyes and felt a deep ache in her stomach. Wait? For what? She didn't want to see Cayetano again. She needed to make a run for it. She had thought about him for the last two weeks, about how much she had liked him, and then how dirty she felt when she found out he was married. The man she saw just now was the man she knew, Cayetano Morales, the scruffy man in the bullfighting bar. The guy who took her to dinner. The man who spent the night in her hotel room. But he wasn't real. She heard his deep, robust voice say her name again, now much closer. With great reluctance, she turned around and there he was behind her on his crutches, his breath laboured. He must have dashed after her on those things. "What?" she spat out.

"I… I just… how are you?"

"Hot. Annoyed. I came today under the impression that there had been an appointment for me because something I had requested had turned up. Only it was your sister who felt obligated to stay after closing time in her office. Why would you do that?"

"I like you."

"Well, I don't like being made a fool of."

"*Señor* Beltrán? Cayetano Beltrán," a man's voice interrupted, and they turned to see an older gentleman approach them. "*Señor* Beltrán," he said again. "What an honour! I am such a fan of both you and your father. How is the leg? I hope you recover soon."

"*Gracias,* my leg is healing well," Cayetano said, and watched the man pull a pen and piece of paper from the old satchel he carried. "Would you like an autograph?"

"*Por favor.* I got one from your father at a fight back in 1967. What a magnificent performance it was. My name is Manuel. I never thought there would be another great like your father, but here you are."

"Dear Manuel, thank you for the well wishes and support. Regards, Cayetano Beltrán Morales," he said out loud as he wrote on the paper. "Here you go."

"*Gracias,*" the grateful man said, and gestured with his hat. "I'll let you charm the lady again."

"A *torero's* work is never done," Cayetano joked, and the man laughed as he walked off.

"So," Luna said and folded her arms, "your father was a bullfighter, was he? So all night you lied to me about who you were, your job, your family, everything. Not just about your wife."

"Can I at least explain myself?"

"What for? We had a cheap one-night stand, and that doesn't need explanations. We will just never see each other again. We don't need to share private information."

"I would have thought we have already shared a lot of private things. I think I already know you very well. In fact, I know every inch of you in a very weak moment."

Luna's eyes flared. Flames were ready to shoot from them. "You don't know me. You may have seen me, but that is not the same thing. Leave me alone."

"Hey, who said we were a one-night stand?"

"I don't know, your wife maybe?"

Cayetano reached out and grabbed her arm when she spun away from him. "Damn it, Luna. Let me explain!" This time when she spun back she looked even more irate. "Please."

"No, I need to catch the train back to Valencia."

"They have trains all day. What's the rush?"

"I would like to get back to see my children."

Cayetano dropped his hand from around her arm. *Mierda.* Shit, there was a revelation.

"What do you know, in an instant he has no interest," Luna said with a sarcastic smile. "Are we done now?"

"I love kids," Cayetano replied. "I just don't have any."

"Well, at least that makes me a little less of a home wrecker." Luna turned and left. It didn't matter how much she liked him, there was no need to drag this out. She heard him call her name out again, this time in anger, but she didn't turn back until she heard him call out in pain. She looked over her shoulder; he was in a heap on the path. She cringed, that must have been extremely painful for him. His bandaged leg stuck straight out in front of him on the uneven cobbles. The dozen or so people between the two of them rushed to his aid, but he looked up at Luna. She came back over and picked up his crutches for him.

Cayetano thanked the people who had helped him, and he sighed. "That was not how to win over a lady," he said to Luna. "I'm sorry."

"Are you all right?"

"No."

She looked at the defeated look on his face, lined with the pain that came from his leg. She realised she quite liked the cheeky smile that usually graced his face. "Is there anything I can do to help?"

"I need to get a taxi home."

Luna helped Cayetano into a nearby taxi outside the building, and she was genuinely concerned at how much pain he seemed to be in. She could imagine what the wound he had looked like. How many ways could she mess up with the man?

"You aren't coming with me?" he asked. He sat in the taxi with his crutches over his lap. "Please? It's not far."

Luna glanced from him to the driver, who seemed rather proud to have Cayetano Beltrán in the back of his car. Cayetano would need help to get inside his building at the other end. With some reluctance, she got in the taxi, and they set off through the busy Madrid streets. The driver wouldn't shut up, and he barely even looked at the road. It seemed he had caught every second of Cayetano's performance in the ring, and was more than happy to offer suggestions on how to fight next time. Cayetano sat there and spoke to the man, despite the discussion being about how much he had fucked up in the ring. She may not have known who Cayetano was, but everyone else in Madrid did.

The day was one surprise after another. When the taxi pulled up outside Cayetano's building, she couldn't believe it. So he was wealthy. Of course he was. The restored building was a marvel, only a few blocks away from the hotel that Luna had been a few weeks ago. It was one of Madrid's treasures. The grey and white stone work was as beautiful as the day it was built. The moment they stepped out of the car, the *portero* came out to help. Cayetano didn't want the aid of the doorman, and he told the older man that his friend would help him upstairs.

Luna sighed and got in the elevator with Cayetano, and watched the doorman slide the metal door shut and hit the button for the sixth floor. The old elevator was slow as it took them up the centre of the winding staircase to the top of the building.

"Thank you," Cayetano said when Luna pulled the metal lattice gate across, and helped him over the gap onto the white floor of the dark hallway.

"If you're fine now, I will leave you. I need to catch my train."

"You won't come in?"

"Yeah, your wife and I can have coffee," she scoffed.

"My ex-wife lives across town with her parents," Cayetano said. "Which you would have already known if you had let me talk."

"I'm sorry! Look, this isn't even about you. I'm embarrassed by my behaviour enough."

"I see, you used me and now you don't want to see me again." A smile spread over his face while he unlocked the front door to his apartment.

Luna couldn't help but return it. "Cayetano, I'm sorry. I'm just outside my comfort zone here, for a lot of reasons. Reasons you don't talk to strangers about."

"Then why don't you come in and not be a stranger anymore?"

"Is your leg even sore?"

"Yes, I have 36 stitches. Every one hurt like hell when I fell over like a fool."

"Does it hurt enough that you needed me to help you up here?"

"Maybe. Don't hate me because I didn't call. I was in the hospital!"

"I never expected you to call." She stepped into the entrance way of the huge apartment, and watched him hop over and close the door behind her.

Cayetano gestured for her to turn right into the kitchen, and he hobbled without his crutches into the large room with her. The place was immaculate; the all-white marble kitchen sparkled in every corner of the room. They sat down on the stools along the island counter in the centre of the kitchen. Cayetano was eager to rest his injured leg, and more eager to have the lovely lady next to him. "How did you find out I was married?" he asked.

"I saw your fight on the news. The presenter mentioned your wife was there."

"I can see why you hate me. I didn't mean to lie to you about so many things. It's like you say, you don't tell your life story on the first date."

"Was it even a date?"

"Don't ask me, it's been years since I have been on one," Cayetano half-smiled. He realised how pathetic that sounded. "I liked that you didn't know who I was, and I didn't want to ruin it. But I realise that was selfish, especially since you were very clear about who you are."

"What do you mean that I didn't know who you were?"

"I meet women, and they know me as the bullfighter, the famous guy. Their intentions are never genuine. My wife and I split eight months ago, and she moved out. But no one knows that, other than our families. But I'm single. It's complicated."

"Clearly," Luna sighed. "I watched you hurt your leg. Did you really mess up with the bull because of exhaustion, as was suggested? They said that you were late for preparation the day of the fight. This all happened because you were with me?"

"I knew what I was doing when I went out with you that night. Trust me, if a man is interested, he doesn't care if he is busy the next day. He stays the night anyway."

"You could have been killed."

"It's my job. Please don't worry, I will be fine in a few weeks, and other than the public humiliation and the anger of my father over me losing, there is no harm done."

"That sounds like a lot of harm."

"It hasn't been my best few weeks, I will agree with you," Cayetano said. He stood up from his seat and shuffled across the room to the fridge and opened it. "How about we have another date here in my kitchen? I suggest lunch."

"You can cook?"

Cayetano pulled an enormous chocolate cake from the fridge. "Cake counts as lunch doesn't it?"

Luna chuckled while he placed it on the counter between them, and pulled two forks from the drawer. "No, I can't cook at all, I won't lie," he said. "My Mamá made it and put it in my fridge."

"Ah, a mother. That explains how a man can have such a beautiful home."

Cayetano scoffed lightheartedly and pulled a bottle of red wine from the rack and sat back down with her. "As I said, my family is around me all the time. Mamá was only 15 when I was born, and she has been ... how you say ... *sobrecompensando ... "*

"Overcompensating?"

"*Sí,* overcompensating my whole life, by trying to do a good job. My father, he is much older than her, and her family were not happy when they found their daughter was pregnant to a bullfighter twice her age. She felt she had to prove that Papá was good for her and that she could raise my little sister and me."

"And your parents are still together now?"

"*Sí,* very much so. I work with my father and uncles every day, and my mother is the protector of everyone. And since María left me, she has fussed over me, even though I'm 40."

"You're her baby. Mothers will always love their sons."

"Do you have a son?" Cayetano asked with caution.

"Two. They're five years old."

"Twins?"

"Yes."

"Wow... that must be amazing. What are their names?"

"Giacomo was born a few minutes before Enzo."

"Italian. Like their father," Cayetano commented. "Luna, I'm sorry."

"What?"

"I mean... you told me all about Fabrizio's death, and now I find you also have children."

"Trust me, I didn't tell you even half of the story. But... Fabrizio died only a few years ago, and it's been hard. So when I threw myself at you the other week, it... forget it."

"How can I forget it?"

"I'm angry at myself, not you, please don't get me wrong. I feel guilty for cheating on my husband, and I know that sounds ridiculous..."

"Not really. At least when your wife of ten years cheats on you, you can kick her out without feeling bad. I can't imagine what it's like for you, to raise the children alone after the one you love dies."

"I don't raise them alone. My friend, Darren, lives with me. He took Fabrizio's place... on the cycling team. He is the boys' godfather."

"He is your... lover? Boyfriend?"

"No! No... maybe. Christ, I should go."

Cayetano reached out and grabbed Luna's hands when she stood up from her stool. "Can I just say something first?"

"Okay."

"I like you. I thought you liked me. I thought we had a good time. I had an amazing time. I just don't know what to do, you're a widow, and I didn't know how far I could push. Then I had my accident, but if I hadn't I would have called you. I want to see you again, but I can understand if you don't like me."

Luna stood on the spot, and watched the hopeful man before him. His eyes were so full of anticipation, those green flecks in the honey brown back again. What was it about this man? The second he touched her hands, the short, sharp shot of attraction and promise ran through her again. She had felt it every time she had thought about him, and that was a lot. Now she was here in his apartment, and for what? No one would ever know she was there, and now that he wasn't married… "I like you," she managed to say with her dry mouth, "in spite of myself."

"I'm just asking for you to… try my cake." His voice was gentle and coaxed her closer to him.

Luna let him pull her into him, and she stood in between his legs that were balanced on the edge of the stool. A lock of his curly jet-black hair had fallen forward on his forehead and the curl begged to be twirled around her finger. She just had to tell herself that it was okay to like a man. Because she liked his one, whoever he was. "I will try your cake."

"Good," he said, and let her hands go. "If you don't like Mamá's cake, I can't ask you out on a second date."

"I thought this was a date." She watched him stab a fork into the moist cake.

"Shh… it's our little secret," he whispered, and held the fork to her lips. "Go on." He waited until she went to bite it and pulled it away and sniggered.

"That was mean."

"I'm sorry," he said in mock apology. "Try the cake."

Luna tried to bite the cake off the fork, and he snatched it away again and laughed at the look on her face. "Fine, forget the cake," she said. "I might go and get that train now."

"Aww… come on," he said and offered it again, but she didn't budge. "Please?"

"No," she said with a grin. "Keep it."

"I'll make you eat it."

"How?"

Cayetano wrapped one arm around her waist, spun her around and held her back against him while she struggled. "Fight me all you want, *preciosa*. I do two hours in the gym every day. I will beat you." He dug his fingers into her ribs and started to tickle her, which resulted in high-pitched shrieking while she tried to make him stop. "You need to beg for mercy," he joked.

Luna grabbed the piece of cake off the fork and mashed it against Cayetano's stubbled cheek and rubbed it into his skin. "How's the cake?" she asked.

"I'm going to make you eat it," he replied, and let her go, and she turned to face him. "You know that, don't you?"

"How, chase me on your crutches?"

Cayetano pulled her to him again, his hands firm on her back. He could feel her heart pound against him. He was ravenous when he brought his lips to hers, and smothered her in his desire – and cake. Either her initial anger at him was gone, or she had channeled it, because the way she held herself to him and kissed showed no mercy at all. This was the girl that had been on his mind for the last two weeks. She was so different to what he was used to. She left Cayetano feeling upbeat and inspired about life. Luna was so beautiful that she would stop traffic, only she hadn't noticed. He could pretend to be the well-known popular bullfighter and the occasional celebrity, and that would work well if he wanted to take home a soulless but attractive woman, and he had done that more times that he wanted to admit. But Luna didn't know that man, and she didn't ask about that life. She liked him for who he was himself – and Cayetano didn't even know that man all that well. It was a pure attraction to each other, every complicated detail aside.

Cayetano reached out and fumbled on the counter until he found the cake, and stuck a finger into it. He brought his hand to her neck and ran his cake-covered finger down her neck and chest, which made her pull away from him in surprise.

"You bastard!" she cried with a grin on her face.

"Don't you like my cake?" He smirked at the chocolate smeared on her face.

Luna couldn't help but laugh when she looked down at herself. "That was the best thing I have ever tasted. Cake isn't bad either."

"You like the famous Beltrán *torta de diablo* then?"

"Devil's cake? I believe that. How am I supposed to go home covered in cake?"

"You don't have to," his deep voice said, and he brought his mouth to the smudge of cake on her throat. Her kissed her skin, and gently licked some of the chocolate icing from her body. A burning feeling shot through him when she sighed, letting his lips and his hands become lost on her. Maybe it was that they didn't know each other, or that they, in fact, knew quite a few private details about each other, neither of them knew. There was an unquestionable attraction between them. He didn't just want her, he wanted to know her, and talk to her, touch her, listen to her, to watch her, and none of it made any sense. Maybe that was the best part. They were a secret from the world, and none of it needed to make sense.

"Cayetano," Luna muttered. She had her fingers in his hair as his lips trailed down her body. His fingers were nimble in undoing the third button on her blouse. She knew that she needed to make him stop. The night she had met him, she had felt awoken for the first time in years, and today had the same effect. After a private adult life, to act like this with a stranger also brought out the worst emotion – guilt. "Cayetano," she stuttered again. "I have to go."

Cayetano brought his eyes to her, not worried in the least that his face was covered in chocolate. "You don't," he purred.

"I do. I'm not proud of what I did the other week, and… I don't even know why I'm here…"

"Give me one reason why what we're doing is wrong. Tell me that you don't feel what is going on here."

"I'm not ready to see anyone," Luna said. "I'm sorry. I don't know what I want."

Cayetano sat back on his stool. He couldn't argue with that. He couldn't convince her, and he couldn't persuade her. "Okay. I understand." In all reality, it was moving at a lightning pace for him. The pain that María had caused was still pretty fresh in his mind, and while one-night stands might be able to block it out for a moment, this was not the same. "What if I just suggested we wipe up the cake and you stay in the city, and we go out for lunch?"

"I need to go home to Valencia."

"Why?"

"I want to see my children. I don't like leaving them."

"Of course, I'm sorry." Cayetano got up awkwardly from his seat. He wet a cloth under the tap over the sink. "Who has them now?"

"Darren does."

"And Darren is only your friend?"

"I don't want to talk about that."

Cayetano gently wiped her neck with the cloth, and the smudge of licked chocolate icing came off her pale skin. She let him rub her neck and chest, before he wiped her cheeks clean. Her young, fresh face enchanted him, and he didn't realise that he was staring. He put the cloth down on the counter and gently pulled her to him again, to give her a deep and tender kiss, to which she returned. They just had to go slow with one another. Pleasure was as fragile as glass, she had said. Her heart seemed just as fragile, so much so that he was worried he would break it when he touched her. "If I let you go, will you promise me that you will go out with me again?"

"What about your leg, don't you need to recuperate?" she asked, her arms around his waist, her body tucked up into his.

"I would cut the bloody thing off for you," he said through gritted teeth. He didn't want to admit it, but the pain in his leg beat the desire he had for the woman in his arms. He would love to sever the entire limb to avoid the pain and take her to bed.

"I can see that you're in pain," she said while he wiped the cake from her face again. "You need to sit down."

"I'm fine."

"Liar."

"I won't be injured much longer. When are you coming to Madrid again?"

"I have no need to come back at all. I think I need to go to Cuenca instead. But kids, work… who knows…"

"My father's family is from Cuenca, but I've never been there. What about next weekend? We could both go, and I can be your assistant and translator."

"Hablo español."

"I know you speak Spanish, very well. But maybe I can help you anyway?"

"Maybe."

"Bring the children along. I love children! We will have a great time."

Introduce him to the kids? She barely knew him. Darren would be away in the coming weeks, to coach some riders during the Vuelta a España, but she wanted to go to Cuenca now. "Maybe."

"My heart can wait on a maybe."

"I'm sorry I was rude to you earlier at the *Registro Civil.*"

"It's all forgiven. Go home to your children."

"Thank you for the cake," she joked. "It's my favourite flavour."

"What a coincidence, I'm really enjoying the taste myself."

6

Madrid, España ~ septiembre de 2009

"It's looking good," the physiotherapist said to Cayetano. "Another week or so and I think you will start to see some improvement. Have you been doing your exercises?"

"Of course he has," Paco grumbled from his seat across the small doctor's office.

Cayetano sighed, and nodded to the kind woman who assessed his thigh muscles to see if he could have his stitches removed. He had been coming to twice-weekly appointments at the private clinic in the hope that the staff could help him regain some strength in his leg. His father had to come to every appointment with him. He had to answer every question on his behalf. Paco was a strong man for his age, and not just physically. He was 70 years old, yet his jet-black hair and strong, demanding attitude had not at all diminished with age. Paco may have been too old to enter the bullring on a competitive level, but that did not stop him from forcing his only son into the spotlight. Cayetano was an asset that needed protecting.

"Gracias," Cayetano said to the young woman. He didn't even pretend that he didn't enjoy her soft, supple hands rubbing his bare thigh. Not only did it ease the pain, it distracted him from the thoughts of a certain woman in Valencia that had followed him wherever he went.

"When can he start back at the gym?" Paco asked her as Cayetano carefully got off the massage table and pulled on his trousers. "Cayetano needs to be back in the bullring as soon as possible."

"You should consult your doctor about that on your next visit," she said. "You were very lucky that the main artery was missed during your accident, Cayetano. So you shouldn't worry that you can't go back to your training. Your leg needs to rest."

"This isn't a game," Paco snapped. "We have his public and his sponsors to consider."

And male pride to repair. Paco had been ashamed of his son taking a fall in public like that. Cayetano knew that fact. The famous Paco Beltrán Caño had never fallen in the bullring, and neither had his prodigy. Until now. Cayetano's first major injury had been in training and Paco had been grateful that no one had seen it. "I appreciate all your help," Cayetano said to the therapist. "I will come on my own next week," he whispered and winked at her, and she smiled. Not many people could deal with the attitude that Paco carried with him.

The two men left the quiet clinic and stepped out of its air-conditioned comfort and onto the street where the heat of the September day wafted over them. Cayetano had to be careful every time he took a step with his black cane; the cobbled path was very uneven, and he didn't need a repeat of the fall at the *Registro Civil* last week. "Papá, you don't need to watch me. My treatment is fine."

"I care, Caya," Paco said without a glance at his son. "It's important we get you the best treatment."

"I'm getting good care, Papá. I'm 40 years old. I can look after my own treatment."

"You wouldn't have fallen in the ring if you could look after yourself."

Cayetano gritted his teeth. There was no sense in arguing. "Should we go for a walk in the park?" he suggested. "Give me a chance to use my leg."

Paco raised his eyebrows. "Certainly. That's a good idea. I'm glad you are ready to push your recovery."

Cayetano rolled his eyes as the men crossed the quiet, narrow street. He could rely on his mother for support, but all he was ever likely to get from his father was pressure. They stepped into El Retiro park, and wandered down the smooth and empty pathway, covered from the sun by overhanging trees. The whole park was unusually green despite a dry summer.

"I walked through here a few weeks ago," Cayetano said casually. "I met a woman."

"Was that the one that Raul said you saved from the bag-snatcher when you were at the bar?"

"I didn't save her. She was pretty tough on her own. She fought the guy, but he punched her in the face."

"Disgusting. Raul said she was very beautiful."

"She was. She came to Madrid to find her grandfather."

"Did she find him?"

"No, he died in the civil war, and she can't find any records."

"Some things don't need to be discovered," Paco said in a grave tone.

"It's important to her. Very important. She wants to know where she comes from."

"You speak as if you had quite a conversation with this girl."

"She told me that I have very good English."

"She is not Spanish?"

"No, she is from New Zealand, but lives in Valencia now and speaks Spanish. Her grandfather was Spanish, but not her grandmother."

"Nueva Zelanda? I knew of a woman that came from there. She was a wicked woman."

"Something you would like to tell me, Papá?"

"No, no," the old man smiled. "I loved your mother from the first moment I saw her. This woman was with someone else. But she was trouble."

"Mamá has told me the story of you falling in love with her on the same day you met. I thought perhaps she was just saying it… you know women…"

Paco chuckled. "No, your Mamá is right. She had come to the bullring with her father one day while I was training, and that was it. As soon as I looked over at her, I knew she would be my wife. I just knew it."

The conversation stalled for a moment as a young woman came towards them, out for an afternoon run. She gave Cayetano a wave with a cheeky smile, and he waved back when she went past them. He looked back over his shoulder to see the woman check him out.

"I see that the cane doesn't put the ladies off my son," Paco said, and glanced over his shoulder at the young blonde who then disappeared around a corner.

"Just looking, Papá. I'm not interested."

"I never thought I would hear that from you."

Cayetano just shrugged. He had already forgotten the girl. "Papá, why have you never told me about your parents?"

"There's nothing to know. They died a long time ago. You have your mother's parents who have loved you since you were born. You don't need to worry about anything else."

"But you were born in Cuenca?"

"Why all the questions, Cayetano?" Paco snapped. "Just because this girl you met wants to find her family, it doesn't mean you need to go digging up your own."

"I… just wondered, that's all."

"Wondered about things which have no importance just because of some girl you spoke to?"

"Her name is Luna, not some girl."

The two men walked in silence for a minute. Cayetano set the pace on his cane. "Your grandmother's name was Luna."

"Really?"

"Yes. Luna Beltrán Caño. She was the most beautiful woman. She had long curly black hair. I guess that is where you and Sofía got your curly hair from."

Cayetano smiled while Paco spoke. He couldn't imagine what could possibly make his father want to keep his life a secret for over 40 years.

Paco sighed. "My father died when I was very young. Mamá told me that he had been sick for a while, but she never wanted to talk about it. She raised me on her own until she died in 1960."

"You were already fighting in the bullring by then."

"*Sí*. She always told me that my father loved bullfighting, but never had the chance to try it for himself."

"I never knew that," Cayetano said. "Even after all this time."

"I didn't want you to be a *torero* just because I was, Cayetano."

"Why would you not tell me that?"

"Because it doesn't matter. My mother asked me to stay quiet on the subject of my father. None of this is anyone's business!"

"Papá, don't yell at me," Cayetano said, trying to calm his father. "I was just curious, that's all. You have that chest that sits in your office, and it's locked. I know it's full of things you had before you met Mamá. You act as if your parents were murderers, and yet you tell me family and tradition are the most important things."

"I can promise you that your grandmother was not a murderer. She was a wonderful woman. She was heartbroken after my father died. She was wealthy after her husband passed away, and she cared for me very well in a time when our nation was starving. I don't know how she coped. There were men interested in her, but she refused them all. She said she had already had her great love. She told me that I was all she needed. It was her who pushed me to be a *torero*. She was the one who gave me the opportunity. She was the one who wanted me to build a family with a woman I loved. That is why, when I fell in love with your mother in a heartbeat, I knew I was doing the right thing. Mamá told me that when you lock eyes with your true love, you know it. That is what she did."

"So… you push for this life of family ties and bullfighting because that is what she wanted for you?"

"She wanted me to honour my father, and to have the happy life that she didn't have."

"So why keep her a secret?" Cayetano asked with a frown. It made no sense. "What is wrong with any of that?"

"Things are never that simple. My reasons are just that – mine."

"So who was my grandfather? Was I named after him?"

"My mother married a man named Ignacio Reyes Paz. Of course, I have no memories of him. But she did say to me once, one night when she was particularly teary, that if I had a son, that I should name him Cayetano."

"Why?"

"It was her brother's name."

"You have an uncle?"

"No, he died before I was born."

"In the war? Was he a soldier?"

"*¡No escarbes el pasado!*" Paco cried.

"I'm not digging up the past! I'm not trying to cause trouble."

"Then don't. Let's go back to the car."

Father and son turned and headed back in the direction they had walked in; the total silence failed to fill the awkward space between them. Cayetano didn't think that he had any reason to apologise to his father. Paco had no reason to stay quiet about his family. They were just normal people who had been through a difficult time. Every family in Spain had grandparents who could say the same.

"You and your mother are right about one thing," he said.

Paco sighed. "What?"

"About knowing when you love someone. The moment you look into their eyes, you know you have found something special. I know how you felt when you first looked at Mamá, and how *abuela* would have looked at *abuelo*. I have felt that."

Paco frowned at his son. "I thought you said you were sure that you and María were over."

"Who? No, not María, Papá. María was a mistake. I shouldn't have married her. No… I am in love with another woman. I knew it the moment I looked at her."

"Cayetano…"

"It's Luna, Papá. The girl I saved from the bag-snatcher. I helped her up off the path, and I swear, the moment I looked at her, something in my life changed."

"Don't be ridiculous, boy," Paco barked.

"How is that ridiculous?" Cayetano scoffed. "You said that was how you felt when you saw Mamá for the first time."

"Yes, I was infatuated with her. It was lust as well."

Lust between his parents? Pass. "But you just told me about this romantic story of love at first sight that happened to you, and the same happened to your own mother! Did you just make that up? Why is it so hard to believe I felt like that?"

"Because you make mistakes, and you're already married."

"I recall it was you and Mamá who pushed me to marry María. Marry the girl from the wealthy and well-connected Medina family. I was the reluctant one, remember?"

"Oh yes, blame us for your mistakes. That wouldn't be new. At your age, Cayetano…"

"At my age?" Cayetano cried. "I'm able to run my own life! But instead, I have my father as my manager, who wants to control my whole career and my personal life! I'm surprised I was even allowed to move out of home! At least Sofía has a life, even if it is not of a high enough standard for you and Mamá. Don't tell me what I can and can't feel!"

"Yes, all right! Your mother and I… I loved her as soon as we met. And what happened? I got her pregnant, Cayetano. She was 15 years old. I was 30. What went on between us caused a lot of pain. Yes, it all worked out. Yes, you came into the world, and we loved you. Yes, the rifts it caused in her family did heal over time. But don't think love at first sight is an instant happy ending."

"I'm not saying that my life has become a fairytale. I nearly lost my leg three weeks ago. My mind is in reality. But I am in love with Luna."

"Really? Do you even know her surnames?"

"Luna Montgomery Merlini. At least… I think that is what her name is…"

Paco rolled his eyes. *"Terrífico."*

"No… I mean… her surname is Montgomery. She is not Spanish, so she only has one family name. Merlini is her married name. I don't know if she uses both or…"

"She is another man's wife? This just gets better."

"No!" Cayetano practically squealed in frustration. "Do you remember, a few years ago, there was one of those Tour de France cyclists, an Italian guy, who was killed in Valencia by some drunk driver?"

Paco's face screwed up. "Vaguely."

"That was Fabrizio Merlini. Luna was his wife."

Paco fell silent for a moment. "I am sorry to hear that. But…"

"But even so, I'm in love with her! I know how crazy that sounds. You know I'm not one to speak like this, not to anyone. Papá, you only have to look at her and you will understand. There is something about Luna, like she is someone I already know. I swear to God…"

"I swear to God that you want this New Zealand girl to seduce you. Think with your head, Cayetano."

"I seduced her," Cayetano shot back.

"Jesucristo en el cielo," Paco swore under his breath. "She is as loose as the other women from her country."

"Papá! Just because you knew one woman, once, who was from New Zealand, and you didn't like her, doesn't mean a thing. I don't know where you get your ideas from, but you have her all wrong. She is a good person, and strong, and a dedicated mother…"

"She has children? A gold-digger then…"

"Damn it!" Cayetano yelled as the pair reached Paco's car parked near the entrance to the park. "Is it too much to ask to get a bit of support from you?"

Paco fumbled in his pocket for his keys and eyed his son again. "When did you meet her?"

"Three weeks ago."

"Before your goring."

"The day before."

"I couldn't get hold of you the night before your performance. That morning you were late for preparation… were you with this woman? This grand seduction you speak of maybe? Did you fall and destroy the Beltrán name because you were with this woman who gives it away for free?"

"I'm walking home. I can't do this anymore."

"You can't walk, it's miles. You will hurt your leg."

"It can't hurt any more than you hurt me, Papá," he replied, and turned away from his father.

"That suits me just fine. Maybe you can have a moment to think about how you're being ridiculous."

Cayetano hobbled away from his father, and didn't bother to look back. He would walk with his cane all the way to Valencia just to prove his father wrong. He was in love with Luna. He had only seen her a few times, and his father was right – he didn't know her. Yet, somehow there was something that bound her to him.

Once around the corner and out of sight, Cayetano stopped and leaned against the wall of the building. He rested his cane against the rough old brickwork and pulled his phone out, and flicked through the numbers. Luna Montgomery. It had been a week since she had left his kitchen. He had just admitted to his father – and himself – that he was in love with her, so there was no reason not to call her.

Fidgeting with his cane, Cayetano looked around him at the others going about their day on the street as the phone rang and rang. Now he had worked up the courage, she wasn't going to answer. Maybe she was at work. He could almost imagine her on her bike – yellow she had said it was – in the park that weaved through Valencia city, as she pointed out the sights to English tourists. When the call clicked over to the answerphone, he became struck with panic. Leave a message? And say what?

"Hola, este es Luna Merlini. Me dejan un mensaje. This is Luna Merlini. Please leave me a message."

Screw it. There was only thing to do – go to Valencia.

7

Cuenca, España ~ marzo de 1939

Luna Beltrán stood in her bedroom and looked at her dress that hung on the single hook on the wall. It had hung there for some time, and she had wanted to wear it to the annual fiesta. It was made of beautiful, pure white full-length silk, which was something hard to get hold of at the moment. It was overlaid with delicate white lace, with delicate lace sleeves. Her father had got it made in Francia for Luna while she cared for her ailing mother. No one else had a beautiful dress like this. Luna knew that she lived in a nation where every day could be your last, but to have something so simple yet so precious lifted her spirits. The dress was a reminder of a better time than now. This white dress in Luna's room was the single thing she owned that reminded her that life could be different. Better.

It was almost time to head up to the plaza for the town meeting that had taken the place of the now cancelled fiesta, but Alejandro and Sofía were nowhere to be found. Her brother had gone to the hospital to meet his wife when she finished her shift, and neither had returned. Go on, Luna. Try on the dress. Of course, there was no reason to wear it tonight. This year they would bring the remaining people of the town together, who would get emotional about how they would to fight to save their lives.

She changed into the gown and felt the softness of it against her body. If the day came that she had to flee Cuenca, the dress would be the only thing she would take with her.

She turned sharply at the sound of a knock on the door. Alejandro had probably forgotten his key again. He did it all the time. No doubt her brother would tease her about the dress again. It had been Sofía's wedding dress, but she wouldn't mind Luna wearing it.

"La chispa."

Luna's eyes widened in surprise when she opened the door. There stood Cayetano Ortega; he looked all tidied up for a change. He wore a simple black suit, complete with tie. When he said he would dress up on the night of the fiesta, he had meant it. His curly black hair was shining under the single light that hung outside the door, and was bright as his smile. La chispa. *The spark. "What is* la chispa?*" she asked.*

"You are. You're the spark that sets off a blazing fire in me."

Luna couldn't help but giggle and look away from him. Her cheeks that felt as if they were on fire. She had no idea what it was about her brother's friend. She had known him for years. He had come to Cuenca from Madrid 10 years ago, when he was only 15, and alone. He was charming, and funny, and sensual, and so, so wrong for her. He was the man she couldn't lust after. She had once been a proud Catholic girl – she shouldn't have lusted after anyone. She was old enough to know that all women lusted for men, and this man, who was clearly very interested in her, was the man she loved. Not the man she had promised to marry at her father's request.

"Alejandro isn't here," she said. "He has gone to the hospital to get Sofía."

"That was a while ago," Cayetano frowned. "He left me at the Libertad on the corner at least half an hour ago."

"You and Alejandro keep that bar in business. Any time I need to look for him, I know to check the Libertad."

"We men have much to discuss."

"You mean you and Alejandro talk on and on about all the bullfighting you both love but don't get to enjoy anymore?"

"That also. We don't want to trouble you fine ladies with the details."

"You take Scarlett to the bar."

"Señorita Beltrán, are you jealous?"

"Jealous? No," she scoffed. "That bar is disgusting, as are the men who frequent the place."

"Men like me? I might head back there now. They have a fire, unlike my place. It's cold out here."

Luna rolled her eyes. The cheeky look on his face was too sweet to deny. "Come in, the fire is on."

Cayetano stepped inside the dark living room and went straight over the dull orange glow of the fire in the stove and held out his hands, and felt them tingle in response to the warmth. "Thank you," he said to Luna and watched her close the front door. "I realise it's improper for me to come in when you're at home alone."

"It's you, Cayetano." Luna stepped carefully over the wooden

floorboards in her long dress. "I trust you." It was herself that she didn't trust.

"You shouldn't. I don't trust myself. I have done things I'm not proud of."

"There's a war on. What goes on in wartime is against all the rules that we live by. After all the battles you've fought in, the world can't be the same for you."

"So... if I said that I came around here, even though I knew that Alejandro wasn't home... would you mind?"

"Why would you do that?" she said. Her heart jumped in her chest. She knew why; she hoped so anyway.

"Because I have sat by for years, watching you at every opportunity. People are scared of what is about to happen. Life is about to change for us, and I have wasted too much time."

"What do you mean?"

"The Republicano leaders have left to live in exile, in Francia. We have been abandoned by those whose cause we fight. It's bad enough that the Británico government endorsed the Nacionales government a few weeks ago. As soon as Franco's troops get here, they will take our town, and that's it. They will win. We are all as good as dead."

Luna ran her hands over her dress and took in the information. It felt so stupid to want the chance to wear a gown to a party when their lives were in danger. "We have to get Papá out of Madrid."

"I'm trying," Cayetano replied and took a few steps over to her. "But an anarchist leader as well-known as Juan Pablo Beltrán is of course in danger. As soon as he is here, we are all going to go to Valencia, and hopefully we can get on a boat and out to Francia. Maybe then we can hide out somewhere. Scarlett is desperate to go home to Nueva Zelanda because... she... she just needs to get out of España. It's been unkind to her."

"I thought Scarlett would have run to the front lines, gun in hand, to fight again."

"Sí, however, this time she can't. She doesn't want to abandon España, but it's complicated. She has to leave."

"I don't want to abandon España," she said with defiance. "None of us should."

"I would kill every soldier to save us if I could do it, Luna. But we need to face reality – we will lose this war. Our chances of success are hindered now that the troops have got through to Vinaròs and cut Valencia off from Barcelona. We're trapped."

"The rebels haven't taken Madrid."

"Not yet they haven't. I just want to move you all out to Valencia."

"You and Alejandro want to take up arms again, don't you?"

"I doubt it would help. I just wanted to tell you that I was sorry that I never danced with you when I had the chance."

"I wish you had asked me. I wish Alejandro or Papá would have allowed it. Juan Pablo and Isabel lost seven children. Alejandro and I were the only ones who made it to adulthood. You can't blame them for being over-protective."

"I suppose that Juan Pablo thinks he has found a good husband for his daughter in Ignacio. He doesn't want a man like me for you."

Luna could barely swallow; a lump of nerves was stuck in her throat. She shouldn't have let him inside. It wasn't proper. She was a good girl, but it was as Cayetano said – they could all be dead very soon. The laws of propriety no longer applied. If the Republicans lost the war, their deaths would be brushed over in the annuals of history, and Cayetano and Luna would be just numbers lost in a war that the world had ignored for their own gain. Only Hitler and Mussolini were allowing their countries to engage in the war, and that brought nothing but misery. "Dance with me now."

Cayetano stepped forward and stood all but against her. "I'm afraid I've never danced before."

Luna took his right hand and placed it on her hip and took his left in hers. She tenderly placed her other hand on his shoulder. "Like this," she said, not sure how close to stand to him, she had only ever danced with her father and brother before now. There was no use in showing him the steps; they could do no more than the slightest shuffle in the tiny dark room. What their feet did was irrelevant to her anyway. She was with the man who awakened her.

"Did you know that love is like water?" he whispered in her ear. He watched her soft brown eyes look up at him innocently. She was so beautiful, so delicate; too good for him. She was Alejandro's sister and Alejandro had told him not to touch Luna, but he couldn't help himself. Alejandro knew about the night Cayetano had spent with Scarlett in Requena. That was proof to Alejandro that Cayetano would never be faithful to Luna. That night with Scarlett was a simple mistake, a moment of comfort. Everyone knew Cayetano wasn't good enough for Luna Beltrán, except Luna. He wanted to be good enough for her. He would have done anything to change who he was to be a proper suitor for her affections.

"How is it like water?"

"Because you can fall in it and you can drown in it. I know that I can't live without your love."

"If you send us away to Valencia, I might never see you again."

"The things that we love always leave us. Holding on to love is like holding on to sunlight – it can't be done. The love you have in your heart can never leave. All you can truly ever have is the love that you have inside you. The love I have moves through my veins, and it's so powerful that it burns me."

Cayetano pulled her body against him and brought his lips to hers. He knew she would be inexperienced; probably had never been kissed before, but the moment his lips lay over hers, he felt her respond. There was an unleashed fire inside Luna Beltrán, a fire she had saved up.

Cayetano reluctantly let her mouth go, and watched her run her tongue over her lips that continued to command his full attention. He loved her so much, and it had always been from afar until tonight. "I have something for you," he said. His hands left her back and fumbled in his pocket and pulled it out. The ring. The Medina ring would be safe with Luna. "I love you, Luna. This is all I have in the world, and I want it to be yours, along with my heart."

Luna looked down at his hand, and her eyes widened. A ring. Not just any ring either. A diamond, and a huge one at that. Cayetano had honourable intentions for her. That was a fortunate thing, because tonight she would have agreed to anything.

"Marry me," Cayetano whispered.

"Caya... where did you get this?"

"It doesn't matter."

"It does," Luna said, unsure of what to do. "It's a diamond."

"It's a white solitaire. A man named Sergio Medina gave it to me. We helped his family out to Valencia just before Christmas. He gave me this as a thank you, and as a hand-up in the world. They are an extremely wealthy family."

"That's quite a thank you!"

"Well, let's say the man owed me a favour. I don't know what is going to happen now, but I need this to be safe. I want the ring to be on your hand, with you as my wife."

"But I have to marry Ignacio."

"You don't have to do anything, la chispa. Run away with me instead."

Luna looked up at Cayetano's hopeful expression. He said it with all the sincerity in the world. Ignacio didn't have an ounce of sincerity in him. "Sí. I will run away with you." She watched him slip the ring on her finger, and his hand shook against hers. "I'm scared, Caya."

"Don't be," he said and brought his hand to her cheek. "We're going to get out of here, and never look back. We're going to be safe. I will protect you, I promise. I love you, Luna, the way you deserve to be loved."

"I want to show you how much I love you," she whispered.

"No," he stuttered. Did he really just say no? "I wouldn't expect you to..."

"I want to. If we are all going to die, then I want to die as a woman." Luna brought her not-so innocent lips to his. She felt hot against him when he drank her in, tasting her sweet and spicy lips. She trembled in Cayetano's arms, and it only served to tease the desire that seared through him. She had a power in her that made the desire in him grow impatient in an instant. He had a dozen reasons to stop her, and only one to give in to her wish. She was right – he could be dead tomorrow.

Their elaborate and romantic outfits seemed heavy and cumbersome as Cayetano led her through to her bedroom. Cayetano managed to take his hands off her long enough to remove his jacket, and tossed it on the floor. He felt her little hands go to the knot in his tie, but she obviously didn't know how to untie one. He helped her undo the tie and then started undid the buttons on his plain shirt. Her eyes watched intently as his body become exposed in front of her. There was no sense of apprehension in the way she touched him. The apprehension came from him. He shivered as her small hands wandered down his chest and rested on his belt buckle.

"Are you sure?" he asked. This would be the first time she had ever been with a man. This wasn't like all the women that came before Luna. Those women were in it for a quick thrill, just like Cayetano was. "We can wait..."

"I don't want to wait," she whispered, and brought her lips to his again. Her heart pounded with exhilaration, and she knew that she wanted nothing else than to be swept away in the moment. "Make love to me."

The lights of the monastery across the dark gorge caught Cayetano's eye briefly as the pair inched past the window toward her little bed. Her hands held on tightly to his shoulders when he found the zip on the back of her dress. The intensity heightened when he discovered she wore nothing at all underneath it. That was the moment his nerves set in; she may have been an innocent, but she wanted him. Wanted him because she was in love with him. It was a dream he thought would never come true.

Cayetano's desire would have overwhelmed Luna if she hadn't been so ready to receive him. Cayetano had her completely overpowered when they lay on the bed. She had his body to touch, experience and memorise. She had long imagined it but now it was hers to enjoy, and God, she wasn't going to waste her chance. She couldn't believe how every inch of her body quivered when he touched her. She had no hesitation in letting him put his hands all over her, to teach her what it felt like to be enticed and teased by a man. She was breathless when Cayetano finally decided that he could no longer deny himself what he desperately wanted. Luna gasped at the feeling of completeness that she got from Cayetano when he gently claimed her. When he cried out in delight with his deep voice, Luna could no longer fight the intensity that raged through her.

They lay in silence on the single bed, curled up against each other, and hoped that their hearts would cease their pounding, to no avail. "Are you all right?" he whispered.

Luna nodded without her eyes leaving his. "Is it always like this?" she asked softly.

"No," he shook his head. "Never in my life has it been like this. I'm in love with you, and it changes everything."

A loud bang on the door brutally interrupted the tender moment. "¡Dios mio!" Luna cried. "What if it's Alejandro?"

"Why would he knock on his own front door?" Cayetano asked, and pulled the blanket up over her. Then he remembered that Alejandro forgot his key all the time. He would stand at his own front door across the street and laugh at his friend whenever he got locked out. There was no escaping this – the drop from Luna's window was straight into the gorge. Even the most desperate man wouldn't jump, but Alejandro's fist in his mouth would be worth it to stand by her. Luna would be his wife very soon.

"Luna?" they heard a woman's voice call.

"That's Scarlett," Cayetano said and sat up in the bed. "You didn't lock the door!"

"Luna, are you here? I need you," they heard her call.

"I... I'm just getting dressed," Luna called back, and hoped that Scarlett wouldn't come through to the bedroom. But no such luck. A moment later the door flew open and there stood Scarlett. Even in her green trousers and shirt she still looked like a flame-haired goddess.

Scarlett paused for a moment in the doorway, and took in the sight, and rolled her eyes. "Luna," she sighed. "I need you."

"Scarlett," Cayetano said. "You have blood on your clothes!"

"I know that," Scarlett said and looked down at the splatters all over her shirt. "It's Sofia's."

"What?" Luna cried while she clutched at the blanket to her naked body. "Where is she?"

"She's in labour at the hospital. Something is wrong. You need to be there, in case the worst happens."

"Is the worst about to happen?" Cayetano asked.

"I would be very surprised if she or the baby are still alive when we get there." Scarlett turned and stepped out, to let them get dressed.

Cayetano appeared by her side a moment later, and roughly tucked his shirt into his trousers. "You're unbelievable," she hissed at him, and hoped Luna wouldn't hear. "You can't just shove girls off to Barcelona to have an abortion anymore, you know that, right?"

"I would never do that," he replied in a hushed tone. "I offered to take care of you, and..."

The conversation halted when Luna came out of the bedroom, dressed in the simple skirt and blouse she had worn earlier in the day. Scarlett noticed in an instant that she had the Medina diamond on her finger. All the work that they had all done to get that diamond, and he had given it to Luna. "Come on," she barked at the pair. "Let's pray your family is still in one piece when we get to the hospital."

8

Valencia, España ~ septiembre de 2009

There went the plan. Not that there was much of a plan at all. Cayetano had paced for days after his fight with his father over Luna and his foolish words. He knew how stupid it sounded – in love with a woman he didn't know. Lust – yes. Besotted – yes. But love? Love was a word thrown around far too often. It had practically lost its meaning. After all, he had claimed to love his wife, and he didn't. He couldn't help it; he felt in love with Luna.

Now he stood outside Excursíones bicicleta del Turia in Valencia, where Luna had said she worked. He had got out of bed that morning and jumped straight in the car. He didn't have the courage to ring her again, and now he had just driven for four hours to a city he didn't know, and found the bike office in the Turia gardens. Office was a stretch of the truth. It was a desk under an umbrella, headed up by a young woman who had zero interest in being there. Cayetano was forced to lay on his charming smile in order to coax information out of the girl, who responded to him immediately. *Luna never does the morning shift here, because she takes her boys to school and then goes for a run. Call her, she will be going past here soon.* Maybe he should call her.... or maybe he could wait and hope to bump into her. That would make him look like less of a stalker. Maybe.

Cayetano strolled away from the desk, which was surrounded by yellow bicycles that waited for tourists, and took in his surroundings.

Just beyond the shade of the Puente del Reina bridge that took traffic over the park, was a children's playground, already full of people for the day. Valencia's park was amazing; he had heard all about it but had never visited. Seven kilometres of riverbed now void of water after it was diverted after the flood of 1957. Now, sunk into the earth, it was a long maze of parks, playgrounds, sports fields, cafés, and even an opera house and science museum that sat at one end, and a zoo at the other. It was marvel. A few metres above him was the buzz of the city that went past both sides of the Turia riverbed, but the oasis just below the city in the park was silent. No wonder tourists wanted to bike through it every day.

Cayetano turned when he heard a noise behind him. There was a group of cyclists that had stopped not too far from him. These were the serious cyclists, all dressed in their racing gear. Cayetano took a quick look at their bikes, not knowing anything about them. That must have been the type that Luna used to work on. The moment he thought about her, he had to tighten his grip on his cane. Just the thought of passing her in the park made his heart beat a little faster.

"If that lazy-ass Darren wants to come riding, he needs to show up on time," one of the cyclists moaned.

"Look, here he comes," said another.

Cayetano turned and looked at the men again. One pointed down the main pathway through the park. He looked through the trees and the locals out strolling, and saw Luna. She ran alongside a man who slowly rode a bike. That must be The Darren. Even from a distance he could see Luna's smile. She must have been talking about something funny, because this Darren guy seemed to be laughing while he pedaled. Her ponytail of black curls bounced back and forward, and she waved her arms around as she told a story.

"He took those kids to school this morning," Cayetano overheard one cyclist say.

"He is a smart man. Pretending to like the kids will get you in the bed of the mother," one joked.

"Fabrizio hasn't been dead that long," another quipped.

"Yeah, but it's so obvious that Darren is banging her already. Moved in to help her with the kids? Please. We all know that they're screwing around."

Cayetano frowned. What a rude thing to say. He would have loved nothing more than to jam his cane into that guy's wheel when he went to leave.

"You're just jealous," another said.

"You bet I am. All the money she has after Fabrizio died? She is rich, and giving herself away in return for a bit of babysitting. I'm next in line to have a turn at riding her."

The group laughed as Darren and Luna approached them, the dirty grins on their faces visible from where Cayetano stood. He took a few steps back and was now completely out of sight behind the huge stone bridge pillar. Now he really was a stalker. He watched as Luna spoke to them for a moment, before Darren joined them and the cyclists headed off in the opposite direction. Darren kissed her cheek before he left.

Cayetano paused for a moment, while Luna fiddled with her phone that she had pulled from her pocket. What the hell was wrong with him? A month ago he had been on top of the world – he was an athlete, a star. A month ago his career was on a high and everyone wanted a piece of him. Now he was reduced to walking on a cane, and too nervous to approach the woman he wanted to see. Seeing Luna with Darren had thrown him – she had said something was going on with him, and the crude comments of the others did nothing to help the situation. *Do it!*

"Luna?"

Luna turned when she heard her name behind her. "Cayetano!" she exclaimed. "Um… hello. What are you doing in Valencia?"

"Well…. I can't work, so I took a holiday," he bluffed. "They say the Valencian beaches are the place to go if you want to avoid the tourists."

"Yeah, yeah, Valencia isn't a tourist trap like further down the coast." *Awkward small talk. Great.* "Where are you staying?"

Shit. "Just over there," he lied and pointed over his shoulder.

"At the Barceló?"

"Yeah."

"Across the street from my apartment building?"

The stalker rating just went off the chart. "No, I'm lying. I drove here to see you."

Luna couldn't help but smile. So much for playing it casual. Just the words were enough to make her want to giggle like a teenager again, and she never did that. "Why didn't you just call me? I figured that after our last meeting that you weren't interested anymore.

Today is the twins' first day back at school after the holidays. You have caught me in my ugly running gear, so you may never want to see me again."

Cayetano eyed her up and down. Didn't she know how beautiful she looked? Not just because of her short shorts and fitted shirt were skin-tight on her body, but because her cheeks were flushed and rosy, and her wild hair all out of place. She looked fresh, young… the opposite of how he felt on his cane. "You're so beautiful it hurts."

"Liar. You're off your crutches. How are you?"

"Good. The leg feels great. I will make a full recovery. This cane? Barely need it."

"Right." She knew what men were like with injuries. "If you didn't know where I lived, how did you plan on finding me?"

"I knew where you worked. Maybe you could show me the Turia on a bike."

"I don't think you're ready for the bike, Cayetano. But you know that. Besides, I'm not working today."

"Maybe there is something else we could do on a date?"

"Are you asking me out?" Luna watched him fidget with his cane. He was a different man since he sustained his injury. It had knocked the confidence out of him. "I might go out with you again if you bring the cane."

"You like the cane, do you?" he teased, and he watched her snigger. "Can I ask you something, *Señorita* Tour Guide?"

"Sure."

"Over here," he said and edged back in the direction of the 200 year-old stone pillar of the bridge. "I saw something in here," he said and pointed around the side of its thick form. "There are little holes in the stones…"

"Oh, yes…" Luna said and followed him. "That was for when…"

Luna was cut off when Cayetano dropped his cane and pulled her into him. He pressed her between him and the stone wall, and said, "we need an icebreaker." She looked at him, his eyes were dark and potent with the desire he had, complete with those trademark green flecks. He wound his arms around her to hold her close, and thrust his lips on her. He tore her mouth open with his tongue and dived deep into her.

The profound spike of want and yearning grew in Cayetano when her body fell into his embrace. Luna practically folded into him, and completely yielded to him, but she wasn't weak to him. She was strong, powerful, as set alight like him. Her hot tongue flicked in his mouth, searching for a release from the wanting that matched his own.

Luna struggled to catch her breath as Cayetano's scorching lips trailed down her neck. He had his legs either side of her, which held her tight in position against the wall, and she giggled at his touch. They were getting too heated for being in public, but she wasn't sure if she cared.

"Cayetano…"

"What?" he muttered, and brought his darkened eyes up to hers.

"I have lived across the street from the Turia for years, so I'm aware of how much 'public affection' goes on in Spain. But you really need to slow down. We are not 16."

"No one will ever know," he whispered. "This is Spain, you don't have to be 16 to come to the park to…"

"Break the ice?"

"Exactly."

"Do you smuggle women into secluded parks for a kiss often, do you?" she asked, and he let her go, and they straightened themselves up again. She bent over and picked up his cane and brushed the yellow Valencian dust from its black paint.

"When I was growing up, I lived with my parents, and my sister, and my grandparents, all in our three bedroom apartment. Privacy was easier in public than it was at home."

They left the private little spot and headed back out onto the main path through the park. She ran her hands through her long black ponytail that started high on her head, and said, "I see couples out here all the time, and they are not always teenagers. I think the close family ties that Spanish families have interrupt romance for couples of all ages. More babies would have been conceived in this park than in homes all over this city."

Cayetano laughed as the two walked along the cobbles, and they stepped out of the shade of the bridge and into the bright Valencian sunshine. Despite only being a few hundred miles from Madrid, the city was totally different. The energy of this city was more relaxed than back home. "I would love to say I took lots of girls for 'a walk' in El Retiro, but my parents didn't let me out very often. I was already in training with the bulls in my teens."

"Wow, they pushed you hard."

"*Sí,* but I wouldn't have all I do if they didn't."

"You do want it, right? I mean, you don't just do it because they want you to be a *torero?*"

"It's me who wants to do it, I suppose. It's an adrenalin rush. My family's reputation is built on it, I have to do it. It's also centuries of tradition, and I'm the one who upholds it for my country. It's an art, not a sport. What I do is a precise and dangerous performance. It's not the bloodletting horror people think it is. The bull will die by my hand, but it dies an honourable death."

"I agree."

"*¿Sí?*"

"Yes. I like bullfighting, I just don't know too much about it. I'm not one of those women who fight to have it stopped. No way. But there are many people who are very critical of bullfighting."

"Trust me, I hear it all. People have told me that I must be sick to want to kill animals. Or that I'm compensating for my lack of masculinity. Or that I call bullfighting an art because I'm not smart enough to understand 'true' art forms."

"Ouch! I read that the financial crisis is harming bullfights. If cities and towns can't afford to run the events, the art will die a slow death, especially with it banned on live television at the moment. It's commercial value has diminished."

"My career hasn't suffered but other people have lost their jobs. The *anti-taurinos* consider all these types of losses a victory. Job losses aren't a victory for anyone. But the *anti-taurinos* don't protest that often, and I don't care what they think."

"I can think of many things I would protest to have removed from today's society before bullfighting."

Cayetano grinned and watched her walk beside him. She had a spring in her step. Her words were full of enthusiasm, no matter what they were talking about. She made him feel old. "Most women hate it."

"That must make it hard to get a date. Other than having a wife, that can't help either."

"Ouch. The lady bites."

"Yes she does."

"I thought I made my position with María clear the other day."

"You did, you did," she dismissed his worried tone. "I'm teasing."

"I don't want to have to smack you with my cane."

"Come on then," she said. She jumped in front of him and bounced up and down in her expensive running shoes. "Give it a shot."

Cayetano reached out to tap her thigh with the rubber end of the cane, but she jumped back out of the way. "Going to have to do better than that," she goaded him.

Cayetano tried to poke her with the cane again, without any attention to where he walked. He tripped in a crack on the cobbles and stumbled forward. Luna grabbed him, but her small frame was barely able to hold his muscular frame. They stood pressed hard against each other for a moment. "This is the best date ever," he said.

"Is that because you landed against me and somehow both of your hands managed to stop on my butt?"

"Maybe." They both sniggered; their matching smiles were only inches apart. "It must be a good sign that you didn't just let me fall."

"Must be," she said quietly. In reality, she felt set on fire, fully clothed in broad daylight. Luna had, of course, experienced sexual attraction but after years of nothing, every sense that made her a woman begged to get out all at once. "Are you all right?"

"No," he sighed, and reluctantly let go to straighten himself up. "I hate that I'm like this."

"You have been injured before, and all sportsmen have injuries from time to time." She watched him smooth the simple white shirt he wore. His hands were very careful and deliberate, as if he wanted to stretch the moment out as long as possible. The trip had hurt his pride, not his leg.

"It's not my leg. It's not even the embarrassment of having to walk with a cane. It's you. You make me like this. I look at you, and I stumble. Even the words stumble out of my mouth. For the first time in years, I have met a woman I like, and I have all the confidence of a 16 year-old boy. I have been moving around on my sore leg for weeks, and I'm not paralysed by it; I'm paralysed by you. I'm besotted with you." He stood silent for a moment, watching her frown. When he swallowed he could feel a heavy lump in his throat. He had no idea what her response would be, but silence only made it so much harder. "Say something. Should I go?"

Luna took the cane from his hand and brought her eyes back to his. "Maybe it's time we got you back on your feet. I'm no great mystery. You just need to get to know me better. But I didn't think you wanted to, because I never heard from you."

"I didn't want to seem too keen," he said with a mischievous smile. "I don't know what the rules are here."

"There are no rules with me. I'm not that kind of woman."

"But I don't want to push too hard... you know... since Fabrizio..."

A serious expression fell over Luna's face. "I need to confess something."

"All right..."

Luna sighed. "Every morning I take my kids to school and then go for a run in the park, as you can see. They say exercise is good for the mind. I have been going through a long bout of depression that has only just lifted. But... when I am alone here, in the park... I go to the café outside the opera house and buy horchata and pastries. I pretend that I like running but instead I only sneak out for sugar for breakfast. Since I haven't visited during the school holidays, I have missed it terribly."

A grin spread over Cayetano's face. "That is a shameful secret," he joked.

"I know. As an athlete yourself, I'm sure you would not approve of such a diet."

"No I don't, I have a strict diet."

"Now that you know, I have to hope that I can trust you with that secret. I'm prepared to buy your silence."

Cayetano cocked one eyebrow. "How?"

"Would you like to come and have pastry for breakfast with me? All the people I know are health-crazy cyclists... and they're all assholes. So I always have to sit alone. I realise if you come with me that this would implicate you in my crimes against nutrition."

"I would love to." It was good to know that she knew that Darren's teammates were assholes. "I have never had horchata."

"What? You call yourself Spanish, and you have never had it?"

"It's a Valencian thing!" he defended himself. "Can I have my cane back?"

"No. I want to you walk with me. Come on. The café is by the rose gardens just there." She pointed across the wide park, and about 200 metres away was the tiny café, where a staff member was just visible while she laid out tables for the day.

They walked towards the little café, with Cayetano stepping carefully without his cane. Luna had her arm weaved through his so he could lean on her, but he tried his best not to. He was left-handed, and it felt good not to have the cane restricting him. "How do you know that I have had previous injuries?"

"I googled you."

"Stalker."

"Hey!" she objected. "I saw you on television, so I decided to find out more about you."

"And what do you know now?"

"I know that you made your *con picadora* novice debut in the ring when you were 22, and did your *alternativa* in the ring, in Madrid, two years later, which made you a *torero*. I know that your bullfighting suit, your suit of lights, is designed in the Goyaesque style, the same kind that your father fought in when he was a *torero*. I know that you had a lot of ears and tails awarded to you in your last season, more than any fighter in Spain. I know that you are known for your noble thrusts."

"Really? How do you like my noble thrusts?"

"Yeah, they're not bad. Skillful and precise I would call them. They get into all the right places."

Cayetano turned to look at her grin a mile wide. "I like to think so, but I thought we were talking about my fighting technique."

"Very funny. You forget I have worked with men my whole life. Penis references make their presence known every day. Nothing shocks me."

"Who said anything about penises? You filthy woman," he scoffed. "I was trying to be a gentleman."

"That's when I also read about your accident," Luna continued.

"I thought all the scars would have given me away."

Of course she knew about the scars. Every time she closed her eyes she saw him naked, ravaged with the silver slivers of battle that ran all over him. "To be gored just below the shoulder and break all those bones, and puncture a lung…"

"*Sí*… broken arm, shoulder, wrist, elbow, collarbone and eight ribs. I had complications after the blood transfusion as well, so recovery was a long time."

"In time to make it up the aisle with celebrity girlfriend María Medina."

"María and my mother planned our wedding while I was in the hospital. I never even proposed. Everyone is allowed one mistake, aren't they?"

"More than one, because I also read that you support Real Madrid football."

Cayetano threw her an incredulous look. "Excuse me? Of course I support them! I am a Madrileño to the bone. I hope you don't support Valencia football."

"Damn right I do! The Valencian soil is in my blood!"

"Do you speak Valencian as well?"

"I do, and so do my children. If you move across the world and make somewhere your home, you need to immerse yourself in the new life you have."

In the shade of the mammoth opera house, the Palau de les Arts Reina Sofía, Cayetano sat down at one of the metal tables and watched Luna talk to the young woman at the café stand. She seemed to know the woman very well. He turned and looked up at the amazing white almond-shaped building that stood over them. The millions of *trencadís,* the white mosaic tiles that adorned the gravity defying building, glistened in the sun and nearly blinded him.

"She's beautiful, isn't she?" he heard her say behind him, and he turned back to see Luna in the chair next to him. "When I first moved to Valencia, I lived in Ruzafa, but moved over here when I was pregnant. They were still sticking the tiles on the building, one by one. Day and night people climbed all over it. When they had one of their famous fireworks displays at the opening, we wondered if the tiles would fall off with all the explosions."

"I think Valencia loves their fireworks even more than Madrid," Cayetano replied. "Where do you live?"

"Right there," Luna said and pointed across the park. On the other side of the nearby Puente de Monteolivete bridge that ferried the traffic through the Arts and Sciences complex, stood a tall white apartment block. "Best view in the city."

The conversation paused when the young girl from the café stand came over with two large glasses filled with horchata and farton pastries on a tray. Cayetano thanked the girl, who did a double take at him, something he was used to happening. "I can see why you love this so much for breakfast," he commented.

"Any self-respecting Valenciano knows that the best horchata comes from Alboraia - made with tiger nuts, water, sugar and nothing else. The farton must be dipped in it. It's essential."

"Alboraia is not far from here, right?" Cayetano asked, and took and a sip from the tall glass. Cold and creamy.

"Yes, it borders the city here. I love Valencia, but I have always wanted to live out of the city in a small town. Beyond the flat lands of the Turia and up into the mountains around here... it's a magical place."

"I have to admit, I don't know the area at all."

"To the north of the city is the Síerra Calderona. I have driven up the mountains through Serra, Naquera, Olocau, Gátova... all great little towns. I would love a place high in the mountains, isolated from everything. But...the kids go to school here, and here is convenient for work for Darren... and me..."

"And horchata."

"Can't forget the horchata," she sighed, and dipped her pastry into the cold drink.

"Can I make a confession?"

"Sure," she said with a mouth of full of pastry. "The way I eat puts you off me, right? Sorry, but I don't care of what people think anymore."

Cayetano chuckled. She had icing sugar all over her face, and a drop of horchata on her chin. It showed a sense of self-confidence that she could act like that in front of someone, and not be embarrassed. Luna knew herself. "I googled you as well."

"Me?" she frowned. "I'm no one."

"That isn't true. The only female bike mechanic on the cycling pro-racing circuit in Europe? Champion of having drunk drivers jailed here in Valencia? Didn't you fight in court for 18 months to have the driver who killed your husband jailed? You are someone."

Luna nodded and wiped her face with a napkin. "I did. I would like to say I did it so people wouldn't make bad choices and hurt others, but I did it for revenge. It was satisfying. My life was destroyed. Someone had to pay."

"Fabrizio was a popular guy... and a very good rider. I can only imagine how hard it is..."

"Cayetano," she interrupted. "Don't get me wrong, I like you, but I don't want to talk about Fabrizio with you. I don't talk about him with anyone. The day might come where I do, but that day isn't now.

It's still all new and fresh and raw, and dwelling on it doesn't help me recover from it all."

"I'm sorry."

"No, I am. The thing is… I'm more than some guy's widow. That is how everyone treats me, as a victim. I met you, and liked you because you didn't know me as that woman. You are the only one who treats me that way, as an individual."

"I don't see you as anything other than an individual. A very strong woman, in fact. You are fascinating and intimidating."

"Me?" she scoffed. "Says the famous bullfighting underwear model."

Cayetano cringed. "Oh, you saw that."

"Saw it? Everyone in Spain has seen you in your boxer briefs. I just didn't recognise you when we met. Probably because you had clothes on! They photo-shopped your scars off."

"Yes, they said my scars would detract from the point of the billboards."

"The point being your big…?"

"Underwear."

"Oh yeah, those."

"I never wanted to do those billboards, it wasn't my idea," he shook his head. "It was all about promotion, I swear."

"Never mind. Only I know that you don't pad your underwear for the photos," she said with wide eyes, trying not to laugh.

"I hope I impressed." How embarrassing. God, his body had been seen by millions, yet the opinion of this woman meant the world to him.

"I'm very impressed," she said, and rested her chin on her hand that was propped up by her elbow on the table. "I like you very much. You're a very intriguing man."

"Good to know. What if I asked you out on another date?"

"I would say yes… but… I need to take it slower this time."

Cayetano reached out and brushed the back of his fingers against her arm. "I'm going through my divorce. Slow is good for me. I won't push too hard this time."

"You didn't push too hard last time. No one pushes me around."

Cayetano leaned forward, the two of them perilously close together. "I could have sworn I pushed you against the bridge just before."

"True, true, but a girl has to have her first public kissing session. I'm 33 years old already."

"You have never been kissed in public?"

"I was in a very, very private relationship before. Fabrizio and I had to have a strictly professional relationship everywhere but at home."

"I want to kiss you now, just to be the man who gets to do that in public with you."

"I think that is a great idea," she whispered. The moment Cayetano lips met hers, Luna's heart leap in her chest. It felt like a wild bird trapped in a cage inside her. His kiss was so tender, but it promised so much. She was afraid to exhale because she wasn't sure she had the power to breathe in again. Over and over he kissed her lips, a guiding and searching kiss that was nothing like the passionate moments they had shared before. This was affectionate, but also offered something, something warm and compassionate.

They could both hear something, but were desperate to ignore it. Luna's phone was ringing. The spell was broken. "Sorry," she sighed. "I need to check it, in case it's the boys' school." She pulled the phone from her pocket and looked at the screen. "Just Darren," she said. "He can wait." She tossed it on the table without answering.

"I'm flattered."

"Don't sound so surprised."

Just as Cayetano leaned in to kiss her again, the phone started to ring, and they both groaned. "Maybe he can't wait, sorry."

"I'm a patient man," Cayetano joked.

"Hey, Darren," Luna said into the phone. "What's up?"

Cayetano frowned when he saw her mood change while she listened. "How bad?" she asked. "And where are you now?" He watched her try and concentrate. She was getting instructions. "Okay... yeah... I guess I can... no, of course, I can do it... right now... just hold on..."

"What's wrong?" Cayetano asked when she ended the call.

"Darren has fallen off his bike. Just outside the city, not far from the Monasterio San Miguel de Los Reyes. It's where you leave the main roads and start to head up towards the mountains. A parked car opened their door and hit him."

"¡Dios! That's bad! Did they call an ambulance?"

"No. He doesn't want one. They wouldn't take his bike anyway, and you can't just leave a €15,000 bike on the side of the road. I'm going to go and pick him up."

Cayetano stood up, worried for her. She had gone pale. "Luna… do you need some help?"

"I don't drive."

"At all?"

"I have a licence, and a car… but I don't like driving anymore…"

Anymore. No doubt since her husband had been run over. Now her friend had been hurt. "I can drive you if you like, if you need help?"

"No, no," she dismissed him. "I have to do this. I'm sorry, Cayetano, I need to go right now."

"Of course."

"Do you need some help?" she asked with a frown. She was now distracted and flustered.

"I can get back to the car on my own," he said. "I'm parked right over there," he said and pointed in the same direction of her apartment building.

"Come on," she said. "I'm sorry, you drove all this way, and now I'm leaving after an hour."

"I don't mind," Cayetano said. He almost had to run on his sore leg just to keep up with her pace as she headed straight across the park and up onto the road. They were back at street level, and the world was noisy and busy around them. "That's my car just there," he said, and pointed to a car down along the row of vehicles parked along the edge of the garden.

"Wow, nice," she commented, in the direction of the immaculate new black Mercedes. She turned to Cayetano, who held his cane horizontally. "Your leg isn't sore? I'm sorry, I just rushed you."

Cayetano looked down at his cane. He hadn't even used it while he crossed the park. "I think you just cured me."

"Well, I hope that made the trip worthwhile then."

"You should go and help your friend. Don't mind me."

"Thank you. It was a nice surprise to see you today." She tried to smile, but her worry was still the biggest emotion in her. "But if you don't call me this time, you will have to work harder to earn my forgiveness."

Cayetano reached out and took her hand and kissed it. *"Hasta luego,* Luna."

Luna reluctantly took her hand from his. "Goodbye, Cayetano," she said, and turned away from him. Cayetano stood at his car and watched her run across the pedestrian crossing and disappear through the self-opening doors of her building, and out of his sight. She had done more for him in an hour of conversation than weeks of recovery. But the way she had panicked when Darren had called – Cayetano was not the only man on her mind. Luna was a still a mystery to him.

9

Valencia, España ~ septiembre de 2009

Wide little eyes. That was what struck Luna when she saw her two sons watch Darren. Their ice-blue eyes stared at the man that they considered their father when they saw him in the living room, battered and bruised after his accident. Luna had driven to where he had come off his bike – a hair-raising journey without the added worry – to find Darren on the path. Blood all down one side. Torn clothing. A mangled bicycle. The same things that haunted her at night when she closed her eyes. Luna had not seen the accident site where Fabrizio had been killed, even though it was only a few blocks from home. She had seen him only when they let her into the room at the hospital, but by then he was already dead. Skull fracture. Dead the moment he hit the ground at high speed and dragged under the car. Now she saw the same thing again, and now her children saw it. The pain would never go away.

A fractured wrist, a dislocated shoulder and multiple cuts and bruises. That was what the hospital had told her. Luna sat in the room with Darren, and watched him be bandaged and stitched back together. He was a mess, all because of some fool opening her car door. Luna had barely spoken to him during the drive to the hospital, or while he was treated. She wasn't sure what to say. She wasn't sure what she felt. Once she had collected Giacomo and Enzo from school it had become even harder; what they saw worried them. Someone they loved had been hurt.

Even with his arm in a sling, Darren had insisted he put the two little feisty redheads into bed that evening. Luna stood out on the balcony of her apartment that overlooked the park on the warm September night. The sea breeze blew, and it lifted her long black ponytail from her neck that was just a little damp with sweat in the heat. With a glass of wine in her hand, she closed her eyes. She felt guilty – she should have been thinking about Darren. She should have been more upset at the images of Fabrizio that kept coming to mind. But she wasn't thinking about either of them.

"Hey, you," she heard Darren say in his smooth accent. Before she could turn around, she felt him weave his good arm around her waist, and his lips came to her neck for a single kiss.

"I don't want you to hurt your arm," she said, and turned her head to face him.

"You couldn't possibly hurt me," he said. He brought his battered arm around to rest against her.

"Where is your sling?"

"I took it off, it was annoying."

"You need it."

"No, I don't. I have painkillers, and you."

"What can I do to help?" she asked, and put her glass down on the small table on the balcony.

"Kiss me and make it all better. My shoulder and arm really hurts."

"Then I shouldn't go kissing it. I know for a fact that a bad fall can make kissing rather difficult."

"No problem, nothing is broken," he whispered. To have her against him in his arms meant the world to him. Even if it did hurt he wouldn't have moved. He dipped his head and tenderly took her lips with his. He took a deep, desperate breath in when he felt her respond to the affection he was so eager to adorn on her. The hesitation in her just needed to be ignored. He would have made love to her right there on the balcony given half the chance.

"Wow," she said breathlessly.

"I like it when women say that."

"You caught me by surprise."

"Really? Because it's been three weeks since you imposed yourself on me, and then went cold again."

"Imposed myself? Is that what I did?"

"Yep. One minute I'm getting out of the shower, next thing you are trying to seduce me in my room when I'm not wearing a thing."

"Then please accept my humble apology, sir." She brought her hand to the bandage that was taped to his face, just below his left ear. "It's been a day of surprises."

"I'm so sorry," Darren said, and cringed when he moved his left shoulder. "I really didn't want to call you. I didn't want you to see me in a mess like this. I called Marco, but he didn't answer... so I called you... and you didn't answer!"

"I'm sorry, I was just... talking to someone. If I had known..."

"This woman just opened her door right in front of me. I didn't even have time to brake. The second I hit the ground all I could think of was you and the kids, and how I have let you down."

"How have you let us down? You mean the world to us."

"So why have you been freezing me out these last few weeks?"

Luna took a deep breath. What to tell him... the story of a hook-up in Madrid was not the right answer. Honesty is not always the best policy. It was more than that, because now she had seen Cayetano twice more. And she liked him. But this was Darren. He took care of her when she was deeply depressed. He helped her with her children, and they loved him as much as he loved them. He was the biggest link to her past and the person most likely to support her in the future. They were comfortable. Comfortable. Cayetano didn't make her comfortable, he shook her violently and left her dizzy. She needed to make herself feel that way about Darren. "I'm sorry. I have been trying to figure out what I want."

"I know, and you said you needed to be pushed. But I can't push you. However, I can't stay the way we are. I smashed face first into the road at high speed today, and all I thought was how I had never been able to be with you. I want a relationship. I want to climb into bed with you every night. I want to make love to you."

Luna couldn't help but smile. "You didn't fall that hard, Darren."

"Only for you."

"Wow, that was cheesy."

"Yeah... I was trying to inject some humour to loosen you up."

"Loosen me up for what?" she asked with a cheeky smile and raised eyebrows.

"Something I can't do when I'm injured," he said through gritted teeth. "I know it's been a while for you..."

Luna couldn't stop an uncomfortable chuckle escape her lips. "Wow, this is awkward..." It was only three weeks since she had ravished a stranger. *Why was that easier than this?*

"I'm still going to go away to help with the team in Cordoba, but..."

"You can't ride. Your shoulder is still swollen after they put it back in place. Your elbow is stitched up, your wrist is bandaged... it's not safe."

"But the team doctors and physiotherapists are going, so I can get my care from them. I'm only coaching. But then I get back... maybe we can explore 'you and me' a little more? Does that give you enough time to decide what you are ready for? I think we just need to avoid this awkwardness and dive right in to each other."

"Yeah," she said genuinely. "That's plenty of time. And you are right, we just need to take the next step."

"And what is the next step?"

Change the subject. "How about I run you a bath and let you soak? You're going to hurt tomorrow."

"That's why I need to make the most of the movement I still have." If only he hadn't come off his bike today, now they could be retiring to a night in her room.

Luna closed herself in Darren's bathroom and let the water fill the tub. *What the hell was going on? What are you doing? Either you want Darren, or you don't. Either you want to move on from the dark patch in your life, or not. Do you want to throw your whole life away just because you have an infatuation for another man you barely know? Of course not. So what was the problem? Darren is the right choice, the comfortable choice, the easy choice. The logical choice. You are not in a position to have a fling. You are not in a position to try something new, or risky, or thrilling. You are a mother of two boys who need you to make the right choice. Your life is not yours, and it hasn't been for a long time.*

Once Darren was in the bathroom, Luna went back to her spot on the balcony, which overlooked the huge opera house and science museum at the Ciutat de les Arts i les Ciències in the park. She watched the couples walking along the paths, and the tourists who shuffled around in their guided groups. She was complacent with her life. When did that happen? One thoughtless drunk ruined the exciting life she had when she was married. Through all the pain she had suffered after Fabrizio died, she knew she needed to work hard with the time she had, but she wasn't doing that. She did the same things every day; same places, same people. She had a million dollar view and barely appreciated it. She was living in limbo, and all of a sudden it didn't seem like enough anymore. That was the problem with Darren. Being in a relationship with Darren would mean things would never change. He was simply a replacement to Fabrizio. It just wasn't enough.

Her daydream was broken when she heard the familiar ring of her phone, and she turned back into the cool air-conditioned living room to find it. When she found it still tucked in her handbag on the couch, she didn't recognise the number. Valencian numbers had a 96 code. Wasn't 91 the code for Madrid? *"Hola, este es Luna."*

"You answer the phone like an *anglosajón.*"

She could recognise that deep, purring, full-bodied voice anywhere. Now Cayetano decided to ring her. "I am an Anglo-Saxon, as you Spaniards love to call us. I haven't learned how to answer the phone rudely with a *sí.*"

"I'm sure not. How are you, *preciosa?* How is your friend? Not serious I hope?"

"Darren is hurt, but he'll be fine. Thanks for asking. How are you? Did you get back to Madrid all right after I rudely abandoned you in the park this morning?"

"My leg is better than it has been for weeks. I just needed your magic touch."

How could it be that both men who were interested in her were simultaneously injured? "I've heard that before."

"May I ask you something, Luna? We didn't talk about your grandfather this morning…"

"Oh, him. I haven't done any more about that. My work permit is valid until the end of the year, so it's not a panic. I can always get it renewed."

"Let me tell you something." There was a sparkle in Cayetano's voice, like a child who had found his stash of Christmas presents under his parents' bed. "I don't know if you had thought of it… but what about looking up the town's census records to see where your grandfather lived?"

Luna raised her eyebrows. "I hadn't thought of that, but how accurate are the records, and how detailed? I thought Spain wasn't very good at census recording."

"They have been doing it since the 12th century. You say your grandfather lived in Cuenca? Cuenca is of course in Castile-La Mancha, and the *municipios* have been keeping census details since the 17th century. The *Directorio de Archivos* has a website that you can easily use to track people in the area."

"Really?"

"I tried it this afternoon when I got home. My sister came by, and she suggested it. Cayetano Ortega did live in Cuenca and was registered to an address in the mid 1930's. They have a scanned copy of the original document that was filled in."

"Bullfighter turned detective, aren't you? Cayetano... thank you."

"That is not all, though. Sofía suggested that if your grandfather lived in Cuenca his whole life, then he may have been baptised at one of the local churches, and they might have records, assuming they weren't destroyed in the war, of course."

"Your suggestion of going to Cuenca seems more and more like something I need to do. But my grandfather was an orphan, so that could be why there is no birth certificate, so maybe the church cannot help me."

"And maybe they can. Who knows what the priests and nuns made records of in those times. All kinds of things went on... babies stolen by the church and housed with Nationalist families after the war..."

"In that case I doubt they will simply hand anything over to me. Especially since I'm a foreigner sticking my nose in."

"You have tried war records? To see if he died in battle?"

"The Republican records are hardly complete in any sense."

"Oh... he was a Republican?"

Luna frowned. She had assumed so – after all, Scarlett had been a nurse who cared for mostly left-wing soldiers, or so she had told her son. "Why? Are your family right-wing supporters?"

"We are nothing more than bullfighters. Politics is not a subject for my family, or me. But yes, I see your problem. The losers of the war are not well-documented."

"What a polite way of putting it." More like forgotten by the world and imprisoned, tortured and murdered, even after they were forced to surrender to Franco's troops. She couldn't be sure her grandfather had ever been a soldier anyway.

"I do have one more suggestion..."

"I would love to hear it. You have got further in an afternoon than I have in months."

"My sister… I had her ring the *Registro Civil* in Cuenca today. They are open on Friday if you want to see them. Also, the cathedral there, the Basílica de Nuestra Señora de Gracia, they could help you. How much I don't know… but it's an adventure."

"It certainly is. Cayetano, you don't have to help me."

"The truth is… I'm not. You see, the cathedral has Unum ex septum signs. If I pray to one, I will be given five years forgiveness for my sins."

"I see, and you can't do that in any of the churches of Madrid?"

"No, none let me in now. They know my reputation for sinning."

Luna knew it, too. Early that morning when she had been loading her dishwasher, she blinked and recalled the moment when his head was between her thighs a few weeks ago. *Focus, Luna.* "So, if I agree to go on this adventure, would you be coming along?"

"The Beltrán family is from Cuenca. I would like to see this beautiful town. It's world famous, and it's part of me. I want to look up where my family lived."

"And pray to the Unum ex septum signs. I don't even speak any Latin."

"Me neither. It means one of the seven, or something. Who cares? I was just trying to win your attention with my overwhelming knowledge."

"Well, I will admit, I'm very intrigued by what you have suggested."

"Do you know of the *parador* there? It is a 16th century monastery that has been made into a hotel. It has a footbridge over the gorge that surrounds the city on the hilltop. They have large rooms, so you could get one with two bedrooms, one for you and one for the children. I, of course, would have my own room. I'm a gentleman."

"What, did you ring the *parador?*"

"Is that too much?"

"Um…" *A weekend with your secret lover. And your children.*

"I'm sorry, if you want to bring Darren as well, I suppose that is no trouble… unless he is too injured…"

"Darren is going to Cordoba on Friday. Cayetano… what you are suggesting is tempting, but I don't know."

"You are in relationship with Darren, ¿no?"

"Yeah, sort of. It's complicated, like you and María."

The conversation fell into silence. The awkward pause grew longer and longer. "Luna… I like you. I want to help you, but it's because I'm interested in you. I got the impression you liked me. Maybe we could spend some time together? I know you have children, so this weekend will be proper. Polite. But I won't lie, I'm attracted to you."

She could remain comfortable and complacent, or let herself be shaken violently by Cayetano again. He made her feel the way she used to; alive and free and young. How a woman in her 30's should feel. "All right. How about this Friday? Can your leg cope?"

"¡Claro! Of course, yes. I can arrange the times we need for the hotel and the meetings. Sofía is a great sister, she knows who to call and who to talk to."

"Please thank your sister, she has been so helpful to me."

"Sofía hates María, so she is happy I have a new girlfriend."

"Girlfriend? Is that what I am?" she joked. She considered herself no more than a one-time lover.

"Since the moment I saw you wrestle a bag-snatcher." Cayetano couldn't help the grin on his face. It never left him when he spoke to Luna, or thought about her, or imagined the shape of her body. The moment broke when he heard his doorbell ring down the long hallway to the entrance of his apartment. Now what? *"Preciosa,* I'm sorry, I need to go. I will call tomorrow. We will make a plan?"

"Thank you for your help, Cayetano."

"De nada. Happy to help."

"Can I just say something?"

"Sure."

"I was thinking about your leg. You need to go down to your local health store and get a cream with hot peppers in it."

"Why?" He heard the doorbell ring again.

"It has capsaicin in it. It's an ingredient that gives the muscles the sensation of being hot. The muscle heats up, and the nerves shut down. It will reduce the pain and loosen up your leg. Cyclists use it."

Cayetano heard a knock on his front door, and turned and started down the hallway. "I haven't heard of that. You are full of secrets."

"Not really, I just married a man who was sore a lot. Capsicum cream is your answer."

"You think about my legs?"

"In the interest of health," she teased.

"I'm sure. I would expect no less from a lady." More banging. "I'm sorry, there is someone really rude at my door."

"I'm sorry. I have taken up your time since breakfast."

"I'm grateful for it. I will call you tomorrow."

10

Madrid, España ~ septiembre de 2009

Cayetano looked at the phone in his hand. He wasn't sure how successful that call had been. Luna seemed genuinely appreciative of his help. She was his girlfriend. He hadn't even thought of that before it spilled out of his mouth. It sounded so juvenile. Maybe it was good that the call suddenly had to end, because she had time to think about that. He wouldn't bother to pretend he would help her as a friend. Life was too short to be coy.

He hobbled to the front door, and he peered through the peephole, to see María there. Fuck. Nothing like an ex-wife to ruin a good day. They had separated eight months ago, and María hadn't come back to their home in all that time. Whatever she wanted, Cayetano wasn't interested. With a sigh, he pulled the heavy door open. The scowl on his face wouldn't confuse María about how he felt.

"Don't frown, Caya, it makes you look old," she said the moment the door opened.

"Perhaps, but you lost the right to use my nickname when you let your cameraman stick his dick in you."

María let out a long whistle and let that moment pass. Her hot-pink lipstick cracked when she did it. "Bitter as ever, I see. Did I interrupt something?"

"Yes, you did. But even if you hadn't, I would have lied and said you had."

María paused and adjusted her purple-framed glasses. At this rate she wouldn't ever win over her husband. "Can I come in?"

Cayetano reluctantly hobbled back a few steps and gestured for her to come in. He shut the door behind her, and watched her welcome herself in their home. His home. He hadn't heard her high heels on the grey marble for a while. The neighbours downstairs always complained about that noise. They probably enjoyed María's absence as much as Cayetano did.

"You have redecorated," she commented and walked into the living room. She gazed around the room, now all done in a simple black and white minimalist style. The room had been in an opulent gold and red when she lived there. Gone were the heavy red curtains in favour of a simple white blind. The deep red rug on the floor was now a simple black rectangle. He had done a great job, even if he had kept his hideous old brown armchair. María sat down on the black leather couch and ran her fingers over one of the white throw pillows. Her long hot-pink nails caught on its fabric. "The place looks great. Did Mamá do it?"

"Sofía helped me," Cayetano said. He limped over to the glass dining table, and pulled out one of the simple leather chairs. "She knew just how to purge you from the place."

"How are you?" She watched him sit awkwardly on the chair across the room.

"Excelente. I am in good hands. I have people who know how to make me well again."

"Good. I have spoken to your Mamá many times, to see how you are. I wasn't sure you would tell me if I called you."

"You're right."

"Seeing you get gored like that was horrific, Caya. I have feared that every day since we met. After your last injury…"

"After my last injury you planned our wedding while I lay in a hospital bed; you didn't even bother to consult me on the subject of marriage."

"Doesn't that show you how much I care about you?"

"You were only at the ring the other week to keep up appearances."

"And because I wanted to see you perform. I still care."

Cayetano pursed his lips and sighed. "There's no need to worry. The week in hospital, and weeks of rest have worked wonders. I'll be fine. This is nothing compared to my last major fall. The pain lessens every day."

"I'm glad," she said, and gently brushed her long blonde hair over her shoulder. "I've been worried. I sit at home and think about you here, discharged from the hospital so soon and trying to get by at home, all on your own."

"I'm never on my own. I have a whole family to care about me. Besides, I'm not crippled."

"Inés said you walk with a cane now."

"I do, but it's temporary, and Mamá should have mentioned that detail. In fact, this morning I went to Valencia and walked in the park with no cane at all."

"You have been to Valencia and back today?"

"Yes, it's a long trip, but it was worth it. María, I don't need to be looked after, and certainly not by you, if that is what you came here for."

"We have been together for over a decade, Caya. Don't brush it all aside because I made a mistake."

"Your mistake, or Paulo as his friends call him, brushed it all aside. The next time I see the man, I will shake his hand. He did me a favour."

"We had a quickie in the office. That's it. You know all this, we have been over it a hundred times." María wasn't a calm woman, she was uptight, and easily wound up. She wanted her own way all the time, and usually got it because people were afraid to say no.

"If you're going to throw your life away, the least you could do is make it a full-blown fling, you know, get your money's worth out of Paulo. I'm having a fling right now, and it's fabulous."

A deep frown clouded María's heavily made-up face. "You're seeing someone? Since when?"

"Since not that long ago."

"Is it serious?"

"No, it's not. It's fun. It's light, and spontaneous, and exciting. It holds a lot of promise but isn't weighed down by it."

María sat and looked at her hands, and played with her wedding ring. "I'm not sure what to say," she mumbled. "We agreed not to see anyone else."

"Yeah, but we agreed to that when we got married, so that rule is easily broken."

"¡*Mierda!* Are you ever going to stop being angry at me? I get it! I fucked up! Has it occurred to you that even though you think I'm an adulterous witch, that I could be the one for you anyway? After everything, don't you think we're soulmates? Even with our mistakes?"

"I have tried to convince myself that we are meant to be," Cayetano said and ran his hand over his sore thigh muscle. "The truth is, María, we don't work. We look nice in photos, and everyone thinks we are a good couple, but we aren't. Your television career is propped up by you being married to a *torero*. It's all bullshit. Life isn't supposed to be this hard. Love isn't supposed to be complicated."

"But it wasn't always like that."

"No, no it wasn't. I loved you. But you broke that."

"Oh come on, Caya! Use your head for a change!"

"My head is to blame for all the mistakes my heart has made. So what if I'm impulsive, and think with my heart and not my head. I was with you because it made sense in my head, but it never made sense in my heart. It didn't make me happy."

"You would seriously throw away everything? What, because of a fling with a woman you don't know?"

"No, it's not about her. Although, the last weeks have been like a new start for me."

"Where is she now that you're injured?"

"She is the only one who doesn't treat me like an invalid. That is what makes me feel better."

"But we are in love."

"Love is like a kiss on the wind. It only sometimes comes your way. You don't know where it's coming from, or where it's going."

"Meaning what?"

"Meaning it's blown my way from the direction of someone else. I'm sorry. I want a divorce."

"What? Because of someone you have known for a matter of weeks? We agreed to no divorce until I had my contract renewed with the station."

"Wouldn't a celebrity divorce raise your profile?"

"I would like an amicable divorce portrayed, if the time ever came."

"Great, works for me. It's not because of Luna, but I have learned some things from her."

"Oh, she has a name now," María quipped and folded her arms

over her chest. "And what has Luna taught you?"

"That even the most broken hearts can move on if they're strong enough."

"I don't believe this crap." María shook her head. "I was on the phone only an hour ago with your mother, getting invited to family lunch this Sunday."

"Go right ahead," Cayetano scoffed. "I'm not going. Neither is Sofía, as usual."

"So you are both abandoning your parents. That's just great. You know how much they value Sunday lunch."

"They turned their backs on Sofía, not the other way around. She is still my best friend." He couldn't resist. "And she likes Luna."

María's eyes widened. "She met your sister?"

Technically, yes. "Sure has." He was really goading her now, and no good could come from that. But it felt great not to be the victim in the relationship for a change.

María grabbed her handbag and stood up. "Do you think I will just wait around while you have a rebound affair?"

"Give me a break, I have slept with plenty of women since I kicked you out." *Liar.* "I'm past the rebound phase."

"So, what, are you skipping off into the sunset with this Luna, are you? House in the country? Children?"

Cayetano rolled his eyes. "You don't have to be so dramatic." She couldn't help it. María seemed to be a shitstorm that was always forecasted to have hurricane force winds. Until they split, he didn't realise how high-maintenance she was. "At least someone as easy-going as Luna would be open to subjects like children, and not just need a man who can drive her to her parties, or plastic surgery appointments. Not that she needs it anyway."

"And we are back to not having a family again. You are like a dog with a bone. I won't give you a baby."

"Good," Cayetano said. He grimaced as he lifted himself from the chair. "That would be like making a pact with the devil."

"You can be impossible sometimes, Caya," María said and threw her bag over her shoulder. "Sometimes I wonder why I bother."

"Probably because I'm richer than you?"

"I doubt that. When did you become this man?" she squinted. "So rude and angry! You have a good reputation, but you're being a fool."

"That reputation is suffocating me. I'm sick of being what

everyone wants. I would rather be happy on my terms. What did you come here for?"

"To tell you that I love you! I care about you! It seems that you are too stupid to realise the mistakes you make."

"At least they are my mistakes, and not just the demands of others forced on me."

"You have everything, Caya. You are a part of a legacy. Don't throw your good fortune away on an affair. You will work all of this out too late."

Cayetano stood on the spot and watched María leave the room. The front door made a loud slam as María exited the apartment. He shouldn't have told her about Luna. That was foolish, but now he felt empowered. He was comfortable in his life. He didn't want to be comfortable anymore. He wanted to feel alive, and so what if he fell on his face? Change was worth the risk.

11

Cuenca, España ~ septiembre de 2009

Drive all the way to Cuenca?
Who are you going with?
Are you sure you can do this on your own?
Why have you planned this for when I'm going to Cordoba?
If you marry me, then you don't need residency in Spain…

Who randomly throws a marriage proposal at a woman over morning coffee in the kitchen? Darren James does, that's who. As soon as Luna told him that she was off to Cuenca in the hope of tracking down her grandfather, he was full of questions. She had told him that she had received help from a woman named Sofía in Madrid.

"How can this Sofía woman help you if she's in Madrid?"

"She called the *Registro Civil* in Cuenca, but there is someone else, Cayetano. He will meet me there and help me out."

"Who is Cayetano? Do you need someone to tell you what you need to look at? Don't you already know?"

"Darren, I'm capable of planning a trip. Don't treat me like an idiot."

"I don't think you're an idiot. You're the boss around here."

"Damn right I am."

"I'm just saying, you don't like to drive and the A3 is a high speed road, and then you would have to get off, at what – the N420? That road is winding through the mountains. Can you do that?"

"I have to learn to drive again sometime," she shrugged.

"Lulu, this is huge. There is no shame in not wanting to drive."

"No, I want to drive again. Who knows, now that I'm unemployed I might get a job that requires me to drive. I can't believe I got fired."

"You weren't fired, you were made redundant, just like most of your workmates. That isn't your fault. People are losing their jobs all over Spain. You're too good for a job that simple anyway."

"I liked it. I needed something simple that got me a bit of time out of the house. It helped me get over my depression."

"Of course, but it's time to move forward," Darren said and put his coffee cup down on the counter. "But don't worry, you don't have to get a job straight away."

"That's good, because I have no idea what goes on with me half the time."

Darren stepped forward and wound his arms around Luna. "You have been a bit funny these last few weeks."

"I'm fine. It's you who is all cut up after the accident."

"I feel much better already. It could also be the painkillers."

"Yeah, it's the drugs."

"Are you sure you can't wait until I get back from Cordoba? I'll come with you. All of us at the *parador* there sounds fantastic. Romantic even. I don't like the idea of you taking the kids and meeting up with some guy."

"He isn't some guy. It will be fine. Nothing weird is going on. I don't make dumb choices, especially not with my boys."

"I don't like it. Why can't you wait?"

I'll tell you why, Darren. Because I feel smothered by you. Of course she didn't say that. But it was true. Protectiveness was a good trait in someone you love, but Darren had become very defensive at the name of another man. He didn't even know a fraction of the story. Good thing she had never told the truth.

"Just think about what I said about getting married, Luna, I mean it."

~~~

Wow, that was enough to sweep a woman right off her feet. Not. Darren had left for Cordoba early that morning. The children were still in bed when they said their goodbyes. His serious words rang in Luna's ears for the whole 200 kilometres to Cuenca. It was a hot day, and even with the air-conditioning on in the car, the boys moaned and fidgeted in their car seats. Darren had announced that he wanted to get married, the kids were loud and difficult, the drama of her grandfather and his disappearing act… and not to mention the drive, Luna's least favourite activity, all made for a stressful day. Only when she pulled up outside the *parador,* the Convento de San Pablo, did she finally let the stress of the day go. Everything needed to be left behind in Valencia.

Luna stood in the cool entrance of the *parador* and took off her sunglasses. The silence of the high-ceiling room didn't stand a chance with the excited footsteps of two eager five-year-olds that jumped up and down on the black and white tiles. The monastery was beautifully restored, and even though the hotel was permanently full of tourists, its stone walls heaved with history. Who knows what the building had seen in its 400 years.

"It looks as if a star has been misplaced."

Luna turned in an instant at the recognisable voice behind her. There stood Cayetano. Her Cayetano. The scruffy guy who walked on a black cane. The Cayetano who wore a suit of lights in the bullring also lurked. His body may have been wounded, but his eyes reminded anyone who came close of the fire that was in him. He possessed an effortless cool, and it threw Luna – her confidence was shaken by the man. Not that he knew that. "A star?" she asked as her two gentlemen companions turned to see who their mother spoke to.

"Yes, a star has fallen and has lit up this room with her presence."

Luna rolled her eyes with a smile. "Good afternoon."

"It wasn't, but is now." Cayetano wanted to step forward and kiss her, but with the boys there, maybe that wasn't a good idea. He looked at the two redheaded cherubs that stood either side of their mother. "Hello, boys," he said. "How are you?"

"Good," they replied in unison.

"This," Luna said, and pointed to her son on her right, "is Giacomo, and this," she gestured left, "is Enzo. Take note, because they will quiz you on it later. Boys, this is my friend, Cayetano. He has come to help me with my work."

"You will test me, will you?" The boys looked identical.

"Yeah," Enzo said. "It's fun. People always mix us up, even though we don't look alike." He flashed his sweet little smile, not shy in the slightest.

"What happened to your leg?" Giacomo asked. "You walk funny."

"Giacomo," Luna chastised him. "That isn't polite."

"No, it's okay," Cayetano said and leaned on his cane. "You really want to know?" He watched them nod. "Are you sure? It's a bloody story." He watched them nod again, vigorously this time. "Okay… there I was… in a bullring…"

"Ooh, this will be good," Giacomo said and rubbed his hands together.

"I stood there, and a 700 kilogram black Iberian bull watched me. He was a smart one. I had my *muleta* out, but I could tell that he wasn't interested in the cape. He looked right into my eyes."

"Did he want to eat you?" Enzo said, almost nervous at the answer.

"Oh, he wanted to eat me," Cayetano replied, and tried not to laugh. "He wanted to go down fighting. He had already got stabbed with *banderillas* in the back of his neck but was still strong. Out I went with my *estoque de verdad,* my sword, and I knew I was in for a fight. The crowd cheered for me to tease the bull and then kill him."

"But you didn't… did you?"

"No, I didn't. You know why? Because a spell had been cast on me."

"What?" Enzo asked with wide eyes. "Really? By a witch?"

"Not a witch, but by an angel. You know, the only thing more dangerous than an angry bull is a beautiful girl."

"How can a girl cast a spell on you?" Giacomo asked.

"I don't know," Cayetano said and shook his head. "This girl, she was the most amazing creature I had ever seen. I had seen her the night before the fight, and all I could think about was her. The world had been shaken and put back together wrong. I was so tired and confused inside that the bull thought he could get me with his horn."

"And he did?" Enzo asked.

Cayetano patted his left thigh muscle through his jeans. "He did. I lifted my arms with my sword in my hands, and he dipped his head and jerked it back up, and got me right in the leg. I fell to the ground and cried like a baby, and blood squirted everywhere."

"Cool," Giacomo grinned.

"What happened to the bull?" Enzo asked.

"They took him away. He got to go to the farm where he lived. I had to go and have an operation at the hospital. When I woke up again, the angel was still in my head. I can't escape her spell."

"So it is the angel's fault that you hurt your leg and a bull tried to kill you," Giacomo said.

"Yeah," Cayetano said and glanced back up to Luna. "Girls are more dangerous than bulls. Remember that."

"Hey!" she said and folded her arms. "Two minutes and already you are all against me?" She watched her sons look up at her and giggle. "All the moaning from you two that I have listened to about not wanting to come with me today, and I thought of doing something fun with you, but now I'm not sure you deserve it...." she taunted them.

"Boys," Cayetano said. He put his hand in his pocket and pulled out two watermelon-flavoured lollipops. "Maybe we should head around to the playground for a while before your Mamá bores us with her work."

They both leaped forward and grabbed the lollipops with a short sharp thank you to appease their mother's stern expression. They all headed in the direction of one of the smaller courtyards within the *parador's* walls at Cayetano's moderate pace.

"A few minutes and you think you have them all worked out, don't you?" Luna asked Cayetano once the boys had run off in front of their mother once they saw the playground across the open courtyard.

"Blood, guts, and a beautiful girl. Boys need nothing else. We are simple creatures."

"Parenting isn't all games and lollipops."

"I know, boys need someone to teach them about girls."

"Can I just make one thing clear?"

"Sure."

Luna watched her boys climb a ladder on the playground for a moment before she decided they didn't need her help. "Cayetano, these are my sons. You can't buy their affections with anything, from the most simple treat in your pocket to the most extravagant gesture. They're here with me, but they're off limits. Don't play games with my kids because you are interested in me."

"You are like a tiger, and I have pulled your tail."

"Yeah, well… even if that comment jumped to conclusions, I have to say it now before today goes any further. I know Spanish people love to spoil kids, and I don't mind that, but you have to appreciate raising sons is not easy, and I have to make careful and considered decisions about them every day. Even bringing them here to meet you is a massive step."

"Of course. I know I asked a lot of you. I just rang and didn't stop to think about whether you were ready to bring the kids, or to drive that distance. I appreciate that you came."

"I don't mean to sound like a bitch. I wouldn't have come at all if I didn't trust you, and let's just say, if you ever pull my tail, you will get bitten."

"I look forward to it," Cayetano said, and gestured for her to sit down on the bench seat by the playground.

Luna sat in the sunshine and looked around. The walls of the *parador* surrounded the leafy courtyard. Who knows what would have happened in this space over the years. If not for the children's playground, it would have been easy to imagine nuns and priests out here enjoying the sunshine. She glanced at some of the other parents; they seemed to all look back at her. "Ah… Cayetano… do you get the impression all the others here are watching us?"

She watched him scan around the playground. "Maybe… but you have said that before."

"Little did I know that the last time I said it, I was walking through Madrid with one of its most famous sons. All the mothers in this courtyard are checking you out."

Cayetano turned and looked at Luna over his sunglasses and saw her cheeky smile. "Wow, that makes this uncomfortable. I'm sure that isn't true."

Luna slid a little closer to him on the seat. "Okay, now that I'm closer to you, let's see if they scowl. That will tell us."

"Maybe I should try the 'stretch and reach' move around you as well, while we're playing silly games."

"Maybe you should."

Luna laughed when he slipped his arm around her, and his large hand rested on her shoulder, and pulled her into him. "Oh come on," he said, "I am sure many men have tried that move on you."

"They have, doesn't mean I let them get away with it."

Cayetano took his sunglasses off and placed them on his head. "I didn't really say hello to you, did I?"

"Not really."

"Buenas tardes, preciosa. ¿Como estás?"

"Estoy mejor ahora que estoy aquí."

"Better now that you're here? I'm flattered."

"You should be. How have you been? Have you tried the capsicum cream on your leg?"

"Not as yet," Cayetano admitted. "I have no one to rub it on me."

"Lucky I bought some with me," she said, and turned to face him. Their faces were only inches apart.

"I thought this trip was strictly business… not that I'm complaining."

"This trip does need to produce something," Luna sighed. "I lost my job yesterday afternoon. I'm unemployed, effective immediately."

"What? Why?"

"The boss laid off at least half of us. He blames the recession. I could see that we had fewer tourists than normal lately, and it seems there isn't enough money to pay us anymore. In turn, the chance of getting my work visa renewed is now zero. I need to be able to prove my Spanishness."

"Spanishness?"

"Yeah, my Spanishness."

"I could hire you. You could be my personal assistant."

"You have a personal assistant?"

"Yes. His name is Hector. I am a brand, not just a person. I run my own company, which needs staff."

"You're a company?" she asked, and looked him up and down. "Where do you keep this staff?" she teased.

"Where you would like to hide on me?"

"Now, now, this is a children's playground. Let's keep it clean. No, you don't have to hire me, but thanks for the offer." She paused for a moment. "You've never had to change jobs before, have you?"

"I've known what I will be for my whole life. I was ready to be in the bullring from age four, so my mother tells me."

"Is it true, what you said before, that I did something that caused your accident?"

Cayetano smiled, touched by her concern. When he sat with Luna, his leg didn't hurt. Everyone else pitied him, or coddled him, but she didn't. "It is my fault that I got hurt. Bullfighting is an art that requires me to draw inspiration for the skill of the performance. I require an emotional connection with the audience in order to concentrate on what I'm doing. However, I wasn't connected, because I was fixated on you."

"Wow… I'm not sure what has blown me away more, the way you speak about what you do, or the fact that I just heard a man use the words 'emotional connection' in a sentence."

"If I don't sound manly, can I remind you that I have a sword to kill an animal when I make the connection? I'm what every woman wants – I can be the man, but I can also write a poem about how sad I feel afterwards, if you like."

"My God, you are unbelievable."

"I thought I was charming and funny."

Luna watched the cheeky grin on his scruffy face grow when he tried not to laugh at himself. "You are very charming, *Señor* Beltrán. Passionate too, but from someone who has been called the greatest *torero* of his generation, I'm not surprised."

"It's my responsibility to keep the tradition alive in this country. The *anti-taurinos* can't be allowed to win just because they incorrectly label bullfighting a blood sport. It's not even a sport, there is no competitive aspect."

"See? Spoken with such passion. That must be the *'El Valiente'* side of your personality."

Cayetano leaned forward to whisper in her ear, his cheek against hers. "There are only two places I would let a woman call me *'El Valiente'*. Since I would never allow a woman in the ring because it would endanger her life, she would have to come with me to the only other place I like to be passionate."

"I think I have already been there."

Cayetano moved to bring his lips almost to hers. "You have been there," his lips murmured against hers, "and there isn't a day that passes when I don't think about you."

"But then I got you hurt," she whispered. She looked into Cayetano's eyes, and there was that flicker of green in the honey brown again.

"We need to get out of the sun," he said and leaned away from her. "I can't take the heat. You scorch me enough. I have no idea how we're supposed to have a platonic visit to Cuenca."

Luna laughed and looked away towards the kids who played together. She felt rather hot herself. Lucky she had brought the boys with her, or who knows where the afternoon would have headed. Not to the *Registro Civil,* that was for certain. "Come on," she said. "We should get on with what we came to Cuenca for."

12

Cuenca, España ~ septiembre de 2009

For all the drama and the dead-ends that Luna had faced on her search for Cayetano Ortega, the moment she got a helpful bullfighter was the moment things started to work. They made it to the *Registro Civil* just before they closed for the afternoon, but the information was ready, thanks to a phone call from Sofía's office. *Enchufe.* It was the only thing that would get this job done. The woman at the desk, a weary looking middle-aged woman named Milagros, thought it was her lucky day when she saw Cayetano walk into her office. A few flirtatious charms and the folder appeared. Now flirting was helping to unwrap the mystery for Luna.

It was refreshing out on the streets of Cuenca in the mid-afternoon. The crowds had all headed indoors for *siesta,* the restaurants and bars all full of the locals and tourists alike enjoying their lunch. The weather in Cuenca was much cooler than the fiery depths of Madrid, or the hot sea breezes of Valencia. It was a chance to wander the maze-like streets and relax. Cayetano watched Giacomo and Enzo both hold their mother's hands and walk along the steep paths between the stone buildings. He still wasn't sure which boy was which. "Who holds my hand?" he joked.

The boys both looked at Cayetano and giggled. "You have full hands," Enzo commented and gestured at his cane and the folder of details from the records office.

"Do you want me to take the folder?" Luna asked him.

"No, a man provides the directions. At least let me have the time-honoured tradition of the man getting the group lost."

"Are you sure you can do this?" she asked. They walked along Calle de San Martín, and it was less of a path and more of a constant set of stairs on the hillside. The entire Barrio San Martín was a cluster of buildings thrown together, with winding staircases through the narrow gaps left between them. On a cane on uneven steps could spell disaster, and Luna couldn't help. She already had to balance two five-year olds.

"Honestly, *preciosa*, you worry too much," Cayetano dismissed her. The walk from the San Pablo bridge that had brought them over the gorge from the *parador* to the area was not that far. "Wait," he said and opened his folder. "This is it. San Martín 16. This is where Cayetano Ortega and Scarlett Montgomery lived."

They all stopped in the shade of the four-storey building and looked up. It was an unassuming place; the light patchwork stone matched the cliffs of the town, as if rising from the land itself. The wooden frames of the windows suggested they had seen serious wear, but the whole thing was very innocuous. But what else could they expect? "Any idea what floor they lived on?" Luna asked. "Or is it one house?"

"No idea," Cayetano replied. "I would say it is all one house, since it's very narrow. Guess we will never know." The wooden arch-shaped door looked original. Cayetano Ortega would have put his hands on there to open it not all that long ago.

"My grandparents lived here once," Luna said to the boys. "Your great-grandfather and great-grandmother."

"Wow, that is so old," Giacomo said.

"Yeah, like about 100 billion years," Enzo said.

"We aren't that old," Cayetano chuckled. Though, with all those stairs, he felt it. "I have a surprise for you."

"Oh, do tell."

Cayetano turned and looked at the building across the narrow path. "Number 15."

Luna looked at the building, which was identical to number 16, except that side of the street was hard against the cliff edge. The view through its windows would have looked straight out over the Huécar gorge towards the *parador*. "What is so special about number 15?"

"That is where my grandmother lived. The house was owned by

Juan Pablo Beltrán Moreno. He lived here with his wife, Isabel. Their son, Alejandro, and his wife, Sofía, and the only daughter of the family, Luna Beltrán Caño, also lived there."

"You're kidding! Did our families live across the lane from each other? That's astonishing!"

"I prefer to think it's a sign."

"Of what?"

"I don't know yet. But everything happens for a reason."

"They could have wandered right by each other. They would have known each other. Who knows… if they were similar ages then they could have been friends… it's almost scary really."

"I wish Papá was here right now. He never talks about his mother. He has never been here. He's missing out on so much."

"Maybe you can bring him one day. What happened to Alejandro? Is he the owner of the building now?"

"I have no idea. Those details aren't listed here, but we could probably find out. I only found out that I have a great-uncle a few weeks ago. I will ask Papá, but he doesn't like to talk about anyone."

"Why not?" Luna asked. She looked at the children, who kicked a stone back and forward to each other, oblivious to the conversation.

"I don't know. Something happened here, and I don't know what just yet."

They stood in the silence of the shaded street. It was almost eerie. This street would have been full of life once. Children would have played. Women would have chatted. Men would have met after work. The end of the road stopped with the drop into the valley. The heavy walls held secrets, but they were locked behind the doors that surrounded them. "No one lives here now, do they?" Luna asked. She stepped forward to the window at number 16 and tried to peer inside. It appeared that the building was derelict, with a thick layer of dust over everything. "I would love to get inside. Who knows how long it's been shut up."

Cayetano stepped across the cobbled path and peered into the window of number 15. He couldn't see anything either. There appeared to be a stove against the wall, but nothing else. "We need to get in there. I will get Sofía to ring and find out who the owner is."

"These buildings shouldn't be left to disintegrate."

"The council probably watches over them, in keeping with the world heritage listing that the town has. But still, who knows…

maybe the owners will let us inside. We will have to come back."

"We certainly will," Luna said and peered in again. She turned around to see Cayetano grimace. "Should we go and sit down somewhere? There was a bar just up around the corner."

"You are such a mother."

"Yep, our Mummy," Enzo added.

"She does all the Mummy stuff," Giacomo added. "Like caring for us and being lovely."

"You have these children well-trained," Cayetano joked, and the group turned back into the direction of the top of the street. "They say all the right things."

"Now Mummy needs someone to look after her so she doesn't cry all night long," Enzo said.

Luna shut her eyes. Kids. Never could keep their mouths shut. She opened her eyes and tried to pretend it never happened. "Would you boys like some lunch?"

"Yay!" they both cheered and started up the stairs of the narrow lane again.

"Luna…" Cayetano began.

"Don't," she interrupted. "Please, just don't ask." Some pain needed to remain private.

It was only a short walk to the bar, the Libertad, on the corner of the street. From there it was only another short stroll to Plaza Mayor and the cathedral, the next stop. The foursome sat outside, to enjoy a lunch of the boys' choosing — tortilla bocadillos and chocolate milkshakes. Luna watched Cayetano in his seat; he was almost back to his old self. He sat straight back, his posture was perfect. His confidence had returned to him. She was happy to see it, because to see him broken was such a shame. He was an interesting and proud man. He possessed a gentility about him that no longer existed in others. It was like there was contemporary sophistication on the outside, but inside was still a very traditional gentleman. She certainly had her hands full with this *torero*. He stared at the table, but his mind was elsewhere. "Penny for your thoughts?" she asked.

"Sorry," he half-smiled. "Just work."

"Do you have to fight again soon?"

"I got an offer to make my comeback after injury already. In Valencia, for Las Fallas in March."

"Wow, that is a big one," Luna said with raised eyebrows. "Fallas means everything to Valencia. It will be an honour to perform."

"Maybe put all these retirement rumours to rest. I would rather die doing what I love than give up."

"Like Daddy," Enzo said innocently. "He died riding his bike."

"Dios mio, Luna, I'm sorry," Cayetano spluttered. The sudden pain in his chest outweighed the pain brought on by any bull horn. His panic-stricken eyes looked at the two boys that sat either side of him at the table. They seemed totally unfazed.

"It's all right," Luna said with a deep breath.

Cayetano could see that it wasn't all right. In quiet moments, he could see that Luna's heart was fragile. She was as delicate as an eggshell that might crack if handled incorrectly. He couldn't think of the right words for this one.

"It all means nothing to the kids. The boys don't know their father. They were too young to know what was going on. I'm both devastated and grateful for it. At least they don't have to be hurt because of it… but they have missed out on a father. Fabrizio was a wonderful man." She paused for a moment. "Sorry, I don't know why I said that."

"Because it's true?" Cayetano offered.

Luna smiled and watched the kids, engaged in their own conversation again. "Yeah," she said slowly. "It is true. You should have seen his face the day that the boys were born. He had two sons, and he was so proud. Then he realised they had red hair… certainly not normal for Italian babies, but he loved it."

"Where does it come from?"

"My father told me that his mother, Scarlett, had red hair. She would have stood out here in Cuenca with red curls."

"It's nice. They wear a bit of fiery family tradition."

"Cayetano Beltrán?"

Cayetano turned to the man who had appeared next to the table and squinted to take a look at him. *"¿Sí?"*

"How's your leg?"

"Fine, thank you."

"After years of brutally killing animals for entertainment, how does it feel to get what you deserve?"

Cayetano rolled his eyes. A great time for an *anti-taurino* to come and hassle him. He never even saw Luna reach for her glass of water before she threw it on the guy. The chilled liquid landed squarely on the front of his beige trousers, and he yelped.

"Ha-ha," Enzo said. "It looks as if that man wet his pants!"

"*Puta*. Bitch," the man spat at Luna and tried, in vain, to wipe his pants. It did look as if he had pissed himself, and Luna had planned it that way.

Cayetano rose from his seat in an instant and towered over the man. He looked straight down on the guy, who took a few steps back. He knew how a bull felt now. Cayetano didn't need to say anything to make his intentions clear – the guy turned and left the table at a brisk pace, and only once dared to glance over his shoulder at the angry *torero* he had left behind. The thunderous scowl on Cayetano's face would have scared the sun itself away had he looked up at it. When he turned back to the group, he still had his shoulders back, his chest out. "I'm very sorry," he implored.

"Don't be," Luna said.

"That was really funny, Mummy. You got him," Enzo said.

"And Cayetano scared him away," Giacomo giggled.

"Come on, boys," Luna said to them. "Let's carry on our day."

They started up the hill along the paths in Plaza Mayor toward the gothic cathedral, the Basílica de Nuestra Señora de Gracia. "I am sorry about that," Cayetano said while he limped along on his cane, and hoped that the children weren't listening. "Unfortunately, I do have to hear the opinions of those who hate bullfighting sometimes. Most don't have the guts to say anything, but every now and then I get an idiot who can't help himself."

"It's okay, really," Luna replied. "Fabrizio was the same. Though his were mostly over-enthusiastic female fans."

"I have those, you know," Cayetano said in an effort to talk himself up.

"Oh, do you now?"

"I rather like it."

"I'm sure you do, you cheeky bastard," she muttered with a smile.

"None from them ever compare to you."

"Keep it clean, we are just friends, remember?" She gestured at the boys, who walked in front of them, and Cayetano saluted back.

Luna helped Cayetano and the twins up the big stone steps to the entrance to the cathedral, and they stepped through the huge iron doors inside the archway of the white stone façade. The cool of the building washed over them; as it did its peacefulness. It had only just opened again after *siesta,* and was empty, except for the young women who were the staff at the entrance way.

"You must be very quiet in here, boys," Cayetano whispered. "There are ghosts in here, and you don't want to disturb them."

"Ghosts?" Enzo asked, instantly convinced.

"It could be anyone. This building has been here for over 700 years. You never know who could be lurking. Look at me back at home, I was just having a beer, and I was struck by an angel. Who knows what could happen in here?" He smiled and watched the boys' eyes widen. "And also, whoever behaves gets more lollipops at the end of the trip."

"Do I get one?" Luna asked.

"Only if you're a good girl. Which I doubt." He smirked at the face that Luna pulled at him, and the boys both giggled. "Why don't you all take a look around, and I will go and see if Father Murillo has any news for us? I spoke to him on the phone yesterday, and he seemed confident he might be able to help us with baptism records."

As Cayetano left them, Luna took the boys to wander the spaces of the cathedral. They walked and took in the stained glass windows, and the only sounds Luna could hear were her high heels shoes on the stone floor, and the excited whispers of the ghost-hunters next to her. Luna always freely confessed to being a fanatical lover of history. She had lost track of how many cathedrals she had seen in Spain, but had lost her faith in God when Fabrizio died.

Cayetano seemed to take a long time, so Luna took the boys in search of their new friend. The place was empty, but he was nowhere to be found. She sat the boys down on a wooden bench seat and took few steps around the confessional towards the altar. There he was. He sat a few rows from the front, his hands clasped in front of him and leaned on the seat in front. She glanced at the golden altar, complete with the obligatory Jesus on the cross in the centre. From the huge vaulted ceiling above them down to the ground was an architectural marvel. Huge stone pillars encased the altar in the centre, which allowed worshipers to sit in a pocket of privacy as the tourists trailed around the outer edges of the masterpiece. She could see that Cayetano had rosary beads between his fingers. He had unrolled his sleeves but hadn't done up the buttons, and the sleeves hung on his taut arms. He hadn't done up the three buttons of his shirt either, and just a faintest hint of chest hair peeked out. *Bloody hell, Luna. You are lusting after a man while he prays.* That had to be a new low. *Look at him, with his curl on his forehead, his eyes closed in concentration while he mouthed something to himself.* It certainly wasn't something she imagined from him.

Luna took a deep breath and tried to purge the image from her mind. Lusting in church. Cayetano Beltrán had no idea what he did to her. *"Señora* Montgomery?"

Luna spun round the see the middle-aged priest there. *"¿Sí?"*

"I'm Father Murillo. Are you here to look at historic baptism records? Would you like to come through to my office to take a look at what I found for you and Cayetano?"

"I... my friend isn't quite ready."

The priest looked over Luna's shoulder, to see Cayetano, and then looked back to Luna with a smile. "You are the woman with him. Now I can see what he was talking about."

"I'm sorry?"

"Nothing," he dismissed her, but his smile remained. "I just spoke with him a moment ago, that's all. Ah, here he is."

Luna turned to see Cayetano come towards the group again, while he pushed his rosary beads in his jeans pocket. "Ready?" he asked to Luna and Father Murillo.

The group headed through into the priest's private office, where a large book sat open. Surely now they had something.

"I'm sorry," Father Murillo said and sat down behind his desk. "I had a look right through 1914 and 1915, and no babies named Cayetano Ortega were baptised here."

"Are you sure?" Cayetano asked, and looked at Luna and the boys.

"There were a few Cayetano's baptised, but none fit what you called and asked me to look for."

Luna sighed. "Maybe he was baptised at another church..."

"Not many churches have records. They were destroyed during the war. Could I suggest hospital records for births?"

"No, already tried that. Nothing."

"Makes sense, many babies weren't born in the hospital during the time period. People lived in a very different world back then."

"So what do you have here?" Cayetano asked.

"You asked me to look up the baptism of Luna Beltrán Caño? I have found her."

"Wow," Cayetano said and looked at Luna. "I just wondered about my family… I hope you don't mind."

"Of course not. I think it's amazing that our families lived here together."

The priest ran his finger down the page to find Luna's name. "Luna Beltrán Caño, born January 3, 1919, and baptised here on January 29, 1919."

Cayetano lifted himself from his seat and rounded the desk to look at the entry. Sure enough, Juan Pablo Beltrán Moreno and Isabel Caño Saenz baptised their baby in this very church. The priest also showed him the baptism of her brother, Alejandro, five years earlier. "It's amazing," Cayetano said. "A piece of my history sits right here. People I know nothing about, yet are part of me, were once here."

"I'm sorry I can't help you with Cayetano Ortega," the priest said, and looked up at Luna. She had an encouraging smile for Cayetano, but she looked disappointed. "As you know, the first 40 years of the last century were tough times here for the cathedral. Much damage… and then the… war… so only a handful of records made by the priests of the time remain. Most were destroyed."

"It's all right," Luna sighed. "I just thought that he might be here. At least I know he lived in the town."

Once Cayetano had copied all the information on his family, they all trailed back out into the warm sunshine on the steps to the cathedral. "I wish you all the best with your search, Luna," Father Murillo said. He looked at Cayetano who stood with to Giacomo and Enzo, who were having a turn each with his cane. "Cayetano tells me that you have been through much pain in the last few years."

"Did he?"

"While you were taking your children through the halls, Cayetano spoke to me about his accident. He is lucky to be healing well."

"I agree."

"I reminded him that all things happen for a reason. Even though he prays before every performance in the ring, he did fall to the bull. God did allow this to happen, but he knows that his angel got sent to watch over him. And don't worry, any concerns you have about late husband, or Cayetano's wife should be able to be smoothed out if you want to marry in the church again."

Luna raised her eyebrows. Okay, that came from nowhere. "Ah…

gracias, for everything."

The priest went back inside and left Luna with Cayetano and the weary-looking children. "So," Cayetano said full of enthusiasm, "what does the rest of our day hold?"

"I might take the kids back to the *parador*. They're tired."

"Oh," Cayetano replied, and looked at the little redheaded darlings next to him. She was right. "Maybe we could have dinner at the *parador?* They have the best Manchego cheese here, and I hear they make a dish with it and that purple garlic from Las Pedroñeras, and they mix it with loads of saffron, and…"

"I would like a break. Let's just walk back to the *parador,* please."

"Is everything all right?"

"Did you talk to the priest about my marriage?"

"Only in passing. He asked about you and me."

"How was our relationship status a factor? Whether I can remarry in the Catholic church? I only met you a month ago. What did you ask, 'the first husband is dead, so what are my chances?'"

"No!" Cayetano cried. They were walking through a tunnel, an archway cut through the stone of a building that led them down to the path back to the bridge across the gorge. His deep voice echoed when he tried to defend himself.

"Father Murillo caught me off guard with that. He spoke as if I needed assurance that I could marry again. I don't want to get married ever again! I have had my love. After your true love, others are just people to pass the time with."

"Thank you very much! So, what, you are just passing time with me? You won't get married again?"

"No."

They stopped on the edge to the bridge, and Luna placed a hand on each of the boys' shoulders when they leaned over to take a look into the gorge. One of the great icons of Cuenca, the *Casas Colgadas,* the hanging houses, sat perched out over the edge of the cliff just behind them. Cayetano knew there would be no more sightseeing today. "You know what? I have had a really crappy year," he said. "All my life things have gone my way, and then just after the new year I found that my wife cheated on me. All I had tried to build with her was gone. Then, my parents, who I love, and my sister, who is my best friend, had a huge fight. I've been stuck into the middle for months, and it's miserable. Then, I get gored at a premiere event, which hurt my entire reputation! But I have always been told that things happen for a reason."

"So, you are deeply religious all of a sudden?"

"No, I'm not. I pray to La Macarena, the patron saint of *toreros* before a fight. It's a tradition. Beyond that, I'm not a strict Catholic, or I would burn in hell. But after so much trouble, I thought 'what-if?' What if fate threw you into my path right when I needed you?"

"We just met!"

"I know, and Father Murillo just jumped to conclusions."

"Or you gave him the wrong idea."

"So, what are we doing there then?" Cayetano asked. "You know I'm interested in you. If you aren't interested in me, are you using me to get what you need?"

"That is a really shitty thing to say," she fired back.

"I suddenly have a really shitty feeling about all of this!"

"I don't believe God has a grand plan, Cayetano. People cheat, they get hurt, and they get killed. There is no reason why. You just have to accept that sometimes life doesn't go well. God can go to hell as far as I'm concerned. If you think that I would use you for a few fucking pieces of paper from the *Registro Civil,* maybe I should just go home to Valencia and accept Darren's proposal."

"What? Are you marrying Darren? You just said you wouldn't marry again."

"Who is getting married?" Enzo asked.

"No one, sweetheart. Let's go back to the hotel, shall we? Say goodbye to Cayetano."

"Goodbye, Cayetano," they both said. "I hope you get better soon. I hope that the angel leaves you alone," Giacomo added.

"That's exactly what she is doing," he said. *"Hasta luego, chicos."*

Cayetano stood on the spot and watched Luna take the boys over the bridge towards the *parador*. She was right; he had asked the priest about marrying again. Clearly that was a fatal mistake.

13

Cuenca, España ~ marzo de 1939

It started to rain as Cayetano, Luna and Scarlett scrambled up the sets of stairs of the Barrio San Martín in the dark. Luna could see why Scarlett wore those heavy boots; Scarlett was able to move much quicker than her. Her mind was in a panic – to be caught in bed with a man was humiliating, but her sister-in-law and her precious child were in peril. Scarlett had Sofía's blood splattered on her; it was a sign. A fatal mistake must have been made.

Scarlett was stone-cold silent. She knew her way through the narrow streets in the dark, and was afraid of nothing when she moved in the night. Other women were tucked away in the safety of their homes when Scarlett was out on her own. She walked a few steps ahead of Cayetano and Luna, and couldn't bring herself to look at either of them. She wasn't surprised; he never shut up about Luna Beltrán. So when, on a lonely night while out on the road just prior to Christmas, when he came to her tent to spend the night, Scarlett had been very surprised. She wasn't going to deny him; no one could deny Cayetano Ortega anything. The man left a trail of broken hearts that could light up the entire road from Madrid to Valencia and back again. He was everything her broken heart longed for – affection and company. Her own husband was killed in the Battle of the Ebro only six months ago. Scarlett had gone to work in a new field hospital, set up in a natural cave at La Bisbal de Falset, under the instruction of a top doctor from Nueva Zelanda. Ulrich was positioned at the front not far away, and she had worried for him. When all in the International Brigade were called to leave España in the October of 1938, Scarlett thought it was her chance to leave with her husband while they still could. But it was too late for Ulrich, who was killed at Ebro before the Brigade retreated. Scarlett buried his body by herself by the Ebro river outside the town of Mequinenza. Only a few people knew she had even married Ulrich, a German man who had come to España in search of adventure. So when Cayetano, who knew about what happened to Ulrich, wanted to be with her that cold night near the town of Requena, her loneliness gave in to what he wanted. Now that night was going to haunt her forever. She wouldn't be able to hide the evidence much longer.

"What can we do to help Sofía?" Cayetano asked Scarlett while he climbed the stairs behind her.

"We need witnesses."

"This is all women's business."

Scarlett glanced over her shoulder at him and Luna. "You have no idea what goes on, do you, Caya?"

"Where is Alejandro?" Luna asked.

"I left him at the back entrance to the hospital with a packet of cigarettes."

"Shouldn't he be with Sofía?"

Scarlett stopped and turned around. In the faint light that came from the window of the building that they stood against, they could see that Scarlett's flaming-red hair had started to go frizzy in the rain. "Okay, I don't know what España you have been living in, princesa, but let me fill you in with some facts. When a young woman comes in to give birth, if she is deemed 'unsuitable' by the nuns who work there, they will take the baby and tell the mother that her child died. The priest then sells the baby to a family that's deemed 'suitable'."

"Should have shot the rest of the nuns," Cayetano muttered.

Luna looked at Cayetano and then back to Scarlett. "Who decides who is suitable? That baby belongs to Sofía!"

"I know, and that is why I am trying to help," Scarlett said. She turned and started up the wet path again, and her companions followed. "Sofía is my best friend, and that is the only reason I was even allowed in to see her while she is giving birth. Alejandro is banned from being in the hospital completely."

"Did you know about this?" Luna asked Cayetano.

"I have heard about this going on in different places, but I don't know of anyone who has had it happen to them," he said.

"That you know of," Scarlett said.

"Why would they say Sofía is unsuitable to be a mother?" Luna asked.

"They know her, she works there."

"Exactly, they know her. They know she was pregnant to Alejandro *before they married. She's only 20, young and stupid."*

"She married Alejandro!"

"Yes, she married Alejandro. *A man with a reputation and an anarchist soldier, and the son of Juan Pablo Beltrán, a well-known* Republicano *activist. The baby could be given to a family that supports Franco. Probably sent off to Zaragoza and then sold on."*

"They wouldn't do this," Luna pleaded. "The priest..."

"The priest who has been lucky not to have been shot?" Scarlett bit back. "Oh yes, he's into this. The Republicans denounced Catholicism. Franco sides with them and the church will get all their power back – and soon. We are about to be on the losing side of the war. Our army is dead after what happened in Ebro, and we can't fight. The church will do anything it has to in order to appease the man who will be our dictator soon. Franco would love 'undesirable' babies to be sold off and given 'better' lives with his own sympathisers, in 'good' Catholic families."

"How long has this been going on?"

"I don't know, but I bet once the war ends, this will keep happening."

"And you are sure this is what is going to happen with Sofía?" Cayetano asked.

"I don't know. It could be fine, but the question is, am I willing to sit back and hope for the best? I have to help. They let me in because I used to work there. Soon after the labour began, she started bleeding. There is so much blood."

"Will they do a caesarean?" Luna asked. "That would terrify Sofía."

"I fear they might," Scarlett said as the group rounded the final corner. The hospital was now in sight. "Something is wrong. I think the placenta has burst. Sofía and the baby are in real danger. If they want to take that baby, they will easily sacrifice her in order to get it."

"So why is Alejandro out the back of the hospital?" Cayetano asked. "His wife could be dying!"

"In case they take the baby and slip out the back. They have many times before." They were outside the front of the hospital now, a stark stone building that was in darkness. "Cayetano, you should go around the back and wait there with Alejandro. Tell him that we're with Sofía and we will take care of her and the baby."

Cayetano nodded. "But will she be all right?"

"I hope so. I will do all I can for them."

"We can trust you, Scarlett." He placed one hand on her shoulder. "You're extraordinario."

Scarlett just scoffed. "Go. I will take Luna in to see Sofía."

Luna watched Cayetano disappear down a dark alley, and turned back to Scarlett. "Are you sure they will let us in?"

"They aren't letting us in," Scarlett said, and beckoned her to follow her up the front stairs. "We are sneaking in."

"But we can't!"

"Do you want your brother to be a widower by morning?"

"Of course not!"

"Then we are sneaking in," Scarlett whispered as the women went in the front entrance. She had jammed the lock when she had left earlier to ensure they could get in later. Normally the hospital got locked at night. "Unless this is all too dangerous for a princesa like you."

"Stop calling me princesa."

"With the Medina ring on your hand, you practically are a princess." Scarlett glanced at Luna. "He didn't tell you where the ring came from, did he?"

Luna glanced at the ring on her finger. "Where did it come from?"

"That is a long story, best left for Cayetano to tell you. The payment from Sergio Medina tells a lot about Cayetano's status in life."

"What you do mean? Cayetano is no one. He is like us."

"Cayetano isn't like us, Luna, trust me. We are all very different people. You are the privileged daughter of a once-wealthy businessman, and your brother is the stereotypical rebel to his father's empire. Sofia is a whore who thinks she fools everyone by playing the sweet young wife..."

"And you are the foreigner with eyes as cold as her heart."

"Do have any idea what I would give in order to be who I was when I came to España? To think I could help, or make a difference in this war? I crossed the entire world on a ship to come and try to save your country. I would love to change all that has happened and to have never seen what I have. Do you know what it's like to see men blown apart by air-raids? To see bodies that have had their eyes gouged out by Falange members, for no reason? To see bodies of pregnant women with smashed skulls and the unborn babies sliced from the womb? To see young girls gang raped? To see the man you love gunned down?"

Luna had no answer to that. "I'm sorry, Scarlett. I suppose that's why Cayetano said that you're leaving España."

"I have my reasons. I'm not surprised that Cayetano didn't tell you the details. I take it that he asked you to marry him?"

"He did, yes."

"Well, I won't ruin that for you," she said coldly. "I hope he didn't suggest you had to sleep with him because he asked..."

"No! It was my idea."

"Yours?"

"Yes, mine. Who knows what the future holds. I'm no fool, Scarlett. I took my chance while I had it."

"I assume that was the first time for you."

"So?"

"Are you all right? Cayetano... sometimes he can be rough with women. If you need anything, you don't have to see a doctor. I can help you."

"I'm fine." Rough? Need a doctor? He wasn't cold and cruel like those fascist soldiers who had raped their way through towns. She wondered briefly if Scarlett had escaped that fate. Women were the spoils of victory, and the rapists had claimed most of the nation. "How do you know what kind of lover he is?"

"You aren't his first, Luna."

"I know that."

"We are on the road together a lot, and we stop in towns. He meets women a lot. Sometimes, he has them in his tent when we're camped, and I hear what happens. Other times it's a quick one out the back of a bar with some girl who works there and her father isn't watching. It's not information that I wish to possess."

Luna glanced at the ring again. She was a woman who thought it best not to pry into what a man did in his own time. Never mind, he loved her. "We aren't innocents."

"You certainly aren't, Señorita Beltrán. I never thought you would be one of those women. You could pray for forgiveness to your priest, if he isn't busy stealing your brother's child." The conversation halted when they heard the sound of voices. Sofía was screaming. "She's alive. We are going to storm in and assess the situation. If it's under control and we think we can trust them, we will step out, unless Sofía wants us to stay. If it looks bad, you will be with Sofía, and I will see to the baby. Are we clear?"

Luna nodded. "How many people are in there? This is a hospital room, not a war zone."

"You may re-think that when we go inside. Right... go!" Scarlett pushed the door and open, and the women ran into the small room. Scarlett was right; it was a war zone. Sofía was on her back on the bed in the centre of the room, covered in her own blood. The bed was soaked. It was all over the floor. The sound of Sofía's screaming overwhelmed her senses.

"Scarlett!" the nurse exclaimed. "What are you doing back here?"

"I went to fetch Sofía's sister-in-law... to comfort her," Scarlett said, and they both approached the bedside. Sofía was extreme weak and pale. Luna rushed to her and took her hand, which was bloody. "That is not a problem, is it?" Scarlett asked the nurse.

The woman looked at the nun assisting her, Sister Rosa. Scarlett had run into her many times when she worked at the hospital. She was a sour-faced old woman. "Nurse Blanca has Sofia in good care," the old nun muttered.

"She has no such thing," Scarlett replied. She had delivered babies before. She knew the difference between a birth and a disaster. "Her placenta has burst, hasn't it?"

"We think so, and the baby is breech."

Scarlett stepped forward to see nothing more than a foot poking from its mother's bloodied body. "We must get this baby out! It will stop breathing!"

"We have called for the doctor. He will be here in the morning."

"The morning?" Luna cried. "It's not even close to midnight!"

"The doctors aren't here tonight."

Scarlett stood for a moment in the blood, to assess the situation. Sofia moaned, a deep, primal groan that only came from a woman when she gave birth. She had lost a lot of blood. There was no way that the baby would slip out. "We need to take care of this ourselves. We need to get the forceps, and she needs blood. Lots of it."

"We can't do that!" Nurse Blanca interrupted. "Certainly not. Let nature take its course."

Scarlett watched the two women share a look. They had no interest whatsoever in helping Sofia. A young mother, another faceless girl in a sea of women who were not going to get the care they deserved. It only took her a second to reach under her shirt and into the back of her trousers where she kept her gun.

Luna glanced up from Sofia when she saw Scarlett make a sharp movement, and her eyes bulged in panic. "Scarlett!" she cried. "What are you doing?"

"Fixing the problem," she replied without moving an inch. Her body stood rigid when she pointed the gun squarely at the two women in front of her. She wasn't going to miss if she fired a shot. "I know what you are doing, Sister Rosa," she said to the nun, who stood firm in the face of the weapon. "You can't have this baby."

"We want to deliver the child safely," Nurse Blanca said.

"And give it to who?"

"You can't stop this, Scarlett," Sister Rosa said. "This girl is going to pay for what she has done. A whore like Sofia doesn't get treated like a virtuous woman. The same way you won't when your time comes."

The only muscle that moved in Scarlett was her index finger when she fired the first shot. Sister Rosa dropped like a stone, and the single shot to her chest barely had time to bleed before her body hit the ground. Nurse

Blanca also didn't have a chance to move before Scarlett put a bullet in her. She fell to the cold floor with blood splattered on her white nurse's uniform. A shot to the stomach wouldn't bring instant death, but it would do the job.

Scarlett stepped over the nurse who was beginning to choke on her own blood, and stood at the end of the bed with Sofía again. This baby couldn't possibly still be alive. Gloves, she needed gloves.

"What the hell have you done?" Luna cried. She clutched at Sofía's hand so tight, but by now Sofía was barely responsive.

"I did what I had to do. I know there aren't any blood supplies in the hospital," Scarlett said while she fumbled through the equipment drawer by the bed. No gloves anywhere. "We can do this on our own."

"I can't!" Luna stuttered. There were two bodies on the floor, neither of them dead just yet, and Sofía looked pale and lifeless. "Sofía isn't moving!"

Scarlett stepped forward to Sofía's side with a face full of concern. "Sofía," she said loudly. "Sofía, can you hear me?"

Sofía opened her dark brown eyes, but there was barely any life in them. She opened her mouth to speak, but nothing more than a whisper came out.

"What's going on?" Luna asked. Her eyes couldn't help but go between Sofía and the two women on the floor. "She was screaming just a moment ago."

"She has gone into shock. I don't know what we can do."

"What? But you said..."

"I know what I said. We need to get her out of the room."

"How?"

"I don't know that either, but it will make life easier if we're not found with the nurse and the torturous witch."

"You shot a nun!"

"Yeah, well, we do what we have to do. Besides, she was going to kill Sofía and steal the baby. She was letting her bleed out."

"So what do we do?"

"A caesarean needs to be performed, but from the swelling, I would say she is bleeding internally. I think the pressure put on her when they were pushing on her stomach has burst her placenta. It must have become unattached prematurely. Even if I knew how to perform a hysterectomy..."

"Can't there be a doctor somewhere?"

"There are none, that bit I believe. There are so many casualties at the moment, and this would be considered non-essential and a waste of supplies. We are on our own. If there were doctors here, they would have responded to the gunshots by now anyway."

"Quiero ir a casa," Sofía whispered.

"No, Sofía, we can't go home," Luna tried to reassure her.

"Por favor, mi bebé..."

Luna's panic-stricken eyes looked up at Scarlett, who had gone to check the baby. "We are in a hospital, we should be able to do something!"

"They don't care, Luna, you don't seem to understand that. If Sofía wants to die at home..."

"She wants to live at home!"

"Luna," Sofía whispered, and the two women stared at the poor woman. She was flat on her back and with her knees bent and her feet strapped to the bed. Her luscious black hair was wet, and it clung to her skin. "El bebé ..."

"I will care for your baby, I promise," Luna said. She looked up at Scarlett. "Scarlett, please help her."

"I could try and pull the baby out. The odds of it surviving are very slim anyway. I just worry that if the placenta has burst it will only increase the blood loss."

"But if she is still bleeding then isn't the blood just building up behind the baby anyway?"

Scarlett's eyes widened when she nodded in agreement. She looked down and kicked Nurse Blanca's arm out of the way. She still made a slight gurgling sound while she drowned on her blood. At least the nun was dead. "We have to get her out of here, or they will catch us. Okay, I'm going to push the baby back in and then hope I can find both feet, and pull."

"Won't it hurt Sofía?" That was when Luna realised that Sofía wasn't holding her hand anymore. "Sofía?" She shook her limp hand, but her dear sister-in-law didn't move. "Scarlett!"

Scarlett stepped forward and put her hand to Sofía's throat. She looked up at Luna and hoped she would feel something. Anything. Scarlett had checked enough pulses in her time, and made the call about whether someone would live or die enough times. But this was Sofía Perez, her best friend, the only person who had befriended her when she first moved to Cuenca. Scarlett may have become a dark soul, but she would always love Sofía. There was nothing. Not even the faintest pulse. She could see the tears coming to Luna's eyes and Scarlett desperately tried to fight back her own, but it was no use. "We have to save the baby," she managed to say, and Luna nodded as she started to cry.

14

Cuenca, España ~ septiembre de 2009

Cayetano straightened his shirt and waited at the door to Luna's hotel room. He hoped that she hadn't driven back to Valencia. The tiniest strip of light shone from under the door, which raised his hopes. The door opened very slowly, she must have seen him through the peephole. A very cautious face appeared.

He held up the red rose he had in his hands. "A truce?" he offered.

Luna swung the door open, and folded her arms over her chest. She was in nothing more than a full-length pale blue silk dressing gown, which was done up very tight at the waist. Her black hair was piled high in a messy bun, and her ice-blue eyes looked brighter than ever. "Did you steal that from the garden in the courtyard?"

"*Sí*, I did. But I asked if I could first." He watched a smile creep over her face and he held it out, and she took it from him. It was as if no one had ever given her flowers. Maybe they hadn't, but it would be hard to believe.

"I'm sorry that I freaked out at you earlier," Luna said.

"I pulled the tiger's tail. You did warn me that I would get bitten."

"Still, it doesn't give me the right to tell you how to deal with the things that you have going on in your life."

"The truth is… I don't know how to talk to you. You have been through something I can't understand. If I get it wrong, then I'm sorry. It's only because I'm lost. Even the simplest things seem new again with you."

"Come in," she said, and opened the door for him. "But you need to be quiet; the boys are asleep."

"Already?" Cayetano asked as Luna closed the door behind him. "It's only nine."

"Long day when you're little." He watched her cross the room, her little feet slid over the dark tiles to the bedroom door which was ajar. She peeked in, and then closed it gently. "They liked you," she said, and the pair sat down on the couch together. "They asked if they get to see the bullfighting man again."

"And do they?"

"I don't know."

"Why?"

"Do you know the expression 'no smoke without fire?' You hit a nerve today. In fact, you do it every time I see you. I never anticipated ever being interested in anyone after my husband was killed. Then you blow in and change everything for me, but that isn't your fault, it happens because I like you. I don't know what to do about it."

"Then do nothing. I'm not asking anything of you."

"It's not that simple, Cayetano. It's opened up so many things."

"Like?"

"I was raised by my father after my mother died. My father was wonderful, but I wanted more for my kids than I had. Two parents, a family, like everyone else takes for granted. Their father was killed, and it made me so angry that this could happen to them. I don't want to be a mother who brings men in and out of her kids' lives. That isn't who I am. I need to be careful with everything I do. My life and decisions don't belong to me. I'm bound by the boys and their needs, and I don't resent that at all. To choose what is good for them is the natural choice for me."

"That leaves us stranded, doesn't it? Because Darren is the safe choice for them."

"I could be happy with Darren, if I try hard enough."

"Love can't be forced, Luna. The harder you try, the further it slips away."

"I have no room for fanciful romance. I can't be flighty and wait for love to come along. I can't be pulled by it. I have two kids that require me to make considered choices."

"How would you feel if they looked back in 20 years and realised that their mother was unhappy for their benefit?"

"I hope they would be grateful. I would also hope that they didn't understand it. I don't want anyone to understand how I feel. I live in an awful place filled with guilt and confusion."

"I can't help you," Cayetano said. "But I do know that being stuck with someone you don't love can destroy you."

"When I met Fabrizio, I loved him so much, from the moment I laid eyes on him. It's so ridiculous but so true. It was mad and passionate. We would have sex until the mattress slipped off the bed." She paused for a moment. "Oh God, I said that out loud."

Cayetano chuckled. "I don't mind."

Luna couldn't wipe the smile from her face. "I thought that he was the only one who could do that to me, love me like that I mean. Madly, passionately and completely. Darren, I love him, and he is important to me, but that feeling doesn't exist with him. But life isn't about passion. It wears off."

"Did it wear off in your marriage?"

"Yeah, it did after a while, as it does. The pressures of work and kids... but then I met you, and that feeling was back. That crazy, lustful feeling of having a connection with someone. I loved it and also hated it, because it meant the connection to Fabrizio wasn't as special and unique as I thought."

"Love is a cruel thing, Luna. Trust me, I know. You can't change the past. What you had once isn't lessened by what you do now. You can't go through life without love."

"I don't want just some excitement and lust, a relationship is so much more than that. Besides, excitement wears off."

"Not always. My parents have been together for 40 years, and they're like lustful teenagers even now. It's hard to watch to be honest."

"That's great, but it's the exception, not the rule. So if I start a relationship with Darren without that passion, then I already know what I am headed for. No disappointments."

"You could start a life with me and have that passion, and it could last forever."

Luna looked up at Cayetano across from her. "Don't ask anything of me. I have nothing to offer."

"I want a shot with you."

"Why? I'm an unemployed mother-of-two with multiple issues."

Cayetano couldn't help it, he had to laugh, and she did the same. At least it broke the ice. "I like you. You are enchanting, and interesting, and deep, and thoughtful. You are beautiful and hot-blooded as hell. I'm not some young idiot who wants to waste his time on himself. Plus I like kids. I've wanted them for years."

"I have always been under the impression that no guy wants to play Papá to another man's kids."

"Families are not always the best just because they are traditional. Life is no fairytale."

"No, it certainly isn't." She looked out the full-length windows that faced back toward the old town. In the dark, the houses along the edges of the cliff illuminated the gorge. "This place is a fairytale."

"Once upon a time, our families lived here. Who knows what went on? We still have to find out where your grandfather came from."

"It would have been a hard life here 70 years ago, with or without the war. I bet they faced deaths of loved ones, and other complications to everyday life, on a scale more serious than you or I."

"Doesn't make our troubles any smaller," Cayetano said and slid forward in his seat. His leg was killing him, and couldn't deny it anymore. All afternoon on those fucking steps had finally hit him. He shut his eyes for a moment and ran his hand over his muscles, and the fabric of his jeans rubbed the tense limb. Bloody accident. He opened his eyes, and Luna had gone, and he looked around. "Luna?"

She came back out of the other bedroom door and was held a small white bottle. His leg was forgotten. When she walked without holding her dressing gown, he could see every inch of her beautiful long legs, they just kept going up and up…

"Capsicum cream, remember?" she said. "I'll rub it on your leg."

"Is that wise?" he asked. Her hands on him right after she had basically told him to back off?

"I'm not doing it to be wise, I'm doing it to be helpful. You could have rested it all day at home today, but instead you helped me out. Take your pants off."

Cayetano stood up and undid his jeans. The moment the pants fell to the floor her eyes lit up. She hadn't seen the wound before. "Wow," she said and knelt down in front of him.

"They all say that," he teased.

"Sit down on the edge of the couch, smart-ass." She waited for him to get comfortable, and then ran her fingers very carefully over the scar on his skin. It had done its best to heal, still purple and dotted by the marks that the stitches had left behind on the flesh. "Is it just the wound that hurts or is it the whole thigh?"

"The whole damn thing," he said, and watched her rub the cream on to her hands. "If it warms my leg to numb it, won't it numb your hands?"

"I will wash them in a few minutes, so no problem."

He groaned the moment she moved her warm hands on his leg. Her smooth hands ran from his knee, over the scar and right up his thigh, and it was the most relieving thing he could have ever imagined. His skin started to warm from the contact, and he almost felt dizzy. No physiotherapist appointment felt that good.

"You are good at this," he said breathlessly. He settled into the joy that she gave him in an instant.

"I have just had a lot of practice. Let me know if I touch you too hard and it hurts," she said without a glance up at him. She continued to knead his leg for him, and could feel the tightness in the muscle.

Cayetano could have sat with her all night. He watched her run her hands back and forward. He felt like a teenage boy the moment she reached the top of his leg. It excited him so much he could barely feel the leg at all. He couldn't hide how much he liked her touch. From her spot between his legs, she could see his enthusiasm. When she leaned forward, her gown would billow open a little, and he could see her breasts sway gently underneath. She had tried to hide the fact she wore nothing under there before, but had now become distracted. María always had herself on show, and even posed nude in a magazine once. Viewers cared less for her news stories and more for the assets she bestowed, all courtesy of her doctor. What Luna had under there was totally different, voluptuous but natural. God, he wanted his hands on her again.

"You okay up there?" she said and glanced up.

"*Sí*, why?"

"You're moaning a lot."

Was he? He hadn't even noticed. "It's the best I have felt since the accident. I can feel it numbed already."

"Good," she said and took her hands off him. "The cream will do the rest for you now that it has soaked in. You will be able to sleep easy now."

"What if I don't want to sleep?"

"Then don't," she smiled. "I need to wash my hands. I like to have full feeling in them."

"You wouldn't want to rub the wrong thing and have 'it' lose feeling." He couldn't help himself.

"No, I wouldn't. Some things are very sensitive and need to be handled just right." The green flecks in his eyes were back, and she couldn't resist. She sat up on her knees and thrust her lips onto his. It went against everything she had just said to him, but she couldn't contain herself. She felt his hands come to her back to hold her against him, firm like the slow kiss her gave her. She wound her arms around him as the urgency in his kiss intensified. She was careful to keep her hands off him; her hands were still covered in the cream.

"I have to wash my hands," she said, still pressed against him. "I shouldn't be kissing you. You're the guilty pleasure I need stay away from."

"The problem with guilty pleasures is that if you suppress your urges, they only fight harder to make you indulge."

"So to be wicked is my only option?" she asked, her lips against his.

"Only after washing your hands."

Luna pulled herself away from him; her hands had started to tingle. She hurried through her bedroom to the bathroom and ran them under hot water. She looked up at herself in the mirror. She was flushed. Bright pink cheeks. There was no shame in feeling this way. She hadn't done anything wrong. Feelings didn't need time to be decided on, either they existed, or they didn't. She had finally been thrown in the path of attraction again.

Luna came out of the bathroom, to find Cayetano in the doorway to her bedroom. There was that stance again; shoulders back, chest out, every inch the man. "How is your leg?"

"I can't even feel it."

"Good. Then close the door behind you," she said and crossed the room.

Cayetano wanted to slam it and grab her, but he shut it as quietly as his patience would let him. His hands went to the tie of blue silk around her waist, and pulled it as they kissed. His hands ran over her shoulders and pushed the gown from her so his hands could roam over her bare body. She let his mouth go and pulled his shirt over his head to let their hot skin touch. Luna managed to wriggle his boxers off him while they fiercely seared their affection on one another. Cayetano certainly hadn't imagined this as the response to his apology when he knocked on the door, but it was clearly the best idea he had ever had in his life. This wasn't like the first night they spent together, neither of them had that kind of patience. This was pure and raw desire.

No sooner than they had fallen onto the bed in a heap, Cayetano pulled her up on him. He had his hands firmly on her hips to guide her body to his. Cayetano couldn't just lie back when she consumed him; just the quiver alone that shot through his body was enough to shock him upright. He could hear his voice cry out, but it sounded like it was somewhere in the foggy distance while she took him to the edge and beyond. He was erotically delighted at the power she held over him, and utterly thrilled at the effect he had over her when she passionately cried out. Every kiss was a desperate, hungry clutch at each other, a search for a way to be as close as possible. Whatever invisible power that drew the two together wasn't finished with them.

It was just light when Cayetano woke the next morning. He opened his eyes to see Luna getting out of the bed next to him. "Hey," he whispered. "Where are you going?"

"I need to start my day." She clutched the sheet to her chest and sat down next to him.

"What time is it?"

"Just after six."

"Why so early? Come back to bed," he said and tugged at her arm.

"I have kids. If I don't get up and shower now, I won't get another chance."

"I will watch them for you." Cayetano pulled her back down into the bed and kissed her. "Or am I the dirty secret that needs to sneak out?"

"Yes, you are. They don't need to know you were here, even if they don't understand what it means."

Cayetano sat up on one elbow and looked at her. "I have snuck out plenty of times before, but never because of the children nearby."

"Well, consider your horizons broadened then."

"Have I broadened yours?"

"You have no idea."

Cayetano's face darkened with a serious expression. "Do you believe in fate?"

"No."

"At all?"

"Nope."

"Why?"

"Fate can't be real. It would mean that I was destined for all the bad things that have happened to me. Fate is believed in by people that have happy endings."

"Our families lived next to each other. Then, 70 years later, we bump into each other in the street and fall in love? You don't think that's fate?" The second he had said it, he realised what he had done. He had just thrown the L word at her.

"Is that fate or coincidence?"

Screw it. "Luna, I have fallen in love with you. Coincidence doesn't do this to a man."

"That's ridiculous."

"It is."

"We barely know each other."

"We can be fast learners."

Luna studied him for a second. "Have you ever used the expression 'need time to decide what we both want' on someone?"

"I used it on María when I kicked her out. It was a polite way of saying 'I have no feelings for you but can't admit it'."

"If you fall in love with someone, you don't need time to figure what to do about it."

"No, you don't."

"I have to tell Darren that I can't marry him. Not when I would rather be here with you."

A greedy grin spread over Cayetano's face. "I thought you were about to tell me that you needed time."

"Time won't change what I think."

"Come away with me, to Madrid."

"I can't. I have a whole life in Valencia."

"Next weekend, come to my country place outside Madrid … you and the kids. We can stay in the city on Friday and then head out. I have a plan. We can relax and continue to search for your grandfather at the same time."

"How?"

"I have a plan, *preciosa*. Trust me."

"Trust you? You are the most wicked man I have ever come across."

"I'll take that as compliment," he whispered, and kissed her. His large hand took the sheet that she still held to her chest and pulled it from her fingers. She let his hands roam on to her body, and forgot that she was supposed to get rid of him.

"Mummy!"

Cayetano and Luna sat bolt upright in bed when they heard the little voice. Only a moment later the door flew open and there stood both Giacomo and Enzo, still in their lime green pajamas. "Mummy, I'm hungry," Enzo said.

"Why is Cayetano in your bed?" Giacomo asked.

Luna and Cayetano shared a panicked look. Even with the covers pulled partly up it was pretty obvious they weren't wearing much. "Um… Cayetano came to visit last night to ask me a question…. and then he was too scared to go back to his own room because he is afraid of the dark. So he had to stay here."

"Hey!" Cayetano objected.

Giacomo and Enzo both giggled at him. "Maybe the angel was hiding out in the hallway?" Giacomo suggested.

"Yes, you're right. You never know when the angel's spell will get you."

"Was it the angel who put your pants out by the couch?"

"Yeah, I don't think they will fit her, but she cast a spell and stole my pants. She is very good at stealing pants."

Luna snorted next to him, desperate to crawl under the covers and laugh. "Why don't you boys get dressed, and we can all go out to breakfast?"

"Can Cayetano come?" Enzo asked.

"Sure," he said. "I just hope that the angel behaves herself."

15

Madrid, España ~ septiembre de 2009

Inés Morales Pena was a remarkable woman. She had the beauty and attitude of a woman much younger than her 55 years. When she and her husband celebrated their 40th wedding anniversary a few months ago, she had dressed up in the same outfit she had worn when she first met him. The simple white dress fitted as well now as it did back then. The world they lived in may have greatly changed in that time, but their love hadn't.

Paco Beltrán and Inés Morales were one of those love stories you read about in poems. The lonely bullfighter who was loved all over Spain, and the young daughter of the fight promoter who happened to meet him quite by accident while out with her father. Within weeks they were in love and only two months later she was pregnant. Any other deeply Catholic family would have been shamed, but the Morales family decided to see it as an opportunity. Their daughter was married off to Paco *'El Potente'* Beltrán Caño, a man with a sketchy religious and political background, but someone loved by the simple man on the street all the way up to dictator Generalissimo Francisco Franco himself. The Morales family were already wealthy and prominent in Madrid, with a reputation for arranging the greatest bullfights and breeding the best bulls in the business. Because Franco had supported and promoted bullfighting as something quintessentially Spanish, the rings were fuller than ever, and he even went to watch *'El Potente'* Beltrán perform. To be aligned with this *torero,* who fought in front of the leader of the country, was good business for the Morales family.

Inés was no fool – she could see what her family were doing when they married her off to Paco. She was head-over-heels in love, so it didn't matter. She was fully willing to be the woman who started the Beltrán Morales dynasty. Her son was born six months after her marriage, and her new husband begged her to call the child Cayetano, after his uncle, the brother of his dear mother, Luna. Five years later when their daughter was born, he had begged her to name the baby Sofía after his aunt, another relative he had never met, but his mother had spoken about so affectionately. Paco had no family now, and rarely spoke of them. Naming her children after members of the Beltrán family was the least Inés could do for her beloved. She had her whole family, and he had nothing but memories. Memories that he hadn't shared in 40 years of marriage.

The door to the Beltrán home was always open. They lived in the luxurious and affluent suburb of La Moraleja, north east from the centre of Madrid. The perfect location for an ex-*torero* like Paco. These days only Inés and Paco lived there with her parents, José and Consuela. Inés' three brothers all lived nearby with their own children and grandchildren. It pained Inés that she had no grandchildren of her own, but with her daughter unable to have children and her son's marriage in tatters, it wasn't going to be. All the relatives that would drop by the Beltrán home would ring the doorbell, so when she heard the front door open without warning, she knew it would only be one person.

"*Mamá, su bebé, Caya, está en casa.*"

Inés smiled and looked up from her book. *Your baby, Caya, is home.* Cayetano used to say it when he got home from school, and now he was still doing it to tease her. "I'm in the *conservatorio,*" she called out.

Cayetano appeared in the doorway a moment later, with a wide smile on his face. "*Hola,* Mamá. Is Papá home?"

"No, your father has gone out with your uncles and grandfather. Much work to be discussed, he said."

Cayetano leaned over and kissed his mother's cheek and sat down in the armchair across from her. The sun was warm through the glass of the conservatory. It was always nice to be home. "Papá needs to remember that he's retired."

"They all need to remember that," Inés said. "But you know your Papá, and your uncles. They love what they do, and they took over the business from my father. They care very much."

"I know, Mamá, I know. But I can take over… if Papá ever trusts me."

"I thought all you ever wanted to do was fight in the ring?"

"A day comes when a man wants more."

Inés raised her eyebrows so high they disappeared under her golden brown hair that fell gently across her forehead. Her son had never been interested in the legacy that her father had wanted for baby Cayetano. "How is your leg, Caya?"

"My leg is good. I have a special cream to rub on it which helps." *The woman that rubs the cream has the magic touch.*

"Then don't you worry about all those retirement rumours, or what your father needs from you."

Cayetano absentmindedly began to wring his hands. "Mamá, did Papá tell you about an argument that we had in the park?"

"He told me that you had decided that you were in love with a married woman."

Cayetano rolled his eyes. *"Gracias,* Papá. Thanks for the vote of confidence."

"I told him that there must be more to it than that, but he wouldn't tell me what went on. Only that he was disappointed. He said that she was the cause of your accident."

"Now that is an outright lie!"

"You have never talked to your father about women, so I didn't believe him. Whatever you said, you upset him. You hurt his pride."

"More than when I got injured and shamed the family name?"

"Don't be sarcastic to me, Cayetano."

Cayetano sighed and took a moment. "I told him that I had spoken with that woman I helped with the bag-snatcher. She wanted to find her grandfather who was killed in the civil war. So I asked about our family."

"Ah…" Inés said and took off her reading glasses. She folded them and placed them on her lap. "Now I understand the argument."

"All I asked him was a little about his parents. Then he told me that his mother's name was Luna. It's taken me 40 years to know that. He told me that she was married to a guy named Ignacio Reyes Paz, but he died when Papá was young. So why does Papá not have his father's name? He has the full name of his mother."

"That is a long story, Cayetano. One you shouldn't pry into."

"And then he told me that his mother's family all loved bullfighting. All this time I didn't know that either. It's like Papá is keeping this huge secret."

"He isn't."

"Then why does it feel like it? Family is everything to us, yet a whole side of the family is hidden away like a dirty secret. So… I went to Cuenca on the weekend, with Luna."

"The bag-snatcher girl?"

"Yes, though I would like another name for her."

"Luna is the girl you are in love with?"

"Yes, but she's not a girl. She is very much a woman. Papá told me that he fell in love with you in a heartbeat, just like his mother fell in love with her great love. I fell in love with Luna like that. After one day and night with her, I was in love. Papá told me that's mad."

"It is mad. Love tends to be."

"So you don't think I'm being ridiculous?"

"When did all this happen?"

"The day before my fall in the ring, but it wasn't Luna's fault. She didn't even know who I was. I lied to her."

"She can't have been happy about that."

"She wasn't, but I've been forgiven."

"So how did Cuenca come into it?"

"Luna is a New Zealander. Her grandmother, Scarlett, was a nurse in Cuenca during the war, and got pregnant to some guy named Cayetano. He abandoned her and she returned home."

"And kept the baby?"

"She kept the boy, Alexander, and raised him on her own."

"Tough in that day and age."

"Very. Luna wants to live here and needs to prove her grandfather was Spanish, but Cayetano Ortega dropped off the earth. We went to find his birth record. But there is nothing, no registration, no baptism, just an address of him living with Scarlett in Cuenca. Since I was there, I looked up the Beltrán family. They lived right across the narrow street from Cayetano and Scarlett. Our families would have known each other."

"That's amazing. Did you tell your father that you looked up the family home?"

"No, I didn't. I thought he would just get mad again. But you told me that I was named after my uncle Cayetano… but Luna's brother was named Alejandro. We found his birth records."

"That can't be right," Inés said with a deep frown. "Your father told me that Cayetano was Luna's brother and the most important person in her life."

"Wouldn't that be her great love, Ignacio, the man who she wouldn't name her son after?"

"Oh, Caya, what have you done?"

"What?"

Inés closed her eyes and rubbed her forehead. "Cayetano… I can't."

"You have to! Why is there no birth record or baptism for Papá? Or a marriage record in the church for Luna and Ignacio?"

"They were married in Madrid, that's why. There is a marriage record. Your father will have it."

"Can I see it? When did they get married?"

"May 1939. Why the urgent desire to dig into your father's life?"

"I'm just curious, that's all."

"Stop it. No wonder your father is furious at you."

"I know you aren't supposed to talk about the war, but like it or not, our family was on the favourable side during the dictatorship."

"We never talk about that," Inés said. "You should not ever bring that up."

"What about that picture Papá posed for with Franco? It's obvious the family has always been right-wing."

"You really want to know? Do you really need to shame your father? Your great-grandfather, Juan Pablo Beltrán, was a Republican, who married off his daughter, Luna, to a businessman's son, Ignacio, in order to make a big profit when he got a foot into the Reyes' business. Only Juan Pablo was murdered at the end of the war, and his daughter became a Nationalist. She was a religious conservative, unlike her Godless anarchist family. Ignacio was not Paco's father. He just agreed to take on the baby Luna was already pregnant with before she moved to Madrid. Your father is a bastard child. He is humiliated by it. His stepfather, Ignacio, died of pneumonia, and Luna inherited all his money, and she was able to raise Paco on her own. Happy now?"

Cayetano sat silently and looked at his hands. He felt like a scolded 10-year-old who had spilled nail polish on his mother's bedcovers while he kicked his football around. "There is no shame in it."

"Maybe now there is no shame in having a child while unmarried. But back then there was. Values still counted for something."

"So who is my real grandfather?"

"I don't know. Your father never said. I don't think he knows. That only adds to his shame. Let's hope it's not this Cayetano Ortega you speak of that lived across the street. Wouldn't want your new girlfriend to be your cousin."

Cayetano scoffed. "No, that is the least of my worries."

"Which brings me to the point of why I asked you to come over. I saw a photo of you in a magazine today."

Cayetano frowned and watched his mother pull a glossy magazine from the drawer under the coffee table that sat between them. He had just learned a huge piece of information about his father. What could be more important? "Mamá, does it matter?"

"I think it does." She flipped the magazine open and handed it to him. "Thank you for telling me that you went to Cuenca, it all makes sense now."

Celebrity bullfighter Cayetano Beltrán Morales was spotted out and about in Cuenca on Friday with a mystery woman. Rumours have circulated for months regarding his tempestuous marriage to Tele 5 star María Medina Cruz. This sensual photo with a beautiful younger woman, taken at the famous parador Convento de San Pablo, does nothing to quell the suggestions of a divorce for the high profile couple...

¿Qué coño? What the fuck? They had been so restrained with their behaviour in Cuenca. Luna didn't want to give the children a confused idea. There it was; that one moment when they sat in the playground, their lips just touched when they joked around. Sensual photo? Oh please. That couldn't have been any more ridiculous if... if María herself had written the article. "Mamá... this is nothing."

"Doesn't look like nothing. The way that woman looks at you says she is head-over-heels in love."

Cayetano brought the photo almost to his face to study it and Inés laughed. "Caya, I'm sure this girl is very nice, but you are married..."

"Separated. I'm separated. You know that. I asked María for a divorce a few weeks ago."

"But you two are good together!"

"Yes, we are… except for all those times when we aren't."

"Don't smart-mouth me."

"She cheated on me!"

"People make mistakes!"

"Have you or Papá ever slept with someone else?"

"No!"

"Well, there you have it. Love doesn't compel people to cheat. María isn't right for me. I know you think she comes from a good family, and maybe she does, but I think we have all learned that family isn't everything."

"I just want you to be sure."

"I'm sure. I don't care if María is seen as suitable for me. I don't love her. Just because her family is rich and has some royal title for doing the King a favour years ago…"

"They are Spanish nobility…"

"Are you kidding me? Sergio Medina was only given a royal title because he married one of the King's mistresses, and he only married her because she was pregnant to the King and someone needed to take over the baby to appease the Queen!"

"One could say he was very noble for doing that."

"Marrying a friend's mistress and getting paid to care for the baby is not a career choice. Just because the Medina family have been wealthy since then doesn't make them noble. Certainly not their great-granddaughter, María, anyway."

"Sometimes life is complicated, Cayetano. Your father tells me that this Luna girl is married, that isn't a simple affair."

"She is widowed. Nearly three years ago her husband was hit by a car."

Inés frowned an expression of genuine sympathy. "That is sad. So young to be a widow."

"And she has children. Gorgeous five-year-old twin boys. They are amazing, so polite, and smart and calm. She is wonderful with them, even with all the upheaval the three of them have faced."

"So you met them?"

"I did, they came along to Cuenca as well, and we spent a few days together. It's the kind of life I could see for myself…"

"*Poco a poco,* little by little, my boy. You must be gentle with this girl if she has lost her husband."

"I know, I know. It's not a simple situation, but it works. Luna is fiery, Mamá. When I step out of line, she tells me so!"

"That could happen often then!" Inés watched her son throw a fake look of indignation. "Who is the husband?"

"An Italian professional cyclist. He was run over in Valencia, where Luna lives. The boys are Spanish, they were born here. But they stand out; they have deep red hair like you've never seen."

"They are not like their mother then," Inés said, and then frowned. "A New Zealander with red hair… reminds me of something your father once said. He told me that his mother had a best friend when she was young, and she was from New Zealand, and had flaming-red hair."

Cayetano's eyes widened dramatically. The wicked woman that Paco had spoken of that afternoon they had argued… "Really? Luna's grandmother, Scarlett, had red hair. Could it be that my *abuela* and Luna's *abuela* were friends? It's fate!"

"Or a coincidence."

"No, there are too many coincidences now. If only Papá would talk about his family…"

"He has his memories locked away in the chest in his office. Perhaps a photo of his Mamá, or her old letters… there could be a hint of something in there. You shouldn't ask him about that. Now is not a good time. Wait for him to calm down a little."

"Will you tell Papá that you told me about how he doesn't know his real father?"

"Of course I will. We didn't make it this far by not talking."

"I don't want to make him mad. Knowing this makes no difference to how I see him."

"Cayetano, you are stirring things that upset him. Why or how is not for us to judge. He loved his mother very much, and Luna died when he was still young. He grew up in the 1940's and came of age in the 1950's. Spain then and Spain now are vastly different. Even in 1969 when we met was different to the world he grew up in. Spain moves at a breakneck speed, and we will never understand what he has been through. His mother did the best that she could on her own. She married well, and it allowed her son to have a lot of opportunities. We have a lot to be grateful for because of Luna Beltrán. It was her that encouraged your father to be a *torero*."

"He told me that his father was a fan of bullfighting."

"That is what he told me."

"Did he say his uncle Cayetano loved bullfighting?"

"Yes."

"Only his uncle's name is Alejandro..."

"I'm sure there is an explanation for that. Your father is not a liar. If your father is one thing, it's very frank and honest."

Cayetano snorted. "Tell me about it. I'm just interested, that's all. It's intriguing."

"Because your girlfriend's family lived across the street?"

"Well, yes. I wouldn't have asked if I hadn't met Luna. She is looking for a man who has disappeared... and more than that. Luna is a lost soul. Both of her parents are dead. She has no siblings, no uncles, no aunts. I think she wants to find a family. Something to hold her here."

"That is sad."

"It is. Especially when we have everything."

"You know what happened to this Cayetano Ortega already, don't you?" Inés said matter-of-factly.

"He was murdered and tossed into a mass grave somewhere?"

"Yes, but people can't go and dig them up. The moment you move the soil over those shallow graves, the agony of Spain will pour out, like fresh blood from a wound. All that pain and hatred is covered with a thin layer, Caya. Don't stir up something you can't understand."

"We would never be able to find him. We don't know anyone who was in his life, so no one could point us in the direction of any graves, let alone the right one. The man could be lying by the side of the road and we'll never know."

"I take it that you and Luna have discussed that?"

"No. I think she has hopes for a good outcome."

"Like the family that belongs to this man?"

"Exactly."

"If Luna looks for peace in a time of atrocious war, she will inevitably be hurt, just like your grandmother was."

"What happened to Papá's uncle?"

"I don't know. Your father never talks about him. He died before Luna married Ignacio."

"Maybe he was murdered."

"Shh..." Inés warned him. "Don't say that."

"Who's going to hear?"

"Nobody wants to hear."

"Do you think I will awaken all the fascists who secretly hide out here in the suburbs?"

"Cayetano, you would be surprised if you knew how close the fascists are. I know you were born during the dictatorship, but you were young when Franco died and…"

"I remember. I remember hearing it on the radio. I remember Papá crying about it. Was he a supporter, or was he relieved that the man was dead?"

"We don't talk about this. Not then and not now."

"It's that silence that hinders Luna."

"Don't let the fact that you have a new lover blind you to what you need to do for our family."

"Lover? At least she was labeled my girlfriend a moment ago."

"Cayetano, I know my son. I can assume she is your lover."

"Now you want to bring up subjects you and I shouldn't discuss."

"I got pregnant at 15. I'm no innocent. You, every mistake you make ends up in the paper. Let's not be coy."

The conversation was halted by the sound of the phone. Cayetano sat back in the sun while Inés went to take the call in the kitchen. His mind drifted back to the wicked redhead that his *abuela* Luna would have known. Surely that was Scarlett. The odds were stacked in that favour. He needed to have a look in the chest that his father had.

Cayetano glanced through the doorway, to see his mother in the kitchen. She fiddled with a plant on the windowsill while she spoke. Perfect. He hobbled down the hallway past the bedrooms to his father's office. Sure enough, tucked away in the corner of the wardrobe, like a heavy burden, was the wooden chest. Cayetano dragged it out into the light of the office and wiped a layer of dust from the top of the old box. The name Beltrán was engraved in it, and it was locked. The lock was old; a little persuasion would solve that. His father wouldn't let him look in it, so it was time to do something that he knew would cause him grief later.

It was only a short walk from the end of the hallway to the front door. Cayetano could carry the heavy box past the kitchen without his mother noticing. He put it on the back seat of his Mercedes where it would be safe. His father wouldn't notice it missing for a few days. He went back inside just in time; Inés had just finished her phone call. "That was your aunt," she said. "She is at the country club with your grandmother, and wants me to meet them for lunch."

"I will leave you alone then."

Cayetano wandered back into the conservatory to pick up his phone that he had left on the coffee table, and picked up the copy of the magazine. "I'll take this home. Papá doesn't need to see it."

"He already has."

Cayetano cringed. Oh for a little privacy. He wasn't 16 anymore, and he certainly didn't need their permission for anything. "Oh well, I will keep it for myself then."

"She is a beautiful woman."

"She is. She's everything I could possibly want, Mamá."

Inés smiled. "Well, maybe you could bring her by one day. But as I said, go slow, Caya."

"She's the one. I'm absolutely sure of it."

"I believe you. Your enthusiasm is obvious. It also explains your mood since your accident. You should have been miserable, and you seem buoyant instead."

"I see a future for myself. Until now, I have been drifting."

"Maybe you are as lost as the lovely Luna. But, Caya, just because this poor girl's family has suffered a tragedy doesn't mean you can stir up our family's past. I don't want to hear you ever speak about this to my parents. They were children during the civil war, haunted by the bombing of Madrid in 1936. Their own parents were killed, so they don't need to be reminded of the horror they faced. They wear the pain enough already."

"Weren't Republican children shipped off to Russia and other places to hide them from the war?" Cayetano asked his mother, and he saw her face grow hard. "We weren't Republicans, were we? We were on the side of the Nationalists. What were we? Monarchists? Religious Carlists? Conservatives? Fascist Falange supporters? Anti-separatist?"

"You don't seem to understand that you can't say these things out loud!" Inés cried.

"So how the hell did that work? Papá was the bastard child of a Republican woman. She and her son would be *rojos,* but they were all murdered during the dictatorship."

"Luna's husband, Ignacio, was a Nationalist, a Falange member. She switched sides to be with him."

"This is Spain – nobody switches sides of anything. Ever."

"Cayetano, these things no longer exist. The country is peaceful, and we can live any way we want."

"It's not peaceful, Mamá. Not as long as people like Cayetano Ortega are lost, like hundreds of thousands of others. Madrid is hiding its secrets, the whole country is. I didn't agree to any kind of pact of forgetting."

"Maybe not, but life is hard enough."

"Not for the rich like us."

"Everything we have could come apart in a second. Don't take your lot in life for granted."

"Let me leave you to your lunch at the country club," Cayetano muttered. "Let's pretend things are fine again. Just like the country that we love has been doing for years."

Inés stood at her front door and watched her only son drive away. Inés Morales may have been a remarkable woman, but she knew she wasn't going to be able to stem the tide of change that was going to hurt her family. The day was coming.

16

Valencia, España ~ septiembre de 2009

Luna's hands had gone red after as she struggled with her overfull plastic shopping bags from the Mercadona supermarket. She always managed to buy more than she could carry home. When she got through her heavy front door, one of Darren's racing bikes sat in the entrance way as an out-of-place welcome home, and she frowned.

"Darren, are you here?" She stood in silence for a moment, no reply to her call. She turned and headed into the kitchen and dumped her shopping bags on the floor. She shivered; the feeling of a presence behind her gave her goosebumps, and when she turned around there he was, with a face as angry as a summer thunderstorm. "Hey," she said, a sudden caution in her voice. "You're home early."

"I felt the need to come home instead of on to Toledo."

Luna wasn't sure what the hell was going on. Darren's tall frame stood over her. It was menacing. It was cold. Darren was never any of those things. "Are we okay?"

Darren thrust the magazine that he held into her hands. "You tell me, Miss. Page 8."

Luna took the magazine from him and flipped through the glossy pages. The magazine had been wrung out, as if life needed to be drained from it in a slow and calculating manner. "Oh shit."

"That wasn't what I said," Darren replied. His voice was sharp.

There it was. A private moment between her and Cayetano in the courtyard in Cuenca. They hadn't even been kissing, just close together, whispering and flirting while the kids played. People had taken second glances at Cayetano, and obviously one person had taken more interest than normal. It was a poor quality shot, most likely taken with someone's phone and sent to this trashy weekly magazine who paraded the lives of celebrities for entertainment. "I can't believe it, someone took photos while I took the kids to the playground?" she said, more asking the page before her than Darren. She shut it and looked at the cover. *Who the hell were these people?*

"That's the least of my concerns," Darren bit back. He snatched the magazine from her little hands and threw it on the floor. "One of the guys saw it while in the hotel lobby in Cordoba. Everyone on the team has seen it now – you whoring yourself to some guy while I'm away for the *Vuelta."*

"Hang on…"

"No, you hang on." Darren pointed at her, the gesture as accusatory as his voice. "You said you were going to Cuenca for your grandfather. You took the children with you, and it was to meet some guy. You lied to me to hook up with a stranger!"

"I did not!" Luna shot back. She stood as tall as she could, though no match to a man of six-foot-five. "You just wait a minute."

Darren grabbed her arm with a fist that promised wrath for what she had done. His injuries didn't diminish his strength. He shook her just a little, enough to scare her quiet. "I asked you to marry me. I went away on the trip to give you a little bit of space as we adjusted to our new relationship, and you cheated on me."

"I never agreed to marry you." Luna was afraid, but she wouldn't admit it. Her voice wasn't going to give her away, it never did. "If you love someone, you don't need time to figure out what you want. It's all or nothing from the start."

"Then what's wrong with you? Did you run off to have a night with a bullfighter? We watched him on television. Did you sit there and lie about not knowing him? Or did you seek him out after that?"

"It's not your business."

"You have strung me along for years, and got me to play Daddy, and not once have you rewarded me."

"Rewarded you?" Her voice had never sounded so indignant. "Let go of my arm, you inconsiderate prick."

Darren shook her when he let her go, but Luna didn't back away from him. "So, what, all this time, have you been biding your time and not really ever been just a friend?"

"For fucks sake, you know what I want. You tease me and string me along, promising that maybe I can have what I want."

"What do you want? Sex in return for helping me out? Like I'm some kind of prostitute?"

"I want to be with you as a partner. An equal partner, not someone you just use! Why is it okay to treat me like this? You wouldn't cheat on Fabrizio. What would he think of you now?"

That was it. Comparing himself to Fabrizio was something she couldn't tolerate. "I never cheated on him because I loved him, completely, without the need to explain it, worry about it, or be afraid of it. I don't feel like that about you. I never will. You were the second choice rider of the team, and you are still second best with me." That was cruel, but she was so angry.

Darren didn't even flinch before he lifted his hand and slapped her across the cheek. He wanted her to feel the physical pain of how infuriated he felt towards her. The moment he did it, he knew that the whole life he had was gone.

The two of them stood in silence for a moment, not able to look one another in the eye. "I think it's time you moved out of my apartment," she said towards the floor.

"Luna…"

"I'm going away for the weekend, as soon as I collect the boys from school. When I get back on Sunday night, you need to be gone."

Darren stood in the kitchen on his own as Luna powered from the room and out of sight. He heard her bedroom door slam shut a moment later. Love wasn't supposed to feel like this, and they both knew it.

17

Madrid, España ~ septiembre de 2009

Cayetano opened the front door of his Madrid apartment and felt the breath sucked from his lungs. There was Luna and her children. She looked hot. Smoking hot. She wore a low cut knee-length dress, which was bright red. Everything was perky and well curved in all right places. Her hair fell gently over her shoulders, the black highlighted by the bright dress, and the very red lipstick she wore. Combined with tall black stilettos on those toned legs, she was killing him without doing a thing. Her two gentleman companions looked tired but happy, two little smiles pleased to see him.

"Hi, lollipop guy!" Giacomo said.

"Good evening, Giacomo. Nice to see you."

"I'm not Giacomo, I'm Enzo."

"I'm Giacomo," Enzo said.

Cayetano looked back and forward between them both, and they started to giggle.

"You're right, lollipop guy," Luna said. "They're messing with you."

"Come in," Cayetano gestured and the boys ran inside ahead of their mother. Cayetano took her small case from her and closed the door. "I have some toys in the living room for you, if you like."

"You're so cool," Enzo commented as the two boys kicked off their black leather shoes. They sprinted off into the living room, and they heard them squeal with delight a moment later.

"Mummy, there are wooden blocks in here. They're so awesome!" they heard Giacomo exclaim.

"Come see!" Enzo yelled.

"Be right there," Luna called to them. She turned to Cayetano with a smile. "How are you, lollipop guy? Anything in your pockets for me?"

"What do you want?"

She placed one hand on his chest and pushed him against the wall, much to his delight. She wound her arms around his waist, and ran her hands ran into the back pockets of his jeans. "I'll take whatever you have."

"Keep it clean, *Señora* Montgomery. There are children present."

"Rule number one of parenting, Cayetano," she whispered and brought her lips to his. "Take every moment you have."

Cayetano needed no more invitation than that. Her lips begged to be kissed, and her body desperately needed to be held. The woman had more sides to her than a flawlessly cut diamond. It didn't matter if she was the enthusiastic and caring mother, the easy-going girl in the park, the flawless beauty in a fine restaurant, the wide-eyed tourist in a small town, or the temptress in his apartment - he was happy to take each and every side of her. When she finally released him from her slow and consuming kiss, he realised he hadn't been this happy in a long time. Luna had rung him earlier that afternoon and said that she wanted to see him, even though she had turned down his offer of a weekend away earlier in the week. Cayetano was so ecstatic he had jumped up and down on the spot like a happy teenage girl.

He watched her poke her head through the doorway to check the boys and then turned back to him. "So, is your offer of going to visit your country place over the weekend still on offer?"

"Absolutely! We will have a great time out there. Plenty for the kids to do."

"You said that you have a surprise for me out there?"

His father's chest of secrets. "I do."

"That can wait for tomorrow then, I'm sure. The children are tired. They probably won't last another hour. Perhaps we can have an evening to ourselves?"

"I like that idea. I was going to suggest we take them out for dinner, but we can do that another time."

Luna glanced at her wrist; still no watch. She hadn't had her last one fixed, but it didn't stop her from instinctively looking at her wrist.

"It's just after nine," Cayetano said.

"Well past bedtime already. The boys ate on the train; they think that is the coolest thing ever."

"I went to the supermarket, which meant braving about 100 grandmothers who wanted to tell me how to heal my leg, to buy things I thought the kids would like. Then I made up the spare room for them. Now they're here, I find all I needed to do was have a few lollipops in my pocket."

"I didn't feel any in your pocket. Can I try again?"

"Yes… later. I want to play with the new blocks I bought. They look fun."

"You didn't need to buy them toys, Cayetano," Luna said and wound her arms around his neck. "But I appreciate it."

"I bought them for me, you just brought the playmates." Cayetano wrapped his arms around her little waist and stole another sneaky kiss. "How are you, *preciosa?*"

"It's been a rough day." Darren's slap had hurt for hours.

"I can help with that." He could barely go more than a sentence or two without kissing her.

"Are you getting married?"

The embrace broke at the sound of the little voice, and Luna turned to see her sons behind her. "What is it with men and marriage today?" she muttered. "Why do you think I'm getting married?" she asked the two innocent faces that looked back at her.

"You're kissing. I saw it on TV," Enzo said, a voice full of authority.

"You don't have to marry every girl you kiss," Cayetano chuckled.

Luna shook her head with a smile. "I'm not getting married. Go and play. I'll put my bag away, and then I'll join you. Go on."

Cayetano and Luna stood in the double doorway to the living room and watched the kids resume their position on the rug. "Sorry," he said under his breath.

"It's okay." Her voice was so soft that her lips barely moved. "You are my lover, and if we are serious, then the boys will need to adjust to that… slowly…"

"We are serious, are we?" Cayetano couldn't hide his smile.

"I brought my children into your home. I consider that serious.

Plus, I have always wanted to take a lover."

"Consider me taken, mistress," he said, and linked one finger through her hand to hold it in his own. "Can we play now?"

Luna sat on the floor with the kids, and watched Giacomo and Enzo talk and play with Cayetano and the toys that he had got them. Luna was not a person who liked children – of course she loved her own, they were an extension of her soul. But Cayetano was one of those people who loved all children, and he was great with the boys. He had all the time in the world for them. Of course, that was easy when you only did it for an hour a week. The games put away when they were exhausted, and the boys were asleep in no time in the spare room down the hallway. Luna wandered back into the living room to find Cayetano clearing away the blocks. "You don't have to do that, I will," she said. "Sitting on the floor must hurt your leg."

"*Gracias,* Mamá," he teased. "I don't mind. If I trip and fall on them, then it might be different. Are they asleep?"

"Yes. The boys will sleep anywhere. It comes in very handy." She looked around the spotless room. "So, what does my Madrileño do on an average Friday night?"

"I usually go out about midnight, and get home just before sunrise."

"Wow, I'm jealous of that."

"Don't be," Cayetano said and got up off the floor. It was easy to see his leg was still not right when he moved. "At home with you appeals far more. Maybe I'm old, but some nights, just sitting in my armchair and doing nothing is great. But I would like company. I get very lonely here."

Luna glanced at the ugly brown leather armchair in the corner. The whole apartment was perfect in black and white, but this stood out for all the wrong reasons. "What's with the old chair?"

"Don't insult the chair!" he cried. "She's my baby. My grandfather José bought it when he was young, and then Papá had it when he was a *torero,* and now I have it. It's a tradition."

"You sit on an old chair that is falling apart as a tradition?"

"You have no idea how many times María tried to get rid of it. She said it embarrassed her when we had parties."

"Was that often?"

"Too often. I like going out, but María liked to show off all the material things she owned. Drove me crazy."

"Well, you have no problem of that with me. I don't own much," Luna said. She crossed the room to look at a few pictures on the wall. "My apartment consists of things I need, not want. We never decorated anything. We weren't interested in 'stuff'. This is your sister, Sofía, right?" she gestured at the photos on the wall.

"Sure is."

"You seem close. That's nice. Wow, you look young in this one." She leaned in to look at the photo of a young Cayetano and Sofía on a walking track in the forest.

"That is Peru. We backpacked through South America when Sofía turned 18. She wanted to go alone, but I suggested I that go with her. Papá was furious when I took a year off work."

"Are Sofía and your parents still not talking?"

"Si," Cayetano sighed, and sat down in his armchair. He pulled the footrest out and leaned back. "It's nothing new."

"That's sad. You never know when you are going to be hit by a car and have everything ruined."

"Shit, sorry."

"No, it's okay." Luna continued to look at the photos. "I'm just saying that you shouldn't assume bad things only happen to other people. They can happen to you. Don't waste time fighting."

Cayetano watched her glance over at him, and he beckoned her. "You have to sit with me. I can't bear to look at you in that dress any longer without having you on my lap."

"I can't sit on you," she said, but came over anyway.

"You can, you are light as a feather."

"Feather? No way." When he took her hand and pulled her, she climbed on his lap and put her arm around his shoulders. She rested her feet on the torn arm of the chair and curled up on him, careful not to put any weight on his leg. She couldn't deny that she loved the spot. "How long were you in South America?"

"A year. Sofía graduated high school and refused to go to law school as Mamá and Papá had arranged. She wanted to travel and be a nanny. I took a year off my work and went with her. At 23, you think you can protect your teenage sister from everything. I did a terrible job."

"Why?"

"Sofía is a free spirit. I don't mind, but that is why she clashes with our parents. Our whole family all work for the family business. Sofía was going to be the lawyer of the family, and she rebelled. I went and trained with a fighter just outside Buenos Aires for three months, and Sofía learnt to dance. I have to admit I made my way through too many young women there, and Sofía was no better. She always manages to find the worst man for her and falls in love."

"We are all guilty of that."

"True! After that we spent six months tripping around south and central America, and then I did another three months training in Mexico City. Again Sofía was madly in love, and I was bed-hopping. We saw all the sights, walked the famous trails, sampled all the local beers, but we needed to come home just to relax from the holiday! I came home to Madrid and ready to take my place as the *torero* of the family, but Sofía came home convinced that she couldn't take her place. She has drifted ever since."

"You can't make her something she isn't."

"No. She met this guy, Garcia, a few years ago. Nice guy. Mamá and Papá loved him. Since she hasn't been what they wanted, instead they saw her as a wife and mother with Garcia. But Sofía isn't into marriage. About a year ago, she got pregnant, but was *ectópico*... ectopic... and now she can't have children. It split the relationship."

"That's terrible."

"Mamá and Papá were upset that she split with Garcia, and Sofía just lost it. She won't speak to them now. She's still hurting over it all. I sit in the middle."

"It's all you can do."

"Then I split with María, but somehow they supported me more than they supported Sofía, which creates tension."

"So, when you see a chance to meet a stranger on the street who doesn't know you, it's an opportunity have a bit of fun after all this is going on?"

Cayetano smiled a warm, genuine smile. "Yeah, but it's far more than that now. I thought you said that you weren't sure about bringing the kids here. Then you turn up, looking so smoking hot that I can barely breathe."

"Very funny."

"I'm serious, you might set off my smoke alarm. Although, standing under cold sprinklers might do me some good."

"Darren came home from Cordoba. He knows all about us now."

"Awkward?"

"I just told my best friend of 15 years that I don't want to be with him, or marry him. I feel like shit."

Cayetano raised his eyebrows and thought about that. He wasn't sure what to say.

Luna could see what went through his mind. "No! Cayetano, no. I don't regret it, so don't think that. Even if I didn't know you, I still would have said no. Especially with the way he acted today."

"What did he do?"

"He acted as if I owed him. He has put in the hours, and now I have to love him. I have to give him what he wants. He slapped me."

"What? The mother-fucker!"

"Don't even go there. I want to pretend it didn't happen."

"I'm afraid my fist won't feel the same if I ever run into this guy."

"After we fought, I just thought 'why not just go to Madrid?' I want to be with you, and I don't want to be in my apartment feeling bad about any of this. I don't have to do anything for anyone."

"Do you need me to punch him for you?"

"No thanks, I can punch on my own."

"I have no doubt."

"I'm not with Darren. I never was. There is only one man I have ever loved before, and he died. All this is just complicated and stupid."

"I will never hurt you," Cayetano said in a quiet voice. His eyes were soft as they gazed upon her. "I don't want you to feel as if you have to do more than you can cope with."

"I can cope. I'm ready to move on… because of you. Not because I am ready for a relationship… I'm only ready for you. A year ago I wouldn't have even looked at you, but now… now I'm happy… I'm ready. But I can't imagine the future, I can only deal with right now."

"We live our lives on our terms. No one exists here, other than the boys."

"They determine the decisions I make. It has to be that way."

"I know."

"When you get married, it's forever. I thought it would be. I'm in uncharted territory, and I've been second guessing every move I make these last few months. It's killing me."

"I knew, the day I married María, that we wouldn't last. I was too gutless to do anything about it. I thought a divorce would release me and everyone around me from my mistakes. But it didn't. You do that. I love you, Luna. More than I have ever loved anyone ever before. A moment like this should have a grand gesture, but…"

"I don't like grand gestures. I do love you, though."

Cayetano rubbed his cheek against hers. "Do you?" he whispered in her ear.

"Yes… and it scares the shit out of me."

Cayetano couldn't help but laugh. "You have no need to worry."

"I know." Luna looked right at him; his eyes sparkled like his smile. "We just need to keep doing what we're doing."

"Maybe just a little more often? A phone call every day and a meet-up every few weeks just isn't enough anymore."

"Maybe we could see each other more often. I thought I would sell my apartment. I need to start over, and a new place will help."

"You could move much, much closer to me."

"To Madrid? And leave Valencia? No way, my blood is in the soil. I don't know why, but I'm drawn to the place."

"I'm drawn to you."

"Then I guess we will just have to see how we go." She gathered his lips with hers, and could feel every ounce of how he felt for her.

"You could just move in here."

"Please tell me that you're kidding."

"I am. Are you sure you want to move? It's not just because you had an argument with Darren is it?"

"No. I have wanted to for a long time. Fabrizio and I always planned to move out of the city, and there's no reason why I can't do it on my own. I stayed in the apartment because it was a part of my marriage that I still had. I could feel him around me when I was there. But he isn't there anymore. I don't feel the pull anymore. I need to move and cope with it. Rip it off like a Band-Aid."

"You can talk about him, and anything you want with me. I promise."

"Are you sure?" she asked sceptically.

"It's Darren who wants to be a replacement, not me."

"What do you want to be?"

Cayetano shrugged. "I don't know. A new start? Both of us need one. Like you said, we just need to keep doing what we're doing. There's no rush to do anything."

"Not a rush to go to bed? I know it's very early by Madrid

standards."

"Either you're very tired or are being very suggestive."

"I guess that depends on where I'm sleeping tonight."

"Well, the children are in the spare room. I converted the other two rooms into my dressing room a few years ago, so that only leaves my bedroom."

Luna raised her eyebrows. "You have a giant dressing room?"

"Yes, for my performances. I get dressed in there, relax in there, I have my home office in there. I keep all my gear in there."

"It's a man cave."

Cayetano chuckled at the title. "Yeah, it is. No one can go inside but me. It's my private space."

"Not even María?"

"Never. When I prepare for a fight, I am alone. She never even asked to go inside. Hop up, I'll show you."

Luna crawled off his lap and helped him up from his seat. "You just said no one goes in there."

"I'll open the door for you," he said and took her hand. They headed out of the living room and down the silent hallway.

Luna could see his bedroom at the end of the hall, but they stopped at another door. He opened the door without a sound and walked into the dark room. She waited while Cayetano turned on a lamp that sat on a big oak desk in the corner of the room, and she looked around. Underneath the huge arch window, there was the biggest white couch she had ever seen. One wall of the room was a gigantic wardrobe closed up tight. On the other wall was a mirror, floor to ceiling in size. On a hook, next to the mirror was one of his *traje de luces,* his bullfighting costume. "Oh my God," she said. "There are blood splatters all over your suit."

"That was the one I wore when I got hurt," he said, quite casual about the fact. "I hung it up in here and wasn't sure what to do with it. It's one of the best I have had made."

Luna fingered the red fabric of the *chaquetilla,* the jacket. Blood had stained the fine and detailed golden embroidery. The pants, the *taleguillas,* were torn, a huge hole punctured through the pliable and strong fabric. Even though the fabric was deep red, the gush of blood that had come from his leg was still visible. Even the *tirantes,* his braces to hold up the pants, were bloody, as was his *corbatín,* his tie. That showed how far the blood had splattered after the accident.

"Oh, Cayetano," she sighed. "This makes the accident real. I…"

"You don't need to say anything," he said. He took the *montera*, his *torero's* hat, from the hook and placed it on her head. "Very nice," he said.

"Do you get a kick out of dressing girls up in your gear, do you?" she joked.

He slid his arms around her waist and laughed. "I haven't let anyone touch my suits before, so not really."

"So why am I in here, wearing your hat?"

"Those lips look beautiful when they're smiling," he whispered. "They entice me into letting you into my life more than anyone else."

"I might kiss you with them, since you make me feel so special, even in your silly little hat."

With a quiet yet deep, sensual tone, he murmured in her ear, *"a la luna de Madrid, me robaste el corazon."*

She watched him take the hat off her head, and put it back on the hook with care. "I stole your heart under the Madrid moon?"

"Can I steal your heart again?"

"You always had it."

"I hope so. There's a fire in you. I should call you *la chispa.*"

"I am 'the spark'?"

"Sí, and let it be that you need that fire stoked," he chuckled, and swamped her lips with his. They lost the playful game the moment they kissed; the power that shot through them was very serious, very deep, and very real. Her entire body was behind the force that wanted him. A passionate kiss from her had felt as if she was searching for something, but that had now changed. It had become a window into a private world that only Cayetano got to see. She had no fear in showing how passionate she was, nothing held her back, and those moments only existed because she was with him.

Luna ran her hands across his shoulders and rested around his arms, and felt the tautness in the muscles. She relished every moment, every flick of his hot tongue in her mouth when he teased her senses with his kiss. Her little hands couldn't stay on his arms for very long; they began their natural wander over the rest of his body. They felt the muscles in his back, before they curved around to the front of his pants, and nimbly undid the button of his jeans. She did it just to hear the naughty laugh escape his lips. The childish snigger disappeared the second she slipped her thumbs into the sides of his pants and pulled them from his hips. Now her hands could have every ounce of his body, and the desperate way he began to inhale told her what he felt was something adult.

Cayetano could hardly breathe; the arousal she continued to stimulate made him feel as if he would burst at any moment. His lips left hers only long enough for him to pull her skin-tight dress from her body, and his own shirt so he could feel her against him. He trailed his lips down her neck while he fumbled to get her bra off, before his hands arched around her to her breasts, unable to resist a not-so gentle caress of a nipple. He would have smiled at his success of building the fire that grew in her, but he was much too dizzy in his own desires. He barely had Luna on her back on the couch below the window before his hands continued their journey. They trailed down to her underwear and pushed past them in a heartbeat. She cried out the moment his fingers grazed her sensitive skin, and he brought his lips back up to hers. "Shh..." he muttered. "This is our little secret."

"I don't think I can keep it a secret for much longer," she panted, and clutched at his lips with hers. Her hands had fallen from him, her body unable to perform any task now. Her fists grabbed at the couch cushions beneath her; her toes curled while she tried to silence her cries as he tantalised her. "Poor innocent me, seduced by some hot Spanish guy," she whispered.

"You're a woman who needs an awakening, but the desire is already in you." Just the thought sent that familiar tremble in his veins she elicited every time they came together, their naked flesh pressed hard against each other. His eyes were dark with the desire to give her a dose of the potency and vigour inside him. "Of course I wouldn't want to be anything less than a gentleman with the lady."

"Sometimes, I don't want to be a lady," she replied when he ran his thumb over her bottom lip. She felt his hand drift down her neck, curve down between her breasts, over her stomach, and softly parted her weak thighs again. They were unable to resist him. She took a deep, shuddering breath when he touched her again. "Sometimes I just want to be a woman. One that can't wait any longer."

Cayetano leaned over her, and brought his body to claim her. He loved the helpless cries he could coax from Luna when he made love to her. They added to the erotic sensitivity that ran between them. But the game of having to remain silent only heightened everything, the power that surged through them continued to intensify while they fought to internalise it all. Every nerve Luna had shattered when she felt the familiar shudder of satisfaction in Cayetano, and she let herself go, to let the flood of pleasure and indulgence pour through her. They both slumped back on the couch, desperate to catch their breath, the only sound in the silent apartment.

"Having to be silent is a fun game," she giggled through her laboured breath.

"Yeah," Cayetano replied, the sound of satisfaction in his voice. "That experiment makes it pretty…"

"Wow."

"Wow!"

"Thanks for letting me into your secret room."

Cayetano lifted his head and looked into her eyes that sparkled in the dim light of the room. "Thanks for letting me in."

"Let you into what?"

"Your heart. Time spent in love with you is time very well spent."

18

Cuenca, España ~ marzo de 1939

Scarlett shivered. She had no idea what to do and felt very out of place. The light had begun to creep in the window at the Beltrán house. Daylight made the situation seem more real. A new day had dawned, but the world wouldn't look the same again. How she wished these days would stop dawning.

Alejandro sat across the tiny room at the table. For some time, his head had slumped down on the table top. He was blind drunk. Both Scarlett and Cayetano had also drunk a lot over the last few hours, but Alejandro was close to comatose, and no one would stop him drinking himself to sleep.

Scarlett had scrubbed her hands so many times, but she couldn't get Sofía's blood out from under her nails. She had gone home and ripped off her bloodied clothes and tossed them, and tried to wash herself clean with a bucket of water. The cold water stung like knives on her skin, and she didn't care. Her soul would never be clean.

Cayetano glanced up from the seat beside Alejandro and looked at Scarlett. "Do you want to go home for a while?" he asked her.

Alejandro jolted upright at the sound and looked at his friend. "Please don't leave me!" he cried.

"We aren't leaving you," Scarlett said. "I'll do anything you want."

"How could you do this to me?" he mumbled. His eyes began to fill with tears again. "How could you let my wife die? My beautiful Sofía is dead."

Scarlett bit her lip in an effort to steady her emotions. He was right; she had betrayed them all. She had let Sofía slip away. The moment she had managed to get the baby out, the onslaught of blood just poured from her friend. Her haemorrhage had been horrific, and Scarlett and Luna had been helpless. The baby had the cord wrapped around its little neck, its body as lifeless as its beautiful mother. Scarlett had wiped a heavy veil of tears from Luna's face before she had handed the baby boy to her, and sent her off in the direction of the back entrance to the hospital with the precious bundle. When Cayetano had come in search of Scarlett through the hallways, he had found her on the floor, covered in the blood of her best friend, weeping uncontrollably. There was nothing she could do. She had failed them all.

"I'm sorry," she whispered. "Alejandro... I'm so sorry."

"What do we have left to fight for now?" he asked. "Everything I have ever wanted is gone. In my bed is the body of my wife. Sofía is gone, and there is no reason to go on now." He had witnessed Scarlett and Cayetano carry Sofía's limp body out of the back of the hospital to take her home. He didn't know why they needed to move her out of the hospital, and didn't care.

"Why don't you go and sit with Sofía for a while, mi amigo," Cayetano suggested with caution. "Lie down with her."

"Lie next to her cold body?" Alejandro cried. He was inconsolable. "You don't understand what it's like, Caya! She is not some woman you play with, she's my wife. She was the mother of my son! She's dead!"

"Scarlett put a bullet in each of the people who are responsible," Cayetano replied.

"That helps me in no way at all." He took another drink from the bottle on the bare table and banged it back down, not in control of his own hands with inebriation. "I want to die. Now I have no need to save my country."

Cayetano and Scarlett shared a look while they listened to their friend slur his words. "You do," Cayetano said. "You have many reasons."

The tense silence broke with the faintest sound, the soft and desperate cry of the baby. The sound was enough to pierce the broken hearts around the room. The door through to Alejandro and Sofía's bedroom opened, and there stood Luna with the crying child. She had been sitting with Sofía, to allow the child to lie next to his mother, if only for a little while.

"I don't want to see the baby," Alejandro said at his sister. He didn't even look in her direction.

"You have to," Luna said. She had no idea how to care for a child herself. The baby had fussed for hours, and surely he would be hungry, but his mother would never be able to feed him. "He's your son."

"The child has no mother," Alejandro snapped. "How am I supposed to be what he needs? There's no place for a baby here."

Scarlett stepped forward and took the infant from Luna. When she looked at the squirming boy, Scarlett could see his mother in him. The child would never even be held by Sofía. "Luna, I need your help. I have some tinned *milk in my bag. We need to feed the baby."*

"Good idea," Cayetano commented, and watched Luna rummage through Scarlett's backpack that sat on the third chair at the table. "It was lucky that we got hold of that tinned milk in Barcelona. People thought those supplies the Russians sent weren't going to come in handy. I'm glad I took it when I got the chance. Lucky that shipment had been food and not weapons."

"It's been a while since we have been able to get milk," Luna commented and looked at the blank tin in her hands.

Scarlett was still fixated on the baby in her arms. This poor innocent child, born into a world like this. The baby meant so much to her, and it wasn't even her son. To see his face blue when she freed him from his mother's body was terrifying. She had never performed mouth-to-mouth on a baby until last night. In a matter of minutes, she had murdered two women, watched her friend die and saved a life. It was all too much. "All babies are conceived out of love, or lust," she said, and ran her fingers through the baby's black hair. "All babies are born out of pain. All babies should be raised in joy, not grief."

Luna couldn't hold back her tears. "What are we going to do?" she whispered.

"You are going to hold this hungry baby for me," Scarlett said and handed the wriggling infant to his aunt. Just holding the baby sent a deep ache through her belly, and she couldn't take another ounce of pain. Death lived at number 15 San Martín, and this child didn't belong there.

"We need to think of what we're going to do now," Cayetano said, and watched Scarlett pour the milk into a little glass bottle. It looked to be no more than a few mouthfuls of milk that she had for him. "It's time to get out of Cuenca. It's a miracle we weren't discovered at the hospital!"

"What's the point?" Alejandro spat at him. He still couldn't turn in his seat and face the women who stood behind him by the stove.

"There is every point," Scarlett said and shook the bottle. "Who's going to feed the baby his first drink?" she asked.

"Don't look at me," Alejandro grumbled. "That's a job that belongs to his mother."

Scarlett shared a look with Cayetano. Alejandro was in such a deep pit of despair, and rightly so, but so much hung in the balance now. "Luna," she said and turned to her. "You feed the baby."

"I don't know how," she said. She could barely hold the grizzling baby that squirmed in her arms.

"Time to learn." She handed her the little bottle. "Put the edge to his lips and let him taste the milk. He won't know that it doesn't come from his *mother. Hold the bottle close to your breast, to comfort him."*

Luna held the bottle to the child's mouth, and her hand shook. The shock of everything that had gone on ran through her, and only adrenalin kept her awake. She had taken the baby out of the hospital to her brother and just cried. He knew in a second that his wife was dead. The baby had begun to cry in her arms out in the cold. Not a word needed to be said. Luna had barely spoken since then, not when Scarlett and Cayetano brought Sofia's body home, not when she sat with her sister-in-law on her bed, nothing. Her life was shattered. Now the baby was in her arms, and he grunted furiously while he searched for sustenance from the bottle. He didn't need to be shown what it was; he latched on and began to suckle, much to Luna's relief.

"Don't force him," Scarlett said quietly and ran her hands through his little curls again. "He won't need much."

"Ale," Luna said. "Please, come to your son."

"No," he shook his head. "I can't."

Cayetano just looked at his destroyed friend. Things needed to be sorted out, and he needed to take over. Scarlett could only cope with so much, and Luna had more or less just become a mother. "We need to arrange a burial for Sofia, as soon as possible. Then, we are all leaving Cuenca for Valencia. Tomorrow, if we can."

"How will we arrange a funeral in that time?" Luna asked.

"We don't. We tell everyone that she went into labour last night, here at home, and she died before we could send for a midwife. Neither you, Luna, or Alejandro, had any idea what to do when Sofia began to bleed."

"Won't it seem suspicious that we didn't call for help?" Luna asked.

"There was no help," Alejandro said and sniffed. He didn't even bother to wipe his tears from his face. "When I saw Sofia at the hospital after her shift, she said that the midwife on duty had been called away. That's why Sister Rosa had offered to look her over..."

"Right, in that case, you did send for a midwife, but no one could be found. The hospital was locked up already, being as short-staffed as it is. By the time you got back to the house, you found Luna had managed to deliver the child, but Sofia had bled out."

"Can't we say that Scarlett was here?" Luna asked. She didn't look up from the baby, who was nuzzling the teat on instinct.

"No, Scarlett had already left for Valencia." Cayetano looked at Scarlett, who seemed unsure. "Nurse Montgomery had already left to catch a ship, in order to return home to Nueva Zelanda. That way, Scarlett can't be implicated in the two bodies that have no doubt already been found in the hospital. We arrange for a private burial for Sofia, and we get the hell out of here. All of us. We just get into the truck, and we leave everything behind. It *doesn't matter where we sail for, as long as all of us get out of here."*

"We can't just leave Sofía like that," Luna said. Just the thought made hot tears come to her eyes. She just wanted to fall into Cayetano's arms and sob and couldn't.

"Don't bury her here," Alejandro muttered. "You know the stories of bodies being dug up and paraded to frighten the masses. I don't want that for Sofía."

"That happened to nuns bodies, and it happened in Barcelona, not in Cuenca," Cayetano replied.

"Then we take her body with us," Scarlett said. "We will find a safe place to bury her."

"A quiet place, in the countryside," Alejandro said and turned in the direction of the bedroom. Maybe he would finally go and see his wife. "Sofía wanted to live in the country. She wanted to be far away from all the suffering she saw. She ... she wanted to have lots of babies..." His voice trailed off into sobbing and his head hit the table again.

Scarlett stepped forward and placed her hand on Alejandro's shoulder. "Save her baby, Ale. A part of Sofía is here, and you can save him."

"Let's go to Valencia," Cayetano said. "Let's go today, before they start looking for the killers of the nurse and nun. We have nothing here, let's just run. We can care for the girls and the baby in Valencia, Alejandro. We can find a safe place for Sofía." His voice was gentle and sympathetic. The red rings around his eyes conveyed the pain that the others felt. "Soon Franco's troops will be here. We will be killed and the girls will be raped. We need to get out of here."

"Scarlett," Alejandro's voice croaked. "You take the baby. Take it to Nueva Zelanda with you."

"Ale, no," Luna interrupted. The baby had fallen asleep in her arms, and now that he was calm, Luna had regained some of her confidence. "He's your baby. You can't be separated from him."

"Where will be safe for him?" Alejandro replied.

"Francia?" Cayetano offered. "We could try and go there."

"No, he needs to be far away from this hellhole," Alejandro replied, his voice full of hate now. "Take him, Scarlett. Tell them that he is yours and that you gave birth to him here. They will let him into the country with you. What's the inglés name for Alejandro?"

"Um... Alexander... but I can't do that," Scarlett said. "I can't take your son from you."

"You need to save him!" Alejandro said and took a deep breath. "We're all going to die. Soon even Valencia will be in the hands of the enemy. Take Luna with you."

"No!" Luna said. "I'm staying here, and I'm marrying Cayetano."

Alejandro turned to face his sister and the baby. "What?"

Luna held out her hand and showed him the Medina diamond. "I'm marrying Cayetano. I will not abandon this country, or my family. We will fight. Papá will come home to us, and we will figure this out. Together."

"Papá is as good as dead in Madrid!" Alejandro said and stood up from his seat with great haste. "You can't marry Cayetano!"

"I can, and I will," she said with defiance.

"You don't even know who he is! You don't even know who his father is, or how he got his hands on a piece of the Medina jewellery collection."

"Ale, this isn't the time..." Cayetano said and stood up. His friend was close to losing control. "You know Sergio Medina is not my real father."

"But his wife is your mother..."

"I don't care who Cayetano's family is. I want to be his wife," Luna said.

"You know why Scarlett is leaving España, don't you?" Alejandro goaded his sister. "Did Cayetano tell you?"

"Alejandro, please," Scarlett said. "Love brings people together and there's no stopping it. You and Sofía are proof of that."

"We prove nothing," he fired at her. "What do you know about love?"

"Enough! I've already buried my love out in the countryside!" she cried. "I dug a hole and placed him in it. I won't forget Ulrich, like you won't forget Sofía. I've been where you are right now, Ale. You must let us help you."

"The pain will never cease, will it?"

Scarlett shook her head, and a few tears fell onto her shirt. "No, but for God's sake, don't abandon the baby."

"There is no God out here, and we all know it."

"There is nothing more violent than love. The scars it leaves on your soul will never heal. Nothing that war will do can hurt more than love," Scarlett told him. Her accented voice shook when she spoke. "That doesn't mean we should give up. No pasaran."

"No pasaran," Luna repeated. *They shall not pass.* The slogan for Republicanos all over the country.

Alejandro looked at his little sister and shook his head. "Have you been with Cayetano?" he asked.

"I... what?" she stuttered. She knew what he meant.

"Did you defile my sister?" Alejandro eyed Cayetano. "Did you?"

Cayetano opened his mouth, but had no idea what to say. The truth wasn't an option.

"Yes, I've been with him," Luna said. "Because I wanted to."

"Whore," he spat at his sister. "You're a fool. You know Scarlett is pregnant to your precious Cayetano, don't you?"

Luna's eyes widened, and she looked to her fiancé. The man froze on the spot. The look of fear in his eyes was unmistakable. Then she remembered what Scarlett had said the night before – Cayetano could be rough with women. She knew first hand. She looked down at the infant in her arms, and then to Scarlett, who took a few steps back from the group. The foreigner who didn't belong here was going to ruin everything. "Are you pregnant?" Luna asked her. It was almost an accusation with the tone in her voice.

Scarlett brought her hand to her stomach on instinct, and then realised that the gesture gave away her secret. How she wished that she hadn't told Alejandro about the baby. He already knew about the night in the tent with Cayetano. Her one mistake would ruin everyone's lives, and she knew it. "Yes, I'm pregnant."

"So, I'm faced with the choice of handing my baby to one of Cayetano's whores who both stand in this room," Alejandro said with a sarcastic laugh in his voice. "And to think they called Sofía a whore for getting pregnant before I married her. For all we know, Luna is pregnant to you, Cayetano, right now, just as Scarlett is!"

Luna turned to Scarlett and handed her the sleeping child. "Perhaps you should take him to Nueva Zelanda and tell them that he is yours. When I marry Ignacio, he won't take the child."

"Luna," Cayetano said. He didn't care about the drunken Alejandro anymore; the man wouldn't put up a fight. He could barely stand up. "We can all go to Valencia. The baby can come with us..."

"There is no us!" she yelled. "You slept with Scarlett? How could you? You said you loved me! You said that I was all you wanted!"

"You have been! But... but you were off-limits, and..."

"Scarlett was cheap and available. Did you think a woman whose husband had just died was easy pickings? Just living together as friends... you bastardo!" She stepped forward and shoved him in the chest as hard as she could muster.

Cayetano couldn't believe what he was seeing. Luna had just turned him away only a day after declaring her love for him. "Scarlett!" he cried. "Tell her nothing is going on between us!"

"There isn't!" Scarlett said with a loud and clear voice. "There is nothing. He loves you, Luna. The whole world knows that he loves you. He used me, and I used him. It was one night..."

"One that will haunt generations to come!" Luna yelled at the two of them. "I hope this hurts you and your child. You deserve it." She stepped forward and took the baby from Scarlett, and woke him in the process. "Get out of this house. Both of you! What the Beltrán family decides to do has nothing to do with either of you."

The group hadn't noticed that Alejandro had disappeared until they heard him begin to wail uncontrollably. He had gone in to see Sofía's body at last. The three of them stood together, as if suspended in a moment of unbearable hell. The death and fear and heartache hung in the air.

"Get out," Luna said again. "Leave us to our grief."

"The grief belongs to all of us," Scarlett said.

"You don't get a say in this anymore!"

"Let Scarlett take the baby to Nueva Zelanda..." Cayetano began.

"You don't have any right to tell me what to do!" she screamed. "Get out or I will tell everyone about what happened at the hospital!"

Luna spun and went into the bedroom after her brother, in a flurry of tears. The world no longer made any sense. It barely had before now. Everyone knew that she was a fool to love Cayetano, and none had the guts to tell her the whole story until it was too late.

The sight of Alejandro on his knees at the bedside was the final straw. His head rested on Sofía's chest and cried a desperate and pathetic weep. The cry was raw and inflamed, like a bloody wound, and nothing would heal the man. Luna sank to her knees next him and bawled on his shoulder, the same way the baby cried in her arms. Just for now, the baby was with its mother and father, but Luna knew that Scarlett was the best shot the child had at survival. They were all close to death now... and their souls were already dead.

19

Madrid, España ~ septiembre de 2009

Luna took a deep breath when she woke up in bed. There was absolutely nowhere else in the world she wanted to be. A bed warm because she didn't have to sleep alone for a change. She curled up in Cayetano's arms, one leg slung over his. Her hand meandered across his chest, and peeked out over the top of the quilt as her fingers came to rest on his shoulder. Was there a better place to be? Curled up against the man of her dreams in the silent apartment? She didn't dare open her eyes; this moment needed to be stretched out as long as possible.

Cayetano stirred a little, and she felt him kiss her forehead. The gentle touch brought a smile to her lips. This pocket of the world didn't belong to anyone but them. It didn't matter what anyone thought, or said, or did, because they were not allowed here. The smooth tips of his fingers brushed a few of her curls from her face, and returned his hand to her back. It didn't take much for them to find pleasure; it was hidden away from the world in Cayetano's bedroom where no one could find them.

"You're lucky to have children," Cayetano whispered.

"That wasn't what I expected you to say this morning after the night we had." Luna was still naked and tangled in the sheets. The man had the stamina of a stallion.

"I mean, if we didn't have kids here, we wouldn't get out of bed."

"You should come and visit me in Valencia. The boys are at school all day."

"How about Monday?"

Luna giggled and opened her eyes. The light of a gorgeous autumn day stung her tired pupils. "I have sex ache again."

Cayetano snorted. "Sex ache?"

"You know, after lots of sex, all your muscles hurt."

"It's practically exercise for me. You're doing me a favour."

"Then you're welcome." Luna looked up at him, and he kissed her. "You have red sheets. Who buys red sheets?"

"What's wrong with them?"

"Nothing… other than feeling a little, you know, like a porn film set."

"What?" Cayetano laughed. "Are you also looking for the zebra print pillows?"

"That sounds bad."

"Bad bad… or sexy bad?"

Luna burst out laughing. "Don't go there. But listen… we need to be more careful. Last night, in your dressing room…"

"Yeah, sorry. You just make so impulsive."

"You didn't hear me complain, so I'm to blame. You're not that impulsive, you brought condoms to our first date."

"A man needs to be prepared."

"I appreciate that, but I don't want a remainder of this night nine months from now. I don't want any more kids."

"You don't?"

Luna glanced up at his serious expression. "Wow, this is awkward so early in a relationship."

"Better now than later I guess."

"I gave birth to the twins at home, a month early, in a pool of my own blood on the bedroom floor. Thank God that Fabrizio had come home early, and delivered both the boys before the ambulance arrived. I spent several days in hospital and had a blood transfusion. I won't go through that again."

"I can't blame you. If we're doing awkward, I may as well tell you that there is no chance of a surprise in nine months. A few years ago I did a sperm test, and it came with slow, confused swimmers in small numbers. I'm the sterile bullfighter. María loved to tease me."

"Your wife is a total bitch."

"That's why she's my ex-wife and I'm in bed with you, *preciosa.*"

"We have done all that marriage and babies stuff. We can just concentrate on enjoying ourselves now."

"You so often see couples, and they look so tired. You hear men complaining about their annoying wives, and women moan about their husbands. The joy is gone. My marriage to María was like that. She had become so tiresome. Even before we got married, I was tired of her. I assumed that it's a natural progression to feel that way. Every day I see you, it's like meeting you again of the first time. Every time I see you, I am struck by how beautiful you are. I am struck by how funny you are when you tell me a story. I am struck by how caring you are when I see you with the kids. I am struck by how intelligent you are when you speak. How could any of this ever become tiresome? I am dazzled by you in my life."

Luna opened her mouth to speak, but paused. She could hear chatting down the hallway. "The boys are awake. The peace is over for the day."

"I like all the noise. It makes the place a home. Your place must be great."

"It's more of a mess most of the time."

"Speaking of mess, do the boys like making pancakes?"

"Does a bear shit in the woods?"

Cayetano snorted with laughter. "Okay, then I shall make breakfast with them, and you can have a nice long, hot shower and relax."

"Why did it take so long for me to meet you?"

"I think our timing is perfect."

"Me, too."

Cayetano sat up in bed and watched Luna head in the direction of the bathroom while wearing nothing. Nothing could spoil today.

Cayetano didn't need to encourage the boys to make pancakes with him. He had barely got out of the bedroom before the two perky pajama-clad gentlemen agreed to cook breakfast with him, and they rushed to the kitchen. They sat patiently as Cayetano prepared everything, and waited politely to have turns helping. How on earth had Luna turned out two such amazing children? He expected them to be rowdy, but they were quite the opposite. While the boys were gentle and well-mannered, there was one thing that Cayetano couldn't control – their questions.

"Cayetano?" Enzo asked as he peered at the pancakes in the hot pan.

"Yes?"

"Do you like Mummy?"

"Um... yes, yes I do like her. Very much. She's my new best friend."

"Are you going to marry her?" Giacomo asked.

"She is available," Enzo added.

Oh boy, why did her shower take so damn long? What the hell was the right answer here? "I haven't asked her."

"But you kissed her," Giacomo continued.

"Yes, well, it's something you do to people that are important to you. You kiss her, don't you?"

"Yes," Enzo said. "But you go all red in the face when she kisses you."

Cayetano wasn't sure if he should laugh or not. Did he really go red?

"Is Mummy your girlfriend?" Giacomo asked.

"Maybe you should ask Mamá these questions."

"Our friend, Stefan, at school, his Mummy got a boyfriend. Now he lives in their house, and sleeps in his Mummy's bed," Giacomo said.

"Stefan said that his Mummy and this man wrestle in bed," Enzo said.

Cayetano nearly choked on that one. Lucky his coffee wasn't ready yet, or he would have sprayed the whole kitchen with it. "Wrestle in bed?"

"Yeah," Enzo said, no idea what he was really talking about. "His Mummy says on Sunday that Stefan and his sister have to watch the pirate show on TV, and then she wrestles the man in her bed."

"Really? Did Stefan say who wins the wrestling?" Cayetano couldn't help but ask.

"He said that they can hear the man yelling. He must lose," Giacomo said.

"Or win," Cayetano said under his breath. "I'm sure Stefan's Mamá will take care of everything."

"Why aren't you married?" Enzo asked. "Mummy used to be."

Cayetano frowned. He was out of his depth. He had no idea how

Luna spoke to the children. They were five, how did they know so much? "Ah… I was married. But not now."

"Why?"

"I… I changed my mind." Cayetano watched the two kids sit happily with their pancakes in front of them, as they took everything in without a thought.

"Is Mummy the angel that you talked about?" Giacomo asked. "I think she is."

"Yes. She is the angel."

"Told you," Enzo said to his brother. He turned back to Cayetano. "So, do we have to call you Daddy?"

"No! No, you have a father, a good one," Cayetano said. That he could answer.

"He died," Giacomo said. "It's not fair."

"No, no it's not," Cayetano mumbled. He took the last pancake off the pan and placed it on the plate in front of the kids.

"Daddy is an English word. What do you call your Daddy, Cayetano? Do you call him Papá?" Enzo asked.

"Yes, I do."

"Knew it," Enzo sighed with satisfaction, and Cayetano smiled at the boy's confidence.

"Darren said we should call him Daddy," Giacomo remarked and took a sip of his milk.

"Did he?" Cayetano asked. "Does Mamá know that?"

The boys just shrugged. "It was only the other day. He tried to get us to call him uncle once, but Mummy said no. That was ages ago."

How interesting. She said no. Cayetano was relieved when he saw Luna appear in the doorway to the kitchen, fresh from her shower, her wet hair tied back from her fresh face. "Good morning, gentlemen. How are we? Being good?"

"Yep," they both said. "We ate nearly all the pancakes. Cayetano had one million," Enzo said.

"Come on, you lie. It was only half a million," he replied.

"I have just laid your clothes out on the bed for you, when you're ready. You need to brush your teeth as well," Luna told them. "Then, today Cayetano will take us somewhere new."

"Cool!" Giacomo yelled, and jumped off his stool. "Let's get ready!"

"Do you need help?" she asked, but the boys charged past her.

"No," she heard them both yell back while they sprinted towards the room.

"Pancake?" Cayetano offered.

"Yes! For some reason, I'm starving this morning. It's as if I was kept busy all night…. oh wait…" she teased. "Thank you for watching the boys."

"That's okay. They ask a lot of questions."

"Did they bother you?"

"No, no. I can't blame them for checking out the guy dating their mother."

"Did they?"

"Sure did. They also told me about their friend, Stefan…"

"Oh, and the wrestling? Yeah, I've heard that one. Sorry!"

"It's okay, they were good. They stayed clean, and I didn't."

"I was going to say…" Luna joked and looked at Cayetano's shirt covered in pancake mix. "Do you need help getting dressed?"

"Does it include wrestling?"

The doorbell rang and interrupted the conversation. *"Mierda,"* Cayetano swore. "Who has come to ruin the morning? Oh, no, it will only be the newspaper delivery."

"I'll get it, save you from having to admit you have the eating manners of a newborn." Luna left the kitchen and into the nearby main entrance. She swung the heavy door open, and her heart sank. There went having a good day.

"Oh look," María said and folded her arms. "It's the new girl who got her two minutes of fame last week while cuddled up to my husband."

Luna recognised the woman instantly. She was all done up in her camera-ready best. Behind her purple glasses was a vile stare. No good would come out of this chat. "Cayetano," she called out.

"I'll just jump in the shower while you have your pancakes and then we can go," she heard him say. He appeared behind her a moment later. "Fuck me."

"I think that is what the girl here did to deserve pancakes," María said. "Do you cook them for all the girls you bring home?"

"There is no one else," Cayetano said. "Don't you think it's a bit predictable to come in here and be the bitchy ex-wife?"

"That's not why I'm here, so don't make me out to be…"

"Bat-shit crazy? You are, María."

"I might leave you two to… whatever…" Luna said, and turned away before Cayetano could dispute her.

"Don't run away, little one," María said. "I have to get to work anyway." It was too late; Luna had started to walk away and she had no intention of turning back.

"You are actually leaving the studio for something?" Cayetano asked.

"No, I sent someone else. We just edit it, so it looks like I went out and covered the story. There were protestors in Puerta del Sol, and there was no way I was going to bother with it."

Cayetano just shook his head. "God forbid letting an injustice get in the way of your timetable. What's going on down there?"

"It's some organisation, protesting the civil war. Can you believe it? Who cares? They reckon their relatives were murdered and dumped in mass graves, and they are campaigning the government to pay to have them dug up and placed in cemeteries. Leave the past alone, I say."

"There is no end to how heartless you can be."

"Oh, please, spare me the drama, Caya. It's no big deal. If these people want to go digging up bodies, then they can pay for it by themselves. No one will stop them."

"I haven't heard anything about it."

"You wouldn't. It's not a popular subject, and if the media ignores it, then it doesn't exist. We're the only ones covering it today and only as an attention grabber. Something to get the viewer's complaining about on our Facebook page. Gets the ratings up. It doesn't do us any favours from a journalism point of view. No one cares about these people."

"I do. Who are these people?" Cayetano asked.

"There is a remembrance society that people can be a member of, run by some guy. Why do you care?"

"Just… imagine if you wanted to find a body… never mind. What do you want?"

"I came to talk to you about this magazine photo of you and girly, but I don't want to talk while she's here… where did she disappear off to?"

"Probably to attend to the children." Cayetano folded his arms, an instinctive thing. He felt very defensive of what was going on in his house; it was private, and María was the last person he wanted to be passing judgment on his new life.

"Children? She has kids?"

"She does."

"I can see why you like her then, she has the kind of ovaries you want."

"Okay, we're done now," Cayetano said. "I can assume that you didn't like the photo. We didn't either. But it wasn't planned, and I'm hoping it goes away."

"You and me both. If anyone gets the story of our marriage break-up, it's going to be on my show."

"You mean so you can lie?" Cayetano stopped when he heard his phone ringing. He turned to see Luna coming towards him with it in her hand. *"Gracias, la chispa.* Oh, it's Mamá, I will be right back."

Luna stood in the entrance way with María while Cayetano wandered into the kitchen on the phone. Luna didn't want to be left on her own. If you want to meet your lover's ex-wife, you want to do while dressed up, not in your casual wear while make-free, especially when the ex-wife looks fabulous.

"It's sweet, he gave you a nickname," María said.

"He gave you one, but it's not as nice."

María chuckled through gritted teeth. "Look, girly, I don't know what your game is, but my husband isn't going to play Papá. You need to find someone else to reel in."

Luna smiled. "Yeah, whatever. I don't play games, so whatever little mind-fuck you're trying on me, it's not going to fly."

"I'm trying to give you some advice, Luna. Cayetano is my husband. We go a long way back. I don't know you, but you need to get out of the way, for your own sake. Plus, if you have kids, they're going to get hurt. Cayetano and I… we're not done."

It wasn't María's words that threw Luna. It was her tone. She was serious. "I don't want to have anything to do with your divorce."

"Who said anything about a divorce? Girly, I cheated on my husband, he cheated on me. We go through rough patches. We're solid, not some affair that burns out after a few months."

"Okay." Luna just shook her head. "We can just not talk."

"I'm sorry if this makes you uncomfortable, Luna. If you have kids, then at some point you have had a serious relationship, so you know what they're like. They're not perfect, but you're not going to find a Papá replacement here."

"My first husband died. I'm not looking for a replacement because he was perfect, like my marriage. I'm sorry you didn't have the same." Now Luna was just annoyed.

"The fact you have kids may be the only reason Cayetano's interested in you. He can't have any... or did he not mention that?"

"He did tell me. So we can make impulsive love in his dressing room without any worries... oh wait... he doesn't even let you in there, does he?" Luna mocked her. It was easy to say you want to keep it classy, but it was easier said than done. "I need to go back to my children now."

María spun around without a word, and disappeared through the front door, just as Cayetano came back out of the kitchen. "Where did she go?"

"I don't know, maybe she left her broom unattended," Luna quipped.

"Was she a bitch? I'm sorry about that. You shouldn't have to deal with her."

"No." She sighed. "I don't want to deal with baggage. I know I have loads, and I don't need more. Is everything all right with your mother?"

"Ah... yeah, she's fine. Papá is angry at me." The bastard went and found the chest missing! "It doesn't matter. Like you said, no baggage."

Luna smiled. "Fabrizio's family is the stereotypical larger than life Italian family. Since I came from a family of only two, Max and Paulina seemed like a handful."

"So... would meeting Paco and Inés be an issue?"

"I thought we were just going to have a fun weekend."

"We are... we really are. We're going to have a relaxing weekend out of the city. We're taking it easy."

"Good, because I know little about family or marital problems."

"Did María say something?"

Luna shook her head and looked to the floor. "It's fine. She seems to think you and her aren't getting divorced, and that you cheated on her."

"Hey," Cayetano said calmly and brought his hands to her face. When her eyes came up to his, he said, "I'm not a cheater. Maybe when I was 20 I was stupid and I acted that way. Being married is serious. I had faith, and I'm not quitter. I swear I don't act that way."

"You don't have to explain yourself to me."

He brought his lips to hers for a gentle kiss. "I'm sorry that María suggested that we're an affair."

"You don't need to worry. I don't have a disgruntled ex, or parents, to present you to."

"I would have liked to have met Alexander and Thelma. They must have been wonderful people to produce a daughter like you."

"The charmer turns on the sweet talk," she smiled.

"Anything to see that smile. Now, let's get those boys ready, so we can resume our perfect weekend."

"They're brushing their teeth as we speak."

"I will get myself ready, and we can go." Cayetano kissed her forehead and headed back in the direction of the bedrooms.

Luna sighed. All of a sudden she felt uncomfortable. She had wandered into a whole life and family, and it felt rushed. It was fun when they were alone, but that wasn't reality. The last thing she wanted to do was get the speed wobbles, but she and Cayetano were going pretty fast with each other. She heard Cayetano talk to María, about bodies dumped in mass graves. Luna had thought that it was a possibility that her grandfather had suffered that fate. She didn't want to believe it, and not just because that was no use to her in regards to her visa application. It was a scary business. María was wrong; people couldn't just dig up bodies and put them in cemeteries. These people had kept the graves secret for the whole lives, and they were scared to discuss them. Even some bodies that had been moved to cemeteries were then moved again after locals petitioned councils, saying the bodies couldn't be there. There was hate and fear simmering, and Luna didn't want to get caught in it. Yet, at the same time, she wanted to yell and scream at Spaniards for hiding their secrets. She couldn't quite put her finger on it, but there had been a shift. The simple joy that she and Cayetano had was now gone. Pleasure was as fragile as glass.

20

Madrid, España ~ septiembre de 2009

The country place that belonged to Cayetano's family was far more than Luna expected. The sprawling grounds of the rural property stretched for miles. It was less of a house in the country and more of an expansive working farm. When Cayetano said that they bred bulls, he wasn't kidding. Not only were there fields of pedigree bulls, there were stables with horses, and a large number staff going about their day jobs. There was good money in bull and horse breeding. Even the property's name – Rebelión – fit so well. It seemed the Beltrán and Morales families had defied the odds and been successful for years. No war, or dictatorships, or anti-bullfighting sentiment ever did them any harm.

Luna almost dropped her bags when she stepped through the lavish double glass doors into the entranceway. It was bigger than her living room on its own, complete with grandfather clock. A huge winding white staircase lead upstairs to the bedrooms, and beyond it were the living areas, kitchens, dining rooms, library, and even a music room. Cayetano seemed quite proud of himself when he watched her wide-eyed at the Morales property.

"Wow, this is quite a place," she said. They stood at the floor to ceiling windows that looked out over the enclosed yard, luscious and green in contrast to the dusty paddocks that were beyond it. The kids had already charged out to play on the grass between the trees.

Cayetano glanced around the living room, all white and immaculately presented. He had seen her look up at the chandelier earlier and shake her head in disbelief. "Thanks. It was a mess when my grandparents first bought it, but Papá worked hard on it. Once I took over I had it restored properly. It's an 18th century building, so pretty new, but it still needs a lot of work."

"But who lives here? No one?"

"Papá comes a lot and brings *abuelo* José and *abuela* Consuela. Technically it's their home, but they live most of the time with Papá and Mamá now, in the city. It's easier. We have staff here to run things day-to-day, and me and Sofía, or our cousins come for the weekends. It belongs to everyone. Mamá and Papá will retire out here soon, and I inherit the house in La Moraleja, so they tell me."

"Wow, La Moraleja, with all the movie stars, and footballers, and celebrities... I guess you are one of them."

"I don't feel like one of them. I like my little place in the city."

"I would love to live in the country."

"Country life is for you?"

"For sure. Sure, the streets of the city are filled with possibility, but the open spaces are lined with freedom."

"Not at Rebelión, I have 15 cousins and we can all fit in here at once. You should see Christmas gatherings. No freedom to be had, it's crazy."

"Nice, though." Luna's voice was quiet, her attention back to the children outside in the sun. "Do you have Christmas here every year?"

"Sure do, and it can be a circus." Then he remembered; Luna didn't have a family. "I mean... I do appreciate it."

"I'm sure."

"Where... what do you do for Christmas? It's only few months away."

"I take the kids to Sicily to see Fabrizio's parents, and they usually come to Valencia for Easter. Though... oh, never mind."

"What?"

"We usually also have Darren's parents come over from Australia for Christmas. I guess we won't now. It's a shame, they're good to Giacomo and Enzo. Sorry, this doesn't matter..."

Cayetano gritted his teeth. There was nothing to say here. Sure, he and Luna were together, but there were so many complications, like this morning's incident with María. "Are you all right?"

"Yeah, yeah," she dismissed him. "It will be nice to see the

Merlini's. They are nice people, even when they quiz my Italian skills. They're fantastic grandparents. They never did like Darren much, though."

"That's funny, I don't like him either."

Luna turned and threw him a smirk. "The Merlini's think no one could match their son. They would shoot you down, you know. I don't want to think about it. Christmas is months away. Maybe I will just sit at home on my own this year."

"We can't have that!"

"I have a lot on my mind, so what I will do for one day isn't an issue."

"Can I take your mind off your worries with some horse riding with the kids?"

"Prince Charming has a horse to ride? Of course he does," she joked.

"Hey, I need to rescue damsels somehow." He wrapped his arms around her waist while they listened to the squeals of the children who had found a ball to kick around.

"The problem with Prince Charming is that he had little personality or intelligence. Charm isn't enough."

"Good to know. Since I hurt my leg, my charm has disappeared into thin air as I hobble around like a cripple."

"Can you ride with your leg the way it is?"

"I should be able to ride just fine. You might have to rub me back to health later."

"Have you even ridden with a child in the saddle with you? If I was to let you ride with one of my children, and he was to fall…"

"Sure I have! My nieces and nephews love it. You can trust me."

"Let me think about it. The trouble is that I may not be able to live with myself if they got hurt."

"You can't deny them opportunities because of potential risks."

"When your life hasn't been ruined by accidents, it's easy to say."

"Don't bite at me, *preciosa*. I want to have a good day with you."

"I'm sorry. It's hard to break habits that have formed over the years."

"Come and sit out in the sun and relax. You need to relax more."

"I know."

"Can I tell you about the secret I have for you later?"

"Please!"

"I have a box of things that belonged to my grandmother, Luna. It belongs to Papá now. I'm not quite sure what is in there, but maybe if we have a look, there might be a mention of Scarlett and Cayetano."

"Your father let you have a look?"

"Sure." That lie slipped out with too much ease.

"I would love to take a look, even if there's nothing in there relevant to me. Luna's life would be interesting on its own. As long as your father says that it's fine, then I would love see what you have. I'm amazed - there could be photos."

"Mummy!" Giacomo yelled across the yard to the adults in the doorway out onto the balcony. "Come and play football!"

"Okay," she called back.

"Cayetano, come play," Enzo yelled. "Be on my team!"

"That might not be good for your leg," Luna said to him. Around the house he walked alone, but the cane was close at hand.

"Stop mothering me, woman! Even injured, I'm more agile than you."

"That's it. Now I'm just going to kick your ass for fun."

"Bring it on, enchantress. *Me vuelves loca.*"

"I drive you crazy?" she said over her shoulder as she headed in the direction of the kids. "The feeling is mutual!"

Cayetano watched her head out onto his yard with the kids. It amazed him how, after years of having the life everything thought was glamorous and free, all he wanted was what others took for granted – a home and a family. Only a disaster could derail how he felt for Luna. The fact that his father had rung him half a dozen times, wanting to know about the chest, had to remain a secret.

It was a long day before the children were finally asleep in the bedroom next to Cayetano's suite. Giacomo and Enzo all but had to be carried to the room. Luna hadn't relented and let them ride horses, but Cayetano was sure he could wear her down the next day. They had played football, walked around the property, played games with the kids, cooked dinner, and let the kids run wild through the house over the course of the peaceful Saturday. It seemed ridiculous to be so happy after only a few months, but that was how Cayetano felt. But it wasn't time for fanciful notions of having a family of his own. By the time Luna returned from tucking the boys into bed, Cayetano was desperate to open the chest that his father had kept him away from his entire life.

He ran his hands over the square chest. The old wood threatened to put a splinter in his hands. He would have to break the lock, which made him feel a little guilty. But on the rug in the living room miles from his family's home, he had no choice. His father probably had the key, but Cayetano would never get his hands on it. The lid was barely held closed anyway; a bit of force and the old lock would just give up its defence. It almost begged to have its secrets discovered.

"Is this it?"

Cayetano looked up to see Luna. "It sure is," he replied. "The boys are all right?"

"Fine. Enzo is already asleep, and Giacomo is only a moment away. Wow, that's quite a chest you have there."

Cayetano sat still for a moment, and just looked at it. Luna sat down on the rug next to him; the only sound the rare and precious rain that had started to fall. The huge windows were exposed to the outbreak, the water tapped incessantly just behind the seated pair. "I can't promise anything," he said. "I have no idea what's in here."

"Are you sure you want to open it? Was it not easier to go through it with your father?"

"The thing you need to know about Paco is that nothing is ever easy." Cayetano snuck a few fingers in between the chest and its lid. He would only to have to force it a little, and the lock would just snap. With some luck, it wouldn't do too much damage.

"Wait, where is the key?" Luna asked. "You can't just smash it open."

"I don't have the key."

Luna squinted as she looked at him. "Why didn't he give you the key? Is it lost?"

"Well... not exactly."

"Does he know you have the chest?"

"Not exactly."

"Then we can't open it!" Luna raised her voice as she spoke. "I want to see what's in there, but not if it means breaking into someone's life."

"Don't you think we deserve to know? This is my family."

"Yeah, I know that. But... your father has reasons to keep secrets. Don't we all have secrets, or problems, or things we simply want to keep to ourselves? I would be upset if I had my privacy invaded."

Cayetano slipped his fingers from the chest. "I suppose."

"For all we know, it could be a Pandora's box."

"I know the expression, but not the meaning."

"To open a Pandora's box is to spread an evil that cannot be undone. Pandora's curiosity pushed her to open a box, and she couldn't stop the evil that was unleashed by her desire to peer into something she did not have permission to open. The only thing left in Pandora's box was the angel of hope."

"The angel of hope? That sounds good."

"Maybe so, but what if evil hides in here?"

"It belonged to a young woman. How much evil could it hold?" Cayetano asked. It was too late; curiosity had got the better of him. They would forever wonder if the answers lay inside if he didn't open it. He slipped his fingers through the gap under the lid and pushed. The flimsy brass lock surrendered to his strength in an instant. The mechanism fell away and into the box itself with no resistance. It may as well not even have been there.

Cayetano opened the lid, and they both peered inside. What could a box this size possibly hold that would cause a man to hide it for 50 years? The way Paco had behaved, there was a body folded up inside. The sight of white silk greeted them. "Am I the only one who feels disappointed?" he asked.

"Yes, you are," Luna replied. She put her hand into the box and felt the soft fabric. "This is beautiful. Is it your *abuela's* wedding dress?"

"There's a photo of Luna and Ignacio on their wedding day in the library," Cayetano said. "Let's pull this dress out and take a look to compare."

Cayetano had to stand up to pull the flowing fabric from the box. Its length seemed to go on and on. He held it up to Luna while they both examined it. It seemed to be in remarkable condition. Luna had married in 1939, and it was still as white as it would have been on the day she wore it. "Suits you," he said to Luna while she held it to herself.

"Oh, don't even go there. I'm not going to be anyone's bride. I'm enjoying all this 'living in sin' stuff."

"It's good to know that I don't need to make an honest woman of you," Cayetano joked and took the dress from her. He placed it on the couch so they could turn their attentions back to the chest contents. Without the dress, the rest of the secrets were exposed. He reached in and pulled out an old camera. "Amazing," he said. "Imagine how few of these would have been around in Cuenca during the war."

"Maybe she got it in Madrid. You know what that means – there might be photographs." Luna pulled a silver hairbrush from the chest. "Wow, this is pretty. And heavy."

"I guess my grandmother had long hair." Cayetano reached inside the box and pulled out a whole pile of envelopes, bound by a single red ribbon. They were clearly addressed to Luna Beltrán Caño. "They have New Zealand stamps on them."

Luna leaned over and took a look. Sure enough, New Zealand was emblazoned the stamp along the phrase "Keep the Home Fires Burning." World War II stamps, complete with a woman hard at work. "How many strong-minded women would Luna know that lived in New Zealand?" she asked.

"I think we have just hit the jackpot. I think you should have a look, they have come from your grandmother."

Luna took the letters from Cayetano, almost afraid of what she would find. Anything could be found within these pieces of paper, maybe good news, maybe not. One thing was for certain; it seemed Scarlett and Luna kept in contact for quite some time. There were easily 50 letters in the collection. Not only did they know each other, they were friends.

Cayetano pulled out a small wooden box and opened it, to find a whole stack of photographs. "Oh, Luna," he exclaimed. "Look at these!"

Many were photos of a woman and a child; Luna and her baby, Paco. Cayetano recognised his father in an instant. Other than the grainy wedding photo in the library, it was the first time he had seen his grandmother, and he was mesmerised by her. She didn't look anything like his father. No resemblance at all. She was a small woman, petite in height and physique and gave the appearance of a very reserved woman. Her expression was sombre, a smile saved only for when she looked at her young son.

"She's beautiful," Luna remarked. She leaned against Cayetano as he very slowly looked through the photos. They were all mixed up in date order. In some Paco was just an infant, in others a boy of various ages. Some were taken on a simple, narrow street which was probably in Madrid, others taken indoors in what seemed to be a comfortable yet not extravagant home. It was only ever the two of them in the photos, so who knows who had taken the ones of Luna and her son.

"Hang on," he said and stopped at a photo. It was a wedding, and there was the dress. "This isn't Luna's wedding day." There stood a photo of a man and woman, the bride in the white dress, and a man in a simple suit. Luna was there, stood next to the bride. Next to the groom were two men and a woman, but the photo was damaged. Cayetano flipped it – Alejandro and Sofía's revolutionary wedding, 3 September, 1938. Juan Pablo, Ulrich, Scarlett, Cayetano, Alejandro, Sofía, Luna, Isabel.

"This is it!" Cayetano cried and flipped it back. "This is Scarlett and Cayetano in the photo. They were at the wedding with my whole family!"

They studied the photo but the damage done made it so that the whole wedding party practically looked like ghosts in the shot. They were ghosts – Cayetano simply didn't know these people. "Who's Ulrich?" Luna wondered.

"No idea. What's a revolutionary wedding?"

"I've heard of that. It's when the marriage isn't ordained by the church or recognised by the State. They were approved by the various unions. It was popular with anarchists during the civil war."

"How do you know that?"

"I'm a nerd."

Cayetano smiled. "There must be more photos in here. There is another box, see if there are photos in there."

Cayetano continued to sort through the photos. There were many, Luna, Alejandro, Sofía, most with Juan Pablo and Isabel alongside them at the wedding. He only glanced up when he saw Luna looking back at him, very pale all of a sudden. "What?"

Luna turned the small box she was holding and Cayetano eyes lit up like hers. There lay an enormous diamond ring, attached to a simple silver chain. "Is this your grandmother's wedding ring?"

"I suppose it could be," Cayetano replied and took it in his hands. The piece of jewellery was exquisite. He knew that Ignacio Reyes had been a wealthy man, but this... this defied all belief. Surely it couldn't be real. "The photo of my grandparents' wedding is in the library, let's go and take a look and see if this is the ring she has on her hand."

The pair moved down the hallways to the dark room. Cayetano flicked the light on, which lit up a private room filled with framed photos. A whole lifetime hung in silence on the walls. "Over here." Cayetano pointed to a set of black and white photos behind the desk that sat to one side of the room. "This is it."

Luna peered at the photo. "How is it that this has hung here and yet you don't know your grandmother? Haven't the answers about your family been here all along?"

"I was told even as a child that I was never to ask. My Mamá always insisted. After a while, you pass by and simply don't ask any more questions. Look, this isn't the dress from the box. She isn't wearing the ring either."

Cayetano and Luna both leaned close to the wall to study the aging shot. That was Luna they recognised from the pictures, dressed in a very plain dress that looked too dark in the photo to be white. On her diminutive hand was a plain band. "I think your grandmother has secrets we have just uncovered," Luna commented.

"I know what it is. Mamá told me the truth about my grandfather. Ignacio isn't Paco's natural father. Luna was already pregnant when she married him."

"Then who is Paco's father?"

"Excellent question," Cayetano replied and turned his face just a fraction, only inches from Luna's. He saw her ice-blue eyes flick to him. "You don't get it yet, do you?"

"What?" she frowned.

"My *abuela* Luna, and your *abuela* Scarlett, were long-time friends. It doesn't take a genius to work out who you were named after."

Luna's eyes drifted away from Cayetano to the photo of her namesake while she thought about it. "It guess that could be true, but Scarlett died before I came along."

"Maybe your father knew about Luna from his mother. If Scarlett wrote to Luna, then Luna must have written back. Alexander could have had the letters."

"I have everything that belonged to my mother and father. It's not much. I can assure you that I have gone through all of it for hints about Cayetano Ortega. But… you are Cayetano, like my grandfather. If I'm named after your *abuela,* could you be named after my *abuelo?"*

"This is getting weird!"

Luna nodded with wide eyes, and turned to look at some of the other photos. Many were of the man she assumed to be Paco, as he was the spitting image of Cayetano. With Paco dressed as a *torero,* the photos may as well have been Cayetano himself. Her eyes stopped at a photograph, and her eyes widened so much they started hurt. *"¡Mierda!* Shit, Cayetano… is that your father with Francisco Franco?"

Cayetano nodded and folded his arms over his chest, a subconscious defence of what was about to be said. "Papá was the greatest fighter of his generation. In the late sixties, things were going well for Paco's career."

"Well enough for the *Caudillo de España* to want to be photographed with him?"

"Sí, Franco watched Papá perform several times."

Luna shook her head. "I'm sorry, that is… just… surreal. Your father is smiling with a dictator. If my grandfather is lying in a mass grave somewhere with a bullet in his skull, it's because this man created a nation where doing that to people was allowed."

"Not everyone saw it that simply…"

"Okay, I'm sorry, did you just defend the *Generalissimo?"*

"No! No, no, no. I'm just saying that in the time period that this photo was taken, Spain was becoming wealthy, an industrialised nation. People's lives were improving."

"They were improving on the basis things couldn't get a lot worse! It's fine if you have a job that this bastard found entertaining. Women were persecuted, the concentration camps were full, all ideals or beliefs were banned, forget speaking in your own local dialect, and let's not even start on all those babies stolen by the Catholic church… and that is after the brutal war was over!"

"I might have known you would be the type to protest, *la chispa."*

"Inaction does real harm to the world."

"I know that, and all this," he gestured at the photo, "is not a case of condoning or sympathising with any regime or dictator. This is my family working with the cards they were dealt. Like you say, anyone who stepped out of line got a bullet. Sometimes you have to work with what you have."

"But why hang it on the wall?"

"My father was born to a woman who married someone she didn't love for the sake of her baby. That man was a Franco sympathiser. You and I cannot fathom what went on in her lifetime. My father was instilled with a desire to be the best, the strongest, the most successful, all by his mother. However, what we do know now is that Scarlett was obviously someone that Luna could talk to."

"Scarlett was a Republican nurse and yet friends with the wife of a Falange prick?"

"Exactly. This story has a lot left to give us. We need to read those letters."

They headed back into the living room and returned to their spots next to the chest. The ring sat in its box, and shone in the light from the chandelier above them. "I didn't know you thought that your *abuelo* ended up in a shallow grave somewhere," Cayetano commented.

Luna shrugged. "It's a big possibility. He disappeared just as the war ended. He was on the losing side. For all I know, he was rounded up, killed and dumped somewhere. Some guy will walk his dog one day and my grandfather will get dug up by the animal, and just ignored. No sweetheart or family member keeps him safe in his resting place."

"It... it's just something we don't talk about," Cayetano said. "Half the world doesn't even know the war went on here."

"I hate to think of how many people are lost out there somewhere, buried with haste, and their families still keep their whereabouts a secret. How can that be okay? How can we live in a society that hides from its own truths?"

"People are divided. They were divided before the war, and look what happened. Franco's reign heralded Spain's first ever period of peace."

"Peace? Hundreds of thousands of people were not at peace. Just because there is no war, doesn't mean there is peace. If my grandfather is lying in a ditch somewhere and I can't find him, will I ever find peace?"

"Will you find it if you do know where he is?' Cayetano asked. "Really? What will that solve? Curiosity? It wouldn't make this whole ugly situation any better."

"Do you want to help me find my grandfather, or not?"

"Of course I do. Let's not jump to conclusions is all I'm saying.

We need to read these letters from Scarlett. You want your answers, *preciosa*, then we might just have them." Cayetano picked up the box with the ring in it again and studied the diamond. "This is the biggest mystery. Why would Papá have it and keep it locked away?"

"You would think he would give it to your mother," Luna said.

"Not hide it."

"Unless it's stolen? Where the hell does a person get something that size? King Juan Carlos probably has stuff like that buried away, but few others in this country would."

Cayetano took it from the box and held it out. "Does it fit you?"

Luna took the ring from his outstretched hand with reluctance. "I don't want to know the answer. You can't wear a ring that a man has given to another woman. A ring is a circle – which makes it a promise of love that goes around forever."

"It seems that my *abuela* had it on a chain anyway, so she wasn't wearing it."

Luna held the huge ring with her fingertips and watched the light dance through its facets. "Ignacio wasn't your real grandfather?"

"No, seems not. Luna went to him already a mother."

"Then you will probably find that the father of the baby and the owner of this ring are the same man."

Cayetano looked at the ring box; the soft cushion that the ring sat in was damaged. This obviously wasn't the box that belonged to the ring. "I guess I need to decide if I want to find out who my grandfather is."

"If the answer is in here, I'm sure your father already knows. He wouldn't have all this without reading through it."

"If Paco is good at one thing, it's denial," Cayetano mused. He pulled the soft padding the bottom of the ring box out, to find a small piece of paper folded up underneath. "This might give us a clue."

"What is it?" Luna asked. She leaned over to get a glimpse of the old piece of paper that Cayetano had delicately unfolded.

"It's a handwritten note… from Cayetano Ortega."

21

Valencia, España ~ marzo de 1939

Luna almost wished she was dead like Sofía. She sat huddled up in the back of the truck, and let the rhythm of the vehicle on the rough road to Valencia toss her body back and forward. It was freezing. They had left Cuenca under cover of darkness, and taken almost nothing with them. Only what she could carry, Luna was told. All she had was her white dress, her diary, a handful of photographs and the silver hairbrush that her mother had given her. All she had was in a wooden chest of things she and Alejandro had jammed their lives into.

In the darkness, she glanced up to see the outline of her brother next to her, asleep. He lay next to the makeshift coffin Cayetano had gone in search of before they left Cuenca. She was grateful that Alejandro had found sleep at last. He had spent all day drunk, and Luna herself had drunk quite a bit. She wasn't sure how many nightmares could all come true at once; Sofía was dead, Cayetano had got Scarlett pregnant, and her baby nephew was about to set sail for Nueva Zelanda. She faced a very unknown future in an unknown city. Her father was still in Madrid and would almost certainly be murdered any day. Nowhere was safe anymore.

The truck was driven by Cayetano, with Scarlett by his side. The baby was there with them where it was a little warmer for him. Luna had told Cayetano she wouldn't marry him, but here she was, in his truck, with him and his mistress. She had no choice; Cayetano and Scarlett had helped Alejandro and the body of his wife into the truck under the cover of darkness, and if Luna didn't join them, she would be left all alone in Cuenca. She had nothing and no one. She had no choice but to clamber into the dirty old truck, and try to keep herself warm through the nights. She had no idea how long the trip would take, and didn't dare peek out into the night. The trip took two nights on the back roads through the mountains and out towards the city. Two nights freezing and dirty, no food or water. Two days without speaking to her companions who had betrayed her, or even to her grief-stricken brother, whose soul was as dead as Sofia's. The world had gone to hell. The sun may as well not come up tomorrow.

Sleep came to Luna in the cold, and when she woke, light shone through the dirty window on the back door. They had stopped. She watched her brother pull himself up and he looked at her with a frown. Luna could see the confused grief that consumed him with every breath he took.

The back of the truck opened, and there stood Cayetano. His glum expression was not welcome, but the waft of fresh air was a relief, as cold as it was. It was very early, and a fog hung in the air. "We're here," he said.

He put out his hand for Luna to come to him, and she got up from her spot. There was no way she would take his hand. She had come for Alejandro and the baby, not him. She got out next to him and ignored his gesture. She stood tall in her simple brown dress and felt the chill of the... mountain air? Valencia city was on the flat plains against the sea. "Where are we?" she asked.

"We're in the mountains outside Valencia," Scarlett said. She had appeared from around the side of the truck, with the baby in her arms. "We have been up here once before. When we brought the Medina family to Valencia, there was a surprise bombing by the German's. The family own this land up here, and they hid out for a few days before their ship came into the port. Now with them in Francia, there is nothing and no one out here."

"I didn't think we would be back here," Alejandro muttered. He jumped from the truck onto the flaky limestone rock beneath their feet.

"It's a safe place to lay Sofia to rest," Scarlett said. "This is one of the few places that peace still reigns."

"Not for long," Alejandro said as he looked out over the almond trees dotted around them. Their pink flowers had come out for the start of spring. The cloudless blue sky and bright pink flowers did nothing to his dark demeanour.

Luna looked around them. They parked next to a masía, *a large now-derelict farmhouse, its stone walls worn and weary. The area around the house had been cleared, but gorse bushes had crept in. Beyond the truck the almond and fig trees looked ready to flourish with the promise of a new season. The air was so sweet with the smell. Blue bellflowers were scattered about, and the war felt far beyond the safety of the tall white pines that surrounded them.*

"I'm sorry, we don't have long here," Cayetano said. "We should choose a place for Sofía. It's a difficult drive down the narrow road back towards the city. We have a ship to arrange."

"I can't do it," Alejandro said. "I can't bury my wife."

"I'll do it," Scarlett said. She turned and handed the sleeping infant to Luna. "I buried my own husband at Ebro, all but next to his own murderers. I can do this."

Alejandro and Luna stood together as Cayetano and Scarlett headed off with their shovels that had been tucked away on the truck. They watched them wander between the almond trees not far from the house, deep in conversation. "I can't believe this is happening," Luna uttered to her brother.

"For all our pain... for all our suffering... for all our fears and our loves and our ideals... we have nothing."

"We have the baby," Luna said. "Ale, he is your son."

Alejandro looked at the sleeping child in his sister's arms and put his arms around her. He held the three of them together. "The baby must go with Scarlett. Far away from this place. Evil lives here. Blood has poisoned the soil of our country. He must be sent away."

"Where are we going?" she asked. "Why can't he come with us?"

"I don't where we're going. Cayetano will arrange it."

"I don't want to go anywhere with him." Luna turned away from her brother to the pair who had begun to dig a grave.

"You told me that you would marry him two days ago."

"That was before I knew he had got Scarlett pregnant. He has to marry her!"

"No, he doesn't. Scarlett won't have him. She doesn't want him. I think Cayetano will take us to Francia, where the Medina's are."

Luna looked down at her hand. She still wore the Medina diamond. She wasn't sure why. "Who are the Medina family?"

"They are Cayetano's parents. His mother is Pilar Ortega, and she married Sergio Medina. He is not Cayetano's natural father. I don't know who is. Sergio took on Pilar's baby when he was young. He paid us well to get him, his wife and their other children out of España. They have a home just over the border in Francia. They are so many refugees in the area now. We could get there and blend in."

"Cayetano is rich?"

"Cayetano is aristocratic, but he doesn't fit into that life. He ran away from home pretty young. He is not right for you, Luna."

"I know, I don't want him. Please, Ale, let's take the baby with us. I can care for him."

"No, you're young. We can find you a husband. Scarlett is already ruined with the baby in her belly. She wants no man anyway, not after what happened to Ulrich. She can care for the baby."

"How can you just turn your back on him? He's Sofía's child!"

"I love him, and that's why I'm sending him away. Who knows, maybe we could send for him. Where we are going, we will be outcasts. Refugees. We have nothing. With Scarlett, he can go home with her, where there is food, shelter, warm clothes... we have none of those things. Do you think any of the children who were shipped away from España during the war were just abandoned? No, their parents loved them, all 34,000 of them."

"Can't we stay here, blend in, pretend we were never rojos?"

"They will flush us out eventually. The killing won't stop once the war is over. Who knows, maybe the misery has only just begun. We have to leave."

"I would rather be dead," Luna muttered.

"We already are. They have broken our spirits. The only difference between us and Sofía is that she can't feel the pain."

The siblings watched Cayetano and Scarlett stab the hard soil with their shovels, their faces as cold as the early morning in the frosty surroundings. They knew that this wouldn't be the only pain they would experience today.

~~~

Luna again sat in the back of the truck with her brother on the slow and bumpy ride towards Valencia city. He sat next to her, and drank out of a bottle of sherry that Cayetano had got from God-knows-where. After all they had seen, the moment that they placed Sofía in the ground was not a time for tears. The goodbyes had already been said, this was simply like mailing an envelope, which sent the goodbyes on their way. They had no idea what awaited them in the city. If only they could drive forever. If only Luna could sit there, and smell the mixture of fuel and alcohol, and let her joints get constantly jolted by the bumpy roads. They wouldn't stop. The door wouldn't be opened. The world would never come in. When they finally stopped, Luna felt dread in the pit of her stomach. Who knew what was going to happen.

The moment the heavy engine stopped, Luna could hear it; the gentle sound of water. "I know where we are," Alejandro said. He crawled over and pushed the door open and looked out; the late afternoon sun flooded into the enclosed space. "Come and see the Río Turia," he said to his sister.

Luna jumped off the back of the truck and looked around. They parked on the side of the road, hard against a small stone barrier that dropped down into the river below them. Across a bridge that beckoned nearby, there was Valencia city. The Torres de Serranos, the ancient gate to the city, stood tall at the end of the bridge. The road seemed unusually quiet around them, but the road on the other side of the bridge was busy.

"We'll leave the truck here and walk the rest of the way," came Scarlett's voice. She and Cayetano had just jumped out of the front.

"Are we going to César's place?" Alejandro asked.

"Sí," Cayetano said with a sharp, serious tone in his voice and expression. "We will see what he knows. The man can get us anything we want."

Luna looked to Scarlett, who held the baby tight in her arms. He seemed unsettled and she seemed distracted by him. There was so much to do, and she wasn't exactly maternal, that was obvious. "Would you like me to carry the baby?" Luna asked.

"Please," Scarlett said and handed the baby to her. "I did feed him a little, but he is unhappy."

"Good idea," Cayetano said. "If Luna is carrying a child, people are more likely to leave her be. Scarlett, you look scary enough, people won't approach you. Any chance you could look more pregnant? That could help."

"*¿Qué coño? How fucking stupid are you?*" Scarlett snapped. "Look more pregnant... honestly..."

"Why would anyone approach us?" Luna asked.

"Fuck knows what's going on in the city, or who is running the place now," Alejandro said as they started over the bridge. The huge stone structure of Puente de Serranos had run over the Turia river for many years, and had seen many of Valencia's battles, leading to the gate of the once-walled city, the only way in or out of the place via the road north to Barcelona. The narrow yet imposing bridge heaved with history. The Torres de Quart, the gate to Madrid, was in worse wear over on the west side of the city, especially after Napoleon's troops bombardment years ago.

They walked along in the sun, and the sounds of the bustling city ahead got louder and louder as they walked. "The problem is, the war is all but over," Alejandro said to his sister. "We are the losers. We don't have our stories straight. We can't be a few rojos and a foreign woman wandering the streets, looking for trouble. Let's just keep our heads down and see what we find."

Luna looked up at the Torres de Serranos as they walked around it. Its Gothic style was imposing and majestic; once it held the world at bay and now it was alone with the city walls destroyed. Still, the huge stone defence was a remainder of the powerhouse Valencia had once been.

"The Prado museum in Madrid put many of its most valuable artworks in there," Scarlett commented to her as they walked. "When Madrid was getting bombed, everything got shipped out here. Then Valencia got bombed. It's lucky the Serranos is still standing at all. Over 440 aerial bombings of Valencia in two years."

The group headed into the shelter of Calle de Serranos, the road that led directly away from the gate. The stone buildings were only few stories high, but down on the narrow one-lane road, they felt like protection. The road was filled with people, all dashing around as if the world was about to end. Maybe it was.

Luna trailed behind Cayetano and Scarlett, who were in no doubt about where to go. Her brother stood at her side, one arm around her as they darted around corners of streets barely bigger than footpaths. The area they walked in seemed increasingly rundown. They passed a group of gypsy girls standing on a corner; their clothes were ragged, and their cutting remarks gave no illusion to the type of morally corrupt profession they were pedaling. This was a place of survival, not life. It was only when they popped out into a small triangular plaza that had several tiny roads leading off it, did Luna look around her. Plaça de L'Angel, the ceramic tile street sign said above her head. Valencian Catalan. She had never spoken any language other than her own castellano, the main variant of Spanish in the country. Rumour had it that once Franco took over, that was the only Spanish to be spoken. Regional native languages, like Valencian, would be banned.

They stopped at the tall wooden door at the first house in the plaza, a narrow but tall building of four stories, and Cayetano banged his fist on it. "César, que es Cayetano Ortega. ¡Abre la maldita puerta! *Open the damn door!*"

The door swung open, and Luna felt overwhelmed by the heavy smell of cigar smoke. Cayetano, Scarlett and Alejandro all smoked, but that was hideous. The filthy young man gestured for them to come in, and they trailed into the very dark living area, Luna going in last. Even the baby coughed when they went into the cramped space. Smoke wasn't bad for babies, was it?

"¡Ajá, this must be the lovely Sofía!" César said, his arms out wide for a hug from Luna. "The Beltrán Perez baby has come at last!"

"No, this is my sister, Luna," Alejandro said, slumped in a chair at the tiny dining table.

"The famous Luna, the lady who holds Cayetano's heart!" César looked to Cayetano, who scowled back. Now was not the time for sharing stories of drunken nights spent talking about the fantasy girls they couldn't have.

"I am Luna Beltrán Caño, and I don't belong to my brother, or that man over there," she gestured at Cayetano, who stood into the corner of the *windowless room. She was sick of being the weakling of the group. No one would speak to Scarlett as if she was merely a companion of a man. She stood alone, and as much as Luna hated the redhead, she wanted Scarlett's independence.*

"¡Ay! *This one has the fire in her too, like my* feroz princesa," *he said to Scarlett.*

"I'm not your fierce princess, and I still won't sleep with you," Scarlett shot back. "We need information."

"You have money, I have information," César shrugged, and put his cigar in the ashtray on the table.

"I have money, if you have another cigar." She fished into her pants pocket. "Is your wife here?"

"She is upstairs, with her dying mother. I wish she would just give up and die, the old witch." César produced another cigar from a box under the table, lit it, and handed it to Scarlett who stood with Cayetano. "What do you want to know?"

"Sofía is dead." Scarlett blew smoke as she said it. "She died having the baby. It's a long story, but we needed to get out of Cuenca."

"And now, we want out of España," Cayetano added. "We need a ship."

"No ships in Valencia, not since Franco banned shipping on March 8, you know that," César shrugged. "It's why we have no food or anything here. The aid ships can't dock here. The Mar Negro is stationed off the coast, from Sagunto in the north to El Saler in the south and then south down the coast all the way to Jávea, stopping ships from coming in. The Británico ships, the Sussex and Stanhope, both tried to get into Valencia last week, but the Mar Negro and the Mar Cantábrico, they fight off any ship. They captured a ship that left port in Gandia only a few days ago. They capture cruise ships, hospital ships, freighters, they are strong. The Italian ship, the Melilla, they are close to Valencia port and are under orders to stop all ships from landing. But..."

"We have no time for games, we have women we need to get out the country," Cayetano said. He faced the floor, but his dark eyes were firmly fixed on his 'friend'. César was a slimy bastard who had his finger on every illegal pie in Valencia. If something was available for a price, César knew about it.

"The Stanland, a Británico aid ship, has just docked. Franco's high command let her through. But their immunity may be lifted as soon as they dock out, leaving them at the mercy of the Mar Negro or her sister ships. Who knows? There will be no more ships. You heard about Madrid, ¿no?"

"What of Madrid?" Luna asked. Her father was in Madrid and she hadn't got word from him.

"We have been on the road for days," Cayetano said, "high up in the hills."

"Madrid was captured yesterday. The war will be declared over in a few days. Valencia will be the last place to fall, tomorrow they reckon."

"Are troops coming in?" Alejandro asked.

"Most certainly! They're ready to control us all."

"We need to get on this Stanland ship," Cayetano said. "Can you get us on?"

"Everyone in the city wants on the Stanland!" César scoffed. "Every Republican has run to ports up and down the coast of Valencia. In Gandia, a ship was let out to sea with refugees, but then captured. Every rojo in España is now trapped like a rat. They will round us up and shoot us."

"What will it take to get on that ship, César?" Cayetano asked. He leaned off the wall and stood with his arms folded. "Any cost, any job, any lie, you know we can do it. We have helped hundreds of people out of España. Now it's our turn."

"You have left it too late, while you chased all those pesetas from your Madrid passengers," César said, and sat back with a smile. Cayetano Ortega always turned up thinking he could have whatever he wanted and this time he wouldn't get it. He would get a bullet like the rest of his type, if César didn't help him. This time Cayetano and Alejandro would have to pay more – and let César borrow Scarlett or Luna for a few minutes of pleasure. Perhaps both of them, one at a time. "Maybe you could get Scarlett on board, she is Inglés, ¿no?"

"Close enough," Scarlett quipped.

"She looks foreign, and she can speak inglés. But the rest of you.... I don't know. If the ship is captured and you're found, they will give everyone a bullet, not just the four of you."

"Then we get Luna, Scarlett and the baby on the ship," Alejandro said. "Where is it headed?"

"No!" Luna interjected. "We all go. I won't go without you, Ale."

"I don't know where the ship is bound," César said. "Maybe Marseille? Where do you want to go?"

Cayetano was staring at Luna, and she knew it. She wouldn't acknowledge it, instead jiggling the fussing baby in her arms. "Scarlett, you can take the child and we know you will be able to get your way safely to Londres and then bound for home. But Luna, what to do with you?" he said.

"I'm not going anywhere!" she cried.

"She could come with me," Scarlett said. "Once we dock in Nueva

Zelanda, we demand refugee status. They will hold her in custody, but she will be safe until I can get her cleared and free."

"I hate you!" Luna cried. Scarlett's ice-blue eyes were staring right at her, as cold as Luna's tone. "I'm not going anywhere, or giving you the baby!"

"Luna, do as I say!" Alejandro banged his fist on the small table. "Scarlett can save you and the baby. If Cayetano and I die here, then so be it!"

"We need to get down to the port right now," Cayetano said. "When does the ship dock out?"

"No idea," César said. "All I was interested in was the supplies I could get off it. Soon the black market will thrive with food for the damned."

"I need some air," Luna said, and turned away from the group. She pulled the heavy door opened and stepped out into the sun.

"Is she safe out there?" Scarlett asked César.

César shrugged. "Safe enough. Though, if she wanted to make a few pesetas, she could probably earn them in the alley around the corner."

Cayetano sighed, and went after Luna. He didn't care how much she hated him; he worried for her. He went out into the light, to find her a few houses down, cooing to the baby. She looked like a woman, not a young impressionable girl. He had no idea how he was going to convince her to get on that ship. It was their one and only hope, especially if Valencia was only a day from falling to the enemy.

"La chispa," he called, and he saw her roll her eyes. "Luna, preciosa, please come back inside."

"No," she said, defiant. "This is a failed attempt, a desperate act. I should have married Ignacio long ago. Now I would be safe with him in Madrid."

"Safe... saluting fascism, hatred, and oppression."

"Not much different to here then," she scoffed.

"Luna, come with me! I will look after you!"

Luna turned and slapped Cayetano hard across the face. "You betrayed me!" she cried through gritted teeth as she held the baby close.

"Jesús, Luna! I love you! Yes, I slept with Scarlett once, but that's no betrayal to my love for you. I sleep with everyone! I slept with César's wife one time. He was in the room, drunk and asleep! I'm sorry! But I never painted myself as an angel. You know who I am, and where I come from."

"Ale says you come from the Medina's."

"No, my Mamá, she was a whore, a mistress to a rich man. She was sold to Sergio Medina through some arrangement when she got pregnant, and they kept me. I'm no one, but if I marry you, I will be someone. All I want is you. I will take the damn baby if you want! Don't hate Scarlett, she's strong and smart and capable. She can help us. What she has done, what she has seen, who she has killed... please, don't hate her. This isn't her fault. It's not anyone's."

Tears streamed down Luna's face. There was no point in hiding them. "I'm not a kid. I'm not weak. You all treat me like an idiot..."

"No, we love you!" Cayetano said. He placed his hands on her shoulders and she tried to fight him, but he was much too strong. "Luna, now is not the time to be a strong, independent Republican woman. Now is the time that we group together and save our lives!"

"What for? None of us has a future."

"We might! Let's get the others. We will go to the port right now, and see who we can talk to about getting on board the Stanland. I know you love me, you still wear the diamond."

"Then take it back," she spat at him.

"No, I won't. It's safe with you. We aren't going to die." Cayetano thrust his lips on hers, and felt her tears against his skin. There was no way that the love they shared could be broken over one stupid incident months ago. When he let her mouth go, she looked more confused than ever. Confused was fine; it was better than mad. "We will go back to the truck, and we get down to the port. We will get out of España. If you still hate me, then so be it. I can live with that as long as you and the baby are both safe."

22

Madrid, España ~ septiembre de 2009

La chispa,
I hope the ship is offshore before you find this letter. I will find Alejandro, I promise I will. I had no idea he would run after you boarded the ship. I can't leave him behind, even though I want to be with you. I know you say you hate me, but I swear, wherever you land with Scarlett, I will find you. I will marry you. Please, don't let Scarlett's baby end things for you and me. She is happy for me to let her and the child go for good. She longs for her home now. She cannot take any more pain. But you, my preciosa, you and I have so much more to come.

I fear that Alejandro may never overcome his pain of losing Sofía, the same way I would never get over you if I was to lose your love. I know you don't agree with Alejandro's decision to give his son to Scarlett. I'm sorry for the pain this causes you, but only time will prove that the child will be better off. One day you and I can have children of our own.

Por favor, la chispa, keep the ring on your hand. It belongs to a part of a special collection of jewels that was given to my stepfather, Sergio Medina, from my father, the King. Both the King and my family are in exile in Francia. If you get in trouble, go to Sergio with the ring, and he will help you. I can't believe you have left España, and I may never see you again. I will do all I can to find you. Please remember I love you. I will always be searching for you.
Cayetano

"Jesucristo en el cielo," Cayetano muttered.

"What?" Luna asked him. "Do you know what the letter is talking about?"

"I have no idea!" he exclaimed, and waved the note in her direction. "But I know who Sergio Medina is!"

"Who?"

"Medina, as in my ex-wife, María Medina Cruz."

"Oh, come on. So what if my grandfather knew a Medina family? There will be thousands of Medina's in Spain."

"María was born in France. So was her father, Leandro. Sergio and Pilar Medina had two daughters and a son, and they went to France during the Spanish civil war. Their son, Emilio, was María's grandfather. Sergio, her great-grandfather, was given a title and money for marrying Pilar Ortega in 1915. Pilar was one of the King's mistresses. Sergio took on the baby from his friend the King, because the Queen was mad at her husband for having so many illegitimate children."

"How many were there?"

"Officially four illegitimate children, on top of the five children born to the royal couple. But they say there could be more. Pilar was one such mistress, a young maid who worked at the Palace. She and her baby were shoved out the way for a substantial price paid to Sergio Medina to make it look like it was his baby. It wasn't a well-kept secret. In fact, the Medina's are quite proud of their family's history. They have researched it all."

"My grandfather, Cayetano Ortega, was the illegitimate baby of the King's mistress?" Luna said sceptically.

"You may find you can track Cayetano down in the birth records if you look up Cayetano Medina instead. That is why you could never find Cayetano."

Luna looked at the note. "It sounds too far-fetched."

"What part? That you and my ex-wife are related? Or that your father and the King are first-cousins?"

"I'm sure many people in Spain can claim the same. There could be a thousand people who could claim some kind of connection to a royal family that has endured as long as Spain's has."

"Yeah, but first cousins? That is pretty impressive. Your great-grandfather was a King."

"And it's your wife that holds the details to my family, assuming we are correct. María, who I met just this morning and reminded me that you and her are a couple."

"Ex-wife. Don't forget the 'ex' part of that sentence. I'm sure I can work on María. Her father, Leandro, has been a fan of his family tree his whole life. I'm sure he would love to know the whereabouts of the illegitimate baby and his family."

Luna half-smiled. "You know, it never occurred to me that there would be anyone else to find. I never wondered who Cayetano's parents were, or if there were more children. I always assumed that there weren't."

"I will call Sofía tomorrow. She can check Cayetano Medina at work on Monday. No wonder the church records in Cuenca brought up nothing; Cayetano wasn't from there. He must have found his way there from Madrid when he was young."

"Why turn your back on a powerful family?" Luna said. "It could have saved his life during the war. He could have left the country early on."

"More mysteries, *preciosa*. There are still so many. It raises many for my family, too."

"Like how it seems that Cayetano and Luna were getting married and she left Spain."

"As far as I know, that never happened. When Sofía and I went to South America, like I told you about, Papá said it was the first time anyone in our family had travelled aboard."

"So, what the hell is he writing about here? He is sending Scarlett and Luna away. Scarlett seemed to be pregnant in the note. Maybe that was what broke them up."

"I see," Cayetano said. "Maybe my grandmother was engaged to your grandfather, but he cheated on her with Scarlett."

"My grandfather is illegitimate, and a jerk. Wow," Luna said matter-of-factly.

"Shit happens, we know that for sure." Cayetano leaned over and read the note again, as Luna held it gently in her fingers. It had been written in haste with a blunt pencil, and hard to read. "Oh no," he muttered.

"What? Are you looking at the part where it says that Alejandro and Sofía had a baby, but Scarlett had the baby with her on the ship?"

"Yeah, it's weird."

"It says 'Alejandro won't get over his pain'. Did Sofía die?"

"Maybe… no death record for Sofía… no birth record for the baby…"

"Add that to the mystery list."

"What… what if 'the baby' is… your father?"

"What?" Luna squinted. "No, Scarlett had a baby with Cayetano. It says right here that she was pregnant. Scarlett never hid the fact that my father was born to Cayetano, as shameful as it was during those times."

"Was she telling the truth? I mean, your father's name was Alexander…. Alejandro…. Alexander…"

"Yes! Alex was born in New Zealand. Records say so."

"Scarlett was a nurse. She would have access to be able to make fake records."

"It's New Zealand, not the fucking wild west. The records are accurate. Besides, if she had arrived in New Zealand with a baby, they would have recorded that."

"You have checked the shipping records of when Scarlett came home?"

"Well, no," Luna admitted. "I never thought it as relevant. I knew she came home in 1939 and Dad was born soon after in a small local hospital…"

"Sounds suspicious."

"No, I refuse to believe that Scarlett isn't my grandmother," Luna said. "And frankly, I'm offended you suggest otherwise!"

"Sorry, that wasn't my intention, Luna. I promise."

"Already my grandfather is the son of a whore," she muttered. "I guess you need to be careful what you wish for. Of course, we could be totally wrong. You know, my mother, Thelma, her family was completely normal and well-adjusted. None of this crazy shit."

"I hope that Scarlett and Cayetano are your grandparents! Imagine if your father was Alejandro and Sofía's baby! That would make us distant cousins. I really don't want to find that I have been having sex with my cousin for the last two months," Cayetano chuckled.

"That is exactly what you've been doing," came a deep voice.

Cayetano and Luna both looked up, with expressions like naughty teenagers. Paco Beltrán stood in the doorway to the room, with a face far more angry than the storm outside. Luna needed no introduction, it was like looking at Cayetano, 30 years into the future.

"Papá," Cayetano said as he stumbled to his feet, his leg sore from sitting on the floor. He hopped on one foot for a moment to try and feel more comfortable. "What are you doing here?"

"You've done it, haven't you?" Paco said, and approached the pair. "You stole from me, and you have gone against everything I have ever told you."

"Papá, no." Cayetano put a hand out and pulled Luna to her feet. He could see she looked nervous. She had inadvertently walked into the ongoing battle between father and son. "This is Luna. I needed your chest to help her."

"The girl you scooped up off the street?" Paco shot back. "The *mujer* who has caused so much trouble these last few months? Have you any idea of the damage you have done to my son?" he said to Luna.

"She hasn't done anything, Papá…"

"Your bloody leg, and then all the questions you have fired at me! Your mother told me that you have been sniffing around my family home in Cuenca…"

"You mean the building still belongs to us?" Cayetano chose to ignore the rest, he wouldn't dignify the accusations with an answer.

"I don't give a shit about those old buildings in Cuenca," Paco fired back. "You have betrayed me."

"I'm sorry," Luna said. She wasn't afraid of the angry man, but she really hoped he would shut up. The kids were asleep not far away.

"My mother was very important to me," Paco said to her. "All I have is a chest of her things, and it's been violated."

"But, Papá, there are photos and letters about Cayetano Ortega! That's Luna's grandfather. He and Luna's grandmother, Scarlett…"

"Luna? Luna Montgomery?" Paco interrupted his son. "You're Scarlett's daughter… granddaughter? Of course, just look at you. You have the eyes."

"My grandmother died before I was born," Luna said tentatively. "I have never seen a photo of her."

Paco leaned forward, and grabbed another small box from inside the chest. He ripped it open, and photos fell from his hands. He grabbed one and thrust it at her. "Look, that's Scarlett," he said. It was almost some kind of accusation. "It's like looking in a mirror."

Cayetano and Luna held the photo. The picture was black and white, but her hair practically glowed in the picture. It must have been fire-red. Her eyes were eerie in the black and white photo, they looked almost translucent; that was where Luna's ice-blue eyes came from, just like her father before her. "Oh my God," Luna muttered. She was the spitting image of Scarlett Montgomery. Now she was real; she was not just a story, but a woman who ran to Spain for her ideals and went home a troubled single mother.

"That woman, that scheming redhead, destroyed my mother's life," Paco said. "Mamá was in love with a man and Scarlett stole him from her."

Cayetano and Luna shared a look. "She told you that?" Cayetano asked.

"*Sí,*" Paco replied. His tone was so bitter, so angry at a person he never knew. "Cayetano Ortega was going to marry my mother. She loved him so such. She cried every night in her bed. He abandoned her. He took her to Valencia, to protect her when the war ended, and instead he left her in the port, and disappeared. Scarlett turned and went home, and my mother had nothing."

"So, Cayetano was never your uncle, like you told Mamá."

"No, Alejandro was my uncle. Another loser."

"He had a baby? Scarlett took his baby?"

"She tried."

"Where is the baby now, Papá?"

"The baby died very young, my mother told me. So no, Luna, your father is not the baby of Alejandro and his wife."

"No, she is part of María's family. Cayetano is the illegitimate baby of Pilar and the King. Did you know that all this time? You knew María's family always looked for him."

"Yes, I knew," Paco sighed. "I didn't want to tell anyone. I didn't want anyone to know that my mother was in love with a *bastardo* like him."

"So, you lied the whole time I was married to María?" Cayetano fired back.

"I never should have let you marry into the Medina's. It's wrong. Dirty. Like this Luna is!"

"Hey!" Luna spoke up. "I realise this is very ugly, but you can't be rude to me, no matter how much Scarlett hurt your mother."

"Rude? Like you have been? Going through my private things?" Paco said right in her face.

"Damn it, Papá, it's also my family here. It's Luna's family in this box. She doesn't know them. You hold the answers to everyone's lives in your chest and you are in the wrong!" Cayetano yelled.

"You don't want to know the truth!" Paco said. "I should never have let you marry María, and now, with this girl, now I have no choice but to tell you the truth."

"What, Papá?" Cayetano asked, his arms now folded over his chest. This was all too overly-dramatic and ridiculous. "What happened?"

"My mother went to Valencia when the war ended," Paco said, his voice now steady. "Instead of helping her, Cayetano and Alejandro abandoned her there. Scarlett got on a British ship and left her trail of destruction behind. My mother had nowhere to go. She managed to find a phone she could use, and she only knew one number, the house of Ignacio Reyes, where her father was. She rang him, and he was able to tell her where to go to see a friend of his. They arranged to get her to Madrid. Spain was undergoing huge change, and Ignacio was the only one who would help her. These people who claimed to be friends and family, and a lover…. no one cared. Her father, Juan Pablo, was murdered before Luna arrived in Madrid. He got flushed out by troops and killed, to be made an example of what the new government and regime was capable of doing."

"And she married Ignacio to be safe?"

"Ignacio Reyes was gay," Paco said. "That was illegal under Franco. Luna provided a cover for him and he kept her safe. She produced a baby, and Ignacio was listed as the father, for their mutual protection. When Ignacio died a few years later, Mamá was rich and able to raise me."

Luna took a deep breath, and a shudder came from her lungs. "Cayetano Ortega is your father," she said to Paco. "Isn't he?"

"He was," Paco said, his voice now quiet. He had never said that out loud, not even to his own wife in 40 years of marriage.

Cayetano looked to Luna. That was the moment his heart broke. More broken than it had ever been before. "Our fathers are brothers," he mumbled and she nodded. "We are cousins. We are family."

Tears had come to Paco's eyes. "It was all right for you to marry into the Medina family, even though I am member of it myself," Paco said to his son. "You only share a great-grandmother with María. It wasn't enough of a connection to be a problem. I saw you with María Medina, and I thought... this was it... this was the connection I would have with my father. At last. It was like a sign."

"That was why you pushed me to marry María like you did," Cayetano said. "It was good for you." His voice had started to shake. He was the one who felt betrayed. But none of that mattered; he already knew that the potential life he could have with Luna was over.

"I'm sorry," Paco whispered. He had never cried in front of his son. "But if this girl is Scarlett and Cayetano's *nieta...*"

Luna shivered. All of a sudden this whole thing seemed so dirty. They were covered in the shame of actions that were already 70 years old. Their lives and their troubles had been left a secret, only to hurt people later on. Her eyes drifted back up towards Paco. He was her beloved father's brother. She searched of some kind of resemblance. They were born to the same man, yet there was nothing. Both Luna and her father had taken after Scarlett, and Paco must have taken after his mother. There was no point in searching for a connection; there was none.

"Papá," Cayetano said, and swallowed hard. "How sure are you of this?"

"I'm very sure. Mamá wanted to marry Cayetano, and she loved him. There was no doubt. She left him because he had got Scarlett pregnant. Cayetano had admitted it to her, there was no doubt that the baby belonged to him. Scarlett wrote to Mamá for years, and Mamá never wrote back. Not once. The pain was too much, but Scarlett tried so hard."

"Have you read these letters?" Luna asked.

"You can read them, but you won't find anything in there what I haven't told you. But no, I never read any of it."

Cayetano was just... aghast at the situation. He looked at Luna, and she looked as mortified as he did. They were cousins. First cousins. He looked back at his father. "If you weren't such a liar... it would... it..." He couldn't say it. He couldn't tell his father that he could have prevented him having sex with his own cousin, even though Paco already knew what was going on.

"If I had known she was Scarlett Montgomery's girl, I would have told you sooner."

"I think I need to go," Luna said with great hesitation. "I think that you two need to sort this out between you. I'm going to wake up the children. I need to go."

"No, no, no," Cayetano pleaded when she turned away from him. He pulled her back by her elbow, and saw the pained look on her face. "No, stay here. The boys are asleep. Please."

"You have children here?" Paco asked.

"Yes. Luna has two sons, and she never lied to them about who their father was," Cayetano said. "They won't have horrible lies thrown at them, no hidden agendas, no deceitful, selfish, manipulative demands placed on them."

"You need time with your father." Luna pulled her arm from Cayetano's strong hand.

"It's the last thing I bloody want!' Cayetano cried. "I still, after this time, don't get why you kept this a secret!"

"The world was different place back then!" Paco tried to convince him. "People were being killed for their beliefs. A hiding Republican woman, and her gay Nationalist husband, they were scared! I grew up in a house of fear! Even when I was 20 when my mother died, she was still scared! She begged me never to tell anyone the truth, because she was afraid it would come back to hurt me. I promised her when she was dying that I would stay quiet."

"You never had to lie to your own family," Cayetano said. "None of us would have done anything with the information, and it's useless anyway! We have nothing to be afraid of now."

"You are young, you don't understand," Paco replied. "I'm glad of that fact. As far as I could see, it would do no harm to lie."

"Well, it has. It has done me a lot of harm. I'm now in love with a woman…" Cayetano turned to Luna. She had tears in her eyes, but she refused to let them fall. "I'm in love with a woman I now can't have. Your mother's secret will condemn me to the same lonely life she had."

Paco turned his attention to Luna. She looked so small next to the two of them as they yelled at one another. He had seen her fire up a moment ago, though – the woman must have had some of Scarlett in her. "Luna, would you like me to drive you back to Madrid to catch the train?"

"Oh, great," Cayetano scoffed, "now you want to play uncle, do you?"

"You're my uncle," Luna muttered. She looked at Cayetano. "I don't know why, but that makes it weirder. I have no family."

"You do now," Paco replied.

"One I will never be able to know. I don't want to know. Why, if your mother loved Cayetano so much, are there no photos in the piles?"

"There is only one," Paco said. He leaned into the box, and pushed aside the numerous papers and bits and pieces in there. He pulled a framed picture that had been placed upside down on the bottom of the chest, and handed it to her. "This is Cayetano Ortega."

Luna held the photo in her hands and took it in. "I know where this is," she said. "I recognise the buildings in the background. It's the *edificio de reloj* in the Valencia port, the clock tower. It used to be for tickets, and waiting rooms, all that kind of thing for the port. The huge building, there behind all the crowds of people, is one of the *tinglados*, the sheds used for various different activities. Both buildings are there now. I guess this was taken at the port when Scarlett left."

They all looked at the picture. A photo taken in a moment where he seemed not to know he was being watched, but even so, his stature was tall, strong, confident. He looked pensive, a face dominated by a deep frown and a stiff jaw. Like a man who knew he was about to lose everything. He had thick curly black hair, without the typical very short cut of the time. Both of his grandchildren had inherited Cayetano's Ortega curls. What an awful thought.

"Can I pick up my mother's things now?" Paco asked.

"I'll do it, Papá," Cayetano snapped. "Please, can you just leave us? You have done enough damage. Happy now?"

"Of course I'm not happy," Paco said. His deep voice had begun to shake in anguish again. "Why would I have ever thought that this day would come? Scarlett went to the other side of the world. Who would ever consider something like this happening?"

Luna frowned; she could hear crying down the hallway. All the yelling had woken one of the boys. No one ever wanted to wake in the dark of a strange room to hear angry voices. "I'm going to get the kids up," she said. "We need to leave, it's not our place to be here anymore."

Cayetano watched her leave the room, and wiped the tears from his face. He didn't care what his father thought of him crying over a woman. "Have your damn chest," he said, and went after Luna.

Cayetano stopped Luna just as she went to open the bedroom

door. He gently pulled her away and into his bedroom across the hallway. "Luna, please, you don't need to leave."

"I think we do. I think enough has happened here tonight."

"We haven't even heard half the story! What if Papá is wrong?"

"What if he's right?"

"So, what, you are just giving up on me?"

"Look me in the eye and tell you don't find the concept of you and I sleeping together and being closely related as utterly disgusting."

Cayetano couldn't do that. It was a sickening thought. He had plenty of cousins, and the thought of laying a hand on them would never enter his mind. "We are only half-cousins…"

"Meaning?"

"Maybe no one will ever find out."

"We know; we will always know. I want to go back to Madrid, please. I need to stop Enzo crying."

"Let me drive you back to Valencia," Cayetano stopped her. She wiped the tears off her pale cheeks. "Please."

Luna stepped past him and crossed the hallway, and opened the children's door. "All right," she muttered. Her heart felt heavy in her chest. She didn't want to give him up. She had only had the information a matter of minutes, but already, they both knew that the happy future their minds had been entertaining was never going to happen.

23

Valencia, España ~ octobre de 2009

Luna coughed while she sat in the dark of her living room. It was an unusually cold October night in Valencia. Once the boys were asleep in their beds, she sat down on the couch with a bottle of wine and Fabrizio's ashes. Cuddling something as basic as a varnished box seemed ridiculous, but as night crept up on her, it felt more comforting. She had done it many times before, to let her tears fall onto the dark brown box while she held it. It didn't matter how often she spoke to her husband, there was no relief from her pain. Not once.

"*Non ho dimenticato il mio italiano,*" she said to herself in the dark. I haven't forgotten my Italian. She only spoke it for her husband. She missed the sound of his voice, the brisk way he spoke in his mother tongue. He had painstakingly taught her Italian, and also Spanish once they moved to Valencia. Fabrizio had taken such loving care of his family. Luna had been so blissfully happy. One thing always remained in her mind, though – she was never his equal. That was the difference between Fabrizio and Cayetano – when she was with Cayetano, he treated her like the most precious thing in the world, a force to be reckoned with, a woman who he was lucky to have, and wanted to get to know. That had gone forever, just like her husband.

"I miss you," she said to the box. "You were so good to me, and now I don't know what I'm meant to do for the rest of my life." Luna had said that to the box a thousand times before. How was she supposed to live on her own? How was she supposed to raise sons with no father? In stronger moments, which became more and more often as time passed, she could hold her head up and tell herself that she could manage, but on dark, lonely nights, the doubt crept in. The dependence on him crept in.

"I've made such a stupid mistake," she whispered. "I did something so stupid." She couldn't say it out loud – I fell in love with another man. Not only that, she told him that she loved him. She let him into Giacomo and Enzo's lives. Now, combined with losing her job, she had nothing. Luna was a fool to think she was over Fabrizio – she wasn't. It was still too soon. The third anniversary of his death was fast approaching, and she feared she would never get over what had happened to her Italian prince. She would never accept it, never come to terms with it, never stop being angry. Falling on her face with Cayetano only served to remind her that things were never going to be okay.

Luna glanced at the coffee table between her and the full-length windows that separated her isolation from the dark park across the street. Her bottle of wine was empty, and she was drunk. Luna could do many things, but hold her drink was not one of them. She had a rule - she could only drink if there was a sober adult in the house. She and Darren took turns at being able to have a glass of wine over dinner, if they so desired. There always needed to be a sober adult in case of an emergency with the boys, Luna always insisted. But now Darren wasn't here anymore. She had driven him away over a man she could never have. She couldn't blame him for being so hurt.

Luna placed the ashes box down on the coffee table and reached out for her bag that sat on the armchair. She pulled out her phone and looked at it; the bright screen hurt her eyes in the dark. *Come to me, Cayetano, let's run away. No one will ever find out.* She couldn't say that. He was her cousin, their fathers were brothers. Half-brothers. None of that stopped how she felt about the man she hadn't spoken to in three weeks now. He had driven her and the boys back home to Valencia, barely a word spoken between them. Since then, she had wanted to talk to him, but there was a sense of shame in it. They couldn't be together anymore, and that meant they couldn't even speak. He hadn't called her, not once. He must have felt the same way she did.

I'm drunk. That was all the message she sent said. She must have been drunk to write something that pointless and send it off. Luna tossed the phone on the coffee table and picked the ashes box up again. The thought of sitting home alone and depressed again was a scary thought. But having sex with your own cousin wasn't exactly a terrific way to move on with your life. Making love to your cousin. Passionate love. She shivered in the dark; when Luna made a mistake she certainly went all out. She didn't only hurt for the life she had lost with Fabrizio, she was hurting for the life she had imagined with Cayetano that she wouldn't have. She was ashamed of herself for the fact. She should have only thought of Fabrizio. *You are not meant to get over your great love. You are not meant to fall in love a second time. You betray one man by loving another.*

It wasn't long before Luna heard the sound of keys in the front door to her apartment. She didn't bother to turn in her seat when she heard the door open and close. A tiny bit of light pierced the dark with the flick of the lamp out in the entranceway. "I'm drunk?" Darren's voice said behind her.

Luna glanced up when he rounded the side of the couch to stand in front of her. She watched him sigh as he looked at her with the ashes on her lap, with the weight of life's disappointments on her slumped shoulders. "Yep."

Darren shrugged off his coat and tossed it on the armchair. "What happened to one sober adult?"

"It's hard to do when you're on your own, and such an asshole that you have no choice but to drink because you fucked your whole life up."

Darren sat down next to her, and looked at the box in her hands. "What's the matter?"

"I'm here in the dark, thinking of all the stupid things I have ever done. Like yelling at you and kicking you out of the house."

"I hit you. I deserved it," Darren said. "I didn't expect to hear from you any time soon."

"Where have you been?"

"At Santiago and Abril's place around the corner. I will clear out the rest of my stuff here soon. I'm going back to Australia."

"What?" Luna turned to him with a frown. "You love it here!"

"Only for a holiday. It will be warm down there, and I can relax while it's the off-season for riding up here. I haven't been home in a while. My family will wonder why the woman of my dreams never came along."

"Because she doesn't deserve you," Luna mumbled. "The kids miss you."

"I miss them. Very much so."

"They have no idea what's going on. I didn't know what to tell them."

"Leave their innocence alone." He tucked his arm around her and let her lean against him.

"Life does make a habit of sucking out the innocence of our existence."

"It does for us."

"The innocence of the past is like a whisper in a dream."

"But do you wish to be the woman you used to be?"

"I wasn't a woman, I was a girl. A girl swept along with whatever she liked. "Finding I was pregnant ended that carefree existence."

"But look what you have."

"I know, I know, I don't regret it at all. I never have. I had twin boys, to my husband who I adored so, so much. I don't wish my time over again."

"What has happened makes you who you are."

"Tough lessons to learn," she sighed. "Who would have imagined that ten years ago, Fabrizio would be dead and we would be like this."

"Imagine what we will be like in another ten years."

"Giacomo and Enzo will be teenagers, and you will have won the Tour de France."

"Thanks for your optimism! What about you?"

"I have no idea."

"That's the beauty, Lulu. You can be anything. You still have a lot of life ahead of you, no matter what you have already been through."

"It's hard to imagine a future."

"Isn't that what an affair with a married bullfighter is for?"

"There's no affair. Not anymore."

"I see," Darren said softly. "So you aren't missing Fabrizio as usual. This is a new problem."

"It's me full of regret for making a big mistake." It hurt to say it; it wasn't a mistake, it was a disaster. She loved Cayetano and didn't want to admit it to Darren. "I'm sorry."

"I couldn't believe it, you know. You have been seeing someone else and didn't even tell me. Here I was, with you and the boys, and you are off with a guy you barely know, and having him around the kids as well."

"I didn't know what to say to you at the time, that's why I kept it quiet."

"I was in love with you. Always have been."

"I know. But I wasn't single until now."

"I know, trust me, I know. I watched you marry Fabrizio. I saw you have kids with him. I saw you go through hell with his death. I couldn't say a word after he died. I held off because I thought you weren't ready to move on yet. The right time didn't come. Then all of a sudden you started a fling with a man you didn't know."

"I did something that was out of character. And for the first time in a while, I felt alive."

"Was it that the rest of us were not enough anymore?"

"Of course not," Luna replied and she turned to face him. "I'm not saying what you have done for me and the kids isn't enough. It always was. Cayetano didn't know who I was. He didn't look at me with pity. Poor broken Luna, everyone needs to hold her hand. I was just me, not the single mother, not the widow. A woman."

Darren nodded as he listened. "I did what I thought was the right thing to do."

"And you did everything right." Luna paused and saw the defeated look on his face. "You know, there were plenty of times after Fabrizio died that I thought about moving on… with you. I thought about it a lot. When you were with me, even more when you were away…"

"I have been with you most of our adult lives. I know everything about you. I was there for all the key moments for the boys. After Fabrizio passed away, I considered the boys my sons. I considered you my girlfriend. I never even looked at another woman because I had a family."

"I feel as if I have cheated on you."

"You have been, in a weird kind of way."

"Yeah, I have. I had feelings for you, but I slept with Cayetano anyway."

"But you didn't pick me."

"I'm not picking anyone. It's time for me to make a change in my life. It doesn't include Cayetano."

"But you and I, we're too complicated."

"I guess we both just need to move on."

"We have broken up, haven't we?"

"We have, and it's slow and painful. But at least it's over." Luna lifted her head from his shoulder to look at him. He sat steady as she leaned forward and kissed him on the lips, a slow and gentle kiss which he gratefully responded to. She wrapped her arms around him, and the two of them sat in silence.

"Lulu, you get depressed and soppy on alcohol."

"Yep, I do," she sighed. "Do you want to stay the night?"

Darren paused for a moment. "Okay, yeah. I can see Giacomo and Enzo in the morning."

"When did we become adults?"

"Around the time you were a single mother of two and I felt the need to be your hero. Hey, how about a night out?"

"What, now?"

"Why not? I can go and see if Lucía is home across the hallway. You know she loves the kids and offers to babysit."

"Poor girl needs the cash."

"And the boys are fast asleep. They will never know the difference. How about you and me head into the old town? A few of the guys are there tonight, maybe we can meet up with them."

"I don't know," Luna groaned. She hadn't been out for an evening out in the Carmen district in a long time. She had drunk enough wine for it to sound like a good idea.

"Come on, how bad could it be?"

24

Valencia, España ~ octobre de 2009

The evening never had a chance. Only a few hours ago she told Darren how much she didn't want her old life back, and now Luna stood with him in a little bar deep in the Barrio del Carmen, the historical quarter in the heart of Valencia's old town. They were surrounded by his cycling teammates, all happy to be finished work for the Christmas break. It was just after midnight, so the area was just winding up, the bar full with people.

"That face is too beautiful to be sad," Darren said to her.

Luna glanced over and threw him a look. The tiny place was full, and the pair stood shoulder to shoulder among the noisy crowd in the dark building. "Very funny."

"Come on, you got dressed up, got Lucía to babysit, let's have a good time! Don't we deserve a little happiness now and then, even if it's just a night out for drinks?"

Luna playfully saluted her friend as he disappeared off through the crowd. She couldn't deny that the wine in her system relaxed her. She shrugged; her top slipped on her thin frame. It was backless and just hung on her. It wasn't a great choice at this cold time of the year, but it made her feel feminine. After losing so much weight when Fabrizio died, she had finally started to get a figure back, and why wouldn't she be able to show it off? She was single now, and a single girl could do whatever she liked.. She would rather be dressed casual, tracking down Cayetano Ortega, wherever he might be buried.

"Looking stylish tonight, Mrs. Merlini."

Luna rolled her eyes. Paul was one of Darren's lead-out riders during his disappointing Tour de France campaign a few months ago. First-class wanker. "Hello, Paul."

"You haven't said a word to anyone," he slurred. The red-faced Englishman never could hold his drink. "I hear that you're coming back to work with us."

"Oh, that is just a rumour." Luna looked past Paul in Darren's direction. Now, when she needed his company, he had caught the eye of the girl at the bar?

"You always did such a fantastic job as a mechanic on Fabrizio's gear. He was always a happy man."

"He was an excellent, fully-committed rider who rode to his full potential instead of cutting corners and getting drunk too often."

"Being able to screw the mechanic probably helped."

"You would have seen nothing but professionalism from me when I worked for Fabrizio." The guy begged for a kick in the *cojones*.

"Shame, because I have something that would benefit from your hands, polishing my 'gear'." Paul gave her suggestive cock of the eyebrow with a sleazy smile.

"Come on, Paul. I bet the only time any of your 'gear' gets polished, it's done by your own hand."

"Don't be so stubborn. If you aren't giving it away to Darren, there's no reason why you can't share it around."

"Excuse me?" Luna cried. "Who the hell do you think you are?"

"It might hurt a little to start with, but you'll get used to it."

"Yeah, I bet rapists say that."

"Cock tease."

Luna smiled just a little when she saw Darren reach out and grab Paul by the shoulder, and yanked him away from Luna and through the crowd. He was just in the nick of time. He returned a moment later, one annoying Englishman lighter. "Thank you."

Darren held his fist up, and she jabbed hers against it with a smile. "You're welcome," he replied. "Got some food up by the bar, if you like."

"Close to the girl behind the bar?" she asked with a cheeky smile.

"Ha! Knew I could make you jealous," he joked as they made their way through the crowd.

Luna sat down on one of the stools and looked at the plates laid out. Standard tapas fare – patatas bravas, jamón and calamares.

"Another drink?"

"I have had quite a lot already."

"In that case," he said in her ear, so she could hear him over the chat going on all over the small place, "an Agua de Valencia it is."

"Just the orange juice and sugar would be too much, never mind the cava, the vodka and the gin!"

"Oh go on," he laughed. "I'll join you."

"Only if it's really cold," she yelled to him as he slid his way down the bar toward the perky young barmaid.

"What the fuck?"

Luna turned and fixed her cold gaze on Paul, who had returned.

"*¿Qué quieres?*" she spat at him.

"Don't use that shit with me."

"You've lived here for years, dickhead. Surely you speak some of the language. And surely women have yelled 'what do you want?' at you before, you dodgy fuck."

"Darren just told me to stay away from you… but it's only because he's fucking you himself, isn't he? All this innocent friends shit is just that. Fucking bullshit. Or are you still giving it away to that bullfighter we saw you with in that magazine?"

Luna was off her bar stool in a flash. Paul didn't move an inch, not ready for the right hook that swung at him. His nose made a horrid crunch just before his whole frame hit the floor in a heap. Suddenly the group of people around Luna had all turned to see the small woman drop the sportsman to the sticky floor.

Luna pushed her way through the crowd and out the front door; the cold air surrounded her the moment she stepped out onto the street, amongst the cheers from some of the revelers. She dodged those smoking on the narrow path and headed away, angry at herself. As she rounded the corner of the old building, she heard Darren call her name, but she didn't want to talk to him either.

She turned off the street into a small triangular plaza, oddly devoid of people in this bustling and eclectic part of the city. She glanced up at the ceramic street sign on the building above her. Plaça de L'Angel. She felt so terrible that some divine intervention would be good. It was bloody freezing! Drunk and out alone in the middle of the night. Still giving it away to that bullfighter. Luna couldn't even deal with that in private. Everyone looked twice at her since that photo got published. So fucking what if she had an affair. It was about time she was able to do as she pleased. She was entitled to do as she pleased. Luna didn't realise how much of a burden having an unimpeachable reputation was until she had lost it.

Luna fumbled with cold fingers in her pocket of her jeans for her phone. No amount of wine would hide that fact she was freezing, but it did have enough power to make her consider calling Cayetano. And say what? She stared at the black screen; weeks had passed and he hadn't contacted her at all. That hurt.

I miss you

A lousy message, but still, it said all it needed to. She leaned back on the cold wall behind her and looked up at the irritating orange streetlight overhead. Who knew where he was, or if he ever wanted to see her again. But only a moment later the thumping of nearby music got interrupted by the sound of her phone beeping back at her.

I miss you, too. I love you
You love me enough to never talk to me again?
I want to see you, but I will want you and I can't have you
He wasn't alone on that. *I don't think we can be just friends*
I don't know what to do
Are you angry at me?
No! I'm angry at the world. I want to be with you
I kept picking up the phone, not knowing what to say
I don't know what to tell you

The conversation halted. No more drunk texts; now he wanted to talk. "Hello?"

"Marry me." Cayetano's voice was strong and serious. "I agree that it's not ideal over the phone... but there it is. Marry me."

"What?" Luna scoffed. "I'm not ready for that. No... we can't."

"We can! As far as the world knows, Ignacio Reyes is my grandfather. Cayetano Ortega is yours. No one will ever know. Come to Madrid with me. It can be the four of us."

"And the whole country with one eye on you and your life," Luna said.

"To hell with my career. It doesn't give me half the pleasure that you do! So what if we're half-cousins!"

"If it didn't matter then you wouldn't have had any hesitation in contacting me since your father told us the truth about who we are."

"I'm in love with you!"

"And I'm in love with you, but the world has gone to hell!"

"What do you want me to say, Luna? If there was anything I could do to change it, I would. Come to Madrid. Or I'll come to you. I want to see you. We can't just not speak to each other."

"I know."

"Are you going to answer me?"

"What?"

"Will you marry me?" Cayetano heard nothing but a long pause. "No, then."

"I… you're married! I just met you."

"Either you love me, or you don't."

"I do, but it's not that simple, and you know it." The two of them said nothing; there was nothing to say.

"I guess I will go back to my meeting then," Cayetano barked.

"Sorry."

"So am I."

Luna looked at her phone; just like that he was gone. She had hurt his pride. He proposed, and she said no. That couldn't have gone any worse. She looked up when Darren appeared around the corner.

"Lulu! There you are! What the fuck happened?"

"Oh… that… Paul got a bit mouthy at me, and I got a little… punchy."

"Punchy," Darren chuckled. "Come on, let's go home."

Luna was more or less asleep when Darren dragged her up to the apartment and let the babysitter go home. "Right, you," Darren said as he pulled her down the hallway. "Bed."

"No," Luna sighed. "Another night in my marital bed, lying in there alone. I want to sleep with you, in your bed."

"Is that wise?"

"I'm not doing it to be wise."

Darren smiled when he watched Luna slump down on his bed. He pulled the covers out from under her and laid them over her still-clothed body when he jumped in next to her. He lay back on his pillow and sighed.

"What are we going to do with you, Miss?" he asked into the dark.

"I'm going to move out," she mumbled. "I'm going to leave the city. I will get a job, and hope I can get my work permit renewed. It seems my grandfather was probably murdered somewhere and has been forgotten. He's no help to me. I'm going to get myself together… tomorrow… when the wine goes away."

"I can still marry you if you need me to, to help you out."

"Please, the last thing I want is to be married…" she whispered. After all, she would never love anyone again. The thought of loving someone ever again was too much to bear. Luna fell asleep with tears in her eyes, and Darren's arms around her.

25

Madrid, España ~ octobre de 2009

"There you are," Miguel said to Cayetano.

Cayetano tossed his phone on the coffee table that sat in the middle of his living room, and looked around. His father sat there, with his familiar frown. Miguel sat next to him, and Hector, Eduardo and Alonso were also dotted around the room. All of his cousins were involved in the Morales breeding business. They were the inner circle who made a living off Paco's legacy, and Cayetano's fighting skill and sponsorship pulling power. Just what his mood needed – everyone's opinion on his professional life on a night when he couldn't be bothered to talk about work at all.

"Can't a man make a phone call?" Cayetano said, slumping down into his armchair. The bottle of whiskey needed to come a bit closer. Between the six men, a lot of alcohol had already been consumed.

"When do you go back to the physiotherapist?" Alonso asked his older cousin.

"A few days," Cayetano mumbled. "The leg is fine."

"Will you come up to Rebelión this weekend?" Miguel asked. "If you like, we can get you into training."

"Not a good idea," Eduardo interrupted his cousin. "I think more gym work should come first. Have you been monitoring your weight, Caya?"

"Yes, Mamá," Cayetano teased him. "You boys all know I'm an adult, ¿no?"

"And we are your managers, and trainers, and assistants, and stylists…" Paco added.

"Don't remind me, Papá." Cayetano gestured to the bottles of Cruzcampo on the table, and Alonso passed him one. Not his favourite beer on the market, but in times like this, you take what you can get.

Eduardo glanced at his watch. 12:30. "Anyone interested in dinner? I know a place that opens at one."

"Yeah, I know the place you mean. The one you can't get into unless I make a phone call on your behalf first," Cayetano scoffed.

"Is it a crime to want to go and hang out with Madrid's most beautiful?"

"I'm sick of all these early nights since my accident," he admitted.

"There you go," Hector chimed in. "Maybe we need a night out. We haven't been out in a while."

"It keeps you out of trouble," Paco said.

"You're jealous because *tía* Inés will be at home, ready to give you trouble if you have a night out," Alonso said to his uncle.

"There's a reason why your wife left you, boy," Paco replied. "I'm the one married for 40 years. You can't tell me about women."

"Women… who needs them," Hector commented.

They all looked at their gay cousin. "We do!" they all cried back.

"What happened to that woman you were kissing in Cuenca, Caya?" Alonso asked.

"That subject is off-limits," he said, with a voice full of authority.

"Like the subject of your divorce? How long do we need to keep that a secret?" Eduardo asked.

"Don't hassle him about the girl. She was pleasant enough but just…" Paco started, unable to think of what to say.

"You know her too, *tío?*" Miguel asked Paco. "Must be serious."

"No, I don't know her, or her little ones. I just…"

"Wait, kids?" Alonso asked. "Caya, what have you been doing? Never date a single mother. They get serious too fast, having to think of the kids instead of having a good time."

"And they want a new Papá for the kids," Eduardo added. "And they moan about their ex, and want to go on kid-friendly dates…"

"Shows how little you know," Cayetano said to the group, and sipped his beer. "Besides, I like kids. Eduardo, I babysit for you and Elena all the time. I don't want to date some young, single girl who wants a fun time. I've had too many of those."

"So, where is this girl?"

"Don't bother my boy," Paco interjected.

Cayetano threw his father a look. He knew Paco didn't want to defend him, he wanted make it all disappear. "She's gone."

"As your image consultant, I think that may be for the best," Hector said.

"Image consultant," Cayetano muttered to himself. That was Spain – jobs for the boys. Finding a job for his gay cousin who hated bullfighting had been tough, until he needed help with his clothing and presentation when promoting for sponsors. That was when his assistant, Hector, came into his own. Alonso and Eduardo had wanted to be *toreros* once themselves, but that role was for Cayetano, and they were relegated to remaining banderilleros and picadors, Cayetano's entourage in the ring. They also took over their father's role in the Morales business, and now worked for their uncle Paco, just like Miguel did.

"We haven't talked about why we're here," Miguel said.

"I thought this whole fight thing in Valencia in March was all arranged," Cayetano said. "I will make my comeback in the ring then, so what else is there to discuss?"

"Las Fallas is a deeply traditional Valencian *fiesta*. Is it wise to have Caya there for that? We are Madrileños," Eduardo said.

"Las Fallas is popular. I think it's a powerful reason to be there, no matter where we come from. Who cares if it's in Valencia?"

"Watch out; next he will be marching in support of autonomous regions of Spain."

Cayetano rolled his eyes. "Oh calm down. It's not as if I said I want to go into the Basque Country, or in Catalonia were they are about to ban fighting. Valencia isn't like them, they're not pushing to be independent as much as other places. Spain is Spain. We're always going to argue amongst each other. I love Valencia, and I see you lot all lying on the beach at El Saler just south of the city every summer."

"I holiday there," Alonso said. "I'm proud to be from Madrid."

"So am I." Cayetano put his empty beer bottle on the floor next to his chair. "But I like Valencia."

"When was the last time you were there?" Miguel asked.

"Not long ago, but I don't get out there as often as I would sometimes like."

"Maybe there is nothing there for you anymore," Paco said. His voice was loud and clear.

"No, Papá, you may be right," Cayetano sighed, his eyes downcast. *Not when you propose, and Luna says no! What the fuck?* "Look, if you want to go to that place for dinner, I can make a call for you, but I will stay here."

"You all right, Caya?" Hector asked.

"No. I'm not. I have a headache and a sore leg. And nothing is going to help, so don't ask."

Dutifully, Cayetano's four cousins left the apartment, happy to give their boss his space. Paco also left without a word to his son. The pair hadn't spoken at all since the explosive evening out at Rebelión. Inés had called her son and told him how upset Paco was to have to admit the truth about who his father was, and also upset to have ruined things with Luna, no matter how much he disapproved. But Paco was a man of few words, and it would be a while yet before he could talk to Cayetano on any subject, let alone something that shamed him.

After a few hours alone in his chair, Cayetano could swear that he could hear clap of thunder every time he closed his eyes. It may have had something to do with the bottle of whiskey and all the remaining beers. But more likely it had to do with the fact that he had never been so miserable in his whole life. His head continued to pound, just like the pain in his leg, day in and day out. His recovery had gone backwards. He was back to needing to use the cane all the time, even around the house. The loss of his beautiful angel in his life meant his whole body had begun to fail him. She said no. He proposed, and she said no.

Luna Montgomery is your cousin. Luna, *la chispa,* the spark that set the world on fire was related to him. Wow, that sounded cheesy… but she was! Oh how she was the spark of life that he needed! Maybe the whiskey filled him with clichés and melodramatics. Probably.

Cayetano slumped back in his armchair and listened to the clock tick across the room. The clock at Luna's apartment in Valencia couldn't be heard. Her home was full of family and laughter, children and games and love. He would never be part of that. To think he had been running around at Rebelión with Luna and the boys a few weeks ago, wondering what it would be like to be married again, and now he was locked up in his city apartment, his leg aching, and he knew that he couldn't have Luna after all. Proposing was stupid, but it was too late to take it back.

The phone was silent. There was no need for Luna to call back. The argument with Paco had been compelling – they were related and couldn't be in a relationship, especially a physical one. Sure, they could be friends perhaps, discuss in more depth their connection, but to be with her and not touch her, not kiss her, not make love to her? No, it couldn't be done. He couldn't ring her again, and she probably felt the same. But what if Paco was wrong? Maybe they needed DNA tests.

The sound of the doorbell interrupted the tick of the clock, and Cayetano groaned. It didn't matter who wanted to see him, he didn't want to see anyone, especially not his cousins who would now be drunk. They had no idea that Cayetano was going through hell. His heart jumped for a moment – maybe it was Luna. But the pain in his gut said no.

"Buenas noches, querido," María said when he opened the door.

"I'm not your darling," he replied. "And it's not a good evening. It's yet another shit evening."

"Are you going to let me in?"

The size of Cayetano's sigh left María in no doubt of his frustration at seeing her, but she went in anyway. "You stink of alcohol," she commented as they went into the living room.

"Yeah... well... I'm single, and if I want to get trashed on my own, I can do that." Cayetano fell back into his ugly armchair again and stretched out his sore leg.

"You're single?" she commented and placed her expensive handbag on the couch next to her. "Where's girly?"

"At home, in Valencia."

"A long way from here," María mused. "How are things?"

"None of your business."

María raised her bleached eyebrows well over her purple glasses. If he and girly were going well, then he would have rubbed it in her face. "Did you split up?"

"Luna and I are closer than ever before," Cayetano bluffed. It wasn't quite a lie. "What did you come over for?"

"Just to say hello, see how you were doing," she shrugged.

"How's Paulo?" Cayetano asked her. "Still fucking my wife?"

María threw him a glare over her glasses. "At least you acknowledge that I'm your wife."

Cayetano leaned over and pulled the handle to open the footrest on his chair and rested his legs. "In name only, my dear, in name only. I take it that you have the divorce papers."

"I do," she mumbled.

"Signed them yet?"

"No."

"I could change it, petition for divorce for just one party. That could look ugly. Not appropriate for your ever so false 'nice girl' image."

"I have a lot of conditions for the divorce, Cayetano. My lawyer will send a list."

"Hmmm… so you have disputed the divorce, yet have terms and conditions. Obviously you don't want me back as much as you have claimed to in the past. You just want a divorce that looks reasonable to the wider public, who, of course, don't know you or me at all. That's twisted logic."

"We had a strong marriage…"

"No, we didn't," Cayetano cut in. He had his arms folded over his chest, and looked up at the plain white ceiling above him as he spoke. "I never saw you, you worked every evening. I was out every day. We simply came and went from this apartment that we both lived in. We scheduled seeing each other. That isn't a healthy marriage."

"What would be a healthy marriage then?"

"When you love someone so much that you can't breathe."

"Oh, please, that doesn't exist," María scoffed.

"Not for you and me it doesn't."

"We were close once, Cayetano. We were madly in love once."

Cayetano glanced away from the ceiling to his ex-wife across the room. "We were young."

"We're not exactly old now. We belonged together."

"Doesn't mean to say we still do, or could get those feelings back."

"Yeah, I know," María sighed.

"How is living with your parents again? How is your father?" Cayetano asked, and unfolded his arms.

"Okay," María shrugged. "Papá asks about you. I pretend that I have had more contact with you and have something to tell him. He has worried since your accident."

"Does he still have all that stuff on the Medina family history?"

"He wouldn't part with it. Why?"

"Just curious. Did he ever find anything about the mystery baby of Pilar Ortega?"

"No," she shook her head. "The family lost so much when they went to live in France, so any details or letters or anything must have been lost. The identity of the baby and his real father were probably never recorded."

"Everyone knows who the father was. The King."

"True. But there isn't much information."

"I'm sure Leandro would love to find more about the baby and the family he had."

"He would love that, but that's impossible."

"Maybe I should go and pay him a visit one day."

"He would love to see you," María said, her enthusiasm coming back to her voice. "You can come over any time."

"Listen, María, my leg is killing me, and I have a massive headache. Can we save the awkward chat for another time?"

María got up from her chair and wandered over to him. "Do you want me to rub your leg for you?"

Cayetano's mind shot back to Cuenca, with Luna and her miracle cream on his leg, her hands on him. The way she had rubbed him. The way she had groped him. The way she had sat up on him in bed while they made love. "No! Please don't rub my leg. It requires a particular technique."

"You're drunk," she said and stood over him in the chair, her hands either side of him on the armrests. "What's wrong?"

"I don't feel so great, and you don't need to ask why. Can't a man feel like shit and drown it with a few drinks?"

"Caya, you're a wreck. You don't look as if you haven't showered or shaved for weeks. What's going on?"

"I don't want to talk about it to anyone, especially you."

"I love you," she said quietly. She leaned right over him in the chair. "You can talk to me."

"I can't talk to anyone." His short, sharp tone had finally slowed down.

"You can say anything you want to me. It's me, the person you trusted for years with everything."

"But I can't trust you now. I can't trust anyone I know. I can't believe anything anyone says. The people I'm closest to treat me like a pawn, just a piece of a puzzle, not even treated to the truth."

María frowned. "Caya, what happened?"

Cayetano just shook his head gently. "Doesn't matter. Nothing can be changed. Nothing can be undone."

"Anything can be fixed, Cayetano. Anything."

"That isn't true. Some mistakes haunt you forever."

"Come on," she whispered. "Things aren't that bad."

"They are. I will get up in the morning and have no idea what to do with my life. I have nothing to look forward to anymore."

"Me. You have me."

"You betrayed me, just like everyone else."

María leaned forward and kissed Cayetano's lips and tasted the whiskey on them. He didn't say anything; he didn't move away. He had finally let his guard down. She brought her lips again, and this time he responded just a fraction. As she climbed onto his lap, she felt his hands go to her hips, and not to protect his sore leg. It didn't seem to hurt half as much as he had made out a moment ago, or he had forgotten all about it. María had suffered during her long absence from her husband's affectionate company. They had made love in his chair many times before, and she gladly would again. She had finally worn him down. Something had worn him down. All she need was tonight to change his mind about her, and they could get their lives back. He didn't fight her as she undid his pants, let her do all the work. The fight was gone from Cayetano Beltrán, and María would take full advantage of it.

26

Valencia, España ~ noviembre de 2009

Christmas songs played inside the El Corte Inglés, the department store just around the corner from Luna's apartment. It was only November, but it was already cold, and unusually early for Christmas crap by Spain's standards. She was off on an excursion today, and couldn't find her gloves anywhere, and had to stop and buy a pair. It would be even colder in the mountains around Valencia. Giacomo and Enzo had shivered the whole way to school with her this morning.

"Luna?"

Luna turned at the sound of her name. She stood outside the entrance to the El Corte Inglés; the self-opening doors wafted her with warmth and the scent of perfumes from nearby counters every time someone went in or out. She had to get outside and away from the damn Christmas tunes. Luna hated Christmas, all happy families. God, now she resented families. She had become bitter beyond her years. It didn't even have anything to do with her hangover from her night out in the old town. That took nearly a week to get out of her system.

"Michael." Luna put her gloved hand out and shook his. It wasn't the English accent that gave away the fact he was her new real estate agent; it was the way he had hurried along to greet her. Spaniards did a curious thing – even if they were running late, they seemed to try and never show it. Being late was an art in Spain, practically an expectation. This cheery-looking 30-something man harboured no such manner. He was here to work. "Nice to meet you."

Luna watched Michael shake her hand, staring at her. It got a little irritating. It may have not been rude to stare at people in Spain, but having ice-blue eyes made everyone take a second look.

"It's a beautiful day to go and look at houses." Michael gestured at the once-again clear blue sky above them. "Your inquiry surprised me; I have only had two other calls about this property in the year since I listed the place for sale. And they both ran for it when they saw the place."

"That's comforting," Luna joked as they headed for his car that he had double-parked nearby. That was practically parking etiquette in Valencia.

"I think Escondrijo will be perfect for someone, the name is intriguing on its own."

"Hiding place," Luna said while she looked out the window of the car. People clutched their shopping bags as they walked in the cold. "That struck me as an odd name."

"Not the only odd thing," Michael replied. "The guy who owns it is odd. Alejandro has lived there since the 1930's. He's about 95 or something. It's remarkable that he still walks around the property and lives alone up there."

"So why is he selling?"

"No idea why. But he says that he will only sell to the buyer he likes the most."

"What's he looking for?"

"I don't think he knows. I'm not entirely sure he's sober at any time of the day."

"Does he know I'm a foreigner?"

"He doesn't like the fact I'm a foreigner, and I'm helping him," Michael scoffed. "I will tell him that you have your mortgage in place, and maybe that will make him like you more."

"I don't need a mortgage."

"You're never supposed to tell your agent that," Michael chuckled. "I might try and talk you into a bigger place instead."

"I have pretty specific requirements." They turned past Luna's apartment building on Avenida de Francia and started towards the edge of the city.

"You must do. Will Mr. Montgomery come to see the property at some stage?"

"There is no Mr. Montgomery. This place is for me and my sons."

"Oh, I'm sorry."

"Don't be. The love of an extraordinary man may have brought me to Valencia, but my immense love of the place keeps me here."

Michael nodded as he drove. "The love of a great woman brought me here, and my love for both her and this great country keeps me here."

"I'm in good company then."

"I live in Serra, which is the closest town to Escondrijo. Are you going to drive back to Valencia every day for work once you move from the city?"

"No, I need to find myself another job, and a school for the kids."

"School is no trouble. How are your tango skills?"

"Ah… okay, I suppose. I'm *anglosajón,* but I have a bit of Latin blood in me." An extremely unfortunate drop of it.

"There is a guy, Nacho, who works in Serra. He wants to run tango and salsa classes, and he needs a female assistant. He's quite a guy, you could apply there."

"Is there any call for dance classes in Serra?"

"Not really. He wants to extend in Olocau, so he told my wife."

"Olocau is even smaller than Serra!"

"Just saying, if you were desperate and wanted a job where you could get hit on a lot by your boss and get paid terribly…"

"Hmm… tempting. I do need a job. The recession took my last one and my work permit is about to expire."

"Buy Escondrijo and list it as a working farm. Put down a few names as employees, and they will extend your permit. You will be a business owner."

"Hadn't thought of that." Luna looked out of the window; the city had begun to give way to the countryside. She had relied on men for too long, a husband, a friend, a lover, a lost grandfather to achieve her goals. Maybe she didn't need any of them. She knew she didn't.

It seemed as if they had driven a long way through the forests of white pine once they left the town of Serra. It wasn't that far, but the winding, narrow and steep roads made it feel like civilisation had fallen away. The moment they pulled up on the bare limestone outside the house at Escondrijo, Luna knew it was what she wanted. They got out of the car, a thousand things to fill their senses. The views were breathtaking – some trees had been felled to allow the view to stretch out across the flat land towards Valencia city and the sea, and the vista seemed never ending. Almond trees surrounded the house, their branches empty after harvest. Beyond the house was a small olive grove, placed on one of the few places where the terrain was flat. Behind the house, the mountain continued to rise, silent and imposing.

"Feel like you've gone back in time yet?" Michael asked.

"Yes, just like I wanted," Luna said. She looked at the large stone house. It was a mess. No matter; she had her whole life to work on it. "Does it have power?"

"No, no electricity or phone, but it does have water. But all can be accessed for some time and money, so don't worry."

"I'm not worried, it's fine." Luna took her sunglasses off as she looked around. It was cold but fresh out there. There was something unique about the place; the air crackled with excitement and surprise. It was what she and Fabrizio had always wanted. He loved riding his bike up L'Oronet mountain nearby every day. A humble set of small buildings were scattered around, but the main house begged to be inspected. Its stone walls were worn, the roof tiles were patchy, and the wooden windowsills tired, but it was what Luna wanted. A lifetime project.

"Well," Michael said nearby, "you haven't asked to leave. I take that as a good sign."

"I love it. It's just what I want. It has a private road off the main road, views, house to be restored, peace and quiet." How marvellous it would have been to have had the place when Fabrizio died. She was hounded after he was killed. The pretty widow and her adorable little children left behind when her celebrity husband was taken from them. Peace would have been nice. That was it – Luna needed to convalesce. Fabrizio had been dead nearly three years and she had struggled ever since, fighting through everything. It was time to stop. "I want it."

"If only it was that simple."

"The land is right where it needs to be, and the house doesn't need to be anything special. That is changeable. I have time, I have money." Not an endless pot, but enough to make a home for her kids. Fabrizio had left her money specifically to take care of them, and this was their dream together.

"I would be happy to sell it to you," Michael said. "But it's not completely up to me." He gestured behind Luna, and she turned. There was the owner. In his nineties? All that mountain air worked wonders. "Alejandro," he called. *"Buenos dias, soy* Michael Holden." He paused for a moment as the old man approached them. "Sorry, Luna, I never even asked you how your Spanish is."

"I have pretty good Spanish. What dialect do I need? Valencian?"

"It's easier to take cues from him."

"¿Qué quieres?" the old man snapped when he came to a stop beside the pair.

"Hola, esta mujer quiere comprar Escondrijo..."

"You spoke English to her," the man barked.

"Sí, she speaks English..." Michael began, unaware that Alejandro spoke the language. "She wants to buy Escondrijo."

"No. No guiri puede comprar Escondrijo."

Luna rolled her eyes. *Guiri.* How charming. She was foreign, but she lived in Spain, made a life here. *"Yo soy un extranjera, pero vivo aquí ahora ..."* she began.

The old man turned to face her directly, and his mouth dropped open. Luna frowned; he had gone pale. He stared as if he had seen a ghost. He looked scared. *"Jesucristo en el cielo,"* he muttered. *"¿Cómo me has encontrado?"*

How did she find him? Luna wasn't sure what to say. She stood still as he reached out and placed his hands on her cheeks. *"Su cabello es negro,"* he mumbled.

Your hair is black? What the hell? "Ah... *sí....*"

"No." Alejandro snapped his hands away. "No, I won't sell Escondrijo. No."

"Pero, Alejandro..." Michael began.

"No," he said again. "No, leave me."

Luna and Michael stood on the spot as the old man retreated into what must be a cold, lonely house. "Okay," Luna began. "I think I just scared the shit out of an old guy."

"I'm sorry, Luna, I don't know what to say," Michael said. "Maybe I will come and see him again in a day or two. Perhaps he will have changed his mind."

The pair went back into the direction of the car, Luna felt

especially unsettled by the man. Was it her appearance? Or just the fact she was an *extranjero*, a foreigner? It felt intensely personal. "I don't think he will change his mind," Luna commented as they got back into Michael's car.

"It's my job to talk people into things. Don't worry. We will get you up here again. We can get around this."

As the car trailed off down the unsealed track toward the main road again, Luna glanced out the window at the house, the old man nowhere to be seen. What a weird feeling.

"Some people I can't understand, no matter how long I live in Spain," Michael commented.

"Ten years in Spain, and I don't pretend to know Spanish people all that well yet," Luna chuckled.

"I tell you, last night I went to a meeting in Serra. I only went out of curiosity, but wow, the tension in there!"

"What was it about?"

"One of the properties just outside the town, they have a *fosa*, mass grave pit, on it…"

"As in civil war graves?"

"Yes. It's been known about for years, but the owner, he's getting old, and he knows his father is in the grave along with many others. Now, he wants to move his father to the local cemetery, and it's caused an uproar."

"No one wants him to?"

"The families of the others buried there are not so keen. The rumour is…. and it's only a rumour… that one the Falange members who shot them all is still living in Serra."

"What?" Luna frowned. "The killer lives in the town with his victims' families?"

"That's what they say." Michael's voice didn't hold as much scepticism as Luna's. "Nothing surprises me. Mostly this was a meeting of older people who want the past to stay packed away. Locked in an innocuous hole in the ground. They seem to be worried about old grievances."

"My grandfather is missing."

"Really? As in a Spanish grandfather?"

"Yes, last seen at Valencia Port, March 1939. Disappeared off the face of the earth, and left several women pregnant and alone."

"Bad choice of words."

"Which ones?"

"Disappeared off the face of the earth. He may he just beneath the surface instead. Sorry, that was a bit heartless."

"It's okay," Luna shrugged. "I'm not sure I want to know him. But it seems like he is one of many who have just been forgotten."

"There was a concentration camp not far from here after the war. Who knows who will find a body next. Many people disappeared in that time, here and everywhere around Spain. People rarely talk about it. These people are not forgotten, just spoken about privately. That's why I was interested in this meeting about getting bodies put in the cemetery. They had a speaker come in from Madrid to help out."

"What was the result?"

"There wasn't one. The man who wants to rebury his father ended up storming out in tears. It took a lot of courage for him to bring it up after all these years. It's remarkable that animosity can last for so long."

"Got to wonder what they're afraid of." Luna looked out the window. There could be bodies anywhere out here, and no one would ever know. Or maybe they did… maybe they were sat in long buried secrets.

"We're of a generation that doesn't have the horrors of war on our minds. Who are we to judge what others say or feel?"

"Very, very true," Luna agreed.

"The war may be old news, but the tough life that followed isn't that distant. Franco still signed death warrants from his death bed in 1975. That isn't stuff in history books for people over 40, that was part of life. Spaniards deserve a lot of credit for the work they have done to form the country they have, despite all the ups and downs since the 1978 constitution."

"The conservative media, the army, the church, the Royal House, all like to think the wounds have healed, but not all of them have."

"Maybe they haven't, but there's no quick fix."

27

Valencia, España ~ noviembre de 2009

"There you are!" Darren said when Luna came in the front door of the apartment.

"What, is something wrong?" She pulled her scarf from her neck. "I thought you would pick the boys up from school."

"I did! No, no, everything is fine with the kids, but I wanted to talk to you. Tomás came by earlier."

"You're babysitting, not having friends over. What are you, a 15-year old girl?" Luna teased.

"Very funny. No, he had something interesting to say."

"All right, one minute."

Darren stood in the living room, and heard the sound of squeals of delight when the boys saw their mother in the doorway to their bedroom where they had played. It was several minutes before Luna returned, with a smile on her face.

"So, have you become a real estate tycoon yet?" he asked as they sat down together.

"I own one apartment, and want one house. It's hardly an empire," she snorted. "It was a fascinating trip. The place was perfect, but... I don't know..."

"Good, because I have a counter offer to you going off on your life of country living. Tomás asked if you would be interested in coming back to work for the team."

"As a bike mechanic?"

"Yes. You have been out for three years, and he wondered if you would like to come back. One of the guys has quit, so there is a space for you. The team is finished for the year anyway, so next year you could join us on the road. We are sending a team to the Giro D'Italia, the Tour de France, and the Vuelta a España, plus some smaller tours, like Switzerland, Austria, Ireland. I won't ride all of them, but you could work on them all."

"With you."

"And the others."

"The others. Your teammates are assholes. I always knew that. They seem to think that since I'm a woman, they can speak to me like I'm a piece of shit."

"But we all worked together for years…"

"Yeah, I did that because Fabrizio needed all his lesser men around him for work. It wasn't because I was happy."

"But it gives you a job, which extends your permit here. You could sign the contact and always bail out later."

"I'm not that kind of person."

"I thought you would be pleased I got you a job. One you liked… or I assumed you liked."

Luna sighed. "I love being a bike mechanic. I appreciate that you want to help. But… but you and I don't need to spend that much time together, do we? Plus, the kids are older now, it's hard for me to move around for work and have them with me. They need things they can't get on the road. It's not like when they were infants on the tour bus with the team. It's harder now."

"Since when did something like that stop you? We will still be based in Valencia most of the time."

"It's not the life I want for myself anymore."

"What's so bad about what we have?"

"We don't have anything."

"You know what I mean. Who would want to leave Valencia?"

"I don't; I want to enjoy more of it, outside the city."

"It was Fabrizio's idea to leave the city, you always wanted to move into the old town. Rescue an old building here instead of out in the middle of nowhere."

"I know that. Sometimes plans change."

"You don't have to change your plans. It's your life, Lulu."

"Exactly! My life! Why would I want to work for a cycling team that is funded by the Valencian government, as a tourism promotion tool? That money was spent on bike racing, which I love, but it has come at the expense of essential services to this city. There is so many problematic areas in Valencia not being addressed, yet they can pay for you to ride your bike!"

"The money spent on the team wouldn't be enough to save the world, Luna."

"No, it wouldn't, but it would be a bloody good start!"

"Since when did it matter where the money came from, as long as the team got paid? Neither of us got rich by saving the world."

"I care about the place I live in," Luna said with a shake of her head. "Spain is the home of my kids. It's their country. Am I bitter? Of course! I spent years fighting the legal system that was happy to let some guy off the hook for killing an innocent man. I have seen the in-fighting and the disdain that this region's government has for its people. The thought of taking money for a cycling campaign, after all the money already blown on stupid things…"

"Then take your part of the cash and do good things with it!"

Luna shut her eyes for a moment. Why did life have to be so fucking hard? Now she was moaning about some moral code of not accepting money that was a foolishly spent by the government. She was far from the only person who didn't trust the leaders of the region of Valencia, but they all would probably take money from them given the chance. *Stop fighting everything, Luna.* That was never going to happen. What she wanted was to run off with her half-cousin, and that creepy thought clouded everything she did. That wouldn't happen – Cayetano was a famous man, he was never going escape the life he had. The good life, in his swanky Madrid apartment. His family was rich of the back of entertaining a dictator in the sixties. Okay, that was mean. If only Paco was wrong about it all, but he had got the information first hand from his mother.

"Lulu, I'm sorry," Darren said. "I thought I could help."

Luna opened her eyes and looked at the man across from her. "I know, I'm sorry. I don't mean to snap. I'll have to think about it. I'm just sick of lurching from one disaster to another. I don't know what I want anymore."

"It's not like that. You're too hard on yourself."

"I know what my problem is. My life is devoid of people. I stand here and say I am proud to have come to Valencia and made it my home. I say I belong here, like my blood is in the soil. I don't belong here! I'm not living a life like an average Spaniard. How many people come home to their large new apartment, that is fully paid for, after a day of not working for a living? I'm not living with many generations of my family because life is a struggle. I have nothing in common with the people around me. I don't have any friends. I know people who were friends with my husband, either real or superficially, but I'm not an extension of him. Whatever bond I had with Fabrizio and his life is over. It hurts, but it's true. I came here because I was pulled along, but I'm here now because I want to be. At least if I moved I might have a chance to genuinely, meaningfully integrate into the place I'm raising my children in. Like the guy I met today, when I went to look at his property. He took one look at me and wrote me off. I can't blame him."

"If only you had found Cayetano Ortega. Maybe that would have given you a bit of peace."

Maybe she was the King's long lost cousin. No, she still refused to believe that ludicrous scenario. "I'm the daughter of Alex Montgomery, and granddaughter of Scarlett Montgomery. That is all that matters. Surely what I do with my two little Montgomery's will define me."

The sound of two little raised voices echoed down the hallway, and Luna rolled her eyes. They had Fabrizio's temper in them, that was for certain. "I will go and see what international crisis has been sparked in there," Darren chuckled.

"You don't have to," Luna said, but he was already on his feet.

"You and I may not be a couple anymore, but I still care about them as much as ever."

"You're going to make an excellent wife one day," she teased.

"Anything that means I can ride every day works for me," he called back as he went down the hallway.

The phone rang the moment Luna sat back in her seat, and she groaned. She pulled from her pocket and looked at the screen. Michael. "Hey, back so soon."

"All part of the service," he replied. "I just wanted to apologise again for today. It wasn't my best viewing."

"Not your fault," Luna said as she examined her slightly chipped blue fingernail polish. "Honestly, don't worry."

"I might have time to go back up there tomorrow and talk to Alejandro, if you like. Maybe tomorrow will be a better day."

"Don't trouble yourself."

"It's my job. Who knows, maybe I will get inside his messy little house full of bullfighting memorabilia again yet."

"Bullfighting?" Christ, who didn't like bullfighting?

"Yeah, the guy is a massive fan. We all love something. If you want to buy Alejandro Beltrán's property, I will make it happen, don't worry."

Luna's polite farewell to Michael was distracted at best. Alejandro Beltrán, who loved bullfighting? No way. *How did you find me?* What else had he said? *Your hair is black.* Luna Montgomery, the black-haired mirror image of Scarlett. Scarlett, who once knew a man named Alejandro Beltrán. *Shit.*

28

Valencia, España ~ noviembre de 2009

The blue rock thrush birds chirped when Luna stepped from her car at Escondrijo. The roads had been silent as she made the steep and winding trip. Being up here was a splendid example of the Spain that she loved – the differences that made up the country. Not long ago she was in the city, a vibrant and modern place to live, and now she was not just out in the country, but isolated. A whole community lived out here, tucked away, living a decidedly different life to the Spaniards in the city. When Luna had first come to Valencia, she only had to drive five minutes south, and she would come to where donkeys and carts were still a legitimate form of transportation. While the city grew and changed right in front of her over the last ten years, out here on the mountain was the same as it had been for countless years. Spain was like that – embracing the new and holding on to their traditions all at the same time. A 40-minute drive had transported her to a different world.

A few purple heather flowers clung to life in the rapidly cooling November weather as she walked towards the house. The silence almost overwhelmed Rebalsadors mountain. Not too far away there would be cyclists and hikers, but in this cold weather, only the hardy souls would be out. Fabrizio would often ride L'Oronet mountain nearby, along past Rebalsadors and on to the Olocau and Gátova townships nearby. Luna had time to stop and take in the view from the house again. The house was built just back from the limestone cliff, and the world dropped away, spread out along the flat Turia land to the city, and the Mediterranean was beyond it, shining in the sunlight. What had gone on in the hills and out on the plain over the last several thousand years was mind-boggling.

"You again."

Luna spun to see Alejandro there, covered in dust. "Me again," she replied and took her hands out of her pockets.

"Whatever you're looking for, it's not here." Alejandro marched straight past her in the direction of the front door to the old house.

"How do you know what I'm looking for?" she called over her shoulder; she didn't bother to turn and face him. She heard his rough footsteps stop on the flaky ground.

"You're another one of them," she heard him call back. "You come to Spain, no idea what it's like here, taking over the place without any thought of what it means to be a Spaniard."

"Is that why you are out here, not even speaking Valencian? You're also a foreigner around here, aren't you?" Anyone who wasn't a native of Valencia could be considered a foreigner.

"Where I come from doesn't matter," he snapped. "You don't belong out here."

Luna turned around and faced him. He stood tall in an attempt to be intimidating, but it wasn't going to work. "Why are you surprised that I found you?" Luna had no idea why he had said that to her on her last visit, but she may as well see where it lead.

"I was mistaken."

"Mistaken for someone that you used to know?"

"I don't know anyone."

"Not even Scarlett?"

Alejandro's gaze fell to the ground. He was looking for a lie, and she knew it. But she saw him glance back up. "Who are you?"

"Luna Montgomery."

She saw him raise his eyebrows. "Luna?"

"Are you Alejandro Beltrán Caño?"

"No." Alejandro turned away again and started back towards the house.

"I know you are," Luna called. Now that she thought about it, he bore a resemblance to Paco Beltrán.

"What the hell do you want?"

"I'll tell you what I want!" Luna cried. "All I bloody wanted was to find a place to live out here, somewhere to hide away from the world. None of it had anything to do with you."

"For some skinny little girl, you seem damn sure of yourself. What would you have to hide from?"

"You would be surprised." For a man who wanted nothing to do with her, he seemed to have an interest in what she had to say. "But, the question is, why do we know each other?"

"We don't."

"Fine." Luna passed the dusty man by the house in the direction of her car. "I can hide out anywhere. I will leave you to hide out here on your own."

"You shouldn't mess with things you know nothing about."

Luna stopped and turned around again. "I know more than you would think. Besides, once you have your husband die, most things in life don't seem like such a big deal."

"You lost your husband?" He couldn't suppress his interest.

"Yes."

"Any kids?"

"Two boys."

"You poor girl," he muttered.

"I'm no poor girl," she fired back. "I'm perfectly capable of carrying on alone. If there is another property out here that would happily take my money, then so be it. You can rot out here. But remember, I know where you are now."

"You wouldn't do anything with that information."

"So you are Alejandro Beltrán Caño."

He sighed. *"La chispa."*

Luna frowned. "Meaning?"

"You have the spark in you."

"Are you, or are you not the man who knew my grandmother during the war in Cuenca?"

"You're the spitting image of her. You have the eyes… and the attitude. But I have no idea what happened to her."

"She died in 1973, in a small town, in New Zealand."

Alejandro's head hung as he listened to the words. "She was such a wicked woman. I hope she had a happy life."

"I didn't know her."

They stood in silence as they looked at the expansive view before them down the mountain. "You're looking at the monastery."

"Yes," Luna said. "That's Porta Coeli monastery, *¿no?*"

"*Sí.*"

"The one used as a concentration camp after the civil war?"

Alejandro sighed. She had said those words out loud without any hesitation. "The place has been down there for over 700 years. It's seen worse."

Luna glanced over at him. "That doesn't make it right."

"It was a long time ago now."

"Time doesn't heal all wounds, because grief is infinite."

"Some things don't heal."

"They say that thousands of prisoners in that monastery are listed as dying of tuberculosis, but they were murdered and dumped in graves around here."

"It was more people than they claim it to be. But those details are hidden away. The courts have made sure those papers aren't released."

"You lived here back then?"

Alejandro just shook his head. "I don't look back if I can help it."

"You were a Republican, weren't you? I know Scarlett was."

"I... I can't... some things just..."

"Did you hide out here, you know... when they were rounding people up to kill once the war was won?"

"*La chispa,* you have to stop."

"Who will hear us out here?"

"The dead can hear you. I can hear them. You won't ever understand."

"Try me."

"Why?"

"Somewhere out there, I bet some bastard killed my grandfather, and he's dumped in a grave. I'm one of thousands of people whose identity is in the soil here, along with the blood of our family members."

"I know that. But surely you have more immediate family. Scarlett had a baby, I take it that the baby is your...?"

"Father. Alexander was my father. Both of my parents died a long time ago."

Alejandro squinted at the young woman. "You've had it tough."

"Haven't we all?"

"Scarlett named the baby Alexander after everything."

Luna turned to him. "You spoke to her about her baby?"

"I knew Scarlett exceptionally well. My wife, Sofía, was drawn to Scarlett when she came to town."

"Cuenca."

"Yes. We were close. Cayetano lived across the street from me, and he offered Scarlett a place to stay. They met at a meeting about the war. The war was not kind to your *abuela*."

"My father told me that she was a tough, outspoken woman."

"She was when she came to us." Alejandro almost smiled. "But she came to Spain to change the world, and reality taught her some harsh lessons. After she was raped out in Huete just before the camp was bombed…"

"What?"

"Maybe I shouldn't have told you that."

"Are you sure?"

"She told Sofía about it. Raped by a group of Falange members who thought women deserved it. Scarlett was darkened by it. The fact she met Ulrich was a relief, and then all that business…"

"Who?"

"Ulrich Hahn was a German volunteer with the International Brigade, like Scarlett. They got married during a visit to Barcelona before he went to fight at Ebro. She buried him a month later, and returned to Cuenca instead of going home, as all foreigners were asked to do."

"I had no idea she was married."

"All wartime Republican marriages were annulled by Franco. I guess there was no sense to mention it."

"But she would have carried that pain her whole life."

"We all carry something."

"So, how did she ever get pregnant to Cayetano Ortega?" Luna's heart leapt in her chest. If Ulrich fathered the baby, then she and her own Cayetano wouldn't be related…

"That was just a one-time mix-up. A night drinking in Requena… it happens." He had no idea how much hope that comment crushed.

"Are you sure?"

"I was in the next tent. I remember more than I ever wanted to know."

"Cayetano was definitely the father?"

"*La chispa,* my body is old, but my mind isn't. Why?"

"What happened to Cayetano? He was your best friend."

Alejandro shook his head, his gaze at the uneven ground beneath their feet. "He's gone."

"Murdered?"

He nodded his head. "Like so many."

"And dumped somewhere?"

"You better come inside."

The house was sparse at best. While the stone building was enormous, Alejandro's whole life appeared to be jammed in one room in the front. It consisted of no more than a single kitchen sink and table in the corner, with a gas cooker on the floor. A single bed lined the opposite wall of the large room, and all else in there was a small table and chairs in the centre of the room. But papers, they were everywhere. So many newspapers and magazines and books, in piles, all seemingly put around the room at random. The table was covered in newspapers, which Alejandro hastily tried to move away.

"Don't go to any effort on my account," Luna said.

"I don't want you prying through my things," he shot back.

Bullfighting. So many things about bullfighting. "You follow your family."

"They're not my family." He didn't bother to look at her as they both sat down at the table.

"How can you sit here, knowing who they are and not go to them?"

"I haven't left this place in years. I will never go to Madrid."

"Not home to Cuenca?"

"I shut my home, and the building across the street in 1939 and never went back."

"You own them?"

"I can only presume they're still there. I get a bill from the town hall now and then."

"Then why not sell them, and not this place?"

"I want nothing to do with them."

"I was there, not long ago."

Alejandro frowned. "In Cuenca?"

"Yes. Not much there. I looked for any trace of Cayetano Ortega. There isn't one."

"You need to look under his full name."

"Medina."

"You have been doing well, *la chispa*. That's a hefty secret."

"Cayetano wrote it in a note to your sister, Luna. I found the letter."

"A letter to my sister? How did you get it?"

"It's a long story." Luna's eyes were on her hands on her lap. Across the table was a magazine article about Cayetano and his accident a few months ago and she didn't want to look at it.

"Isn't all of this?"

"Cayetano Beltrán and I… we looked together to figure out a story. He has so much from your sister. His father, Paco, kept it all."

"What is Paco like?"

"You have never met him?"

"Never."

"He's a hard man. Strong. Fanatical about bullfighting and his family. Your sister, Luna, told him that his family loved it."

"We did," Alejandro smiled. "We did love it. There was a bar… up from our house, the Libertad. We would spend hours in there talking bullfighting with others from around the town. But… the war ended that love for me…"

"But your sister saw to it that Paco grew to love it. And he does."

"Paco has done well. I have followed his career. He did well marrying that Morales girl."

"Inés. I hear they're happy. They have a daughter, Sofía."

"I didn't know that," Alejandro whispered.

"Sofía likes to stay away from the family business."

"You know much about the Beltrán family."

"Yes… well… Cayetano and I…"

Alejandro watched the woman across the tiny table from him. "How well do you know Cayetano?"

"Pretty well."

"Like I said, my body is old, but my mind isn't. The boy…"

"He's hardly a boy."

"He is when you're my age. I thought you were married. So is he."

"I was. I am."

"Look me in the eye and tell me that there is nothing going on with Cayetano Beltrán."

"Nothing is going on," Luna said sternly. "Anymore."

"So, your end has as many secrets as mine. You won't even look up at the boy in the paper here. Did he break your heart? I doubt you're the first."

"I'm not." The moment she said it, Luna realised she had given herself away.

"I see. You have had a rough time."

"So don't chastise me for wanting to come out here. From the cavemen of the Bronze Age, to the Romans to the Muslims to the Christians, hiding out here has been popular."

"Are you as eager to leave your mark as them?"

"No. I want a bit of peace."

"It's not out here, Luna." Alejandro wished he could say something to the woman to make her feel better, but he knew the same pain she was going through. "As the saying goes... we are all curious about the things that can hurt us."

"Your nephew's son doesn't need to take the blame. None of it was Cayetano's fault."

"Paco isn't my nephew."

Luna finally looked up at the old man. "Luna had a baby..."

"My sister had a baby? With who? Ignacio was gay. That's why we married her off to him, because we knew he wouldn't touch her. It was all part of a kind of 'insurance' deal, somewhere to hide her if we lost the war."

"I mean Paco. He knows that Ignacio isn't his real father..."

"I knew that Luna would tell him the truth about that. But we can't deny that Ignacio provided for my sister and the baby, even if he was a Nationalist. Gave my sister to a Falange member," he muttered to himself. "Our father, what a fool. He sealed his own fate."

"It's the problem of Cayetano Ortega being my *abuelo,* and also being Cayetano Beltrán's *abuelo...*"

"Cayetano wasn't Paco's father." Alejandro looked at her as if she were stupid.

"Luna Beltrán and Cayetano Ortega's baby is Paco. Paco told us."

"Paco is wrong. I think I need to tell you the whole truth."

29

Valencia, España ~ marzo de 1939

Luna stopped for a moment outside a church, the Santa María del Mar. "What happened here?" It was a mess. "Was it bombed?"

"They used the bell tower as a point of defence," Scarlett said. "Made the church a target."

They carried on past the damaged church that sat at the end of Avenida del Puerto where they had left the truck. A white building stood at the port, a beautiful clock on top. It too had been bombed; rubble sat around the largely roofless building. There were people everywhere. "Is that where we're going?" Luna asked. The baby in her arms cried out in protest; the sun was in his eyes, and he rubbed his little face against her coat in an attempt to get away from it.

"Sí, that's where you go to get a ticket to get on a boat from the Valencia port," Alejandro said as they walked down the crowded street. "But there are no tickets or boats to be had anymore."

Cayetano couldn't waste any time. He left Scarlett and Luna outside in the sun, and he and Alejandro pushed their way through the busy crowd and into a room in the damaged building, all seemingly patched up after its destruction. They found the man at a desk, a cigarette in his hand. He looked exhausted.

"Back so soon," he said to the pair, who looked as desperate as the tired man. "You know there are no ships coming into Valencia port. I told you that on your last trip. Whoever you have in your truck, you need to send them to Gandia."

"Is anything getting out of the port in Gandia? Jávea? Alicante?" Cayetano asked.

"No, not that I know of."

"It's different this time," Cayetano said and pulled a chair out from under the filthy table. "This time we need to get ourselves out."

"You?" Antonio looked at Cayetano's face across from him. He watched Alejandro sit next to his friend, the man was dirty and worn out. Normally these two good-time guys looked their best. "Why?"

"We don't want to live in a country ruled by Franco and his ultra-conservative religious pigs."

"We need to get used to it. Madrid yesterday, Valencia tomorrow. They have won this war."

"Doesn't mean we have to like it," Alejandro snapped.

"Yes it does, or you will get a bullet. I'm surprised that you two men aren't dead already. Everyone knows which side you're on. It's a miracle that you weren't marched from your home in the night, shot and dumped in a ditch."

"We weren't home often enough," Cayetano quipped.

"How many poor families from Madrid did you transport to Valencia? Around 100? More?"

"Don't know," Cayetano shrugged. "We want on the Stanland. We know it's the Británico ship ready to leave Valencia."

"It's carrying aid, it's not taking passengers."

"Surely there's room for four of us."

"And why should I get you on there and not many of the others who would like to leave the country? Franco might open the ports to ships again, I don't know. Maybe you can wait…"

Alejandro looked at his friend for a moment and turned back to Antonio. "What about just two people? My sister Luna has a child, and Scarlett, you remember her…"

"The redhead with the icy eyes. We all remember her."

"She's pregnant. Surely we could slip the pair of them onto the ship. Scarlett is Inglés, she wouldn't stick out on the ship. And Luna, bless her, she is still young…"

"What about your wife, Sofía?" Antonio asked with a frown.

"She passed away," Cayetano answered for his friend. "It's very sad, but now we can only think of the other women in our lives."

"Luna is the one you liked, ¿no?" Antonio asked. "Is the baby yours?"

"No, Scarlett's baby is mine."

Antonio rolled his eyes. "Anyone else and I would be surprised, but not you, Ortega."

"Can you help us, or not?" Alejandro asked. "And if you want money,

I'll pay."

"Why do you think I can convince a ship captain to help you?" Antonio asked.

"We don't, we know you can sneak us on that ship. Hide somewhere on board if we have to."

"The four of you? I doubt it." He took a long drag on his cigarette. "I might know someone who is working on the ship. Maybe we can get the girls on... but no guarantees."

The air was fresh back outside the office, but the streets were filled with worry. People hurried everywhere, and Cayetano was at a loss. If he told Luna and Scarlett that they were going alone, he wasn't sure what their reaction was going to be. Scarlett needed to go home; he wouldn't see her again after that ship left port. The spring sun may have held a little warmth, but Cayetano couldn't feel it on his skin. There was too much on his mind – Sofía's bloody death, Alejandro's grief, Scarlett's worry, Luna's anger.

"Caya," Alejandro said. "Caya, are we doing the right thing here?"

"What do you mean?" He squinted in the sun at his friend.

"I mean, do we need to run? Maybe we will be okay."

"It was you just yesterday going on about getting your son out of España for good."

"I know... but..."

"But?"

"Do you want to send Scarlett and Luna away?"

"I want to get Scarlett safely home. She deserves that. What I've done to her, and the rest of her life, is unforgivable."

"Had it been easier to travel to Barcelona, she could have got rid of that baby."

"It would be safer to stand on the front line and get shot than to take up one of those abortions in Barcelona. There is only so much pain a woman can, and should ever have to, take."

"And Luna?"

"You know how I feel about your sister."

"That's a subject we don't need to discuss."

"I want her to be safe. She's got my diamond. That could get her a long way."

"But where? It's one thing for Scarlett to travel to Nueva Zelanda, but what about Luna? It's not that simple. She doesn't even own a passport or anything to identify herself. Who knows where that would leave her."

"I don't know, Ale!" Cayetano cried. "I don't know what to do here!"

"What if we go back up to Escondrijo in the mountains and just hold tight. Scarlett can still go home."

"Let's go to Francia. The Medina's told us that any time we needed help, they would take us in. Pilar is my mother. Luna would be safer there in Pau than here."

"Pau is a long way from here! We would need to get over the Pyrenees and head a long way west to get there. If we get there at all."

"We have the truck."

"And need to drive it through regions all already captured by Franco's troops. And what about the rumours of refugees being arrested and imprisoned in camps, in Francia, for the sole crime of being from España?"

"That is in the east, not in the west."

"That we know of. Plus, there's all those rumours that now that Hitler has practiced bombing our magnificent country that he's going to take on the rest of Europe. Nowhere is safe."

"Maybe the suggestion of Argentina isn't so stupid. This is the kind of thing we have been saving up for. There is a lot of cash in the chest that Luna is sitting on with Scarlett right now."

"And no ships leaving port here!"

"Do you want to die?" Cayetano asked. "You haven't come up with anything."

"Everything I hold dear is already dead and hidden away on a mountain. I loved Sofía, and if I can find a safe place for her baby, then I'll do it."

"Ale, I'm not saying what you have suffered with Sofía isn't important."

"Then stop pushing me. I can't make a decision. I don't want to leave. Let Scarlett go, and Luna, but only if she wants to. We don't need to make decisions for these girls; they're perfectly capable of looking after themselves."

Cayetano turned and looked through the crowds, to see Scarlett standing there with the camera out of the chest. What had she been taking photos of? Hopefully not the desperate look on his face.

"Going to enlighten me on what happened during this meeting I'm not even allowed to sit in on?" Scarlett asked the pair when they approached them at their spot against the wall of one of tinglados, *the work buildings along the water's edge.*

"It's still a big maybe," Cayetano said to the women.

"This is stupid," Luna said. She sat on her chest, and tried to calm the fussing baby.

"That saves asking her what she wants to do," Alejandro scoffed.

"We are better off leaving the country. After all, what do we all have to stay for?" Cayetano asked the group.

They all looked at each other; he was right. They had nothing. Scarlett was a foreigner, Alejandro had lost his wife, and Luna had no family left with her father off to Madrid and her mother dead. The man she was in love with had betrayed her, so nothing was enough to keep her there.

"You know I love you all..." Scarlett began.

"You need to go home," Cayetano said. "Please, don't feel as if you have to stay."

"I want to stay," Luna said.

"Preciosa..." Cayetano replied.

"Don't call me that!"

"Luna, stop being so difficult," Alejandro said.

"I thought that Republican women were supposed to be treated equal to men," she replied. "I thought the role of women was considered essential. So stop telling me what to do!"

"Fine," Alejandro sighed. "Tell us, where will you go? Will you go home to Cuenca? Alone, unable to find your way, let alone have an income to look after yourself? Cuenca will be full of Franco supporters, full of men ready to tear apart a girl like you, one cock at a time."

"Fuck, Ale, calm down," Cayetano interrupted him.

"I don't know what I will do," Luna said. "I can figure it out."

"You're young and have never looked beyond being married, you can't look after yourself."

"Ale," Scarlett interrupted. "Don't speak to her as if she's a fool. I didn't hear you complain while she played nurse to your mother, or cared for the household you live in. You were more than happy to accept her cooking, washing, housekeeping skills then. Don't judge her now."

"I don't need you to tell me what to do," Luna said.

"You know what?" Scarlett fired back at her. "I'm leaving España, one way or another. As a foreigner, I'm in less danger than the rest of you. I will go home. My country's government knows I'm here and expect my return. I have sponsors through the New Zealand Spanish Medical Aid Committee who will assist me in any way I need. I broke the non-intervention agreement my country has with other European nations, so my whereabouts are well-documented. I will go home, and you won't see me again. I won't get in the way of you and Cayetano, so don't be so indignant. Life is short – way too short. If Cayetano wants to run away with you, then do it!"

"Cayetano!"

They all turned to the sound of the voice, to see Antonio through the crowd. The heavy-set man was sweating by the time he reached the despondent group. "You want on this ship?" he said, his voice lowered.

"Yes," Cayetano said.

"Right now."

"Now?"

"They have unloaded the aid off the ship. You will have to go in the hold of the ship, but you will all be able to fit. I don't know where the ship is bound for, because the ship is unsure themselves. They're waiting for clearance to leave without being stopped by the Mar Negro off the coast. But they won't be stopping in España again. This is your chance. Now or never."

"Luna," Cayetano said and grabbed her by the shoulders. "Don't let the anger you have now endanger our lives. Please. Come with us."

Luna looked at her brother. "Only if I can take the baby."

"No, the baby needs to go with Scarlett," Alejandro replied.

"Well?" Antonio asked. "I just got a message." The group huddled together. The people around them all wanted out of Valencia one way or another, and there was no reason to panic them. "They told me that Valencia has surrendered. Troops will be here tomorrow. There are no ships in Alicante. There are 20,000 Republicans trapped at the port there. Reports of people committing suicide, all sorts going on. For all we know, they will round us all up and shoot us. If you don't get on this aid ship, you could die."

"Don't you want on this ship?" Luna asked.

"I can't leave, I have five young children and a sick wife, I have to stay. When the church bells toll to announce Franco's victory over España, I will be here to hear them."

"If things are getting out of hand in Alicante then things could go wrong here – and fast," Cayetano said. "We have to leave this place."

"Come." Antonio gestured towards his office. "All of you. Let's see what we can do."

They pushed their way through the crowds and back to the broken and sorry building, which was surrounded by women who sat with their children. The faces told of their despondency. Of their fear. Of wondering what would be their fate. Cayetano stopped when he saw Luna lag behind them with the baby in her arms. He put the chest down and went back for her. "Luna, what is it?"

"I don't want to go," she said in a quiet voice. "Why should we escape, but not these people?"

"You think they would stop and think of you, given a change in fortune?"

"No, no one seems to care about anyone. Why would God do this to us?"

Alejandro stormed over to his sister. "God? What God? How can you persist in believing in a higher power when we live in the world that we do? There is no God, the lives we have are what we carve out for ourselves."

"So, what? We did this to ourselves?" Luna challenged him.

"Now isn't time for this," Cayetano said.

"We're anarchists!" Alejandro cried. "We stand by our beliefs!"

"Your beliefs!" Luna yelled her brother. "Who ever said they were my beliefs? No one ever asked me what I wanted!"

Scarlett charged out of the office towards the group. "This isn't the time for this," she said. "Come on!"

They filed into the building, where another tired-looking man stood. "This is Mark," Scarlett said for him. "He doesn't speak any español. He works on the Stanland."

"Hello," Alejandro and Cayetano both replied. They had learned some inglés from Scarlett on those trips on the road with her. Luna, however, didn't have a single word.

"You have to appreciate my problem," Mark said to Scarlett, aware that most in the office couldn't understand him. "It was hard enough for us to get our ship here. We're ready to leave, and we're aware that there are a lot of people who want out of España. I can't just fill the ship with people who have nowhere to go. I can take you, Scarlett, if you need to get to London, but I can't fill our decks with refugees. We barely made it into Valencia. The British consul has been in mediation to get us out again. If we set sail with a boat full of refugees, the Mar Negro or the Mar Cantábrico off the coast will capture us, and then who knows what will happen. I wouldn't put it past them to sink the whole ship and everyone on it. Let's not forget what happened to the Ciudad de Barcelona."

"There was a New Zealander on that ship when the Italian submarine torpedoed it," Scarlett said. "He drowned along with 60 other Republican soldiers."

"It would have been even worse if those Spanish fishing boats hadn't sailed out to their rescue."

"The Republican planes trying to fire at the submarine were no help, they killed many innocent souls in the water. What a disaster. Mark, I'm not asking you to save the world, just these few," Scarlett said. "It's different for you and I, we can commission other governments to help us, but what about ordinary Spaniards? They have nothing."

Mark looked at the group. "How can you stand here with a child and expect me to say no?" He sighed. "Yes, all right, as I told Antonio, I can get you on, but it won't be a comfortable ride. You can't bring anything with you. We have no room, not even beds for you."

"We don't need anything," Scarlett said. "We have provisions for the baby, and that is all we have to take." She turned to Luna. "Sorry, we can't take the Beltrán chest with us."

"If you're coming, you need to come right now," Mark said. "We are getting ready to dock out, and the moment we think we're safe to set sail, we will. There will be no waiting."

"I would rather die like a dog in the street than run away," Alejandro said.

Scarlett spun around. "What? I'm standing right here, trying to help you!"

"I don't want help! If the rebel bastards want my country, they will have to shoot me." He turned to Luna and took the baby off her, the first time he had held him. "Name him Paco," he said. "It was what Sofia wanted to name him, after her father." He kissed the child on the head. "You will do great things one day," he whispered. "Remember me then."

"Ale, what are you doing?" Luna said as he handed the bundle back to her.

"Now is the time I stay and fight."

"Don't be a fool, it's much too late for that," Scarlett said.

"I would rather be dead with Sofia than live the rest of my life without her," he replied.

"Ale!" Cayetano yelled after his friend who turned and darted out of the office.

"I'll go get him," Scarlett sighed.

"No, I'll go," Cayetano said. "You ladies need to get on the ship."

Mark looked to Scarlett, unsure what was going on. "Scarlett, we need to leave. I have things I need to do. Like I said, we are readying the ship for dock out."

"I thought all you wanted was to get the women on board and not yourselves anyway," Antonio said to Cayetano.

"You planned to abandon us on the ship?" Scarlett asked.

"No!" Cayetano said. He looked at Luna, who had an equally unhappy face. "I wouldn't do that."

"After everything, you treat me as the weak one of the group," Scarlett shot at him. "I don't need to be rescued."

"You're four months pregnant, you need to be helped, whether you like it or not. I'll go after Alejandro. You both have to get on the ship. I will get Ale, and bring him back here. We will meet you on board."

"You... you're coming... aren't you?" Luna asked Cayetano.

"Get on the ship, la chispa. Please. I love you. I want you to be safe."

"Come on, Luna," Scarlett said. "If we don't get on, they won't hold a place for any of us," Scarlett said. "Let's take baby Paco, and get him fed and settled."

Cayetano placed one hand on Scarlett's stomach for a moment, and held her gaze. They looked as frightened as each other. Without a word, she turned away from him, and he knew she never expected to see him again.

He watched the women be taken from the building. Luna looked back at him, worried about what would happen next. He followed them from the building, guided by Mark in the direction of the ship nearby until they had disappeared from sight, Scarlett's red hair no longer visible through the crowds. He turned with a heavy heart and went back into Antonio's office, where the man stood with Luna's chest of the Beltrán belongings.

"You're not going, are you?" Antonio asked him.

"Not if I can't find Alejandro. I can't go without him."

"We're all going to die, aren't we?"

"We've been on the losing side of this war for a while. We live in a world of locked minds, so it's impossible to be safe." Cayetano sighed. "What are the chances of getting a letter on board that ship?"

"I could try. I have a guy who is working with the loading."

"Just in case... just in case I never see them again."

30

Madrid, España ~ noviembre de 2009

Luna should have paid more attention to the ball going back and forth. Not that it went terribly far. The under-6s pelota teams weren't exactly the pinnacle of the handball sport, but today, Giacomo and Enzo got to play the game at the trinquet de Pelayo, the main pelota court in Valencia. Normally they played the outdoor version the game, Llargues, but it was their 'big match' against another local school, slotted ahead of the adult game later in the afternoon. Most of the time the ball didn't even make it over the net between the two pint-sized teams of five, but regularly bounced awkwardly amongst the parents that sat on the stairs that ran along one side of the concrete indoor court.

She had wanted to sit with Alejandro all day and talk, but the school bell and subsequent pelota match had called Luna away. There was still more to learn from him. Cayetano Ortega's body was still buried somewhere in the secrets of time and lies. She had to go back to Escondrijo, and soon, but the most pertinent fact was already known – she was not related Cayetano Beltrán. That not-so minor detail distracted her from her sons playing the proudly traditional local sport in front of her.

It was one thing to go to Madrid and tell a man you haven't seen in a while that you are in love with him. That you want to be with him, despite all your own hurdles and hang-ups. But if only it was that simple. The main fact was that Paco Beltrán was the son of Alejandro Beltrán and Sofía Perez, not Luna Beltrán and Cayetano

Ortega. She was about to go there and have to tell Cayetano that his father didn't know who his own parents were. Paco loved his mother so much, and she wasn't his mother, but his aunt. She had lied to him his whole life. It didn't matter how old someone grew, the desire to have their parents love them and be proud of them never went away. The life Paco had developed through his family wasn't real. The man was already mad at Cayetano and Luna for pulling apart the dubious history he tried to hide, and this would only make things worse. So many questions still needed to be asked to Alejandro. Cayetano Ortega was still missing, but he didn't get Luna Beltrán pregnant, and right now that was all that mattered.

A night of tossing and turning in bed yielded no results. Luna could have called Cayetano, but there were no words for this. She had to see him. By the time dawn had broken, she was up and early to leave Valencia for the capital city, her victorious pelota players in tow. This needed to be a face-to-face meeting.

It was considerably colder in Madrid than Valencia when they arrived. The kids talked continuously the entire trip and Luna was frazzled. Even the most loving mother can get sick of nonsense spoken by five-year-olds. She didn't even bother to get their bag out of the car, they just went straight into the grand old building and up to the sixth floor. What if he wasn't home? What if he didn't want anything to do with her? Even if he didn't, Cayetano needed to know that his real grandfather was still alive in the mountains outside Valencia.

There was no time to think of something profound to say, no time to stand in the dimly lit hallway and procrastinate. No time to think of a way out of this if it all went wrong. Enzo pressed the doorbell about ten times and that could be enough to make any man turn away guests.

The door swung open and there stood Cayetano, leaning on his cane. His eyes grew wide at the sight before him. Luna could see his eyes go between the two spirited redheads who jumped up and down and Luna's stiff and nervous smile.

"*¿Te acuerdas de nosotros?*" Giacomo asked.

"Do I remember you? Of course! Hello, welcome back!" The boys were delighted by the broad smile that greeted them.

"We haven't seen you in ages," Enzo moaned.

"I know, and I'm sorry. Would you like to come inside and play? It's cold out there."

Giacomo and Enzo darted in, and Luna cautiously moved in the doorway as well, next to the man she just wanted to grab onto and never let go. But with the kids there, and neither of them were quite sure what to say.

"We drove four hours to see you. We saw the wind farm," Enzo said.

"There was no wind," his brother shot at him.

"It was still there!"

"I have your blocks here," Cayetano said. "If you would like to play, the box is still in the living room."

The boys dashed off, more than happy to make themselves at home again. Cayetano and Luna stood eye to eye for a moment; the ice needed to be broken.

"Sorry," she said.

"What for?"

"For turning up unannounced. For drunk dialling you a few weeks ago. For… saying no…"

"Like you say, shit happens, who cares."

"Your leg isn't better?"

Cayetano dropped his cane; the wooden stick banged against the grey marble tiles. "I'm fine… no, I'm miserable. I don't know what to say."

Luna cheeks had puffed out while she held her breath. "We're not related after all," she blurted out.

"What?"

"I know, it's crazy but true."

"Good enough for me!"

It was a relief more than anything when she could finally kiss him again. He held her so tight that her ribs hurt, but she didn't care. You can't just stop loving someone. It doesn't just go away. All the thoughts of rushing to him in the hopes of a passionate, sensual reunion were nothing more than a fantasy. When she kissed him, it was significantly more than that. She loved him. It seemed impossible to love someone she hardly knew, but she did. The relief of being back with him was laced with an element of surprise of how much she felt for the man. The hot-blooded attraction that pulled them together was there, along with sensitive and compassionate craving to be part of each other's lives, proven in a tender kiss.

Cayetano held her tight against him, not sure of what to say. In her high heels, she was tall enough to rest her cheek against his, and she could feel the dampness of his tear run between their faces. "You leave me so undone, woman, I hope you know that," he whispered.

"I'm not sure if that's a good thing or not."

"It's good. You turn the world on its head."

Luna leant away to look him in the eye, to see them wet with tears. "I hope you like that, because that's what I have come to do."

"You found Cayetano Ortega?"

"Kind of. Have I upset you?"

"No." His face broke into a smile. "I just… I thought you weren't coming back. I… I have something I need to tell you."

"Okay."

"Maybe when the kids aren't listening…"

"I have a lot to tell you. Big stuff."

"It doesn't matter what it is. I love you."

"Then why do you look terrified?"

"When I admit my feelings to a woman, shouldn't it be far grander than standing in the entranceway to my apartment?"

"I don't know," Luna tightened her embrace around him. "It's cold outside, but we are safe and warm in here, and I can hear my children playing and laughing together. Sounds like a good place to be."

"If you ever leave here, you will break my heart."

"I think enough hearts have already been broken. I have always thought romantic love to be dangerous."

"Who cares if it is?"

"It's already nearly cost you your leg."

"It's a small price to pay to leave behind the life I had before I met you on the path that day."

"Cayetano!" Giacomo called out. "Why don't you have a Christmas tree yet?"

"We put up our Christmas tree earlier than Spanish people, sweetheart," Luna called back to them.

"Would you like to go shopping with me to get one? I'll need help decorating it," Cayetano replied.

They both smiled at the sound of the kids getting excited. "You'll be staying in Madrid tonight, I take it?"

"If you'll have us."

"It's all I want. You take my life from black and white into colour."

"You're too much."

"I thought you liked that."

"I do."

The pair sat on the couch, close to one another, a physical connection needed at every moment while the children played and talked. For a woman who rushed herself to Madrid on that cold Saturday morning, Luna was more than happy to take her time to tell him what she had learned on Rebalsadors mountain.

"Can we talk about what you have learned in front of the children?" Cayetano asked as he watched them play on the floor.

"I guess so. It's not like they pay much attention anyway."

"So? What happened? Is Cayetano not your grandfather after all?"

"He is. What Scarlett told my father about his heritage was all true. Cayetano Ortega was murdered, after the end of the civil war."

"You know for sure?"

"Yes. Most likely shot in a concentration camp set up outside Valencia. I wasn't able to coax out any details about his death, but I will try again. Now I know where he was, the possibility of finding records on him is higher. I know what happened to Cayetano, and Luna, and Scarlett, everyone after they disappeared from Cuenca."

"Don't hold me in suspense!"

"Sofía, Alejandro's wife, died giving birth to their baby. So the whole group fled Cuenca for Valencia, to get on a ship and leave the country for good. Only Alejandro, devastated by the loss of his wife, left the group, and Cayetano went after him. Scarlett and Luna went to board the ship, but for some reason, Luna never got on board. The ship docked out, and Scarlett was gone forever, Luna somehow made it to Madrid and married Ignacio, and Cayetano and Alejandro were rounded up by Nationalist troops and thrown in a concentration camp."

"I wonder if Cayetano knew that Luna was pregnant when they were separated."

"She wasn't pregnant."

"How do you know?"

"Alejandro Beltrán told me."

"What?" Cayetano cried. The boys on the rug in front of them stopped their game in a heartbeat, shocked at the raised voice towards their mother.

"It's okay, boys," she said to them.

"Sorry, your Mamá is telling me a grand story," Cayetano added, and they turned back to their game. "How did this happen?"

"Do you remember that time I told you that I wanted to move into the mountains outside Valencia?" she asked, and he nodded. "I went up there to see a property, and I came across an old man that turned out to be Alejandro. It was all by accident. He recognised me because he knew Scarlett. He's 95."

"And he told you all this?"

"Yes, but with considerable reluctance. There are still holes in the story, but I intend to get the rest. But once I knew that we weren't related, I wanted to come and tell you, even though he begged me not to say anything. I couldn't see how I could not tell you the truth."

"But how are we not related?"

Luna took a deep breath. "Paco is not Luna and Cayetano's son. He is Alejandro and Sofía's only baby. When Sofía died in childbirth, Scarlett was supposed to take the child and go to New Zealand. But somehow, when Luna left for Madrid, she took the baby with her. The baby didn't perish, as Paco thought. Paco is the baby."

"But that means that Luna Beltrán is not his mother, not my grandmother. My Papá idolises her. She meant the world to him, as shown by how angry he was when we went through her things."

"Cayetano Ortega did love Luna and did propose to her. When she found Scarlett was pregnant to Cayetano, she changed her mind. Alejandro said that while her pride was hurt by the mistake, she still loved him. But they were torn apart by the war."

"It's all terribly sad, but I still can't grasp the fact that we know Paco is not who he thinks he is."

"Luna had a great love, and she lost him. She was left with her brother's child, and raised him as the product of the great love she couldn't have."

"The pain involved in that is horrendous. There would have been no peace for her, only misery."

"Luna and Cayetano are an extraordinarily sad love story. And Scarlett, she had fallen in love with some German man who was also killed, and lived her life alone with Cayetano's baby."

"But if she hadn't had the baby, then I couldn't have you now.

You're my great love. I told you, it's fate we met."

"Fate has been cruel."

"I can't be sure that telling Paco would be wise. He could easily go the rest of his life thinking Luna and Cayetano are his parents."

"Paco seems ashamed of the fact he is Cayetano's Ortega's son. He thinks he's the bastard child of an affair, and that his father was the same thing. He is, in fact, the product of a young couple who married in a revolutionary wedding, and had their lives destroyed."

"But would that information give Paco any peace? It means his mother lied until the day she died."

"It means that his natural father is still alive. He could have the chance to meet him. Alejandro is ashamed of all he has done and that he never came to find Paco, instead he let him be the son of his sister. He has followed Paco's career, and yours."

"He could have tracked down my father his whole life and chose not to. He abandoned his own family."

"I don't think it's that simple. We don't have the whole story."

"How sure is he of all this?"

"Alejandro looks like Paco. You only have to take one look at him!"

"Cayetano?" Giacomo interrupted. "You look funny."

"Do I?"

"You look a little pale," Luna smiled.

"Well, you did surprise me. Hey, little gentlemen, in my kitchen I have Christmas treats. I've got some *turrón*, some *polvorones* and some *mazapan*. Would you like some?" He watched two pairs of ice-blue eyes light up. "You wait here, and your Mamá can help me with the treats."

Luna followed her limping companion into the kitchen. "You cook now? Or did your mother do it again?"

"Mamá."

Luna went in to find the traditional Spanish treats, on the huge plate on the island counter. He had *turrón duro,* the hard almond nougat treat, along with the sweet almond and honey *mazapan.* The *polvorones* were the flaky rich almond shortbread cookies. "You're a 40 year-old man, and your Mamá still bakes you sweet treats?"

The moment she turned back to him, he grabbed her and thrust his lips on hers. There was the heated passionate moment she had longed for, out of sight of the little ones. She found herself pinned between her bullfighter and his extra-large fridge as his hands searched her body for the best way to hold on to her.

"Next time you suggest we 'get some almond treats', I will come better prepared," she joked.

"I missed you. Did I mention that?" His intense gaze may have been fixed on her, but one of his hands roaming her body.

"I missed you, too. But we will have two savages on our hands if we don't produce sweets, and I don't want you to serve my sons while with a raging hot *erección.*"

Cayetano let out an evil laugh. "You noticed."

"How could I not?" She giggled as he brought his lips to her neck to nibble at her skin. "Later, Caya, later."

"I know," he mumbled, his lips against her neck, the rain of gentle kisses slowly made their way back to her mouth. "First treats, Christmas tree shopping, and a bit of happiness."

"I was worried you would be mad at what I came to tell you."

Cayetano stood up straight, a serious look on his face. *"Preciosa,* not at all. All this isn't our fault. In 1939, Luna and Cayetano were split up by circumstance. It's our duty to make sure that history doesn't repeat itself."

31

Madrid, España ~ noviembre de 2009

Cayetano's face started to hurt; he smiled so much that his cheeks stung in the cold air. People went about their days unaware of how lucky they were. Taking Luna and the boys shopping wasn't a chore. The way he heard other parents moan about such excursions seemed like overkill. The department store was packed with Madrileños getting into the early Christmas spirit with some reluctance, but not Cayetano Beltrán. He bought a stupidly large Christmas tree and all the decorations they could carry. Jamming it all in the Mercedes was a mission in itself. He liked the way the kids had to stop and touch everything they laid their eyes on. He liked looking his rear vision mirror to see them in their booster seats. He liked the way Luna graciously smiled every time she heard someone yell, *"mirar, mirar, pelirrojo."* Look, look, red hair. It obviously got on Luna's nerves. Strangers came to inform her of something that thousands would have already mentioned in the past, and in a tone that suggested she hadn't noticed that her sons were redheads. The boys seemed to know exactly how handsome they were; they just stood there and grinned every time they heard it.

What was the point of being well-known in Madrid, if you couldn't use it to impress your girlfriend? Trudging up to a popular restaurant at three in the afternoon, no reservation, and getting straight in was a perk of the job. Yes, people did take a second glance when they saw him there with a woman who wasn't his wife, and two little children, but he didn't care. He wasn't about to let anyone get confused either. It was clear she was his lover. The way he held her hand across the table told its own story, while he listened to the children who sat politely in their seats against a window that let in the weak winter sun. The occasional kiss to the back of Luna's hand sealed it for those still in doubt about their relationship. Cayetano knew this was what it felt like to have a family, something he could have as long as no one messed it up for him again.

There was the problem. Cayetano was smiling and happy, and grateful Luna had come to see him, but there was an obstacle. Maybe not as big as being related, but a significant one all the same. Luna had mentioned he looked terrified when she came in. He was. When she had turned down his stupid phone proposal, he had gone and had quick sex with María, in the armchair. It was nothing more than a drunken biological moment, one minute's reprieve from the lonely world he had cultivated for himself. He had to tell Luna what he had done. But it would ruin everything, surely. Or would it? They had been in a state of confusion for over a month, not clear on whether they had broken up or not. He had told himself that they hadn't split, but had acted as if they had. What had Luna been doing? Had Darren been hovering, waiting for her? This conversation would ruin all the joy. So, behind the smiles and chats and kisses, Cayetano sat in his chair at the restaurant and watched the kids make a mess of a fine dish of suckling pork, not sure if everything he dreamed of would last another day.

The day continued and Cayetano's concern grew. It was dark by the time he had decorated his Christmas tree with the kids, their bright little faces so happy when they flicked on the twinkling white lights. The four of them sat in the dark, only illuminated by the Christmas tree.

"Why don't you normally have a tree?" Giacomo asked him.

"I have Christmas at Rebelión, the farm," he explained. "I'm not here much at Christmas time, so I never got a tree for myself."

"So, when do you have Christmas? We get presents on December 25 in Italy from Nona Paulina and Poppy Max. Santa Claus knows we are there. But the three wise men leave presents under our tree at home on January 6."

"That's the same for me. I go to church on December 25 with my family, but we have gifts on Three Kings Day in January." He turned to Luna, who sat next to him on the rug by the tree. "Are you going to Italy for Christmas again this year?"

"Yes. Fabrizio's relatives are all the family the boys have. I want to give them a relationship with the Merlini family."

"You're a selfless mother. I hope people tell you that."

"Never."

"Well, they should."

"When my father was dying, I wanted to thank him for all he had done for me. He raised me alone after Mum died. He asked me not to thank him for anything. He said if he had done his job right, to shield me from the burdens of the world, I wouldn't have noticed what he had done for me. I hadn't; he had done a terrific job, just the two of us."

Cayetano watched her face turn into a frown. She tried not to cry. The kids sat nearby; she considered everything she did and said for their benefit, like her father had obviously taught her to do. "It doesn't get easier, does it?"

"No, it doesn't. Dad died ten years ago, and it still hurts. He was dying, and worrying about what would happen to me. He said that being 23 made me still a baby. That's why I was so grateful to Fabrizio, he reassured Dad that he would look after me, and they thought that I didn't hear their conversations."

"That's a noble thing for a man to do."

"Dad went to Italy for our wedding. It was the first time he had ever left New Zealand. At least he was there to share that with me."

"You were young to be married."

"I was ready, and Fabrizio was a lot older than me, and wanted to get married. I already knew that it's the little things you do, the way you act when you think no one can see you, they're the things that define you and your character. To see Fabrizio at my father's bedside, telling him that he promised to look after me, it left me in no doubt that I had married the right man."

"Was that Daddy?" Enzo asked.

"Sure is."

Cayetano watched Luna turn her attention to the boys for a moment, who sat so close to the tree that they may as well have started to climb it while they admired their decorating skills. "Marry me," he whispered.

Luna turned her face back to him. "What?"

"I can be noble, if that's what you want. I would devote the rest of my life to finding a way to prove it. Marry me."

"Cool, can we move to Madrid?" Giacomo asked.

"No!" Luna said. "I mean, no to moving to Madrid."

"Oh yeah, you are going to work on the bikes with Darren," Enzo said.

"No… well… maybe…"

"Maybe to the bikes… or…?" Cayetano asked. *"La chispa,* I can't live another day without you, and I kind of hoped you felt the same way."

A little smile crept over Luna's face as she nodded gently. "Yes."

"*¿Sí?*"

"But I'm no rush to get married…"

"Me neither, all I need is the promise I can be with you." He didn't even notice that his leg didn't hurt when he leant over to give her a kiss.

"Will there be more kissing?" Giacomo asked, his little nose screwed up.

"At least they will be married, so it's okay," Enzo added.

"There's always a critic," Cayetano joked.

The doorbell rang, and he rolled his eyes. "Seems like a day of people just turning up unannounced."

"We can go if you like?" Luna said.

"Don't you dare!" He grabbed his cane and pointed it at her. "I won't let any of you go."

Cayetano didn't even stop to consider who might be there. Right now he felt like any problem could be solved. But that feeling was lost the moment he saw María. That was back. His eyes were still adjusting from in the dim lighting of the living room to the harsh reality of what he was faced with. "Not now."

"It has to be now." María pushed passed him and went into the large entranceway. "Why are you in the dark? Are you in need of company again?"

"Luna and the boys are here," he hissed at her. "I need you to leave."

"Luna and the children are here?" Her voice was loud and clear, more than enough for Luna to hear her. "Well, in that case perhaps she would like to join us?"

Cayetano saw Luna flick the lamp on the living room, and come towards the angry pair in the entranceway. "María. Is there something I can do for you?"

"Not really," she said. "I need to talk to my husband, but you may as well hear what I have to say."

"I don't need to be part of your business."

"But if you and I are getting married, you are entitled to be part of anything you want," Cayetano replied. Hopefully Luna wouldn't call his bluff. He didn't want her anywhere near María.

"You're getting married?" María spluttered. "You forgot one thing."

"No, I asked you for a divorce. I think you need to leave." Cayetano was not angry, he was defensive. The last thing he needed was María's fat mouth to ruin things.

Luna turned and shut the double glass doors from the living room into the entranceway, so the boys didn't hear the argument. "Look, if you two need space or whatever, I'm fine with that."

"I don't need space," María shot back. "I needed to tell my husband that I'm pregnant."

"Congratulations," Cayetano said. "You and your adulterous cameraman will be able to raise your little Satanic baby together."

María looked at Luna and back to Cayetano. "You never told her, did you?"

"What?" Luna shrugged.

"María, you need to shut up!" Cayetano yelled, which surprised both women. "I want you to leave." His heart had begun to pound in his chest.

"Cayetano and I spent the night together, a few weeks ago. I guess it's a miracle, we sleep together on the one right day of the month he decided to fire live rounds instead of his usual blanks. I found out today, we're having a baby. Just like my Caya always wanted."

Cayetano felt cold to the bone. Just when he thought he had got his shit together, his whole life started to slip away. The look on Luna's face said it all. "I don't believe you," he shot out.

"I have the test I took at the doctor's office." She fished around in her large handbag. "It's still very early days, Luna, so I would appreciate your discretion on this happy occasion."

"I don't want to see it!" Cayetano didn't dare look at the little white stick that María had produced. "Even if you are pregnant, how do I know it's mine? You're seeing someone else."

"It's fate," María said.

"There's no such thing as fate." Cayetano looked over at Luna. He had tried to convince her that fate was real.

"No, there's not," Luna replied. "But history can repeat itself." She turned and opened the glass doors to the living room. "Come on, boys, we're going home now."

"No, no, no, no, no," Cayetano begged as he grabbed Luna by the arm. "Please, no, please don't leave me."

"There are things going on here that have nothing to do with me, and certainly nothing to do with my boys."

Cayetano let Luna go. "María, get out." He turned and opened the front door with force.

"You would toss me out, pregnant with your baby?"

"Even if I believed you, it would make no difference. I will never love you. Don't make me throw you out."

María dragged herself into the doorway and turned back. "I will come and see you tomorrow, when you have calmed down."

"I will never calm down. Don't ever talk to me again!"

"But…"

She got cut off when the door slammed in her face. Cayetano turned to find Luna with the boys. "Please, don't leave. What are you going to do? Drive all the way home now?"

"It's 350 kilometres. It's not that far," Luna snapped.

"So, what? You just give up on me, just like that? Again?"

Luna paused while she watched the boys pull their shoes on. She grabbed their coats off the rack. "No, but I can't have this conversation in front of the kids."

"Then let's sit down, and talk about it later."

"How many elephants do we need in the room?" she cried. "If she wasn't pregnant, were you even going to tell me that you and her…" she glanced at the kids' innocent faces, "were together?"

"Yes… but…" he gestured in the general direction Giacomo and Enzo. Jesus Christ, this was hard with them in earshot. It was probably the reason she hadn't spit in his face with disgust. Her expression suggested she wanted to. "Everything was going so well."

"We were only apart for a month. That's all it took for you to cheat on me? Were we even apart?"

"I thought so… I don't know! Luna, please, it was nothing!"

"It was something! Something I can't get my head around right now. When was this?"

Cayetano glanced at the boys. "You rang me, and I asked you to marry me... and you said no. You said no! I was angry, and drinking..."

"You told me that you loved me."

"I did! I do!"

"But to do that when I said no... I said no for a very good reason!"

"And today, just now, you said yes!"

"Maybe we're cursed. The first Luna and Cayetano couldn't work it out over an accidental baby, and maybe we can't either."

"Why not?"

Luna opened the door and gestured to the boys to head out into the hallway. "Because I feel like a fool. I was just sitting there with you, and I told you something intensely private about my father and my husband. Now I'm not sure I can trust you."

"I thought we were staying the night," Enzo said as he and his brother stepped into the cold hallway with their mother.

"We can't," she replied.

"You can!" Cayetano said. "I'll beg if you want me to!"

"Please don't make a scene in front of my kids." Her eyes were filled with tears, but she refused to let them go.

"What do you want me to do? Please, anything."

"You offered nobility. I want noble. What you've done is the exact opposite. What I need is space. Boys, say goodbye to Cayetano."

Cayetano stood helplessly in the doorway to his apartment and watched the group walk away. The twins waved goodbye with sad faces, until they disappeared down the stairs and out of sight. He gripped his cane tight in his hand; there was no point in running after her. Don't make a scene, she said. The boys looked confused enough already. Everything he wanted was gone, just like it had happened to his namesake years ago. And he knew he deserved it.

32

Valencia, España ~ diciembre de 2009

When things went wrong for Luna, she tried to take heart in the fact that things could be worse. It rarely helped. It was okay to be upset, or angry, or both. Screw being grateful for all you have. Luna was upset. Very upset. She drove home at high speed to Valencia, her foot hard on the accelerator along the A3 that took her through Castile-La Mancha and back to her home region. Although there was plenty to see out there during the day, in the dark she had her eyes forward the entire time, briskly overtaking people who moved along at regular speeds. Luna just wanted to get as far away from Madrid as possible. If she didn't live right on the coast, she probably would have kept driving. The boys sat in the back, and dozed most of the way, which allowed her to let silent tears roll down her face without any questions asked.

From the most crucial things, like raising sons without a father, to minor things, like getting two children out of the car in the parking garage and up to the apartment while they were asleep, Luna was convinced that children needed two parents. Struggling with the boys up to the apartment in the cold was just one more little reminder that she had to live her life alone. Like she needed a reminder. She carried the children into their room, and barely got them to stand to take off their shoes and coats before they both crawled into their beds still fully clothed. No matter. It may have been midnight, but they were safe and home in bed. Eight hours in the car was a long way for anyone in a day, let alone a child that age.

Luna sighed a breath of relief when she closed their bedroom door. The apartment was totally dark, except for the kitchen light. Darren had been vague about his weekend plans, and he must have gone out and left the light on. Luna shuffled her way to the kitchen and frowned. On the floor was a black bra. Luna never bought anything in black, she used bright colours to hide her despondent moods. She picked it up and looked at it. C cup. Two sizes too small for her. She turned, and there stood Darren, shirtless.

"I know you gained weight, but I don't think you need a C cup," she said to him.

"I didn't know you were coming home tonight. You said you were staying in Madrid. Are you okay?"

"You have a girl in your room, don't you? Did you strip her down in the kitchen?"

"Like I said, I thought you wouldn't be back." Darren reached out for the bra and Luna tossed it to him.

"Hygiene, Darren. No sex in the kitchen."

"We've all done it."

"I know. But if you want awkward position sex, use the vanity in your bathroom, not the kitchen counter."

"It's not like that," he chuckled. "I swear. We were only talking in here, and then things…"

"Got fun? It's okay, everyone needs to get laid. Just make better choices about who you sleep with than I do. And keep the noise down, the boys are asleep."

"I'll send her home."

"No, it's okay."

"Are you all right? You look as if you've been bawling."

"I have been." Luna rubbed her tired face. "I don't think you would believe me if I told you what's been happening. In fact, I couldn't tell you, because I've failed to mention so many things that it wouldn't make any sense."

"Look, I will tell Lucía to go home, and…"

"Lucía, as in our babysitter, Lucía? Who lives across the hall? Did you fuck the babysitter? She's 20." Luna shook her head. "I'm not surprised. Thank you for lightening the mood."

"She came over because she had some plumbing problem, and she wanted to see if we had the same issue…"

"And let me guess, you let her inspect your pipes?"

Darren had gone red in the face. "Oh don't tease," he moaned, and tried not to laugh." I just… it… a man needs to take a moment to be satisfied."

"Don't I know it! You're all as untrustworthy as each other. Go back to your lady friend. I will take a bottle of wine and some headphones to bed. Just don't wake the kids."

"No, no, I will ask her to go. It's fine, she understands that it's your home…"

"It's your home, too… what do you mean? You have brought her in here before, haven't you?"

Darren shrugged in an attempt to suppress a smile. "It's a casual thing."

"For how long?"

"About a year."

"A year! Why can't men just be honest about who they fuck?"

"It's every few months or so, when her boyfriend is away in Salamanca."

"Does he go away, and you and her lie in bed and talk about what… school? It's that easy is it, just wait until poor Diego's back is turned so you and her can get to quick sex?"

"Stop with the jokes." He reached out for her. "You need a hug."

"I don't know where you've been. Don't touch me."

"Actually yeah, I should wash my hands first."

"Gross. Please let me wallow in my misery. Go back aiding Lucía's desire to be a cheating whore."

Darren disappeared, bra in hand, and Luna turned her attention to a bottle of wine in the fridge. Why bother with a glass when she could slurp it out of the bottle, just like she used to after Fabrizio died? Cayetano shouldn't be able to hurt her as much as he did. After what life had already dealt her, Cayetano turning out to be cheater shouldn't hurt as much as it did. She took the bottle of wine and wandered into the living room and slumped down the couch. Only a few moments later, Darren reappeared, this time dressed, with young Lucía behind him.

"You don't have to leave because I'm home," Luna said across the room to her, and didn't bother to get up. "But I won't keep your secrets for you either."

"No, Luna, I'll go." The girl looked almost afraid. "I'm sorry."

Darren saw Lucía out and came back into the living room. "I reckon she thinks we had an affair behind your back."

"Trust me, I know what that feels like."

"What happened, Lulu?"

Luna sat still for a moment, and then burst into heavy tears, and Darren sat down next to her. She cried often, but this was a deep, heavy pain that wouldn't go away, and she knew it.

~~~

The hangover. The punishment for making alcohol related decisions late at night, then amplified by the sound of happy children waiting for attention the next day. Luna needed to shake it off, and she knew exactly where she wanted to do it. Hours of drinking and crying on the couch as she poured out all the details of the last few months to Darren had been a fitting yet miserable end to an awful day. Now she had to avoid her phone, because it had rung eight times, all from Cayetano. The man was hell-bent on explaining himself, or apologising, or something. Luna didn't want to listen to his messages. He had slept with María and hadn't told her. When they first met, he had lied about who he was, and that he was married. Now he had slept with María. A pattern of lying had emerged.

Luna and the boys drove Darren to the airport, his time in Australia with his family had come. He had been reluctant to go, given that things at home were so difficult. But it wasn't his problem, it was Luna's. She had created this mess, and she needed to fix it. They needed time apart, things were still very awkward between them.

The threesome didn't go home, and instead Luna headed straight for the mountains. As sharp and argumentative as Alejandro was, she liked him. He offered a window into the past that wouldn't be around to look through for much longer. Escondrijo offered an opportunity for a new way of life, one Luna needed and deserved. All this sitting around worrying and crying over men wasn't who she was, and she was tired of it.

It was cold at Escondrijo. The sky was clouded over, Valencia's characteristic blue sky hidden behind the threat of precious rain. Maybe even snow. When Luna pulled her car up outside the main house, Alejandro was just coming towards them, his arms full with chopped wood.

"Back so soon, *la chispa,*" he said as he walked over. "I thought maybe you had all you ever needed to know from me."

"You won't get rid of me that easy." She turned to pull the back door of the car open for the twins to get out.

Alejandro looked in amazement at the two quiet and well-dressed children that climbed out the car. *"Pelirrojo!"* he exclaimed. "It looks like Scarlett is alive in your family's looks."

"It doesn't come any redder than this." Luna ran her hands through Enzo's hair. "You should have seen the look on their father's face when they were born."

"I can imagine." Alejandro grinned, the first time Luna had seen him in anything less than a frown. "Come inside, it's cold out here."

As they wandered in, Giacomo asked, "Mummy, why are we here?"

"I hoped we could live here, if this man will let us," Luna replied.

"I haven't decided if you are up to the job," Alejandro remarked.

The fire was on in the corner of the room, and the boys both went over to the warmth and sat down. There was something about an open fire that appealed to everyone, but Luna's motherly instinct kicked in as soon as they got anywhere near it. Luna glanced over at Alejandro; he watched the children, his eyes switched back and forward between the boys.

"Do you need some things to burn, *niños?*" Alejandro asked them. The two young ones nodded excitedly, and he handed them some twigs to throw onto the flames.

"What brings you back here, Luna? It's cold and lonely. No place for you. I thought I told you that."

"Why don't you want me here?"

"It's not that I don't want you." He gestured for her to sit down at the table. "You have a whole life ahead of you. One you could have better in the city."

"Then why did you live your whole life up here?"

"I'm bound to this place. My blood is in the soil."

"Why?"

Alejandro looked up from his aged hands on the wooden table. "This is where my Sofía is buried. I couldn't leave her."

"Here?"

"After she died, and we left Cuenca, we stopped here to bury her. We knew the family who owned the place had gone to France and wouldn't be back."

"Who's we?"

"I came here, with my sister, and the baby, and Scarlett and Cayetano. We buried Sofía and left to go to the city to leave Spain."

"But didn't leave."

"I'm glad Scarlett got out." He had turned to look at the children again. "I never heard about her again. I wondered sometimes, you know, what had become of her and her baby. She meant so much to me, and we parted on unpleasant terms. I wasn't myself the day she boarded the Stanland. You know, if I hadn't met Sofía, I would have been all over Scarlett like a rash. Cayetano was just the same."

"But he loved Luna, didn't he?"

"Oh, very much so. I was protective of my sister, our country was at war, and the least I could do was look after her. You see things, you hear things... I wanted Luna to be shielded from it. She was only 20 when I last saw her. The thought of her being hurt shocked me. I was a soldier, and it changed who I was. I didn't want to become like our father. Juan Pablo was a cold man, a man whose ideas about politics meant more than his family. He went to Madrid to fight for the cause, and didn't even care when his wife died. I heard that he was killed on the streets in Madrid a few days after the war ended; pulled from the house and had his throat slit on the street. He was used as an example of what would happen to those of us who had rejected Franco. I didn't care. I only ever saw him when Cayetano, Scarlett and I went to Madrid to collect families who needed help leaving Spain. We collected mostly poor families, families who could barely afford a ticket to sail, and let them travel to Valencia with us. We would sometimes help wealthier families move their belongings, and that how we made our money. Enough, in theory, to leave Spain ourselves. But we never did."

"That's a kind thing for you to do, to help people trapped by war," Luna said quietly.

Alejandro shrugged. "I think about it, but I don't talk about it."

"I'm grateful that you speak to me."

"You're Cayetano and Scarlett's family. I never expected to see you. I did wonder sometimes what happened to the child."

"Alexander was born a few months after Scarlett returned to New

Zealand. She lived the rest of her life alone, to raise my father. She worked in small hospitals, in small towns, where they lacked money and equipment. She wanted to help those who couldn't get to the city for care."

"That sounds like Scarlett. She hated the rich, those who had everything. She had this fight in her, to right all the wrongs of the world. I'm glad it never went away. I'm not surprised she never got over Ulrich being killed at Ebro. She was devastated. But I'm glad she raised the baby, that must have been hard."

"Very tough, especially where she came from. Single mothers were given no sympathy."

"I'm sure Scarlett could rip the head off anyone who dared cross her path," Alejandro chuckled.

"My husband used to say that about me."

"I'm sure there's plenty of Scarlett in you. You look like her."

"My father used to say I looked like my mother, but I think that was Dad being nostalgic."

"You have no parents now?"

"No, my mother died when I was a child, my father died when I was 23. Scarlett died before I was born. Cancer, all three."

"It's a horrible illness."

Luna watched him bring his hand to his stomach, and she frowned. "Why are you selling this place, if you have lived most of your life on it?"

"I don't actually have any choice. It's a big property, I can't tend to what I grow, or to the animals I keep. I can't plant trees and take proper care of the house. I haven't been able to for a while."

"You are sick?"

"At my age, who isn't? That's not your concern. So, did you tell your bullfighter what you know?"

"I told him that you're his grandfather."

"I wish you hadn't. But you did it for yourself, didn't you?"

Luna glanced at the children, who happily sat back from the fire. "I wish I hadn't."

"Why? They hate me, don't they?"

"No! I only told Cayetano. But I wish I had never been there."

"Why?"

"It makes no difference." Her voice quiet as she shivered in the cold. "He is married, and now his wife is pregnant."

Alejandro took a deep breath. "You've been messing around with him, haven't you?"

"He left María nearly a year ago, and then he and I met. But… but after we discovered that we shared a grandfather, or so Paco told us, we spent some time apart."

"And he went back to his wife."

"He said it was one night only. One minute only to be exact."

"And now?"

"And now he has asked me to marry him, but how can I?"

"Sounds like you have the curse of Cayetano and Luna, how fitting."

"It's bizarre. My grandmother got pregnant in a one-night stand to Cayetano, which broke Luna's heart. Scarlett wrote to Luna many times and ever heard back."

"Scarlett wanted to right the wrongs that she did in Spain."

"Scarlett named her baby Alexander, awfully close to your name."

"When she was first going to take Paco away, I asked her to call him Alexander. I guess she honoured that in her own way, with her own baby." Alejandro's eyes were wet when he said it.

"Do you know why Paco called his son Cayetano?"

"I guess because Luna told him of her great love."

"Yes, but he told his own family that Cayetano was Luna's brother."

"Paco said Cayetano was Luna's brother?"

"Paco treated you and Cayetano as the same man. He always knew he had an uncle. I guess Luna just wanted your baby for herself and never told him that she wasn't his mother. I guess it was hard for him to understand, and even harder to explain."

"I can't blame her, she raised the boy. I told her to name him Paco. I'm glad she did that, and raised him to be a bullfighter. I wish I had been able to see her again."

"She died of tuberculosis in 1960."

"I was in the concentration camp at Porta Coeli until 1944, and in prison until 1956. After that, I came up here and never wanted to see another person again. I assumed Luna would have washed her hands of me."

"You were in the concentration camp at the monastery?"

"I was. I got caught not long after I refused to leave on the Stanland, but they didn't kill me because they thought I would be useful for labour. The camp was full so they moved some of us into prisons, and we were eventually released."

"What was it like? I have heard of people talk about the giant camp at Albatera, inland from Alicante…"

"I can't talk about that, *la chispa,* I'm sorry." The old man looked thoroughly defeated by his own history. "They killed at will, at random. They hated us. We were 'enemies of the State.' A lot of people starved to death or died of infections. When they shut the camp in 1956, I still didn't feel free. I still don't now. I wish they had killed me."

"Did they kill Cayetano?" Luna whispered.

"He was shot and buried."

"Where?"

"I can't say."

"Because you don't know, or don't want to tell me?"

"Please, don't ask me anymore. Your grandfather was my best friend, like a brother to me. He and Scarlett were all I had in the world, along with my sister and my wife. I'm grateful you have come here, but please, those years I can't talk about."

"Do you think that Luna would have ever overcome the pain of Scarlett getting pregnant to Cayetano?"

"You mean, should you forgive your Cayetano for his indiscretion with María? That's up to you. What I know is that the love that my friend had for my sister was so strong it could have sunk a ship or moved a mountain. His last moments were spent thinking of her."

"You witnessed his end?"

"Every moment. And when I close my eyes at night, I can still hear the gunshot that went in his back, and the sound of the flies buzzing around his lifeless body."

The conversation fell silent with that. The room was filled with the sound of the fire in the corner, and the quiet voices of the boys chatting away to one another. The only window was covered in condensation from the fire that warmed the stone structure in contrast to the bleak winter outside.

"I hate what this has done to me, and others," Luna said to break the silence between them. "I'm just a regular person, getting on with my life, and then I met Cayetano by accident. We uncovered all this, and in the process have unravelled our own families. It has hurt Paco, and you, having to bring all this back up. I'm hurting, Cayetano's hurting… it's a disaster, and all my fault. It's made a miserable and whining mess of me."

"If you lost your husband you can be excused for being sad about your life," Alejandro said. "I carry the same type of weight, and it doesn't get lighter. You just learn to carry it around."

"It's been three years," Luna said. "I have only adjusted because I met Cayetano."

"That's good. To meet another person you love is a blessing."

"Then why has it become a curse?"

"Sofía's kisses still linger on my lips. Her whispers in my ear can still be heard. Her touch can still be felt on my body. The smell of her skin, the softness of her hair, I still have all those things. I'm sure you have those things, from your husband."

"I do."

"They won't leave you. But I hid myself away, unable to move past Sofía's violent death. Your grandmother delivered Paco, after shooting the nun and the nurse who were going to take our baby and give him to a God-fearing Nationalist family. The whole thing ripped my heart out. I couldn't get past it, and I have lived my life alone with my demons. If you have found love a second time, then you should do anything you can for it. If you deny your desires, they will hurt you. Don't come here to hide away."

"I like it here, I feel drawn to the place."

"Do you know who the last owners were? The Medina family, they bought it for a summer home. They abandoned it, and I was able to purchase it. It could have been Cayetano's land, had he lived. Maybe that's why it's suitable for you here."

"I can't believe it," she muttered. Maybe fate was real after all.

"I'll let you have Escondrijo, if you want it that much, but only once I know you haven't wasted your second chance on fixing the Luna and Cayetano curse first."

33

Valencia, España ~ diciembre de 2009

Luna shivered in the morning winter sun. She sat in the café that was on the bottom floor of her apartment building, with the sun that streamed in the enormous window next to her. The place bustled with people going about their daily lives. Luna glanced down at her table; a cup of *café con leche*, a glass of orange juice, and a little chocolate pastry. Everyone needs chocolate for breakfast. She glanced her watch; 9:45. The jeweller had done a superb job, Fabrizio's watch looked like it had never been broken in Madrid. She had stressed she needed it perfect, as if that day never happened. She didn't want to look at its silver face and links, and remember the day she met Cayetano. Whether she liked it or not, she had to forget the man. He obviously didn't love her as much as he had claimed to.

Luna's eyes gazed around some of the people in the café. In the far corner was a young couple. Satchels lay at their feet, the symbol of the Universitat de València visible. They sat across from one another, hands held over their cups of coffee. Luna knew them; she was the daughter of an older couple who lived in her building, and her boyfriend who had recently moved in. They were both studying law and wanted a career in the public sector. Luna couldn't fathom why. The old-fashioned notion of job security may have enticed them.

There was a group of three men at the counter, who ordered coffee, beer and toast with olive oil. They were construction workers;

she had seen them at the apartment block nearby. They had whistled at Luna a number of times, and each time she had given them the international one finger salute. As they moved away to sit down, she saw Bonita, the elderly woman who lived alone on the first floor; her daily bread sat in a bag on the table as she sipped her drink. Bonita would rush over every time she saw Giacomo and Enzo, to tell Luna to dress them warm. Bonita's husband had died nearly 50 years ago, leaving her alone and childless. She would wander the building late at night, mumbling to herself, her knitting in tow. Luna felt sorry for her, and hoped her own grief wouldn't last that long. Bonita had told her that she hoped the same thing for her sake.

"Luna, *bon dia.*"

Her friend and former work colleague, Tomás Vega, stood there with a wide smile. She hadn't seen him since his 40th birthday earlier in the year. Before he sat down at her table, he gestured the young girl at the counter to get him a round of everything Luna had.

"*Bon dia.*" Luna smiled; now that Tomás ran a Valencian cycling team, he was eager to practice his Valencian dialect.

They kissed on both cheeks, and Tomás sat down across from her. "How are you, beautiful?"

"I won't lie, I've been better."

Tomás nodded. "Wow, I can't believe the three year anniversary of Fabrizio's accident is already upon us. I swear, when we're riding, I can still hear his voice on the team radio in my car."

Luna brought her hand to her face in an effort to hold back the tears that instantly sprung to her eyes. "I'm sorry," he implored, and reached out to her. "I don't want to upset you."

"It's okay," Luna said with a sniff. "You think you're over it, and then little things remind you of it all."

"Where are the boys? At school?"

"Yeah. They have no idea that it's the anniversary of their father's death this week. It means nothing to them. I'm glad; that way it doesn't hurt them."

Tomás shook his head. His solemn face spoke of true sympathy. "I think that maybe if I had told the guys to take a week off training…"

"It would have made no difference. Fabrizio wasn't riding because his manager told him to. He did it because he wanted to every day. Thousands of moments lead up to that accident and we didn't have the power to change any of them. Trust me; I have been over every one of them."

"Killed only a few weeks before Christmas. Nothing could be crueller."

"I don't find much joy in Christmas, that's for sure." Luna sighed as the waitress brought over Tomás' breakfast. "With no family I never did like it, but now, even less so."

"Will you go to Palermo for Christmas this year?"

"Yes, in a couple of days. A few weeks in Italy will do me good. I will bury Fabrizio's ashes on his family's property."

"That's a great idea!"

"I thought so. I wanted to do it here, since he loved it so much. But his parents and sisters are all still in Sicily, so I thought he should go home to them. It's time I did it."

"He would appreciate that. He was such a family man."

"He was."

"I remember him, on the podium in Paris when he won the Tour de France, unable to wave to the fans because he had two one-year olds in his arms."

"That photo is on the wall in the boys' bedroom."

"That's nice." Tomás took a sip of his coffee. "What did you ring me for, Luna? Anything you need, I can help you."

"Darren told me that you have a job for me on the team."

"He told me that you had reservations. I also saw you punch Paul in the face."

"You did? I can understand if you didn't want to hire me after that."

"Actually, I told Paul to go back to England to think about his career. We will have 20 riders on our team, and I won't waste a space on him. There are plenty of splendid Spanish riders we can hire, and Valencian locals would be even better. Good for our image."

"Darren will still be the number one rider?"

"Yes, we need to take the best we can get, and Darren's the best with Fabrizio gone. If we want to win grand tours, we will do it with Darren. We are in need of another mechanic, so the job is yours, if you want it."

"I want it." Luna was certain of that.

"Are you sure?"

"I am. I want my career back. It's an odd life, but I enjoy it. I can't work full time for you, 10 months a year on the road isn't something I can do. If Darren is the top rider on the team, he needs his own mechanic anyway. I want that job."

"Have you told Darren?"

"No, he went to Australia a week ago, and I haven't heard from him. This is my choice."

"Luna, I would love to have you on the team with us," Tomás said. "Marco is the team leader, and I have already spoken to him about hiring you. He is behind it. We are doing a photoshoot, the team on bikes around the main sites of the city, to use as promotion for the city tourism board. Marco said that having you there would help. After the loss of Fabrizio Merlini, Luna Montgomery is back on the team. He thinks that would be a delightful story. You in Fabrizio's gear, at the famous sites of the city…"

"Using my husband's fame and death to promote the team? Classy."

"I know. I told him to fuck off." They both smiled. "Unless you wanted to?"

"I'll think about it." Luna took a deep breath. Time to go back to work in pro-cycling without her husband. There was a sense of freedom in that. "I need to get my work permit renewed if I work for you next year."

"No problem, Luis is still working as our lawyer. We can get him to sort it so you don't have too much hassle. I know the process can be difficult for New Zealanders. What about the kids?"

"Any chance I can ride in the team car with you and put their car seats in with us? They would love it."

"For you, anything."

"Great. When I get back from Italy, I'll sign a contract. New year, new start."

"Did you ever find your grandfather? Darren told me all about it."

"Sort of, I know that he was here in Valencia at the end of the war. He was an anarchist who was killed in a concentration camp when Franco took power. What happened to him after that, I may never know."

Tomás nodded thoughtfully. "My grandfather was the same."

"Yeah?"

"My family lived in Barcelona when the war started. They were fascists, but Barcelona was the stronghold of the Republicans. My grandfather was dragged out of the house one night and shot. My grandmother saw it, and so did my mother, though she was young. His body was carted away and dumped. They never did find out where his body was buried. Doesn't matter what side your family was on, you were still wronged, one way or another. When the Nationalists won the war, those who had killed my grandfather were murdered in reprisal killings. My grandmother said justice wasn't done in that, it's all just misery."

"No one is innocent. They were all as bad as each other."

"I agree, but you have to just leave that all alone. Why bring it up? We are the future of Spain, and life is hard enough now. If I hear the words *'crisis económico'* one more time…"

"Let's just race bikes and be happy."

Tomás smiled. "Now that is a plan."

34

Valencia, España ~ diciembre de 2009

The dry weather had given away to unusually heavy rain in the night. Valencia's paths and streets cascaded with flowing water by the time darkness had fallen. Luna had packed her bags for Italy and sent her children to bed. They were excited to finish school early to go on a Christmas adventure. The apartment was clean, the gifts wrapped, and the paperwork that allowed her to carry human ashes on a flight were all arranged and put in her bag.

Luna flicked off her hairdryer and put it on the dresser. She looked a mess in the reflection of the mirror. She had stepped out of the shower and put her short fluffy white robe on, and between her tired face and flat hair, she looked as if she had aged 20 years in a matter of weeks. She felt as if she had. Going to see Alejandro more often didn't do her any good. He wouldn't talk about his life anymore, instead he took her for walks around Escondrijo and talked about the area. All the same it was company. She gave him a kiss on the cheek on her last visit since she would be away for several weeks. He had protested but gave in. She liked him. But her heart was heavy in her chest. Heavy from the weight of lost love. Now she had the sting of that misery to carry around for more than one man.

She fluffed her now-dry black curls and tried to smile at herself, in an effort to look a bit better. Nope. The sound of the rain dominated the room, and she hoped the children wouldn't be woken with the tapping against their window. It had been hard enough to get them to sleep with their excitement of a plane ride to Palermo. Her concern turned to annoyance when she heard the doorbell ring. It was late, and friends, neighbours and colleagues all knew not to ring the Merlini doorbell, because the children went to bed earlier than the traditional late bedtimes enjoyed by Spanish children. She pulled her robe tight around her otherwise naked body, and headed down the dark hallway to see who was there.

On tiptoe to the high peephole, she looked into the hallway, worried about who would come to her door while she was alone. Luna could have sworn her heart stopped beating when she saw who was there. Her *torero*.

"Luna?" She heard his muffled voice through the heavy door. "*¿Estás en casa?*"

She hesitantly turned the key in the lock; the deadbolts clunked undone to let the door open. Cayetano stood there, soaking wet. In one hand was an enormous bouquet of red roses, all wet and mushed, limp on their long stems. In his other hand was a long brown tube, which dripped as much as the man who held it. He looked cold and miserable, his clothes stuck to his magnificent body, and water ran out of his hair and over his face. "I thought it never rained in Valencia!" he cried.

Luna stood back, and he took it as an invitation to step inside. "Why are you here?" They hadn't spoken in weeks, and she thought that the silence was pretty telling; she didn't condone his behaviour and he knew it.

"I bought you a present," he said, and gingerly handed her the soaking wet tube.

Luna read the now barely visible label on it – *Soft Construction with Boiled Beans (Premonition of Civil War) by Salvador Dalí*. She loved that painting.

"I thought you might like a copy of the painting, since it doesn't hang in the Prado." His voice was hesitant as he spoke, almost worried. "But perhaps now it's ruined."

"If something is destroyed on the outside, it can still be intact on the inside," she said softly and placed it against the wall behind her.

Cayetano dropped the drowned roses to the floor and closed the door behind him, but didn't take his eyes off her. He didn't have any more words. He left countless messages for her, to say sorry and to ask for forgiveness, but the words had lost their meaning. Luna gasped, almost cried out when he grabbed her and threw a kiss on her lips. She found herself pinned between him and the full length mirror on the wall, the gasp elicited more from the chill of his cold hands on her than the surprise of the intense moment. He was cold and wet, but she didn't care. She wanted to push him off her, slap him, send him away. But she couldn't. The urge to hold him close outweighed the desire to do the 'right' thing.

Meeting Cayetano Beltrán was a painful experience. He turned her intensely fragile world into a jumbled mess – love, then pain, then love, then betrayal, then confusion. And yet she found herself peeling his wet shirt from his body; she didn't hear the slap it made when the fabric hit the floor somewhere behind him. She could barely feel her bathrobe get damp and heavy as it absorbed the water from him. His cold hand had gone up under the edge of the robe, and between her legs. The cold sensation overpowered the heat she felt inside her the moment his hands went to her body. The man had only just stepped in the door, barely a word spoken, and already she wanted to tear his pants off. Goosebumps appeared all over Luna's body; it could have been the cold, or it could have the force of how he made her feel.

"Stop," she managed to whisper.

They both froze in the moment, their hands on each other, their faces still touching, their eyes closed. Luna could feel his wet body against her, and his warm breath on her neck. He breathed as heavy as she did. Her robe had come untied in the tousle, which left her bare against him. The hand that had tantalised between her legs rested on the inside of her thigh, the other at the back of her neck, and wouldn't let her go from his embrace. The pause stretched longer, and longer, and Luna could feel the heavy weight of all the drama that had gone on between them seep away.

Cayetano turned his face slightly against her hand that lay on his cheek; he kissed her palm once, twice, a third time, each slowly moved up her fingers. He reached her fingertips, and let her move her fingers over his bottom lip, gently rubbing back and forward as he brought his eyes to hers. She could feel his pulse sear through his veins, as if he had run all the way from Madrid in the rain.

The anticipation grew as they leant against one another. There was no going back, no moment for a rational conversation; there was nothing more to say. She had wanted him to stop because she felt prisoner to his desires, but she liked it too much to send him away.

"Where?" he whispered.

Cayetano suddenly felt weak in her arms. She stepped forward to release herself from his embrace, and took his hand to guide him down the dark hallway. Everything was silent, in slow motion, smooth but with a heightened consciousness of how each of them wanted to unleash themselves. Luna shut her bedroom door behind him. She could feel his eyes on her every move. The second she turned to him, his dominance took over the moment again, and his now dry hands pushed her robe from her shoulders. They stumbled towards her bed in the dark, four hands desperate get his jeans off, the stubborn wet fabric made the task difficult. The infuriating trousers discarded, they fell into the warm bed. Their hot bodies were unable to feel anything but one another.

Every nerve was shattered. Her heels dug into the bed as she forced her body against his. Her impatience made her unguarded, it left her on her back, and Cayetano was free to do as he pleased. He took immense delight in every whimper she gave out when he stroked inside her to see how far he could push her. She didn't dare to release his mouth from hers to speak, and brought her hand gently to his arm so he would stop teasing her. She needed more.

The man knew what more was. She didn't recognise the noise she made when she came, a deep groan that cried of surrender. She felt him burst, the powerful force of his own release leave his body and into hers. He held on to her so tight that the tips of his fingers dug into her back, and she loved it. She could feel tears in her eyes, but wasn't sure if they were a relief, or if they had been literally squeezed from her body by some libidinous power.

Luna loved his muscular weight on top of her, not a word said. He lay there, his breath erratic as he came slowly back to earth. Her mind was still caught up in a fog of indulgence when he lifted his head and kissed her, his affection now gentle and composed. She could feel the same equal parts invigoration and exhaustion in him that she felt. They finally parted, and he rested his head between her breasts, his arms wrapped around her waist. She ran her hand through his hair, still a little damp. She was surprised the water hadn't turned to steam. She was that hot underneath him, even the moisture between her thighs that was now against his stomach felt hot.

Cayetano's voice broke the silence first. "It's never felt like this before." His voice was only just above a whisper.

"Actions speak when words fail."

"I miss you."
"Please, don't. Can't we just have some peace?"
"No, I fear not."

Sleep came and went. Luna was up early, in order to complete the last tasks she had to do before she set off for her early flight to Palermo. She had dried Cayetano's clothes for him. When she went back into her bedroom with them, she found him awake in bed, a disorientated look on his face. It was still dark, only a thin strip of light shone through the tiny gap under the ensuite door. He looked almost fearful when Luna came in.

"I thought I lost you," he said as she sat down next to him.
"In my own house?"
A grin spread over his tired face. "Good point. Why are you up?"
"I'm going to Italy today. Soon, in fact. I need to wake the boys."
"Can I see them?"
"Is that a good idea?"
"I don't know, is it?"
"Why are you here?"
"Because I love you, and you left me."
"You know why."
"No, I don't." Cayetano sat up in the bed and reached out to her. "Luna, please I made one mistake."
Luna looked down at her hands on her lap. One of his hands almost encircled both of hers. "One really big mistake."
"So what was last night?"
"I... I don't know."
"Love. Lust. Luna, you overpower me."
"So does your wife."
Cayetano sighed as he hung his head. "No, she doesn't. It was one moment, one stupid moment that I can barely recall. I thought that my whole life was ruined, and... I don't know... she was there..."
"She was there. How many more times will she be there? Or will anyone do? You can't love me and do that."
"I was angry. At everything. I felt as if we're cursed."
"Feels a bit that way."
"Scarlett may have broken up our grandparents, but that doesn't mean that María can do it to us. We don't need to let her win."
"This isn't fate. This is real life. These are our own mistakes. We

can't blame some magic higher power. It's not fate, or a curse… coincidence maybe. We all live and die by our own sword."

"This is killing me."

"Me too." Luna wiped a tear from her eye; she couldn't dare look at him. "But I've had my heart broken before. All you can do is keep going. I'm pushing ahead with my life. I'm going to bury Fabrizio ashes, and spend time with his family for the boys, and then I'm going back to work as a bike mechanic. You just have to keep going."

"I can't."

"You're going to be a father, like you always wanted. It's something I can't give you. This could be your only chance to have the child you have long wanted."

"I can't forget you. I love you."

Luna brought her wet eyes up to the man in her bed. "I love you." Her voice began to shake. "And I worry that I won't ever get over it."

Tears had started to run down Cayetano's face, and he didn't even care. "Please… I'm begging you… don't leave me."

"I'm going to Italy for three weeks."

"Can I call you?"

"While I'm with my in-laws? I would prefer if you didn't. This trip is always hard."

"I'm sure. Emotionally charged."

"I have a lot people to think of. To me, burying ashes isn't goodbye. I have said goodbye. But it's the homecoming of the only son of the Merlini family for everyone else. My children go through a lot, and most of it isn't easy for them to understand."

"One day, when you're ready, you can think of yourself."

"I have been doing that for months. I've made a mess of my life."

"Mine is also a mess, if that helps."

"Not really, that's my fault."

"Is it María's baby? Is that the problem? I can't turn my back on the child, I'm sorry."

"I know you can't do that," she dismissed him. "But for you to have a child with someone who isn't me can't go well for us. It's complicated."

Cayetano inched closer to her in the bed. "What about when you come home from Italy?"

"How do I know you won't be back with María in that time?"

"Did last night not show you anything? I love you. You can't ask why, there's no answer. We are bound together, by love, and time, and fate. If you tell me that you don't feel that, I will walk away. But I will be forever broken."

"I can't tell you that," she whispered.

"Whenever you're ready, I will be here. But before you leave, is there any chance for us?"

"Maybe."

"I will wait forever on a maybe."

35

Madrid, España ~ diciembre de 2009

December 24. Christmas Eve at the Beltrán Morales home in La Moraleja. Cayetano was at his parents' place, along with his grandparents for lunch. He didn't want to be there, but at least it kept him away from María. She hadn't dared show her face since her bombshell a few weeks ago, but he had received a message to say she wanted him to go to her ultrasound. Screw that.

Paco looked over at him. He knew that life had broken open for his only son. Cayetano sat across the room with his shoulders slumped, his mood despondent. He wanted to avoid conversation with everyone. Paco had been hard on Cayetano his whole life, he argued that he and his son were too different, but Inés argued that they were too alike. Maybe his mother was right. Right now, Cayetano ached with the agony of being away from Luna; he hadn't heard from her in nearly three weeks.

Paco turned to his father-in-law, José. The man was only 10 years older than him, and they were close friends. *"Padre."* He leaned over to speak to José, who he had always addressed so formally, as his wife did. *"Padre,* I need your help with the boy."

José Morales Ruiz was a strict man, imposing in attitude and stature, even at 80 years old. That was part of the reason he always got along so well with the stubborn Paco Beltrán. The old man glanced away from his son-in-law to his grandson. He loved Cayetano, had done everything he could for him, and was so proud of all his achievements. If Cayetano suffered, so did José. He possessed all the pride that the man half his age did but was far softer with Cayetano than Paco. When Cayetano had fallen in the ring back in August, it had taken a toll on his grandfather. "What's wrong? Is he sulking over the girl that Inés told me about?"

Paco nodded. "We need to talk with him." He turned in his seat, to see his wife and her mother Consuela in the kitchen, gossiping as usual. *"Princesa,"* he called to his wife. "We are just going down to my office for a moment. Work to discuss."

"What work?" Inés stood in the doorway with her hands on her hips. She glanced toward her son in the corner. "Can't it wait for another day?"

"It can't wait one more day. I've wasted enough days." Paco stood up from his seat and kissed her on the cheek. "Go and do your womanly things."

Cayetano heard his mother scoff, and he smiled. He never did understand why she put up with Paco. "You don't need me," he mumbled towards his father.

"I need you." José stood up, and gestured for his grandson to do the same. "Come and talk with me."

The three men trailed down the hallway and closed themselves in Paco's office. The Beltrán chest still sat in the corner, with its broken lock, and it looked sad. It looked as miserable as Cayetano did. They sat down, Paco behind his desk, José on the dark leather couch across the room. Cayetano sat down on a single chair by the window in the sun, the hard seat better for his sore leg.

"Right, from the beginning, Caya. Tell me everything, *nieto,"* José said.

"About what?" Cayetano shrugged.

"The girl, Cayetano," Paco's sharp tone said. "The thing that's making you fucking miserable."

"I don't want to talk about it."

"I didn't ask if you wanted to talk about it," José said.

Cayetano took a breath. He still hadn't told anyone that María was pregnant. He was surprised that she hadn't rung Inés and told her. He had expected it. In fact, for someone so keen to split him and Luna up, María had been quiet. She must not have expected his response to the bad news. Probably expected him to cave in and take her back.

"I will start," Paco said. "Cayetano met a young girl, Luna. They went out a few times, and in his eagerness to impress her, he made some rather grandiose errors."

"Whatever," Cayetano muttered.

"The way I hear it, Cayetano fell in love with this girl and ended up with his leg injury. But she is also the reason he has been so keen to recover."

"Every man needs a vice, and beautiful girls are the most dangerous, but most enjoyable option," José said.

"Luna is a New Zealand girl, here looking for her Spanish grandfather. He died in the civil war, ¿no?" Paco asked.

"Sí," Cayetano replied.

"Luna's family lived across the street from my family in Cuenca, in the 1930's," Paco told José.

"¡Oh! That is interesting. You never mention the Beltrán family, Paco."

"I know. That's the problem." Paco took a pause. "I have been keeping secrets, and it has accidentally hurt Cayetano. For that, I'm sorry. I never thought it would happen."

Cayetano looked up to his father. He hadn't seen that coming. He wasn't sure his father had ever uttered the word 'sorry' in his life.

"Maybe it's time you told us everything," José said. "The dead can't argue with you."

"My mother and father, Luna and Ignacio, are the problem." Paco swallowed hard. "Ignacio isn't my real father."

"I see. I assumed it was because he died when you were young that you never spoke of him."

"Ignacio died when I was only four. Pneumonia got him."

"Are you sure?" Cayetano asked. "I mean, have you ever seen a death certificate?"

"No, but my mother told me. She wouldn't lie."

"Oh yes she would," Cayetano snorted. He turned to José. "Ignacio was gay."

José cocked one eyebrow. "That explains why he isn't your father then, Paco."

"How do you know he wasn't just dragged from his home in the night by his fascist comrades and shot for his sexuality? Being gay was seriously out of step with the perilous conservative stronghold of the time."

José gave his grandson a stern look. "Caya, that's enough."

"I call it as I see it."

"Not on something so sensitive you don't. Don't speak so ill of Falange members."

"I'm sorry, what? Are we defending fascists now?"

"Just ignore him, Caya," Paco interrupted.

"It seems like all people do is lie to suit themselves! My opinions don't need to be censored! I never agreed to any pact of forgetting."

"You shouldn't judge what you don't understand," José sighed. "I was only a child during the war. Life was hard, I hid all the time amongst the Republicans who held the city. Madrid was surrounded on three sides by Nationalist troops, who tried to rescue the city, and we were trapped for years, and had to live amongst so much hate. Hate was the only survivor in those times."

"And yet you prospered under the following dictatorship, didn't you, Papí?" Cayetano watched his grandfather shift uncomfortably in his seat. "You were always safe, weren't you? Deeply religious your whole life, and you support Spain as one nation – none of that autonomy rubbish would agree with you, would it? You had Rebelión, which made you a landowner, something many only would have dreamed of. There were no years of hunger for your family, were there? People who only thought of themselves flourished under the regime. Like Papá here, fighting in the ring, loved by Franco himself."

"Cayetano, you have lived your life in this family, why is any of this news to you?" José asked.

"Our family has never denied who we are," Paco said.

"Yes, but it's the Morales family who believe all these things, isn't it, Papá? I have never seen you force your opinions on me, not political opinions anyway. Please tell me, why is that?"

"Caya, you are dragging up remarkably old issues. Grievances long lost."

"Not that old. This happened all in my lifetime."

"What's the point here? I thought this was about the girl," José said. "Did she find her family?"

"Her grandmother was a member of the International Brigade, and her grandfather was an anarchist."

José raised his eyebrows. "I see. You shouldn't need to worry about that. It's old news now."

"I'm not put off Luna because of the beliefs of her family. She was raised in New Zealand, free of hate and the shackles of old ideas."

"I'm still lost on where all this is going."

"You see, Papá's mother, Luna, had an affair with a man named Cayetano."

José watched his grandson sit back in his seat. "The fact you have the same name as the man worries me."

"It should, Papí. This other Cayetano was her lover."

José's eyes flicked from Cayetano to Paco. "Boys will be boys. We have all had lovers."

"True," Cayetano continued. "But the problem for Paco is that the Beltrán family were anarchists, as was this Cayetano. Papá seems ashamed of this."

"I'm not ashamed that the Beltrán's were Republican supporters," Paco said. "But I have nothing to do with it. My mother was not an anarchist, her family was, but in her heart she was conservative. She happily left her family and moved to Madrid to live in a fascist family."

"Is that so?" José asked. "How fascinating. She had extraordinary courage. Let me guess, you're the bastard child of your mother and this *rojo* bastard that she slept with?"

Paco nodded. "I'm not proud of it, but that's the case. She married Ignacio, but he died. I can assure you that my mother was right-wing in her political and religious beliefs."

"She turned her back on the whole family?" Cayetano asked.

"She told me that she did. The trouble is that this girl of Caya's, this Luna, is also the grandchild of Cayetano Ortega. Luna's father is my half-brother."

José looked between the two men. "*Jesucristo.* The *rojo* bastard was obviously trouble. I hope he got a bullet."

"He did, in a concentration camp after the war," Cayetano said.

"Good."

"How do you know?" Paco asked his son, while he watched the indignant look Cayetano gave José.

"Luna told me," Cayetano said without a look at his father. "Papí, how can you be so callous? You were a child during the war. You were poisoned by the misguided opinions fed to you."

"I know what I believe," José said. "Call me Falangist,

conservative, Carlist, monarchist, I don't care. I know what I wanted for Spain, and we won the war. We prospered as a result of the dictatorship. You are, as a result, rich and successful. You are who you are, Cayetano, because of what I have done. My hard work was handed to your father, and now to you."

"You mean by breeding bulls and horses?"

"Where do you think I earned the money to buy Rebelión?"

Cayetano swallowed hard. Did he want the answer?

"José, I have asked you all of Cayetano's life not to tell him what you used to do for a living," Paco said.

"Maybe it's time he knew," José replied. "And it wasn't just a job, it was something I believed in. It was my contribution to our country."

"Okay, I'll bite," Cayetano said. "What was it that you did?"

"I started out as a member of Guardia Civil, but then was asked to join a special brigade. Franco wanted to flush out all those who had defied him. So many bastards thought that they could defy the regime, even long after Franco took power. They were enemies of the State. We were paid well to find these people."

"And do what with them?" Murder, torture, rape? Fuck, this was about to go down as the worst Christmas in history.

"The dissidents needed to be taught a lesson."

"Dissidents? You mean anyone with left-wing views?"

"I think this discussion has gone too far off-course," Paco said.

"No, I want to hear more," Cayetano said. "Please, Papí, tell me."

"No." Paco's voice showed his anger.

"I have a right to know if my grandfather is a murderer."

"No, you don't."

"I'm not ashamed of anything I have done," José said. "Yes, Caya, I did have to kill people. It was part of the job. These *rojos* are so disgusting that even now, the ground that we dumped them in, it rejects them. And now, people have the nerve to think they can dig these pigs up."

"They are people. Husbands, fathers, children, siblings, lovers," Cayetano said. "Other people cared about those you hurt."

"Lovely little wives may have wanted to see their husbands while they were in prison, but we taught those girls a lesson. You should have heard them cry when we stripped them and…"

"That's enough," Cayetano butted in, and jumped from his seat.

The thought of his grandfather raping girls was too much to bear. He could have gone his whole life without knowing the truth. Now it was too late. The ghosts of the past had woken up. "What about Alejandro Beltrán?" He was riled up enough to tell them some truths of his own now. "Would you round up innocent men like him?"

"Who?" José asked.

"Luna Beltrán's brother. Papá, do you know what happened to your uncle Alejandro?"

"No. Mamá never knew what happened to him. She said it was his decision to disappear from her life," Paco said.

"She kept photos of him, didn't she? Photos, letters, little bits and pieces. He was the one who loved bullfighting, the one who prompted her to push you into the art of bullfighting."

"Caya, I don't care. Yes, my family were left-wingers. I have lived my life not believing in the same things that my family did. I have had a happy life with the people I surrounded myself with. I met your mother, and yes, the Morales family are a strong conservative family, and I didn't care. It's as your *abuelo* told you, it's all old grievances. None of this matters."

"The bitterness in Papí's voice is still there when says that he thinks the *rojos* all deserved to be shot."

"And I won't change my opinion!" José cried. "History only favours the winner, Caya. Stick with the winners, it's who we are."

"Alejandro Beltrán is still alive," Cayetano said lightheartedly, and looked out the window. "He lives just outside Valencia. He and Luna have been spending quite a lot of time together."

Paco had gone pale. Very pale. "How can you be sure?"

"They have been chatting. Alejandro has taken quite a shine to her. Cayetano Ortega and Scarlett Montgomery were his best friends. The man has lived a terribly lonely life, far from home, and his son."

"Who is his son?" José asked.

"He sits at the desk here. Paco Beltrán is the son of Alejandro Beltrán, an anarchist supporter from Cuenca, and Sofía Perez, a young nurse. They were married in a revolutionary wedding, not even a marriage sanctioned by the church or the State, but instead by the unions. And you thought my civil wedding to María was a slap in the face of Catholicism!"

"Paco?" José asked. "Is that true?"

"No, Luna was my mother."

"You know Alejandro and Sofía had a child. You said the baby died," Cayetano said.

"Mamá told me that the baby died."

"You are the baby," Cayetano told his father. "Alejandro named you Paco. He has been reading about you in the paper ever since, he watched you in favour with the political parties that tried to kill him, who killed his father, and who murdered his best friend, Cayetano Ortega. Whether we like it or not, there is a political hangover in this country. Those with crazy right-wing opinions still make their presence known." Cayetano looked at his grandfather. "I have a feeling one of them is sitting across the room."

"Franco saved us," José said. "I will never apologise for my support to the man. Socialist ideals won't be forced on me by some downtrodden, working class fanatics." He stood up from his seat and left the office, not another word said.

Cayetano and Paco sat eye to eye for a moment. "What I don't understand, is that for the last 40 years, we never had these conversations. I have never considered us political," Cayetano said.

"We're Spanish; were all political."

"But we live with a Francoist."

"José can believe whatever he wants."

"What do you believe, Papá?"

"I believe there are no innocent or honest parties where politics are concerned."

"That we can all agree on," Cayetano scoffed.

"Caya, I left all this behind when my mother died. She left me a lot of money, money she had got from Ignacio. Having money allowed me to make decisions for myself. It gave me choices. Many here were starving, but I was able to pursue a career in fighting bulls. This put me in the path of the conservatives, the wealthy right-wingers who controlled the country. The middle classes and the rich were happy. It was easy to blend in and get by. I had no allegiance to anyone; it was only when I met your mother that I was considered right-wing also. But all I have ever done is get by. I won't form a political opinion based on a war that happened before my time. I make my own decisions, just like my mother did."

"Your life hasn't been as cosy as you claim, has it?"

"I grew up watching unrestrained vengeances being carried out. I decided that I wouldn't take sides."

"Is that possible?"

"No. But I loved your mother, and that drove most of my life's decisions. I make no apologies for that."

"I want my life's decisions to be based on being able to be with Luna, Papá. You and I aren't that different."

Paco paused. "You have fallen in love with a foreigner, maybe you are the lucky one." He watched Cayetano smile. "Don't ever tell your mother, but the left-wing candidates always get my vote. I like the ideas of freedom and of the State and the church being separate."

"Yet you sit in church every week with Mamá and her parents."

Paco shrugged. "Women. What can you do?"

Cayetano nodded in agreement. "I know all of this is irrelevant. I have opened a can of worms, and for nothing, none of this has anything to do with me and Luna."

"Well, if she is telling the truth, and I doubt she has a reason to lie, then you are not related to her."

"How do you feel about this?"

"I have nothing against Luna personally, I don't know her."

"I mean, how do you feel about Alejandro being your father, and Sofía being your mother?"

"Luna Beltrán was my mother as far as I'm concerned. We lived a lonely existence together. None of that can be changed. But I don't want to know Alejandro Beltrán, if that's what you're getting at. The past can stay buried."

"How did you keep all this a secret from me all this time?"

"Do you feel better for knowing the truth?"

"No!" Cayetano cried.

"There you have it. It's ugly. I don't condone your grandfather's behaviour, but I can't change it either. He had already given up that life for country living when I met him."

"Does his wife know he's a rapist? Does Mamá know that her father is a murderer?"

"No, and it needs to stay that way. Can you see why I tell you to not dig into your family's history?"

"It does make sense now."

"It wasn't about Luna, Caya. Never. She wasn't the problem; she simply woke you up to things that we were lying about."

"I've done something terrible, Papá."

"What? Besides enflaming your psychotic grandfather?"

"María is pregnant."

Paco's face dropped. "What? When? How?"

"How? The usual way. Drunk and stupid and miserable."

"And Luna knows this?"

"She does."

"And?"

"And I think she hates me."

"So you're not related, but still can't be together?"

"Seems not. But I still want a divorce from María."

"Then, if Luna forgives you, then you can be with her?"

"You support me now? After everything?"

"This time, I'm not going to let my own defiant attitude influence your choices. It's not my place to tell you what to you, Caya. Where is Luna? Don't *extranjeros* celebrate Christmas on December 25? That's tomorrow. You should go and see her."

"She is in Italy with her dead husband's family."

"That is very kind. When is she back?"

"This week."

"Then fuck Cayetano Ortega and all the drama he has created. We all need to get out of his shadow and be happy. You need to win that girl back. I would do anything for your mother. It's time you did the same for your girl."

"I don't deserve her."

"No, I agree. But that doesn't mean you need to give up."

36

Palermo, Italia ~ diciembre de 2009

Sending an envelope on its way. That was how it felt to let Fabrizio's ashes go on Max and Paulina Merlini's Italian olive grove. He had ridden his bike through the grove as a kid, while he dreamed of a life as a cyclist. Now, after passing away at the age of only 37, Fabrizio was buried in the centre of the grove, where a large tree stood. Max and Paulina spent time there, to enjoy the peace of their property, and now their son could rest there. For Fabrizio's parents, it was a painful and emotional homecoming, with a sense of relief that their son was back with them. For his three younger sisters, it was upsetting; the shining star of the family had dimmed, and only now were they able to bid farewell to him. For his sons, it was confusing; all the adults in their lives were sad, and they were still not old enough to understand.

For Luna, it was many things. It was sad; she had kept Fabrizio with her much longer than was probably healthy. But when she curled up the little piece of paper she had written a poem on, and placed the varnished box into the earth, she felt free. Not of her husband, but of the pain that his death had caused. So much had gone through her mind over three years — did he know he would die when the car hit him, did he see the car coming, did he feel any pain, what crossed his mind at his final moment? None of these questions would be answered, but her dreams weren't haunted by the uncertainty of not knowing, as they used to be. Luna didn't wish for him to be with her all the time, as she once used to. She didn't feel helpless, as she once used to. She didn't feel bound to a ghost, as she once did. Now, the misery of their whole ordeal had let her go. Now, she accepted what had happened.

Luna had no recollection of her own mother, and to spend time with Fabrizio's mother was always an experience. She never had a woman she could turn to for advice, love, or comfort. It was hard to know how to interact with Paulina and her husband Max, even when Fabrizio was alive. Christmas Day saw 40 family members in attendance, parents, sisters, aunts, uncles, nieces and nephews of the man they had laid to rest. Luna loved to see Giacomo and Enzo so welcomed, and so happy with the other children. While the comfort she gained from her husband was long gone, the Merlini's still cared for Fabrizio's boys like they had once cared for their son. That was all Luna needed from them.

"Qualcosa di sbagliato, Luna?"

Luna looked up from her full wine glass and looked at her mother-in-law across the living room from her. Paulina and Max had chatted in her direction most of the evening while they sat together near the fireplace, but she hadn't listened. "Nothing's wrong. I'm fine."

"You haven't touched your wine – again."

Luna looked back at the drink, a heavy red wine. She didn't have the heart to tell them that she didn't like it; it was Fabrizio's favourite. "I'm just tired."

"It has been nice to have you here," Max said. "You know how much it means to us to have Fabrizio's children here."

"We know you have to move on with your life, so we appreciate you coming, Luna, really," Paulina added.

"You never have to worry about me not bringing them here." Luna looked out the window, the sky dark over the olive grove. "It's been really enjoyable to be here, calming. Relaxing. It's good to get away from the world."

"Is there something you have forgotten to mention to us?" Paulina asked. "You won't drink your wine, you're tired all the time, you have a glow…"

Luna just shook her head.

"Are you pregnant?"

"No!" she scoffed. "Please, no, never again. Besides, it would be hard to get pregnant, given the state of my marriage."

"I would hate to think you are as sad as you seem because of Fabrizio. Of course, we all miss him very much. But I would be seriously worried if you still suffer as much now as you did when he died. You are young; you have a lot of life left."

"Moving forward has been a lot harder than I imagined." Luna set her glass down on the table in front of her but couldn't bring her eyes back to the pair.

"Who is Cayetano?" Max asked. "I've heard the boys mention him a few times, and when I asked them who he was, they said that he was the man that Mummy would marry, but they couldn't tell anyone."

Luna covered her eyes with her hand and sighed. Five-year-olds simply couldn't lie. All the bribes in the world wouldn't win them over. "He is a guy I met a few months ago."

"You are seeing him? Is it serious?"

"No. It's not. It's nothing."

"Luna." Paulina waited until she made eye contact again. "Luna, is this man the reason you're sad?"

"It's a long story, and not one appropriate for here. I came to see you, and celebrate Fabrizio's life. Nothing else."

"That doesn't mean you can't talk about your life, or see another man. It's horrible to think of you so alone in the world. Everyone needs someone that can count on."

"No, that won't happen. No man will come before Fabrizio."

"Fabrizio is gone," Max said in a serious tone.

"No one will replace him."

"No one has to, but you can still be happy with someone new."

"I wish it was that simple."

Paulina sat forward in her seat. "Luna, you had two children with Fabrizio. You will always be bound to him. You will see him in their faces. You can't raise them in a home of grief and guilt. They won't thrive in that world. Fabrizio loved you when you were young, free, spontaneous, vibrant. Honour him by being the girl he loved."

37

Valencia, España ~ diciembre de 2009

Luna wasn't sure what she had hoped for when she arrived home to the sunny shores of Valencia. The house was as she left it, empty and lonely. Darren had phoned a few times, to report that he was on his way back to Spain. Luna had put her suitcase in her room and exited quickly – she could swear that she could smell Cayetano on the sheets on her bed. They needed to be washed right away. But there was one surprise; a package had arrived for her, and the *portero* had kept it for her until they returned. Expressed couriered from Madrid by Paco Beltrán. Could be anything.

Late into the evening, Luna sat down with her package. How did Paco even know her address? Cayetano knew, obviously, so it was safe to assume the men were speaking again. At least that harm had been undone. She opened the box and pulled out a short note –

Dear Luna,
I have enclosed the letters written by Scarlett Montgomery to my mother. We felt you should read them first. Also, enclosed is one of my mother's diaries, which I never had the courage to read. I never kept them in the chest, so that is why you haven't seen them before. Maybe these will help you put some of the pieces of your family together. If you find it in your heart to forgive my idiota *son for what he has done, return the diary to him. If we do not see it again, we will know the secrets are safe with you.*
Kind regards
Paco Beltrán Caño

Luna looked at the treasure before her. The bundle of letters from Scarlett she had seen in the chest. The diary was a new thing, and it could house secrets. With care, she slipped the old ribbon from the pile, to free the mystery. This was her grandmother writing to Cayetano's grandmother. She briefly considered whether Paco knew the truth about his parentage now, but brushed it aside. Luna Beltrán had been his adoptive mother, and maybe that was all that mattered. She picked up the first letter, eager to all read 50 or so.

14 July 1945

My dear Luna,
I know this letter may come as a surprise. We have not seen one another for six years now. It is almost impossible to get information out of España, especially something as detailed as your address. I sincerely hope this letter finds you well.

Nothing I could write will ever right any of the wrongs that have been committed between us all. I do worry for you. I feel guilty for being here, safe and well with my son, Alexander. I do not know what life you have come to live. I do not know what has become of the baby. Is his name Paco? I have never heard from Ale or Caya. I try, with all my might, to believe they are safe. If anyone can save themselves, it is them.

I told myself that you would be well, because a smart woman like yourself would know how to take care in a difficult world. But alas, I sit in bed at night, and am haunted of the news we hear from España, and indeed from all of Europe during the war. I would have come back, but I worried for the safety of my son. I have no help with the boy. I am on my own. My family turned their backs on me.

Alexander is about to turn six and is such a delight. I have many regrets from España, but he is not one. Paco must be very similar to my Alex. If only they could meet.

If you ever need anything, please contact me on the address on the envelope.

Forever your friend,
Scarlett Montgomery

Luna read the note a few times; obviously the first in the series of letters. She flicked through the pile; they carried on for years. Luna had died in 1960, and the letters stopped soon after. Luna picked up the last in the pile.

10 November 1960

Dearest Paco,

Thank you for your letter. I will admit that my heart jumped in my chest when I received the mail. I have been writing to your mother for 15 years and have never received a reply. It is heartening to know that she received the letters. But your news of your dear mother's passing fills me with enormous sadness. If your mother has kept my letters, please read them. Luna and I shared a moment in our lives that we could not forget, whether we wanted to or not. Your mother is one of the strongest women I have ever known, to have taken care of you as she has. I search constantly for news on life in Madrid and have seen your name several times. I see that you are a young bullfighter. Alejandro and Cayetano would be so proud of you.

Please remember that I am here, and if you ever wish to write to me, I would love to hear from you. Your mother can never be replaced, but as a friend of your family, if you ever need a moment in time filled with memories, perhaps I can help. Thank you for taking the time to inform me of your sad news. Luna will forever be in my heart.

Deepest sympathises,
Scarlett Montgomery

Paco had always known who Scarlett Montgomery was. The wicked redhead. What had his mother said about her? Surely, somewhere deep in her soul, Luna had forgiven Scarlett. The woman had gone to considerable lengths over many years to beg forgiveness. If Luna kept the letters, that meant something.

Luna read every letter; she read so much about the early life of her own father, something she never thought she would be able to learn. Tiny pockets of history were wrapped up in the letters, and she could swear she could almost feel her father's comforting presence as she read about him, and his mother's life, through the 1940's and 1950's.

What would Alex have made of all this? Had he ever wanted to know his father? Scarlett had clearly spared him all the gruesome details of her fateful time with the man.

It was well into the wee hours of the morning when Luna completed the letters, but now her mind was more awake than ever. Next was Luna Beltrán's diary. It must have been difficult for Paco to have parted with such a special item. How could she not return it? The man was cunning; the book arriving home would be a sign that Cayetano was forgiven. Luna Beltrán's reluctance to forgive Cayetano Ortega hurt so many people over such a long period of time. Was she prepared to make the same mistake 70 years later?

Maybe Luna Beltrán had the answer. She opened the old leather bound book, and began to read the carefully penned Spanish. Pleasure was as fragile as glass, but maybe held with care, love could live forever. This diary surely knew that.

A man's sins cannot be warmed up once you have let them cool...

38

Valencia, España ~ marzo de 1939

Luna watched Scarlett push through the crowd ahead of her. They moved towards the ship, which only had one entry ramp. All they had to do was get on, and they might be safe. She looked back; there was no sight of Cayetano or Alejandro. What if they didn't come? What if they weren't coming at all?
"Scarlett."
The tall redhead turned around. "What?"
"Is this the right thing to do?"
"Do you have a better suggestion?"
Luna glanced down at the baby. "Do you want to leave?"
"It's not about wanting, Luna. I'm listed as an officer in the Republican army, but I came to España to represent the Spanish Medical Aid Committee, and if they want me back in Nueva Zelanda, it's my responsibility to go home. The reality is that there's no place for me here."
"Why did you ever come?"
Scarlett sighed and watched Mark gesture to her through the crowd. "Because I knew there would be people, people like you, who would be caught in a war being fought out for the desires of others. They claim that this is a battle for all of España, but it's not. It doesn't matter who wins the war, everyone is still a loser. Will anything change tomorrow when Franco's forces stake their claim on Valencia? Will life in España be fair? Of course not. I have done all that I can."
"You give up."
"I haven't given up on España, I have been beaten back by the flames that rage here. Maybe I could come back, maybe under another name... who

knows. War is imminent through all of Europe, so who knows what comes next."

"You have a baby now."

"Then maybe it's best I do disappear. I'm sorry for what I've done here, but I won't let a baby be blamed for the sins of its mother."

"No," Luna shook her head, "that's not what I meant."

"I know what you meant. Luna, why is this so hard for you?"

"Caya and Ale aren't coming, are they?"

"I really don't know the answer to that." Scarlett paused for a moment. "You're not coming, either, are you?"

Luna turned back and looked at the view back toward the clock tower where she had left Alejandro and Cayetano behind, but didn't say anything.

"Luna, can you live with yourself if you don't see Cayetano again?"

"No, I can't."

Scarlett pulled her bag off her back and pulled it open, to fetch her passport and a few papers she had with it. "Here." She handed her the bag. "Here is all the money I have, and milk for the baby. Take it and go. I know that's what you stopped me for, so let's not pretend otherwise."

Luna took her bag in one hand and awkwardly slipped it over one shoulder. "I can't take your money."

"Then keep it for the baby, because I know you won't hand him over to me."

"I can't."

"Where are you going to go?"

"I have no idea. I have never even been in a city before."

"Okay, go back to where we parked the truck by the church and stay there. Either one or both of the men will end up there, for sure. And take the chest with you. I know Alejandro's money is in there. I can't believe he worked for all that time, only to leave it behind. The man is crazy."

"That's why I can't let him make decisions for the baby."

"If, for any reason, you don't find the guys, there's a building in town, the Pelayo trinquet. It's a pelota court that the trade union took over. There is a guy there, his name is Alvaro. Tell him that I sent you, and that you need a place to stay. He's a nice guy; we have stayed at his home before. He also has a phone, have you ever used one?"

"No."

"I don't know what to suggest... the train line to Madrid is damaged, the roads are blocked... who knows what's going to happen now. Blend in, any way you can. No one knows you here; say you are a religious conservative that has come out of hiding, or something. Put those rosary beads of yours to good use. A woman and her baby will be okay. You have money."

"Maybe I could go to Madrid and find Papá. I know the address of where he is staying... where Ignacio and his family are hiding..."

"Your father is not the saint you think he is, Luna. He is living with a young woman, in Ignacio's family home. He took it for himself, since they are fascists trapped in the Republican zone. I have no idea why your father didn't just shoot them. I can only assume he is no real anarchist at all. Your father makes no sense to me. He doesn't care about the Republican cause; he only cares about squeezing money out of once-wealthy conservative landowners, like the Reyes family, who are now trapped in Madrid. But now that the Nationalists have won, the Reyes family can stop hiding. Your father will probably be killed by the time you get there."

"Then let's hope I find Alejandro and Cayetano."

"You will be safe with them. But do me one favour."

"After all you have done?"

Scarlett pursed her lips for a moment. "One day, when you and Cayetano have a large family and are blissfully happy, and your babies are grown, tell the children they have a sibling in Nueva Zelanda. Please. I will never contact you again, if that is what you want, but don't deny them the truth of what happened here. But remember, a man's sins cannot be warmed up once you have let them cool."

Luna nodded and took a deep breath. "Adios, Scarlett."

Scarlett nodded once and turned away, and edged through the busy crowd towards the ship. Luna stood on the spot and watched her disappear. Now it was too late to change her mind. Baby Paco started to cry, and Luna was ready to do the same. Get the chest, Scarlett said. She needed to go back.

Luna hurried back to the broken building, and straight to Antonio, to find the man at his desk. He looked even more miserable than the first time she met him. "I need my chest."

"You just missed Cayetano," Antonio said. "He left a note, and asked me to get it onto the ship."

"For me, or Scarlett?"

"For you."

Luna took the piece of paper from Antonio's sweaty hand. Cayetano loved her. He promised to find her. He was the illegitimate son of the King in exile, and that is where the ring had come from. She had to find him.

With nothing more than a quick thank you to Antonio, Luna left the clock tower, baby in one arm, and pulled the heavy chest with the other. The short walk from the port to the church seemed so far while juggling the two. She was happy to see the vehicle still there, parked on the small alley off the main port road. She pulled the back door open and put baby Paco down, much to his annoyance. "I'm sorry, Paco," she said while she loaded the heavy chest into the back of the truck, and pushed it in. "I'll give you some milk."

Luna opened the bag that Scarlett had given her, surprised to see how much money was in there. She had never personally had more than a few pesetas in her life, and now here was more than she ever hoped to have. She didn't dare wonder where it all came from. She pulled out the milk and the bottle. It was dirty, but she had no way of washing it, and pouring the tinned milk into the bottle was a challenge. But the basic equipment was all she had for the baby.

She sat on the back of the truck to feed the child, and watched the people pass by out on the main road. Her heart pounded. She wasn't afraid to admit it; she was scared. She was young and naive. The girl from the country was suddenly on her own in the city, with a baby. But if Scarlett could travel across the world in search of adventure, then Luna could see herself through the times that would come. If nothing else, she had the truck to sleep in.

"Luna! What you are doing here?"

There stood Cayetano. He was a mess, his clothes pulled and torn, and breathing heavily, like he had just been in a fight. Luna wasn't quite sure what to say. "I'm not going without you... and Ale. Where is he?"

"You should have got on the ship! Where is Scarlett?"

"She got on board. I saw her. But I'm not going. I can't. And baby Paco isn't either. Scarlett offered to take him, but he belongs here with us."

"Do you have any idea how many people climbed the Pyrenees in the cold winter to try and escape this place? Or the untold thousands of people stranded at ports down the coast who want to get away? This was your chance!"

"I can't go without you!" Luna put the now happy infant down on the truck again, cushioned from the cold metal by his blanket. "I got your note from Antonio."

Cayetano swallowed hard. "I guess you read it?"

"Now I know who you are. You weren't going to get on board, were you? You were going to leave me."

"I thought you didn't love me."

"I do." Luna's deep brown eyes let a few precious tears go.

"You forgive me for what I've done?"

"I don't care what you've done."

In the shade of the burned and damaged church, Cayetano pulled her into his arms, and rewarded her courage and forgiveness with a tender kiss. It was all it took to tell her that she had made the right choice. That tiny moment, tucked away from the sense of worry and panic that crackled in the

Valencian air, Luna knew she had made the right choice not to get on the ship with Scarlett. His body was warm against her, but also stiff, as if he were on guard.

"Did something happen to you?" she asked.

"I found Alejandro, and he punched me. I tried to stop him from running, but we ended up fighting. He is drunk and consumed with grief. It does strange things to a man."

"Where is he now?"

"I don't know. But we have the truck and he doesn't. I bet anything he will go back to Sofía."

"But that's miles, especially on foot."

"Then let's get this baby in the front of the truck, and hope we have enough fuel to get there ourselves, and we find him. If we are going to survive this, we need to stick together."

"We can do this."

"*Of course,* la chispa, *of course we can.*"

39

Valencia, España ~ diciembre de 2009

I need to send you a diary. A man's sins cannot be warmed up once you have let them cool.

One message, received in the middle of the night, was all Cayetano needed to get his ass to Valencia. All he had done was sit at home and think of how much his life had changed with the information about José. The last six months had thrown his life into disarray. But now, things had to change.

Every Thursday, the Tribunal de las Aguas de Valencia, the Water Court, was held at the Door of the Apostles of the Valencia Cathedral. The eight men, dressed in black cloaks, would sit and discuss irrigation matters of the agricultural plains around the city. They spoke Valencian, and never wrote anything down, just as they had done for the last thousand years. Cayetano wandered past them in Plaza de la Virgen as they set themselves up, but didn't pay much attention. Judging by the small crowd it pulled, it seemed more for the amusement to the tourists than anything else. As a bullfighter dressed in his full blue and gold *traje de luces,* hat and red cape included, he drew more of a crowd than the tribunal.

The door that the tribunal sat before was the side entrance to Valencia's cathedral, while people poured in and out of the grand building on the other side, in Plaza de la Reina. Plaza de la Virgen was smaller and was home to the majestic Basilica de la Virgen de los

Desamparados, just a few steps from the cathedral. The stone surface of the *plaza* gleamed in the sun as he walked across the square, between the locals, tourists and pigeons, and over to the fountain. In his full *torero's* suit, he now had the full attention of many around, and he almost looked like a tourist attraction himself, his red cape draped over his shoulder only added to the suggestion he was up to something. No matter how many people were in the square, Luna would spot him soon.

The whole Ciclo Comunitat Valenciana cycling team had assembled, all twenty riders, with team managers Marco and Tomás, and Luna. She looked out of place as Cayetano watched her; as if uncomfortable with the whole set-up. He had no idea what she was up to, and what he was doing almost as much of a mystery. He had gone to her apartment, all dressed up in an effort to surprise her, only to find her not there. It was lucky that he bumped into a beautiful young woman named Lucía, who told him where Luna was today. Now he had found her, dressed in the new-look cycling team jersey, and cycling trousers and riding shoes. She wasn't a rider. Never wanted to be. Her hair was perfectly done, her wavy black curls combed to perfection, and her face all made up. She was doing some kind of promotion work for the team and the tourism board, or maybe as the lone female mechanic on the pro-tour? Maybe as the wife of the adopted son of Valencia, Fabrizio Merlini? Should he speak to her at all?

A large crowd of onlookers were held back while the team posed for photographs with bikes and one another around the fountain. Lucía had told him that Luna and Darren were doing photoshoots in popular areas around the city, today the first day of the work they had to do. Cayetano watched Luna, she stood on the small ledge around the fountain, being extra careful. She must have had pedal cleats on the bottom of her cycling shoes, because she was unsteady. But she radiated beauty in the sunshine that reflected off her shiny black hair while she posed for photos. She had Fabrizio's heavy watch on her wrist again. His heart jumped when he saw her wobble above the water, and even more when Darren jumped forward and grabbed her. The photographer took the opportunity to take a few more photos as he held her steady. The smile that they shared wasn't for the camera; it was a genuine smile while she held his hands. She looked happy with him. Maybe when she said she needed a break from Cayetano, she meant more permanently. But there was the message on the phone in the middle of the night about the diary. He had to go through with talking to her again.

The world was invaded by the sound of a ringing bell. The Miguelete bell tower attached to the cathedral struck twelve, which started the Water Court's session behind him. With the bells ringing in his ears, Cayetano continued to watch Luna, who had her hand out to touch the water pouring into the fountain around the statue of Neptune in the centre. Around the sides of the fountain were seven smaller statues, there to represent the seven ancient irrigation channels to the city. The sound of the bell ringing had made the pigeons jump up off them for a moment, spooked by the sudden noise. He thought they should have been used to the bell by now, apparently not.

You're procrastinating by thinking about pigeons, Caya. What the fuck are you doing? Burst through everyone and talk to her, or go home. The way she had smiled at Darren; it hurt. What if... what if she had changed her mind, and wanted to be with Darren instead? Or what if she had gone to Italy, and found she was truly not over her husband? What if your idea to win her back is so fucking...

"Look! It's *'El Valiente'* Beltrán! Here, in Valencia!"

Too late to run. Someone had recognised him, and about 100 people turned to look at him. The guy had said it loud, just as the bells had stopped. Everyone heard. Including Luna Montgomery. Cayetano watched her, still on the ledge of the fountain, her eyes able to skim over the top of the watching crowd, and he watched her spot him, easy to find his sparkling gold and blue suit. Coincidentally, she was dressed much the same, her cycling uniform the colours of the Valencian flag, yellow, red and blue. He watched the smile drop from her face, frozen on the spot. Now or never.

Cayetano pushed through the crowd, who were more than happy to step aside. The photographer's assistant, who had been constantly asking people to step back didn't say a word as he walked straight over to Luna, and stopped in front of her. Time to say something profound. "Ah... *hola.*"

Her face broke into her smile again. "Hey, dude, what's up?"

"Oh, you know, just hanging out."

"Planning a little bullfighting later on, perhaps?"

Cayetano took a deep breath and relaxed. "Maybe. It depends on how the afternoon goes. You?"

"Just having my photos taken for work, in front of more onlookers that I expected. Hard to blend in when a *torero* comes over to say hi."

"I just wanted to ask you something."

"Here?" Luna looked over him at the others, her friends, colleagues, strangers; all watched their conversation. Even the crowd that the Water Court had drawn watched from across the *plaza,* as did the café-goers that sat in front of the Palau de Generalitat, the imposing but beautiful Valencian government building at the other end of the *plaza.*

"May I?" Cayetano jumped up onto the ledge next to Luna, grateful his leg didn't let him down. He pulled his cape from his shoulder, to the cries of *'¡ole!'* from some in the crowd.

"Señoras y señores." His deep, robust voice echoed out across the open air space. "I have a story to share with you. A long time ago, 70 years to be exact, there was a woman named Luna Beltrán. She was in love with a man, Cayetano Ortega. They lived across the street from each other. But fate, beliefs, mistakes and war hurt these two young people. He had given his beloved a beautiful ring to show her his love, but life intervened and they were parted forever. But, as we all know, you can never lose those you love, because even if loved ones slip away, they are always in your heart."

Cayetano paused for a moment and looked back to Luna. She didn't seem to see where his speech was headed. "But the story didn't end there," he continued to the intrigued crowd. "What happened was, 70 years later, a not-so young bullfighter named Cayetano Beltrán…" he paused as the crowd laughed, "… a bullfighter was sipping a drink, when he saw a beautiful woman fall on the street. Little did he know that when he helped her up, she was Cayetano Ortega's granddaughter, Luna. This woman stands here next to me now."

Luna couldn't help but smile when he said that, and the crowd who commented to each other on the coincidence of it all. "She's a beauty!" someone yelled. "Keep her!" The crowd laughed again.

"I wanted to," Cayetano called back. His voice was loud and clear. "But again, while the Beltrán and Ortega families came back together, fate tried to intervene. Today, I say history will not repeat itself."

Cayetano jumped off the ledge of the fountain, and turned to face

Luna, to the cheers of the crowd when he took her hand. "Luna, love is made up of dreams and reality. Most fall in love with only the dream. Yet, when you find true love, you fall in love with both." His hand started to shake around hers. He desperately needed to take a deep breath, but he had nerves. He fumbled briefly in his tight-fitting sleeve and pulled out the Medina diamond.

"This ring could not fulfill its destiny and bind Luna and Cayetano together in 1939. Today, I ask it to fulfill its destiny with us. I am touched by your tenderness. I am inspired by your love. I am encouraged by your passion. I will drop a tear into this fountain, and whenever they find it, I will stop loving you. Until then, Luna… *¿quieres casarte conmigo?* Will you marry me?"

It seemed that the crowd knew the answer before Luna, a round of applause going up, laced with a sea of *'¡sí!'* replies. He held the ring up hopefully to her, her face stuck in an expression of total surprise. He saw her look away just briefly in Darren's direction. Cayetano knew he had put her on the spot, but he loved her so much, and he didn't care who knew it. She may have not been one for grand gestures, but by Christ, he was and wasn't afraid to put on a show for her, impromptu as it was.

"Please, *la chispa,"* he said, his tone quiet so only they could hear. "I love you. Maybe you could change your mind about us if I explain myself. Even if you say no, please let me talk to you."

"I don't need an explanation," she said to him. She cleared her throat gently and raised her voice. *"¡Sí, me casaré contigo!"*

The crowds around them all gave out a cheer. By now they had the attention of everyone in the *plaza*, several hundred people on the busy morning. "Please, accept the ring, *preciosa."*

"I can't take that ring," she said but held her hand out tentatively anyway. She had only just taken her wedding ring off and put it on her right hand, the tan line still visible on her finger.

"You can, trust me." His own hands were shaking a little bit as he held the ring in his fingers. "Shit, I hope it fits," he muttered. "I only want to do this once."

With a little persuasion, the small band just fitted on her hand. "This is the third time you've proposed. I only want to marry you once."

"Once is enough for me."

"It's always been a dream of mine to have a man propose while we're both wearing tights."

"Oh shut up, *mujer*," Cayetano joked. He grabbed her by the waist. He pulled her from her ledge and slid her body down his enough so their lips could meet, to another round of applause from the crowd.

"Any chance I could whisk you away? Could we just make a run for it?"

Luna looked down at her cycling shoes. "In these things I can't run anywhere. I left my regular shoes in Darren's car." She looked over at him; he stood with his arms folded, his face stuck in an obviously fake smile.

"Kick them off. Do it."

Luna slipped the shoes off, the ground cold beneath her feet. She squealed when Cayetano swept her up into his arms, and grabbed his shoulders, his sequined *chaquetilla* rough on her hands.

"*¡Discúlpeme!*" he called to the crowd, and proceeded to push through them, his bride-to-me in his arms.

"Go through the archway between the cathedral and basilica," Luna said to him. "There are fewer people around that side."

Cayetano continued to carry her right around the cathedral, and came to where his car was double-parked in Plaza de la Reina. He was pleased to see the Mercedes hadn't been towed.

"Were you planning on this not taking very long?" she asked when they got to the car.

"I barely know Valencia, the city is a maze. I wasn't going to waste time finding a parking space."

They got in the car, relieved to have no more eyes on them. Well, Luna seemed to be relieved. Cayetano couldn't care less who saw what he had just done. As far as he was concerned, the whole world could know. He watched Luna pull her keys and phone out of the strange little pockets in the back of her jersey. "Where are we going now? My clothes are in the back of Darren's car."

"Your place then."

Cayetano navigated the busy roads in the direction of the riverbed, through Plaza del Ayuntamiento and past the Plaza de Toros de Valencia, the bullring, and hoped to find a place to cross the Turia. There wasn't a lot of romance in asking a woman for directions. They stopped at a set of lights, and he noticed Luna looking at the precious diamond on her hand. "Not too tight, is it?"

"It was made for a small hand," she commented. "This belongs to your family."

"It belongs to Cayetano Ortega, who is a member of your family. Technically, it's returned home."

"You got my message last night then?"

"I was wide awake in bed when I got it. What do you mean, 'a man's sins cannot be warmed up once you have let them cool?' Am I forgiven?"

"It's something your grandmother wrote in her diary. She forgave my grandfather for what he did. She held everyone's happiness in her hands, and she made the right choice. If I hold the María situation against you, I hurt everyone, and I don't want to do that."

They moved forward, Cayetano relieved when he saw her apartment building across the Turia. *"Preciosa,* in the glove box is an envelope. Inside is a present for you. Open it and take a look."

Luna did as he asked, and pulled a piece of paper out of the envelope on top of the pile things in there. "Semen analysis? Interesting…"

"Fuck! No! The other envelope!"

Luna laughed when he tried to swipe the paper from her, but she wouldn't give it to him. Instead, she reached in and pulled out another envelope. This time he watched her pick up the right one. He saw her face change when she found the old letter and delicately unfolded it. "Oh my God."

"I know," Cayetano said smugly as they crossed the riverbed, the park that teemed with people below them. "Cayetano Medina Ortega, born 31 August, 1914. That is the original birth certificate issued in Madrid. I know it's basic, but it should be enough for your residency paperwork."

"How did you get this?"

"Leandro Medina, María's father, had it. His father is Cayetano's half-brother. I went to tell him that I had found Cayetano's granddaughter. He is an unwell man, and I thought the news would make him happy. He is interested in the history of Ortega."

"You have been with María?"

"Just with her father. Leandro told me about how he was so disappointed that María and Paulo are in a relationship now. He said he hoped I would take María back. So, I had another sperm count test. It says the odds of me becoming a father are not as pathetic as we first thought, but that doesn't mean the baby is mine. She has been seeing someone else."

"You can't go looking for reasons why the baby might not be yours. You have to own your mistakes. Why would she lie?"

"Desperate people do stupid things. There is less glamour in having a baby with a nobody. María is shallow enough to think that way. Either way, I need to know the truth."

Luna let out a deep breath as Cayetano parked his car in a space near the entrance to her building. "Wow, it's a lot to take in all at once."

"I know." Cayetano's stopped the car and turned to her. "I don't expect you to forget all this. I fucked up, I know that. But still, I found Cayetano's birth certificate and you deserved to have it. I have already shown Sofía, to see why it's not in the official records database. She will have the information entered for you."

"It has Sergio Medina is his father."

"Well, maybe once upon a time you could lie about the real identity of a baby's father, but not anymore. Babies and fathers need to know the truth. Your grandfather knew who his real father was anyway, and María's baby will need the whole story, one day."

"I'm just sick of all the drama. I filled my life with people who don't do things like this. Honest people, trustworthy people."

"Noble people."

"Yeah."

"You wanted noble. I can do that, I promise."

"Come inside. I'm sure we can think of more enjoyable things to talk about."

Cayetano dropped the bag of clothes he had brought in from the car the moment he got inside Luna's apartment. He had only been in there in the dark until now. It was just how he imagined, simple and neat. The full-length mirror in the entranceway was familiar. The memorable moment against it would never fade. He watched her put her keys down on a little side table and looked at him in the mirror with a smile. Her short zip on her cycle jersey was undone, and her perky breasts begged to be touched just beneath the opening.

"How did you know where to find me?"

"I didn't. I just got here and found you were out. Your neighbours told me where you were."

"So, your plan was to turn up here, in a costume, and propose?"

"Not much of a plan I admit. But I did worry, I didn't want to make a scene in front of the kids if you said no."

"I appreciate that. It was good timing, they are at the pelota day that the school is running. If Paco turns up and tries to cut my hand off to get the ring back, he needs similar opportune timing."

"No, Papá knows I took it. He knew I had a plan to win you back. He wasn't so impressed when I burst into his house at six this morning to get the ring… but he'll live…. forever probably, knowing my luck…"

"That's enough of that. The only time I have met him was when he told me that I was fucking my cousin, and I needed to get out of his house, but even so, don't wish death on people."

Cayetano took a deep breath, his eyes not leaving hers in the mirror. "I thought you were going to say no… just for a second, I thought you were going to step off that ledge and say no."

Luna turned around, a frown on her face. "I needed just a second to think about it. Things have been hard."

"It crossed my mind that you would go to Italy and not come back."

Luna wrapped her arms around his waist, which sent a shot of excitement through him. "I have plenty of reasons to say no to you, but none of them would make us happy. And just this once, I want to be happy." He felt her soft lips come to his neck and whisper, "I love you. I missed you."

"I'm back now." The moment they kissed, Cayetano felt the pain he had been going through fall away. A deep feeling of lust seared through his body instead. It hurt to be away from Luna, and his body throbbed when his greedy kiss engulfed her mouth. A weight had been lifted. He could feel her hands claw at his back as she tried to keep up with him. He had already experienced all the release he needed, and when she pulled away from him there was a hot pain in his chest.

"Preciosa, I need to ask you something."

"Okay."

"Is it true that cyclists don't wear underwear?"

A cheeky smile spread over her face. "Yes, it's true."

Cayetano turned her in his arms so they both faced the mirror. "So you have nothing underneath your clothes?"

"Not much, no."

Her jersey was easy to peel off. He admired her figure in the mirror, nothing more than skin tight lycra pants and her bra. But it simply wasn't good enough. He did away with the bra. "Getting closer," he muttered.

"To what? Do you have some fantasy where you're in your suit and you have a naked woman against you?"

"I do now!" He watched the mirror, to see her peel off her cycling pants to stand there totally naked, not an ounce shy. His throat had gone dry before she leant against him, her eyes on his in the reflection. His gaze couldn't stay there, instead it wandered up and down the lustful image. He barely saw the smile she had while she watched his desire take over his expression. He slid one hand up her body to clutch at a breast, the other one free to roam wherever it liked, and it caused her confident stance to buckle under the urge that shot through her. Cayetano wanted to touch her until she felt dizzy. She tilted her head back to let him kiss her, happy to surrender to what he wanted to give her. When she turned back into him, and her hands pushed his jacket from his shoulders, he felt a shot of need power through him.

"You once told me that you only let women call you 'El Valiente' in the two places you like to be passionate. You would never allow a woman in the ring with you, but I have you here, in your suit so close to my bedroom…"

"Say no more."

His suit had never felt more cumbersome as he fought it from his body while Luna led him to her bedroom. He watched her look at his naked body for a moment, scarred all over, but fully healed at last. With one quick sweep, he picked her up and carried her over to the unmade bed, and placed her down softly on the white sheets. It was obvious she as stunned as he was at the spontaneous emotions that they invoked in each other. He knew that he should slow down, but the awakening she brought in him must have rushed through her as well. Time was lost as he was swept away by the power she drained from him with her attentions.

Cayetano had no idea how long he had been in bed with her, and didn't care until Luna tried to leave him. "Maybe I should just stay here?" he teased.

"I need to get the kids from school. I felt bad for sending them today, it's supposed to be their holidays. Plus, let's not forget that Darren lives here."

"Can I come with you to the school?"

"I guess so. I assume you have regular clothes."

"I do."

"Are you planning on going home anytime soon?"

Cayetano shrugged. "Don't know."

"I might have to keep you here forever."

"You may be able to entice me. As you can see, this trip didn't have any planning involved."

"I'm going up to Escondrijo later, to see Alejandro. Would you like to come with me?"

"I don't know. Would he want to see me?"

"Maybe. Only one way to find out."

40

Valencia, España ~ diciembre de 2009

Luna was struck by how much she loved Cayetano when Giacomo and Enzo emerged from the school gym. They ran over for a hug, eager to say hello to their Madrileño friend. They genuinely liked the guy. He genuinely liked them. She couldn't take a second look at Cayetano if she didn't have the twins' approval, but she had it and everything else had to stand back, because no more obstacles were going to get in the way. There was no Luna and Cayetano curse, and there never had been.

On the way up to Escondrijo, the Medina diamond sat within Luna's line of sight, on the hand that rested on top of the steering wheel as she navigated the winding tree-lined roads. Surely the ring would stir memories for Alejandro. He knew it had been his sister's ring. He had said she could have Escondrijo, but only if she had made sure she had done her best to see through what was going on with Cayetano. Now Luna was going to present the man with his biological grandson, the bullfighter that he followed with keen interest. Maybe Paco would even want to meet his father. But one step at a time; things had already moved fast enough.

"Wow, you want to live up here?" Cayetano asked as they pulled up to the house.

"It's so cool," Giacomo said from the back seat. "We have walked out here with Alejandro and there is so much stuff to see."

"Mummy, look, the goats are here!" Enzo said.

The foursome exited the car, and noticed that the small herd of goats wandered around by the house, and Luna frowned. Normally Alejandro kept a tight rein on the animals when by the house, but they seemed to have made themselves at home wherever they liked. The house was closed up. "I will see if he is here." She left the boys with Cayetano by the car.

She turned the handle on the wooden door and cracked it open a little, not wanting to be rude. But the moment she opened it, she felt how chilly it was in the house. Ice cold. The most explosive moments in life weren't tangible, they existed in the air. A feeling of something good or bad had no face or name, it was only a sensation. Luna had suffered a few hard moments in life, and she could feel a numbness the moment she poked her head in the door. The feeling of total emptiness. She remembered as a child when her mother was gone, the family home was cold and confusing. When her father had died in his bed at home, the air was filled with a cold, solemn emptiness that could not be identified. Her own home in Valencia had been filled with the same, an ache that hung in the air, reminding her that Fabrizio would never come home. Now, across the room, lay Alejandro in his bed. She didn't need to go inside, she knew he was dead. Death wasn't a tangible entity; it hung in the air, a hollow feeling that engulfed all the senses.

She turned and looked at Cayetano over by the car; she had no idea what her expression was, but she saw him frown in an instant. "Why don't we play outside for a minute and let Mamá talk to Alejandro?" she heard him ask the boys, who nodded. They looked eager to chase a few goats who had wandered in their direction.

Luna stepped inside and shut the door behind her. This couldn't happen; after everything that had gone on, was the man who had unlocked all the answers to the mystery dead before the past and its demons were laid to rest? She moved towards the small single bed against the opposite wall, her eyes locked on him. Alejandro was on his side with his face grey and lifeless. To her relief, his eyes were half closed.

"Oh, Alejandro, what happened?" she whispered. She sat down on the floor next to him and placed a hand on his cold shoulder. He had been dead a while. She knew he was sick; that was obvious, but he wouldn't speak about it. How long had he been there, on his own? How had he died? Cold, alone, in pain? Had he been in bed, and hoped she would arrive? She was off on holiday, and then taking stupid photos for work. She could have been here with him. Instead, he was dying on his own, with no way of contacting her or anyone.

Luna sobbed as she looked around his single room home. The place seemed spotless, a contrast to how it usually was. There was no food anywhere; he hadn't eaten in some time. The fire was long out, nothing more than a few grey ashes. No one had been here, no hint of what had gone on. She looked back at him through a veil of tears, and imagined the horror of having to die alone. She had seen her father die, a terrifying sight, and she hoped it was more peaceful for Alejandro. His body was old and weak, and with some luck, it put up no fight as his last breath came. What would he have thought about, who would have been with him in his mind – Luna would never know. She would never get to speak to him again. Never get to go for a walk with him. She had only met him two months ago, and now he was gone.

"I'm so sorry," she whispered, and rubbed his back gently. It seemed so stupid to rub a man who was dead. The last few months of his life had been confronting, and all because of Luna. She could only hope it brought him some closure, to talk about what went on in the early years of his long life. The diamond on her hand sat on his shoulder; their families had come full circle and he would never know. He would never meet his son, or grandson. But he was finally with his Sofía, the woman he had never been able to get over.

Luna glanced up at the windowsill high above the bed, to see an envelope. She stood up, wiped her tears and picked it up.

It is a great punishment to be consumed with desire and not be able to do anything about it

What a strange thing to write on the front of a letter. But it resonated in the Beltrán family so much. No one ever seemed to be allowed to follow their desires, only doing what they had to – or felt they had no other choice but to do.

La chispa

Soon I will be dead. There are some things a man cannot beat. You are young and have suffered enough troubles, so you do not need to know mine. I want to be alone in my final moments, so please do not be angry at my decision. You are a proud and stubborn girl, who pushes me on things I would rather not talk about, and for that, I am grateful. You are the only person I can trust with Escondrijo and my Sofía's resting place. I have made a will, and the place is yours. If you check on the table, all you need to take over will be there.

Don't be like me, Luna. Don't hide up here. Don't sit alone and grieve for a life that you have lost. I don't ask you to listen to this, I demand it. A long life with pain and regret is the cruellest mistreatment I have suffered. To have died at the hands of another man would not hurt an ounce as much as the pain that I inflicted on myself. In the end, you have nothing but what is inside you. Fill it with what makes you happy, and if that is Cayetano, please forgive him for his mistakes and live your life. If my sister could forgive, so could you. But only if that is what you want.

Please, tell Paco what became of me, but spare him the details. He has had a happy life, and it is not my place to be part of it. I never deserved to know him, and I have always known this. To know that Scarlett and Caya's granddaughter is in love with Paco's boy is the greatest gift you could give me. Take those little boys of yours, and live a decent life. Please, I beg you.

Enclosed is a confession, one I have written and destroyed many times throughout my life. It is my greatest sin laid bare. I prayed one day I would be punished for what I did in a moment of confusion and anger. There is no redemption for what I did. There is no forgiveness. Please, Luna, do not hate me, but I cannot explain myself to you, because there is no answer. Read it, and throw it away. Do not hold on to the misery that lies on the page.

Alejandro Beltrán Caño

Luna smiled. He signed his whole name, a formal end to such a personal note. Paco had done the same thing when he had written a note to her. She looked into the envelope; the other letter still folded up. Instead of reading, she slipped the first note back inside the envelope and wiped more tears from her face. She had to face the boys and Cayetano who were outside.

"Hey," Cayetano said the moment she emerged from the house. "Are you all right?"

Luna just her shook her head, not sure what to tell him.

"You started to worry me. My mind started to panic when I saw the look on your face just before."

"Whatever you imagined, imagine worse. Much worse."

Cayetano left the children and wandered over to her at the door. "What's wrong?"

"He's… um… he's dead in there."

"How dead? I mean… how long…"

"How many types of dead are there?" she shot back. "He died in there! Alone!"

Cayetano wrapped his arms around her as she began to weep again. She didn't care if the kids saw; she wasn't able to hold it in. This was not how the story was meant to end.

~~~

It all seemed surreal. Luna had gone to introduce Alejandro to his grandson, and instead she had helped load his body into the back of the ambulance that Cayetano had called. They told her that he had not been dead long, most likely had died in the night. A quick look through his things neatly lined up on the table yielded his oncologist's phone number. Alejandro had died while she was at home, reading Scarlett's letters. He had stomach cancer, had done for some time. He had been to the city for a hospital visit while she had been away. He knew what was coming, and Luna hadn't been there for him. Maybe that was what he wanted. But it didn't comfort her at all.

She was at a loss once he was gone. She wondered if she should have gone with his body, but there were still the kids to look after. Cayetano sat in the car with them, to keep them out of the way, for their own sake. To watch their mother cry over another dead man would do them no favours. The drive back down to Valencia was a sombre one. This wasn't how the day your soulmate proposes to you should feel like.

The beauty of having children was that Luna always needed to be practical and level-headed for their sakes. She didn't have the opportunity to get upset, she needed to take them home and wait until they were in bed before she could talk to Cayetano about what had happened. Darren had been at home in their absence and had left a note to say he was not going to be home tonight. The conversation between the two of them about her engagement would have to wait quite some time.

"I don't know what to say," Cayetano shrugged when they sat together in the living room, the apartment silent.

"I'm sorry; you probably wondered why you came here now."

"I know why I came. I came to ask you to marry me. I came to put an end to all this drama and sadness. And yet we have the opposite."

"I liked the guy. I did. I'm glad I met him. He knew he was going to die; it's me who is getting the information only now. But that aside, I'm glad I knew him when I had the chance."

"Alejandro was 95 years old; he wasn't going to live forever. Knowing that he met you and could leave Escondrijo with you would have given him a lot of comfort. Maybe even a little release from the pain he was obviously hanging on to."

"He wrote me a letter begging me to move on with my life."

"He is pretty insistent. Good thing you agreed to marry me."

"He doesn't know that. He will never know that. To him, all this is unresolved. I think that's the worst part – he will never know that you and I worked everything out. He will never meet you, or Paco."

"I don't think he really wanted to."

"I think he didn't ever contact Paco, not just for Paco's sake, but also as a way of continuously punishing himself for abandoning his son."

"Well, there is nothing we can do. Some questions don't get answered."

"Yeah, I know." Luna sighed. She had run out of tears at last.

"The facts are the facts. Alejandro filled in so much for us. We know who our real families are, and how they interacted. We know the whole story about our grandparents and their doomed relationship."

"Cayetano Ortega is still a mystery. Maybe he is in one of the *fosas,* the burial pits, near the cemetery in Serra. Maybe I should join that fight to have it dug up and reburied with dignity. At least now I know where he died… more or less."

"There is no dignity in death, only in life."

"True. I did talk to Alejandro a few times about the reburial argument going on in Serra. He asked me to stay away from it."

"Then maybe you should honour that. Are you going to read the other letter he gave you?"

Luna shrugged. "He wants to admit something he has done, something he has never told anyone. Why would I want to know? Maybe I should just burn the letter; if it hurt him, maybe its truth is better left unsaid."

"Alejandro wanted you to know. There has to be a reason why he wants to tell you. Maybe it's about Cayetano, or Scarlett. Maybe it will help you to know. He wouldn't tell you if it might hurt you."

"I think enough harm has been done."

"Then let this be the end. Read the note."

41

Valencia, España ~ marzo de 1939

Luna wondered if Valencia was always loud. Maybe it was just today; maybe it was the knowledge that fascist rebel troops would march through Plaza de Emilio Castelar. Maybe it was part of the adjustment to city life. Luna had spent the night in a building on Calle las Barcas in the centre of the city, a once-grand building now in need of repair. The ceilings were so high; they were on the second floor, but the room height must have been four metres, and the ceiling was black with soot. Families had gathered in these rooms and cooked in there, after they came from surrounding villages and in need of a place to stay. Luna slept with Cayetano and the baby on a floor covered in mosaic tiles. Today, she woke up on a cool morning, in a strange building, with a hungry baby, and it made her wonder what came next.

She smiled when Cayetano reappeared in the small room, with a bucket of water. The courtyard of the building had a well, and they were able to get clean water via a pulley system that came up through the window of room number three.

"Preciosa, *how are you? How is the baby?*" *Cayetano sat down with her on the floor to take a look at the infant in her arms.*

"*He is all right, I suppose. I never cared for a child before.*"

"*You're a natural.*" *He gently kissed her cheek, in the hopes of making her smile.*

"*Do you know what Scarlett said to me?*"

"*What?*"

"*She said, one day, when you and I have many children who are grown, to tell them about their brother or sister in Nueva Zelanda.*"

"*She thought you and I will go on to have a big family?*"

"It seems that way."

"Maybe she's right."

"How are we meant to do that? Here we are, with a child that isn't ours, we are far from home, not married, and we have nothing. We slept on the floor of a borrowed room, shared with strangers."

"Things will improve. I promise you. They won't shoot me. I have dodged fascist bastards for years. Don't worry; I'll take care of you."

Luna shrugged lightly. "I guess."

"What does that mean?"

"It means... why do I need to be looked after?"

"I don't think you need it; I love you, so it's an impulse to want to know you are safe and well. I want to help you."

"Is there any food anywhere in Valencia? We spent all day and night hunting through all your known spots here and never found Alejandro. I hate to say it, but I'm hungry."

"I'm sure we can find something. Alejandro is probably sleeping off the alcohol somewhere. Looking for him can wait until after breakfast. But there isn't much to eat, everyone is starving."

"How can there be a food shortage, but alcohol available?"

"That is a question best left unanswered, Luna. Come and take a look at the view."

The pair wandered out on to the narrow balcony. The streets below were full of people who hurried around, which made all the noise that Luna could hear. She had the baby tucked up under her coat that she had slept in. "That is Plaza de Emilio Castelar over there." Cayetano pointed to the end of the street, which led onto the open plaza. "That building you can see, on the far side, is the town hall building."

Luna looked at the place; a large and elaborate building looked worn and damaged. Who knows what was happening there. That was where the city had been run from, and now their city was close to being taken over. Troops could arrive at any moment. "Can't we just go back to Cuenca? Scarlett is safe and gone, so why not?"

"We don't have anything to go back to."

"Our home, which we own."

"I am an anarchist, I don't believe in private property."

"You seemed to have no problem in living there for free in the home owned by my father. Don't you believe in just having a safe and simple life?"

"I would love to! But that isn't a choice we can make. We are only two people in sea of Spaniards who need to find a way to live together."

"Do you accept that we are on the losing side of the battle? If Franco is in charge of this country, all the rights of the State, church, wealthy landowners, all that will be restored. The army will be in control. Cities like Valencia will be under Franco's control. There is no freedom or autonomy out here anymore."

"I have no answers for you, Luna. I think we should leave here and head back up into the mountains."

"Will we be any safer out there?"

"I don't know, but it's worth a try."

~~~

Alejandro was right where they expected him to be. How the hell he had got from Valencia and up to the secluded spot high above the village of Serra was anyone's guess, but there he was, right where they had left Sofía. Luna just sighed when she saw him. She and Cayetano had parked the truck out of sight behind the old house that stood there and come around to find their companion. Her brother was in agony, totally miserable at the loss of his wife five days on from her death. How could they expect him to carry on with all the pain he suffered?

"At least out here there is no more alcohol," Cayetano muttered.

"Not much of anything out here," Luna said back.

"Not much of anything anywhere, anymore."

"Now what?"

"Well," Cayetano said and looked around, "we may as well stay out here. We have a little food and water, and there is shelter in this old masía here. It will be cold, but we can find ways keep warm."

"It's called fire." Luna gently moved the baby in her arms.

"How practical of you," Cayetano teased. "I was thinking about huddling for warmth again."

"You know I love you," she smiled, "but all I want to do is help my brother."

Cayetano kissed her. "Stay here and I will go and speak to him."

Luna watched Cayetano wander over to Alejandro; the limestone crunched under his heavy boots. Alejandro was on his knees nestled between the almond trees, and just sobbed. She watched Cayetano sit down next to his best friend and place a hand on his shoulder. She wanted Alejandro to at least respond to the kindness, but there was no chance. Alejandro was too grief-stricken, too tired, too drunk, too inconsolable to listen to anyone.

"Leave me!" Alejandro screamed as he scrambled to his feet. "I never want to see you again!"

"Ale, I'm here to help you," Cayetano said and stood up to his friend.

"You? I want nothing to do with you! With anyone!" He turned to see Luna over by the house, the baby in her arms. "Why is that baby not on the ship?"

"Scarlett is gone, and she can't take the baby. Paco is your son," she replied.

"You can do this," Cayetano said to his friend. "We can help you. We are all here for you."

"The world may as well end! I don't care about anyone, and I don't want to look after a child! Let those Francoist bastards find me here! I won't kill myself; I won't do them the favour! If they want to ruin my life and my country then they will have to shoot me!"

"You don't have to worry about any of that, we will be okay. We can live normal lives... once you learn to live without Sofía."

"There is no life without Sofía! How could you say that? You... you have whatever you want. You have a rich family who can look after you. Look what you did to Scarlett, and you're going to get away with it, aren't you? You got her pregnant and made her disappear! You get to have my sister! You get to have your love! I get nothing!"

"You have us, Ale!" Luna cried. She walked over to the men; the sun made her squint when she headed in their direction. But she saw Alejandro's quick movement, one hand underneath his coat to produce a gun.

"Mierda, Ale, don't be so stupid," Cayetano said, and reached out for the weapon pointed his direction.

Luna stopped on the spot just before the almond trees. Cayetano had commented that a few items were missing from the truck, one being Scarlett's handgun. Did it have bullets?

"Alejandro," Luna said, and watched her brother's head snap in her direction. "Please, put the gun down. We're all on the same side. I love you. We love you. We need to stick together."

"I don't want anyone near me, why don't you understand that?" He looked at his sister, but the gun still pointed at Cayetano. "Why can't you just leave me?"

"Because we want to know you're all right. We're a family."

"My family is dead." Alejandro's strength started to fade, and tears came back to his eyes. He didn't see Cayetano step forward to take the gun from him.

"I know," Luna said. She took few steps forward to get the baby out of the sun and under the pink flowering trees. "I miss Sofía. I don't know how we are supposed to live without her. I don't know how baby Paco is meant to live without her. I'm scared of what is going to happen to all of us. But surely we're better together than alone."

"Stay away from me!" Alejandro turned the gun in her direction, and she jumped a step back on instinct.

"Don't you dare point that at her!" Cayetano cried. "You're the one who deserves a bullet right now!"

Alejandro swung the gun back in his best friend's direction, and took aim at him. "Don't tell me what to do!"

"I'm sorry, Ale, but I will defend Luna over you every time. I know your love is gone, but mine isn't. The rest of my life is devoted to Luna's happiness."

Alejandro didn't move when Cayetano ignored him and his gun and walked past him to stand with Luna. Luna couldn't see her brother with him between them. Cayetano smiled just briefly at her as he faced her, and glanced down at the still sleeping baby. All Luna heard was the gun go off. She didn't even see any blood to begin with when Cayetano fell forward onto her, and the three of them fell to the ground. She looked in horror at the bullet wound in his back; barely any blood came from the hole pierced into him. It must have gone straight in his back and straight through his chest, and somehow missed her and Paco. She couldn't even open her mouth to scream. She couldn't look up at the gunman, her brother. She put the baby on the ground in his bundle of blankets, and he cried out when she let him go. The moment she touched Cayetano she knew he was already dead. He didn't move. He may not have even felt the bullet that ended his short life.

Luna rolled him over with all her might, to see a stain of blood on his chest. His eyes hung open, already lifeless. Only then did air hit her lungs and fill them enough to let her cry out. She screamed; every muscle in her body behind its force. The love of her life was dead. He died by her brother's hand. In one second, all she had left was gone. She put her hands to his face, almost willing some kind of reaction from him, but his warm body was now only a shell. The cheeky and loving soul that lived inside was gone.

Luna looked up at Alejandro who just stood there; the gun in his hand, pointed aimlessly at the ground. His face spoke of the same horror. His actions instantly sobered him up. Now they truly had lost everything.

Luna stumbled to her feet, her dirty clothes covered in splatters of Cayetano's blood. "How could you?" she screamed. "Why would you do that? Do you want me to suffer like you do?"

"No!" Alejandro began to cry again as the gun fell from his hands. "I want no one to suffer the way I do."

"Look what you've done," she wept. "Cayetano is dead, and you will have to live with this your whole life, you miserable human being!" Luna wasn't sure how she could even stand anymore. The pain that seared through her body was so profound that she felt as if she had got a bullet in *the chest. She may as well have. She was as good as dead on her own. She fell back to her knees, and her tears fell on Cayetano's shirt as she rested her face on his chest. If only she could feel the faintest flicker of life. All hope was gone. All life was gone. As the last bastions of freedom were surrounded by Franco and his followers, the lives of the Beltrán family were defeated by the grief of lost love, courage and promise.*

42

Valencia, España ~ enero de 2010

Luna slapped tape over the box and patted it. That was the last one. It felt bittersweet to pack Darren's things, but it had to be done.

"Are we finished?" Darren asked when he came down the hallway, a bag in his hand. "That keen to get rid of me, are you?"

"You know I'm not keen to get rid of you."

"It's time I moved out. I don't want to be here when you and Cayetano are naked and chasing each other around the apartment while the kids are asleep."

"Yeah, because that would happen," she shot back. Actually…

"It's going to be weird, not being here with you and the boys. But, a new year, a new start."

"Your new apartment is gorgeous. I wouldn't mind overlooking Mercado Colon every morning. The agent, Michael, did a superb job getting you that place."

"Are you ready for a new year?" Darren put his bag down and leant against the wall.

"No," Luna sighed, and ran her hands through her long hair. "Who knows what will happen. But at least I have had my work permit extended. And eventually, I will get my permanent residency. My Spanish grandfather does exist after all."

"And we know you will be with me as my mechanic. We both will be very happy with that, I know it."

"You couldn't keep me away."

"And you're getting married to Cayetano."

"Yeah, eventually. No rush."

"All the intermingling by your grandparents hasn't left any weirdness?"

"It's weird, for sure. But there are far more pressing issues than that to deal with."

"Like his ex-wife being pregnant?"

"Don't start me on that one. I'm not free of baggage myself."

"If only all girls were as casual as you, Lulu."

"What makes you say that?"

Darren smiled. "When I was in Australia, I met up with Lia, remember her?"

"That girl you were seeing when we first met?"

"Yes. We spent some time together, and now she wants to come to Spain for a holiday."

"Lucky you have a new apartment to show off."

"We only saw each other for a month, and she wants to come over? That's heavy."

"Did you spend a month in bed with her?"

"Maybe."

"That kind of thing insinuates to a woman that you like her. We all have a cross to bear. A girl who likes having sex with you wants to visit. That isn't so bad."

Darren nodded as he thought about it. "True. I'll go pack the car and come say goodbye to Giacomo and Enzo. Are you off to Madrid soon?"

"Very soon."

"Ready to be part of the whole Beltrán family?"

"Not really."

"Are you sure you're okay?"

"Yeah, are you sure you're okay with not seeing the boys for Three Kings Day?"

"It's a Spanish thing, so I don't mind, even though I also didn't get to see them at New Year."

"You went partying in Ruzafa, where all the cool people hang out."

"You all went and sat in the park to see in the New Year with the traditional twelve grapes and cava with Cayetano."

"As you would imagine we would. Please don't make this hard."

"I'm not. You and I are over. You are with him. I won't say the best man won, just the luckiest man."

Luna smiled. "You and me… we just couldn't work things out…"

"No, we couldn't. We aren't meant to be. After 15 years, we both know it. But I still want time with my godsons."

"Of course! Just not in May and June when the bulk of Cayetano's bullfighting season is on in Madrid."

"I can live with that." Darren smiled. "Go meet your future family, Lulu. If it's awful, come home to me."

"You're the only person who still calls me Lulu, now that Fabrizio and Dad are gone."

"Your family is whoever you want it to be. It's you and me, kid, always. Things won't always have an awkward break-up vibe."

Luna smiled when he reached out for a hug. "I hope not. Life is short enough without worrying about things we can't change."

43

Madrid, España ~ enero de 2010

January 5 was never the best day to get anything done. Everyone was usually in a rush to get everything they needed for Three Kings Day. But Luna wasn't at all tired by the time she arrived in Madrid with her boys. She felt more alive than she had in years. Her enthusiasm for whatever lay ahead was matched by the smile that greeted them when the door to Cayetano's apartment opened.

"There you are!" he cried when he answered the door to the children and their fist-pounding.

"We haven't seen you for like… four days," Giacomo complained.

"I know, and it's too long. Quick, come inside. I heard a rumour about presents arriving under my tree a day early, and they have Giacomo and Enzo written on them."

The redheaded pair dashed past their future stepfather and into the living room in search of treasures, which left their mother with all the bags. "Charming as always," she joked.

Cayetano kicked her things inside the door and closed it. All he needed was a kiss from her, which she was more than happy to give him. "The boys are right, four days is too long to be apart."

"We live in different cities, it's going to happen. It was you who was so eager to go home after New Year."

"I had to, not wanted to. I wish I could hide out in Valencia forever. Trying to swallow twelve grapes with cava with you when the clock struck midnight was just what I needed after a very sombre few weeks on my own."

"Oh good, then, if you had such a good time, you will be happy to live in Valencia with me."

Cayetano took a step back and raised his eyebrows. "And leave Madrid? Please, *mujer,* not going to happen."

"Fine, I'll get a part-time lover for when you aren't around."

"You wouldn't dare."

"No, I wouldn't. You're a handful enough."

"How are you, my *preciosa?* I felt so miserable that I left you after all that happened with Alejandro."

"The man died," she shrugged. "I feel awful for him, all alone as he was. He has been cremated and had no funeral. That is sad."

"But that was what he wanted. He had you in his last months, and that would have given him immense comfort. Not only in giving him someone important in his life, but also because it eased the weight of guilt that he had to carry."

Luna watched her children rip into gifts with sheer delight. "But now it's me who carries all that weight. What am I meant to do with that information? We can't tell Paco the truth."

"It was you who was so determined to find Cayetano Ortega, so Alejandro gave you the release you wanted, and in turn battled his own demons. This story was never destined to have a happy ending."

"I thought I would be angry that he murdered Cayetano Ortega. He killed his own best friend and in front of his sister. But I'm not mad."

"He was in a bad place at the time."

"I've been in the bad place that he was in. When I saw Fabrizio at the hospital, all cut up and bloody when he died, I thought my own life was over. I couldn't imagine a life where I could ever do anything without seeing that image in my mind. I still have it there, all the time. I took my anger out on the person who did it, but not with violence. I will admit it crossed my mind to hurt others."

"Society had burst wide open, we can't judge Alejandro."

"I have no intention of judging. It happened. It can stay in 1939 as far as I'm concerned. Only you and I know what that note from Alejandro said. I'm quite happy for Cayetano and Sofía to stay buried in secret at Escondrijo. Everyone involved is dead, let it rest."

"What about Alejandro's ashes?"

"I will put them at Escondrijo with Sofía, I guess."

"Not with his sister, here in Madrid? Luna is buried alone."

"Would she have wanted him with her?"

"Would she have wanted him with Cayetano?"

"I don't know. We will never know. Like you said, the story has no happy ending. How is Paco?"

"I think Papá hasn't even come to terms with the fact Alejandro and Sofía were his biological parents."

"A subject close to my heart," Luna sighed. "Cayetano Ortega is my biological grandfather, but he did nothing to shape my family or my life. I can see why Paco would feel the same way. Luna Beltrán was his mother. She was there when it counted. But," she gestured to the children, "Fabrizio won't be there for my sons. It doesn't mean he is just shoved aside and forgotten. I think it's an individual choice that Paco needs to make about his biological heritage."

"I have no intention of taking Fabrizio's place with the boys, I hope you know that."

"I do know that. I won't ask you to."

"But I do want to be a father. I don't care if they are not my own biological children."

"You have a biological child on the way, with María." Luna turned her attention back to the children who had unwrapped an Xbox. "Cayetano! You can't spend that kind of money! They are only five years-old!"

"Nearly six," Giacomo said.

"He didn't, the three magi left them on his windowsill for us early, right, Cayetano?" Enzo said.

"Right," Cayetano replied, and turned to Luna's guilty expression. "Your Mamá forgets who brings the gifts."

"We have been good this year," Giacomo said.

"You have, that's true," Luna said.

"You're very lucky," Cayetano said.

"Caya, it's too much," Luna said to him.

"Nothing is too much. You're going to be my wife, remember?"

"How could I forget, carrying this thing around?" Luna hung her left hand as if to show the diamond was too bulky to carry.

"Very funny." Cayetano put his arms around her while they watched the kids play. "It's going to take a while to condition you into being my wife, isn't it?"

"In what way?"

"In that you're incredibly stubborn and independent. You don't have to fight the world anymore, *la chispa.*"

"I don't have to fight? That will be new. I have had no one to back me up when things went wrong."

"You do now. You have a whole family now. You're Spanish, not a foreigner."

"I don't know what I am. I do know that I won't be an obedient wife."

"Yeah, I know. You will be difficult to handle. But I fight bulls, so I can fight you."

Luna scoffed, but the doorbell interrupted her reply. Cayetano slipped his arm from around her waist, and went to answer the door. Luna didn't even enquire who it was; she didn't care. She was just happy to be there, in his home. Then she heard Cayetano call her name from the direction of the kitchen. She left the twins with their things and went to find Cayetano leaning against the island counter, with María across the room with her arms folded. Not Luna's first choice for Christmas visitors.

"María has got something to tell us," Cayetano said.

"I saw the photos of your engagement in the paper today," María said. "A two-page spread. Quite a public announcement."

"Not really, just an opportunistic photographer and my boss eager to get the team name out there any way he can," Luna said.

"It came with quite a story. Grandparents torn apart by war, and a romantic speech from a *torero* in full dress."

"All true," Cayetano said, as he looked at the floor.

"I have fielded a lot of questions about my marriage," María said. "Like how my husband is proposing to someone else."

"You're the one who loves a public life, so there is not much I can say about that."

"I signed the divorce papers. It won't look good if I do anything else. I will look like the spiteful *bruja* who got in the way of a love affair."

"It must be exhausting to spend so much time wondering what other people think," Luna said.

"I just like it to sound favourable. It's not all pleasant about you, you know. First a celebrity sports star husband, and now a bullfighter. And a rumour you were involved with a friend of your husband."

"María, shut the fuck up," Cayetano spat out.

"No, it's okay," Luna said. "My first husband wasn't a celebrity, just part of something high profile, something far bigger than he was by himself. The same can be said for Cayetano, one man who is part of something ingrained into society. And if anyone is confused about my private friendship with Darren James, they are welcome to ask me about it. But they will never understand a private bond. People can think what they like, because I have better things to worry about."

"I came here and told you that I slept with Cayetano behind your back. I told you that I was pregnant to him."

"Yet he still wants to be with me. I want to be with him, baby or not. The circumstances of the time when he gave you quick sex, or why I chose to let it go, will never be anyone's business."

"I think I can see María's problem," Cayetano said. "She wants to announce her pregnancy, but the father is marrying someone else. Not the pretty image. Now is your chance, María, you can make me out to be the bad guy. Go ahead, I don't care."

"I don't want to do that," María said. "Papá asked me not to."

"Then Leandro is a kinder person than you. Respect your father, he is a good, and ill, man."

"I asked him what you and he have talked about lately, but he said it was private."

Cayetano smiled, and Luna joined him; Leandro knew that Luna was his uncle's granddaughter and hadn't told María.

"How would you feel if I spoke to your family behind your back?" María asked.

"You have plenty of times. Look, we have things to do. We have two children to spend the evening with. We have a big day tomorrow."

"Meeting the Beltrán's?' María asked Luna. "You have my sympathy."

"I don't think it will be any problem. We have history," Luna said.

"How?"

"None of your business," Cayetano said. "Thank you for signing the divorce papers. As for the baby…"

"It's not your baby."

Cayetano stood up straight the moment that María said that. Luna watched his whole body freeze; the proud, shoulders back, chest out stance was back. She couldn't tell if he was surprised or angry. He seemed to be speechless.

"I already knew I was pregnant when I slept with you. I had just found out. I thought it would starve off the divorce a bit longer…"

"And what? Pin me to a child that wasn't mine? How could you be that cruel?"

"You're happy to be Papá to Luna's kids! They aren't yours!"

"That is my choice. Did you consider the amount of pain a secret like that would cause?"

"Can we keep our voices down, please?" Luna asked. She poked her head out the door to check on the kids nearby.

"Sorry," Cayetano said. "María, I will never love you. Baby or not. That is such a cruel, predictable, and sorry trick to play. Never mind you and I, the pain it could cause the child, and its own children, could be monumental. People have a right to know who they are and where they come from."

"Would you two like to discuss this in private?" Luna asked.

"No." Cayetano reached out and took her hand "I don't think there isn't anything else to discuss. Thank you, María, for coming over here and telling me what I knew – that I made all the right choices this past year."

"Does the real father know about this?" Luna asked.

"No, but he will. Paulo and I have been on a break."

"Tell him the truth," Cayetano said. "Now get the fuck out of my house."

He and Luna stood silent while María left the apartment. Cayetano held his breath until he heard the front door slam shut. *"Jesucristo,"* he sighed.

"Exactly how many bombshells are going to be dropped on us?"

"Preciosa," he mumbled with his large hands over his mouth. "I'm so, so sorry."

Luna pulled his hands away from his face. "It's okay."

"It's not. I let the witch in. I did this. I caused all this trouble between us. As if we didn't have enough hurdles…"

"But as far as major developments go, this one is pretty good for you and me."

"We can be married sooner than planned."

"If you like."

"And there will be no more María in our lives."

"But you don't get the child you want so much."

"But I have you, and I have Giacomo and Enzo."

"Is that enough for you?"

"I can't have children, and you don't want to. I have no choice."

"Maybe you do. Nothing is impossible, there are just some obstacles. You said it was our job to make sure history didn't repeat. So we need to overcome all the hurdles."

"So, you're saying you would want a child with me?"

"Slow down! I'm just saying… anything is possible. One day. A long way off from now. I'm certainly not ready for that."

"I hope you know how much I love you."

"I do. I know I've been pretty hesitant with you the whole time we've been together, but I do love you."

"You agreed to love me, and marry me, even though you thought the baby was mine."

Luna just shrugged with a smile.

"It shows how much you love me. Actions speak louder than words."

"María has given you the best gift ever. Now, we can take the kids to the Three Kings parade at Plaza de Colon, knowing we are free to live our lives."

"Freedom. We are free, our parents, our grandparents, finally, we are all free of what hurts us."

44

Madrid, España ~ enero de 2010

Rebelión on *Dia de los Reyes Magos,* Three Kings Day, was just as Luna expected. Dozens of people to meet, all eager to be introduced to the woman that the future patriarch of the family had been indulging in a private whirlwind relationship with. It was hard to keep up with all the names. José and Consuela Morales, in addition to Cayetano's mother, Inés, had three sons, all married with children and grandchildren of their own, which resulted in a large family. It was Inés that Luna had to impress, and also her husband, Paco, who had been furious with Luna last time they met. But for today, everyone was in a warm mood, and the children were more than happy to play with the other children in the lavish home, which left Luna to try and settle into the notion of having an extended family.

"Taking a look at all our embarrassing moments, are you?"

Luna turned away from the family photos on the wall to see Cayetano's sister, Sofía. "Not at all. They are terrific photos."

"We are a crazy bunch, but you'll get used to it."

"I'm sure I will."

"Just watch cousin Alonso. His wandering hands are the reason his wife left him. He works for Caya, so you will have to avoid him a lot."

"I'll remember that."

"How are you? You must be wondering why you said yes to marrying my brother."

Luna laughed. "He has his crazy moments, that's for sure."

"Caya was a mess without you, Luna. Really. My mother even called me to see if I could do anything to help him. My mother and I don't get along at all. You have brought my parents back to speaking to me. Well, you, and María trying to pin a baby on Caya."

"You all know about that?"

"Only me, and Mamá and Papá. That can fade away. I have to say, you have taken that well."

"It's a long complicated story. The result is that we can move on."

"It's none of our business. My family likes to hold grudges, so you will be a breath of fresh air."

"Or they will hate me."

"I doubt it. If Papá gives his approval of you, everyone will think you're a gift from heaven. Paco is a hard man to please, but he raves about you."

"He does?" Luna squinted when she said it.

"He does to me. I need to get myself another drink, family events are not my favourite thing, but I wanted to come and see you and Caya. Can I get you anything?"

"No, thank you. Unless, you can find where Cayetano went?"

"He will be gossiping somewhere, I guarantee it," Sofía said as she turned away. "He loves being the centre of attention."

That was certainly true. Luna stood and watched her children play in the middle of the room, quite happy to ignore all the adults around and mingle with the kids. She felt proud of them, speaking Spanish as fluently as they did. It had taken years of Fabrizio's teaching her before she picked it up herself.

"Luna?"

She looked up to see Paco there, and she smiled. "Yes, Paco?"

"A moment?" He gestured for them to step through into the dining room, all quiet for now. "I was pleased to hear that you decided to return my mother's diary, even if it didn't give you any good news."

"I got the truth, and I'm grateful to you and your mother for helping me. It has cost you a lot to help me out."

"It shouldn't have been so hard. I should have been more understanding of you and Caya from the beginning. I should have been more honest about the fact I knew who Scarlett was, but I didn't. Can an old man admit he was wrong?"

"He can, but I wouldn't expect him to."

Paco smiled. "I can't pretend that I haven't caused you and Cayetano a lot of problems. I was so busy looking at myself that I wasn't thinking clearly."

"Paco, if it were me then I would be the same. Everyone has secrets. I have two sons, and one day, do I want them to know the whole story of their father's life and death? No. It would hurt them. We all have parts of our lives that deserve privacy."

"My mother will always be a painful story for me. She died when I was only 20, and the pain of it never ends, not even after 50 years. I'm a grown man, so it sounds ridiculous…"

"No it doesn't, I lost my father at that age, and my mother was already long dead. I know exactly how it feels. Seeing one of the most defining people in your life dying of illness is a torment. It doesn't matter what age you are, it's a painful affliction."

"My mother was a liar."

"No, she was a mother with a son. She loved someone, and she witnessed his needless death. She was hurting and tried to spare you the truth."

"I'm not ready to accept the truth."

"Well, we have only known the whole story for a week. It's going to take a lot longer to accept it."

"So, my biological mother, Sofía, is buried at this Escondrijo?"

"Yes, and so is Cayetano Ortega. Alejandro's letter to me said he buried Cayetano next to Sofía after he shot him. Luna took the baby and ran, terrified of her brother. She took you to protect you from him. She never contacted him again."

"That must have been so awful," he all but whispered. "She had to leave Cayetano's body behind there, with the man who killed him."

"I know. I can't believe she could go through something that painful and carry on with her life."

"She didn't; she spent the rest of her days alone, not many friends, and her sham marriage didn't last. She didn't get over what happened."

"It makes me sick to just think about it. I saw my husband when he died. That was horrific. To have just left his body on the bed at the hospital and walk away… I couldn't have done that. I spent days crying beside his coffin before the funeral. I needed that."

"It explains so much about my mother to me. Why she was such a quiet, solemn person."

"Alejandro buried his friend in a safe place, and lived there most of his life, right next to what he had done. That would have been just as bad."

"I don't know what to think of Alejandro Beltrán. He was my real father, and he never wanted me."

"Different times, Paco. He was confused when he gave you away."

"What was he like?"

"He looked just like you," Luna said. She could see the man try and to hold back what that meant to him. His eyes looked damp as he turned his gaze to the view out the window. "He was a surprisingly gentle man. He acted all rough, and brave, a real tough solitary man. But he was, in fact, kind and warm. He tried to hide it, but he couldn't. He recognised me in an instant, from my grandmother's looks, and took me in."

"But he murdered your grandfather and kept it a secret all this time."

"I wish he hadn't killed him, of course I do. I wish your mother hadn't seen that. I wish you hadn't been there, in the first days of your life, there at that bloody moment. But we can't change history. None of them could change the outcome of what happened, and neither can we. Luna took you and drove you to Madrid. A young woman, who had never travelled, managed to get you all the way to Madrid and built a life for you. That is brave. It sounds like an impossible task, but she did it."

"I remember walking the streets with her as a young boy," Paco said. "I was about ten, and we were wandering past a hotel where foreigners were coming in and out, tourists on holiday. I asked her why they came to Spain, and I remember her having no answer. She said a foreigner cannot understand Spain the way that Spaniards do, and that they had romantic notions of the place. She said there was nothing romantic about the awkward fashions of the day. I remember Mamá, tugging at her ill-fitting jacket when she said it. I know that means nothing, but I remember her pulling her coat, wishing for better lives for us. Black, she always wore black."

"She's right. As a foreigner, it is hard to understand Spain. The thing I always notice about Spaniards is that they are never conflicted.

They have beliefs, and they will defend them. They all believe that what they know and what they have is the best way to live. No one changes sides in an argument and will fight to the death to defend themselves."

"That stubbornness has caused many dramas."

"I like stubborn." Luna smiled, and Paco returned it.

"When I saw you here that night, with Cayetano, going through my mother's things… I was rude."

"We shouldn't have gone through the chest without your permission."

"I shouldn't have hidden her things away. I should have looked at it, and read her diaries. I was being an idiot. You looked for a family amongst it; I have had one most of my life, and I shouldn't deprive you of that."

"I found no such thing. Cayetano Ortega merely got a New Zealand nurse pregnant; he isn't a member of my family. I do imagine him to be a charming man, if not cheeky and a womaniser, but he would have been entertaining. But he isn't family."

"He might have been, had he not died. Your father may have gotten to know him, somehow."

"Maybe. Alexander didn't suffer without his father. Scarlett was a devoted mother to him. Family consists of whoever we want it be."

Paco nodded and glanced over his shoulder, to double check everyone was out of earshot. "I met Inés, and I wanted to be with her, and that meant becoming a member of the Morales family. My mother… can I still call Luna that? She wasn't my biological mother…"

"I would call her that. Alejandro and Sofía produced you, but Luna raised you."

"My mother was deeply religious, like her mother was, but had the independent anarchist ideals of her father and brother… and, I suppose, Cayetano and Scarlett. She was a torn woman."

"An exception to the rule."

"Exactly. But the Morales family… a family of Falangists… so conservative, almost fanatical, religious members of society. Consuela was raised to be a wife and mother, a decent God-fearing woman, submissive to her husband. José, whose father was killed in the early days of fighting against the Republicans in 1936, was, and still is, a strong Franco supporter. Did Cayetano talk to you about that?"

"Yes, he told me that you, he and José had a talk about it. Cayetano said he had no idea that his grandfather worked for Franco."

"I told José to keep a lid on his political views in front of Cayetano, for his sake. I told him that Cayetano would do better by having no clear political alliance. He can appeal to everyone that way. José may be a murderer, but he does care for Cayetano."

"These are old ideals that shouldn't shackle anyone. But I won't lie, hearing about what José was like once upon a time is scary."

"You adjust, I suppose. We aren't the only family in Spain with this kind of history."

"I know."

"I grew up to be like my mother, believe what you like in private, and just blend in. The Morales ideals go in one ear, and out the other."

"I won't hold anyone's ideals against anyone, Paco. I'm a foreigner, I don't get an opinion."

"Are you eligible to vote in Spain?"

"No, no yet."

"Lucky you. But you aren't a foreigner. You are the product of a Spanish man, and he was the product of the King himself. You can't get more Spanish than that."

"That link means nothing as far as I'm concerned. Leandro Medina knows I'm Cayetano Ortega's granddaughter, and that is enough."

"Leandro Medina is an upstanding man. Pity María is his daughter. The woman is a bad seed. I tried to like her, I truly did. I wanted her and Caya to work out."

"I guess I need to do a lot of work to impress you and Inés."

Paco shook his head and turned around to the face the groups of relatives spread out around the huge room through the doorway into the living room. "Look at Caya," he said. He gestured towards his son who had reappeared. "The boy has never been happier than he is right now. You did that to him. Inés, she is so pleased to see her son as well as he is, that she will do anything to keep you around. Me, well, I have long wanted a loving woman for my son. I know that I had made a mistake wanting him to marry María. She wasn't any good for him. I wanted him to have what I have with Inés. Happy wife, happy life. That way, he would have no woman troubles and stop being such a pain in the ass."

Luna burst out laughing along with Paco as they went back into the living room. "Yeah, I can see that," she said through her wide smile. "I can imagine Cayetano being a pain in the ass."

"Show me this ring on your hand again," Paco said and took her fingers in his. "This shouldn't be hidden away. I didn't want to give it to Inés. I wanted to buy her a ring, to prove what a rich man I was. I was young and stupid. Now, I'm old and stupid. This ring belongs to your grandfather, and to you."

"But given to me, by Cayetano. He got it from his grandmother and that makes it unique."

"I guess we all got what we wanted, it just took 70 years to feel that way."

"What's going on over here?" Cayetano said as he approached the pair. "I hear laughing, that has to be good."

"It is good; it's all your expense," Paco said, and he and Luna laughed again.

"Touching, *preciosa*," he said to Luna and slipped an arm around her. "Have I lost you already?"

"She's a woman, Cayetano," Paco chastised him. "You can't control them, never could, never will."

Luna chuckled as Paco left the pair. "At least Paco doesn't hate me for all the secrets I have dug up."

"He discovered who his real father was, and now the guy is dead. He's hurting, but just won't admit it."

"Aren't we all? This isn't how it was meant to end. Alejandro murdered Cayetano, and now I have his body, and also Sofía's body, hidden where I want to raise my kids."

"Leave them there. Let them rest. We have the rest of our own lives to live."

Luna watched her sons play with two little girls, Cayetano's cousin Eduardo's daughters. "I guess the boys would have cousins when we get married."

"Surrogate cousins, aunts and uncles, grandparents, as well as a father… and perhaps brothers and sisters…"

"I mention it once and already you are taking it as gospel. I said I wasn't ready for more kids."

"Is there something wrong with wanting to be happy?"

"No. You're not alone in wanting to be happy."

"It's all on your own terms, *la chispa*. I said I won't be a replacement for your family, or husband, but something new instead, and I meant it. I will only adopt the boys if you want me to, but I won't push for it. And we can marry and adjust to a new life in your own time. I can wait, I'm happy."

"Thank you. I'm ready to marry you, by the way. It also has to be on your terms."

"Good, because Mamá already asked me about when the wedding will be."

Luna rolled her eyes with a smile. "Let me guess, they have already picked the date, dress and venue?"

"Yeah... yeah, that's true."

"Grandiose wedding in Madrid, early summer time before the three months of hell starts?"

"Of course, no one wants to sweat through a wedding in a Madrid summer. But maybe... you and I can change the plan a little?"

"How?"

"What if you and I, and Giacomo and Enzo, go to Cuenca and get married? Right in the middle of Madrid and Valencia, where the story between our families started? We can marry where the first Luna and Cayetano would have gotten married given the chance, 70 years after they missed out on happiness. Just the four of us."

"You don't need to shut everyone out."

"But I do need to make you happy."

"I am happy. So happy that I barely recognise myself."

"I will be glad to take the credit." When he kissed her, she forgot that she was in a house full of people she didn't know. They faded into the background.

"Give it a rest," Cayetano's cousin Hector called from across the room. "Children are present."

"They kiss all the time," Giacomo said from his spot on the floor with a wooden train set.

"It's true, they do," Enzo agreed. "And then Cayetano goes all silly."

Cayetano shook his head while the group laughed at him. "Mock me if you like," he said over the top of them all. "I'm taking a momentous step forward with my life with Luna, Giacomo and Enzo. It's a joy to feel so convinced in my belief that I'm on the right path with my life. Our whole family, and even all of Spain, could learn from us. If you shake off the ghosts that weigh you down, extraordinary things can happen. Core values and traditions can be held onto, without needing to hold on to the bitterness that comes with bad or even gruesome experiences. The future doesn't have to hold worry or fear. No person, no belief, no sickness, no pain can break the bond between Luna and I."

Luna gave him another kiss. This time no one teased, because he spoke all truthful words and everyone knew it. Here in front of everyone that mattered in Cayetano's life, Luna couldn't have felt any more comfort than what he provided. All she had to do was return the favour for a lifetime, which didn't seem like a big task at all.

45

Valencia, España ~ febrero de 2010

Escondrijo hadn't yet been handed over to Luna, and no doubt that would be another long-winded bureaucratic process. But it didn't stop her from wanting to spend time there, as cold as the snowy winter was up on the mountain.

Luna and Cayetano walked around the property; their boots crunched the latest dusting of snow that covered the surroundings of the *masía*. The children ran just ahead, which shattered the peace that the place provided. Cayetano was due to fight in the Valencia's bullring at the end of Las Fallas, the city premier *fiesta* in March, and time to relax up on the mountain was called for before life became crazy again.

"*Preciosa,* I don't want to be negative about Escondrijo…"

"Don't then," she said with a smile while they wandered the property together, the kids just ahead of them.

"I mean, this place is a mess. I can't imagine what you're going to do with it. It's steep and rocky, and overgrown."

"But you have Rebelión, and it's flat and pristine for breeding animals. This is a totally different environment. I will grow a few things, raise a few goats, and take it easy up here. It's not a large operation."

"Then why have all this space?"

"Because I can."

"Oh, I see, queen of all she surveys."

"I wish." The pair stopped; before them was a drop down the rocky mountainside. The kids had dashed off behind them to run around some pines nearby, their giggling echoed back towards their parents. Luna looked out across the enormous view, the flatlands of the Turia that lead to Valencia city in the distance, along with Albufera lake and the glistening Mediterranean.

"What are you thinking about?" Cayetano asked.

"About whether I correctly set up Darren's seat post torque setting when I tuned his bike for today's ride."

"Will he fall off if you didn't?"

"No."

"Pity."

Luna scoffed. "Not particularly nice. I know you and Darren don't get on, but you will need to learn. Besides, Fabrizio fell off his bike and it killed him, so please don't wish that."

"Sorry."

"It's okay. It doesn't bother me. Watching you trying to be stabbed by a bull again bothers me. All those months of pain…"

"My leg wasn't that sore. My pride hurt the most. It felt better when I was in favour with you and in pain when you were gone. Most of the pain was in my head."

"Most of the bull's horn was in your thigh."

"You have watched me practice, you know it's safe enough."

"Yeah, I do. I can watch you stand there and satisfy the bloodlust of others."

"Bullfighting is like dancing the tango. It is a collection of human emotions – passion, love, anger, jealousy, happiness… all illuminated distinctly in the performance."

"I don't need the *'I love bullfighting'* speech, Caya. I get it," she smiled. She turned to check the children, and then focused back on him. "I enjoy watching you practice at Rebelión."

"I'm telling you… passion, love, anger, jealousy, happiness… you can't resist me when I'm performing. It builds up a fire of lust and desire in you."

"Confident much?"

"Hey, I get more women's underwear given to me per season than I get ears awarded to me."

"Maybe that says something about your efforts."

"Are you saying I'm not the greatest fighter in this great land?" He tried to sound offended as he gestured out at Spain laid before them, but she didn't fall for it. "Are you saying you feel nothing when I'm performing?"

"Oh, I'm hot of you," she said quietly. "I just keep a lid on it. Besides, if you want my underwear, do my laundry for me."

"I can think of more fun ways to get them."

"Well, now you don't have your cane to walk on. That was hot. But you always impress me."

"One day, when I'm old, I promise to wander around Escondrijo with a cane, just to get you all worked up."

"Promise?"

"I promise. I'm not going anywhere."

"You're as bound to Escondrijo as I am."

Cayetano nodded and looked out over the view again. "I guess I am. Our families rest here in the soil."

"Your weird grandfather, José, must love that."

"The man whose job it was to round up 'enemies of the State?' He loves hearing stories about *rojos* who were killed."

"That guy makes me uncomfortable. Your father said we would adjust, like he is adjusting to all this, but... I spent all this time wanting to find my grandfather, and in turn exposed something very sickening about your family."

"I know. Yet I feel compelled to know more about what José did during that part of his life. It's like watching a train wreck, I can't help myself."

"I guess it's a part of this story that isn't finished yet. Like my involvement with the Medina family. Do I let that go, or get to know them, María included?"

"There is plenty of time for us to figure all this out. For now, we can worry about happier things. One day, the house will be finished for us to live in, and we can settle here, instead of going back and forward between Valencia and Madrid, if that's what you want."

"It is, but only if you agree."

"I don't care where I live. I won't be Spain's best *torero* forever, my life is flexible. Plus, I'm not sure I want to be part of the Morales family business anymore."

"It's the Beltrán family business, too. Don't make any hasty decisions. You need to be flexible."

"Are you going to be flexible? Maybe we could live in Madrid, and just travel out here now and then."

"I don't know… I would have to give up work for that. How flexible do you want me to be?"

"I like where this is going! I thought you said only one of your legs over my shoulder at a time in bed… are you suggesting both legs now?"

Luna threw him a look, and he smirked. "I meant a bigger family."

"Now my interest has peaked."

"Before or after you imagined me 'flexible' one sexual way or another?"

"Are you pregnant?"

"We aren't married yet."

"Marriage doesn't get you pregnant. Nor can a sterile *torero.*"

"Maybe he can."

"Really?"

"Maybe. Might be worth checking."

"Why didn't you tell me? You're pregnant?"

"I'm telling you now. I'm not sure yet. But I really hope I'm not."

"Mummy!" Giacomo said. "Mummy, come and look at this! We found bones!"

"Good. Interrupted by the 'let's poke dead stuff with a stick'. My favourite game," she teased as they headed in the boys' direction.

"I think the boys are getting more Spanish by the day, they love bloody stories, and now they love death in general. One day it will be girls they love…"

"You talk crap sometimes."

"You love it."

"No, I only love you."

"Look, Mummy," Enzo said when the pair reached the children. "We were stomping in the snow, and the bones are sticking out."

"Are you sure they aren't just bits of branches off the trees?"

"Luna…"

She looked in the direction Cayetano pointed; a human skull.

"Mummy, why are there dead people at our new house?" Giacomo asked. "Skeletons are scary."

"Why can't they be put in boxes when they die?" Enzo asked. "There's another one over there."

Cayetano went over to where Enzo directed, and sure enough, there was a damaged skull, and other bits of bone scattered around.

They must have been washed to the surface by the recent unusually heavy rain before the snow had set in.

"Come on, boys, it's not a good idea for you to be here," Luna said.

"Are they real, Mummy?" Giacomo asked.

"No, honey." Luna was prepared to lie to save them a life of therapy after discovering bodies on their own farm.

"We need to… something…" Cayetano said with a frown. "Let's not jump to conclusions."

"Other properties out here have *fosas* from the war."

"Wait, we are jumping to the conclusion that this is a burial pit?"

"Who knows, maybe they are victims of evil people like José Morales."

"Do we want to know?" Cayetano knew he had no choice but find out.

"Clearly the story of what happened out here still isn't finished."

To be continued…

ALSO BY CAROLINE ANGUS BAKER

THE 'CANNA MEDICI' SERIES
PART I - NIGHT WANTS TO FORGET

Canna Medici is a hedonistic young woman who flees her home and an abusive relationship in Italy, and finds herself in a new life in London. She becomes the new assistant of Virtuosi, a small opera group who are about to embark on a tour of ten of Europe's greatest opera houses. When Canna soon becomes romantically involved with English tenor Dane Porter, trouble comes in the form of fellow Virtuosi singer Claudio Ramos Ibáñez, the dark, brooding Spanish baritone. Canna and Claudio have crossed paths once before with vicious consequences, and each are desperate for the truth to remain hidden.

As Claudio becomes more and more entangled in Canna's violent and addictive secrets, Dane is forced to re-evaluate his life – his morals and stereotypes are going to be tested in order to accept her dark past. Canna continues to pursue pleasure at any cost, exploiting the weaknesses of those around her in an effort to hide her demons. All of the men and women in Virtuosi are going to be hurt by Canna's narcissism unless she can overcome her inner torment.

Canna is night and Dane is day, and while the night wants to forget, another night is calling to her in a form very close to home, and love holds on too tight...

PART II – VIOLENT DAYLIGHT
Forgetting the night and coming into the daylight isn't as easy as first thought...

Canna Medici is free. Her tyrant husband, Giuseppe Savelli, is dead and can't hurt her anymore. Or so she thought. Now that the recovering drug-addict is the head of Caraceni Industries and heiress to Giuseppe's billions, Canna finds that the riches are more dangerous than ever. Giorgio Savelli, the charismatic but volatile nephew of the deceased family patriarch, wants the Caraceni fortune, and Canna needs to decide how to eliminate Giorgio and be the sole heir of the dirty money.

Operatic music group Virtuosi are in the throes of stardom; world tours, new albums and legions of fans beckon. All baritone Claudio Ramos Ibáñez wants is to be with his lover, Canna, whose business dealings take her to Milan far more often than he likes. The Virtuosi group adapt to the new relationship between Canna and Claudio, but tenor Dane Porter isn't sure of how he feels about Canna. Dane finds himself in a situation where he can destroy Canna and Claudio's already strained 'happily ever after', and Virtuosi risk a descent into jealousy and madness.

When a brutal murder occurs, and Virtuosi get caught up in the scandal, Canna begins to question if she can have a future with Claudio. As the bodies of enemies and loved ones begin to pile up, the dark desires of drugs and self-mutilation dominate Canna's mind. The truth won't set anyone free, and Canna's life is again under threat, this time from her most dangerous adversary – herself.

ACKNOWLEDGEMENTS

The thanks for this book goes to four fine young gentlemen – Grayson, Torben, Espen and Lachlan, who (mostly) give their mother space to write. Special thanks needs to go to Martyn Baker, my help, support and occasional human thesaurus, for all time and space given to me. There are no words to express my gratitude.

Thanks to Stuart Angus, for being genuinely interested in this novel. All we have be through this year, and you still stopped to ask how the book was coming along. I've always got your back.

To Christine Holmwood, what you have done for me cannot be thanked enough. I can only hope I have been enough for you in return.

There are many people based in Spain to thank, especially the Writers and Bloggers about Spain group, with all their help with the modern day storyline. Even the simplest things you say make their way into my work. I am looking forward to meeting people and getting lost in Valencia again really soon. Thank you to the International Brigade Memorial Trust with help on the wartime storyline.

The plight of New Zealanders who fought to save Spain during the civil war has gone largely undocumented and unrecognised. The kiwi attitude of "making do and getting by" did all it could, far from home. Thank you to the families of the New Zealand men and women who took the time to share their relatives' experiences in Spain with me, especially the family of New Zealand nurse René Shadbolt.

Lastly, and most importantly, to my father, Scott Angus, who passed away before I managed to finish the book. All those years of watching war documentaries must have rubbed off on me. And don't worry, the next book in the series will follow the thread you suggested. You leave behind a hole that cannot ever be filled.

Printed in Great Britain
by Amazon